Dedalus Original Fiction in Paperpack

LIFE IS LIKE A FAIRY TALE

Y:

a

P   rt Irwin (born 1946) is a novelist, historian, critic and

v   olar. He is a Fellow of the Royal Society of Literature.

       the author of seven previous novels, all published by
D   us: *The Arabian Nightmare*, *The Limits of Vision*, *The
My eries of Algiers*, *Exquisite Corpse*, *Prayer-Cushions of
th. Flesh*, *Satan Wants Me* and *Wonders Will Never Cease*.

All of Robert's novels have enjoyed substantial publicity
and commercial success although he is best known for *The
Arabian Nightmare* (1983) which has been translated into
twenty languages and is considered by many critics to be one
of the greatest literary fantasy novels of the twentieth century.

D1613161

Robert Irwin

MY LIFE
IS LIKE
A
FAIRY TALE

Dedalus

Supported using public funding by
ARTS COUNCIL ENGLAND

Published in the UK by Dedalus Limited
24-26, St Judith's Lane, Sawtry, Cambs, PE28 5XE
email: info@dedalusbooks.com
www.dedalusbooks.com

ISBN printed book 978 1 912868 19 3
ISBN ebook 978 1 912868 25 4

Dedalus is distributed in the USA & Canada by SCB Distributors
15608 South New Century Drive, Gardena, CA 90248
email: info@scbdistributors.com web: www.scbdistributors.com

Dedalus is distributed in Australia by Peribo Pty Ltd.
58, Beaumont Road, Mount Kuring-gai, N.S.W. 2080
email: info@peribo.com.au

First published by Dedalus in 2019

My Life is like a Fairy Tale copyright © Robert Irwin 2019

Printed and bound in Great Britain by Clays Elcograf S.p.A
Typeset by Marie Lane

A C.I.P. listing for this book is available on request.

Acknowledgements

The Rainer Maria Rilke poem 'Autumn Day' on page 199 has been translated by Tom Beck.

The film images used on the cover and at the beginning and end of the text are courtesy of Barbara and Ted Irwin Collectables.

Chapter One

A shot rang out. After a momentary pause the young man who had fired the shot screamed and then fell to the floor in front of the large mirror which could now be seen to be cracked from top to bottom. Where before there had been silence there was now an excited babble.

Sonja disliked films with lots of snow in them, films featuring cripples, anything with Emil Jannings in it, documentaries, any film by or starring Leni Riefenstahl, foreign language films, sad films about women who end up committing suicide like those ones that Kristina Söderbaum kept starring in, and, above all, she hated horror films: symphonies of grey, exotic hook-nosed faces, claw-like hands, candlelit cellars, yawning sepulchres, panic-stricken drives across desolate moors, and bafflingly mysterious plots about man's dual nature, at once angelic and bestial, or some such bogusly profound theme. There were enough horrors in real life. One did not need them on the screen as well. She had just been watching the shooting of the final scene of a remake of the 1926 version of *The Student of Prague* and, though this was the only shoot that she had stayed to watch, it was obviously a horror film and she would not bother with it when it reached the cinemas.

Needing some fresh air, she walked out of the studio. The

Great Hall where the really big scenes were shot towered over the other long huts of Universum-Film AG studios which were laid out in an orderly fashion, as if the place was a barracks or a work camp. Well, it was a sort of work camp she supposed, but quite a pleasant one, and not like the ones to which the communists and Jews were being sent. The huts, comprising the studios (some of which were glass-roofed), the workshops, the props store, the costume store and the make-up room, had all been set up to facilitate the industrialised production of fantasy.

At length, feeling the cold, she entered the UFA canteen and fished out the big new notebook from her bag. How to begin? Where should she start her story? Some films started in the middle of the story, before going on to work with flashbacks, but probably it would be easier to start with her birth, her childhood schooling and all that. Now she thought about it, flashbacks only really came in during the thirties. In the same way, close-ups were rare in the films she had watched as a child. It took some getting used to, seeing heads with no bodies or people moving about with no visible legs. But she was drifting. Back to the autobiography. If only she had had a more exciting childhood and if only she had realised then that she was going to want some early excitement in her life in order to make the mature woman's proposed book work. If only it was possible to literally flashback and return to one of her younger selves. But no, she was rambling again. She must make a proper start, once, that is, she had got a cigarette alight. Now for the start. She was about to put pen to paper when she felt a hand upon her shoulder. It was Werner, one of the focus pullers. Had he come as messenger to tell her that a new part had been found for her? But no. It was not good news.

'There was a man at the gate asking questions about you. He was very persistent. Apparently they had a lot of trouble sending him on his way.' Then seeing the expression on her face, Werner continued, 'Don't worry. He didn't look anything like Gestapo.'

If only it had been someone from the Gestapo. Sonja had nothing to fear from them. Dear Joseph would continue to look after her. It must be Wieland, still haunting her. She wished that he were dead, so that his haunting was only that of a ghost. Inside the empire of the UFA studios at Neue Babelsberg she might be safe from him, but only there, and the filming of *The Woman of My Dreams* was nearly complete and, unless she secured the role that she thought she had been promised in *Kolberg*, she would be unemployed and find herself to be, like Wieland, vainly seeking entrance to the dream factory. After Marika Rökk's big dance number that was just now being filmed, there were a few remaining outdoor scenes to shoot and then inevitably there would be some retakes, particularly since the crew still had limited experience in lighting sets for a film in colour. But the work might be finished in a matter of weeks or even days.

Werner interrupted her reverie, 'The man left a message. It was that he had something of yours. Something which you badly need to have back. He said that he would be in touch.'

Sonja nodded and tried to dismiss Wieland and the world outside Babelsberg from her mind and for a while she succeeded. She was very good at not thinking about things that she did not want to think about. She could switch off thinking about Wieland, or Rommel's retreat from Libya, or the

Russian advance on Kursk, or the poor reception of *Baghdad Capers*, or her mislaid ration card, or the imminence of her next birthday.

Instead she thought back to the big dance scene towards the end of *The Woman of My Dreams*. Marika had performed her third ethnic dance on a vast glittery set that was painted orange and gold and dominated by an enormous white cascade of a staircase whose steps led nowhere and which was there for no better reason than to demonstrate Marika's ability to tap dance up and down staircases. The supporting chorines, dressed in a romantically bogus Spanish fashion, wore mantillas and sported fans. Sonja had been one of them. They paraded like eerily disciplined goldfish behind Marika, who swayed sinuously and, as she did so, showed a lot of thigh. Sonja doubted whether that was going to get past the Reich Minister for Public Enlightenment and Propaganda. Anyway Marika's legs were too fat and her body was stubby. The camera and lighting crews had to work hard to conceal this. She had been leaping about like a kangaroo. Sonja did not call that dancing. In an interview to the press, Marika had described herself as 'volcanic'. But who wants to see a dancing volcano?

Belatedly Sonja decided that it was also time to dismiss Marika from her mind. The autobiography was more important. She picked up her pencil again and looked down on the notebook which was still empty. She needed to summon up memories of growing up in Dordrecht. There were memories of peacetime and childish innocence and of the gabled houses and their wavering reflection in the water of the canals. Beside those canals old men in blue linen jackets and baggy trousers sat on stoops and smoked clay pipes or chewed tobacco. It was all a bit boring. There always seemed to be jackdaws hovering round the belfry of Dordrecht's main church. The cobbled streets had been eerily quiet. Yes, certainly quiet – and this was not personal enough. She should start instead with her family and her toys. Memories... memories. It was like that game where one had to look at a medley of objects on a tray and then, once they had been covered by a cloth, one tried to list them all. She had had two china dolls. There was a board game based on a battle in the Franco-Prussian War, a small collection of musical boxes, a glass box containing a maze which a silver ball had to find its way through, a tiny wooden ape that could climb its wooden ladder and a large volume containing the Dutch syndicated version of comic strips featuring the misadventures of Little Nemo in his dream world.

Still much too dull? It was a bit like a séance in which the only message that comes to her from the spirit world is that she has forgotten to buy potatoes earlier that morning. She had supposed that one should start at the beginning and go on to the end. But why should German readers be at all interested in her childhood in Holland? And then there was the awkward fact that Dordrecht had suffered horribly during the German invasion of 1940. It had been a garrison town, there had been heavy fighting and many of the historic buildings that she should be describing had been destroyed. On the one hand, it might be a good idea to paint a picture of girlhood in a dull, provincial town in order to make a contrast with the glamorous life she now led. On the other hand, dullness was dullness. Perhaps it would be best to start with Wieland after all – the serpent who had found its way into the garden of innocence. What could be said for Wieland was that he would be interesting to read about. But then there was the danger that he was so interesting that he might take over her autobiography.

Perhaps childhood in Dordrecht was the wrong place to start the memoirs of a film star? Rather, she should begin with her starring role in *Baghdad Capers* and then present her younger self in a series of flashbacks? Or perhaps she should give an account of what she could call her 'friendship' with Goebbels. What is the best way to write a memoir? And what should her title be? *My Path to Stardom* sounded arrogant and, come to that, a little premature. How about *Memories of the Dream Factory*? No, that seemed to imply that her career was almost over. Maybe *Everything Has Gone Well*? Or *From Clogs to...* to something or other.

The book should be produced on proper creamy white paper, not the brittle stuff that things were printed on nowadays and which went brown so quickly. There was no point in publishing her book before Hitler launched his secret weapon and the Russians, who were fighting on over-extended supply lines, would be forced into a humiliating retreat. Only then, with the war won and the time of hardships over, would the public be ready to read her inspiring story. It occurred to Sonja that her book should contain snapshots. A star pupil at dance school receiving her prize. Her appearance in her first supporting role, in *Habanera*. Her lunch with Goebbels and his delightful family. At a birthday party for Emil Jannings. At the premiere of *The Great Love*. Her big star number in *Baghdad Capers*. Her name in big letters above the entrance to the UFA Palace by the zoo. Chatting with Hans Albers on the set of *Munchausen*. Being presented to Hitler at the Berghof.

Everybody's life should be like a film. In *The Woman of My Dreams*, Julia, the famous stage performer (played, curse it, by Marika) clad only in a fur coat and her underwear, suddenly flees stardom and having disembarked from the train at the wrong place, she gets lost in an Alpine snowstorm. But then she finds refuge in the mountain cabin of two handsome young engineers, Peter and Erwin. Both are struck by Julia's beauty and vivacity (this last madly overplayed by Marika). Julia keeps her identity as a big star a secret and in what follows all sorts of misunderstandings transpire and she is almost killed by a landslide when she tries to run away. Eventually she does make her way back to Berlin and reassumes her role as the big star, signing autographs and contracts and making it up with her manager. Peter, who had resolved never to see her again, nevertheless does see her performing in a series of spectacular dances of which the Spanish sequence was one and he realises that she is the only woman for him, the woman of his dreams. As a final twist, they quarrel when he visits her in her changing room. The film ends with Julia realising that she loves him after all and so she has to rush out of the theatre and chase after him. The two are reunited in each other's arms.

Our life is no film, but it can and should become one. Once Sonja reached the pinnacle of her career she hoped that she would do as Julia did and renounce the trappings of fame for love. She would abandon her former life as a femme fatale and settle down in comfortable domesticity. Yet it seemed to her necessary to become famous before rejecting all that fame might bring. She believed that one day she would come to prefer the love of one strong man to the adoration of so many admirers. Would she settle for Peter the engineer? Played by

Wolfgang Lukschy in this film, he was very handsome, but oh so serious – and apparently not rich.

So far as she was concerned there was no man alive who could match Rudolph Valentino. At least she had not met one yet. Her parents had not allowed her to see *Blood and Sand* or *The Sheik*. That would have been unthinkable, but Sonja had covertly studied the stills of Valentino in film magazines and much later when he died in 1926 she read everything she could about his funeral. It was rumoured that he had been poisoned by a former mistress. A hundred thousand people marched behind his coffin. Apparently four Blackshirts delivered a wreath from Mussolini. Pola Negri, who claimed to be Valentino's fiancée, collapsed over his grave. All over America women committed suicide on hearing of the death of the Latin Lover. Every year, on the anniversary of that death, a veiled woman dressed in black and carrying a red rose appeared at his grave. It was only after Sonja fled to Germany that she was able to see the actual films, starting with *The Four Horsemen of the Apocalypse*. That picture was now banned by the Nazis for being anti-war, but this was too late for Sonja, since by then she had irrevocably fallen in love with a dead man. Was it possible to be in love with a handful of dust? None of the German film stars could come near Valentino, not even Hans Albers. In Germany the men of the SS and the Wehrmacht strutted about and gave orders, but on the Nazi cinema screens it was the women who ruled – Zarah Leander, Christina Söderbaum, Lida Baarova, Ilse Werner and (curse it) Marika Rökk.

Of course, the part of Julia should have been given to Sonja. Though Sonja had only been given a small part, she took comfort from Tilde having quoted Stanislavski to her:

'Remember: there are no small parts, only small actors'. The reason that Sonja had agreed to appear as a hat-check girl and then again in the Japanese dance sequence in *The Woman of My Dreams* is that she hoped that Joseph would give her a bigger part in *Kolberg*. Everybody was talking about *Kolberg*. Planning for this film was far advanced and not only would it again be in colour, but it would be by far the biggest, most expensive, most spectacular film ever shot in Germany. It would be superlative and the world would watch it and marvel.

Cigarette break.

Maybe Wieland had her missing ration card? If so, so what? It would certainly be troublesome, but she could get another one and, if there were difficulties, she could appeal to Joseph for help. She was not going to go on her knees before Wieland for an old ration card.

Now it occurred to her that she should write her memoir in such a way that it cried out to be made into a film. To that end she must make her story visual. So, as well as flashbacks, it should have fade-ins, dissolves, jump cuts, montage and all sorts of other filmic tricks that she was a bit vague about. Also her life story ought to have the same sort of happy ending that *The Woman of My Dreams* was offering.

While it was tempting to skip over her dull childhood in Dordrecht, it was important that her readers should realise the humble and quite ordinary beginnings she started from. And that they should be aware that, despite her somewhat oriental appearance, she has no Jewish blood in her. There were no Jews in Dordrecht. At least she never saw any. Anyway, back to the dullness. Except for Sundays, every day was the same and Tuesday seemed the same as Monday, for only the name

17

of the day had changed and then Wednesday was the same as Tuesday... the only promise of another world and the presage of future glamour, love, violence and the exotic came from films. This was where she should start, since that there led to this here. Then she was distracted by her memory of Wieland starting a campaign to abolish Wednesdays so that the working week would be shortened.

But no, back to her memories of a Dutch childhood. At first there was no bioscope or cinematograph house in Dordrecht, but travelling showmen brought screens and projectors with them and presented their shows where they could. Several competing booths were set up in July when the summer fair took place and the local women paraded in traditional dress. Film barkers in top hats stood in front of the tents and bellowed out the details of forthcoming attractions. Sonja's parents had reluctantly permitted her to go to films which might be thought to have some religious content. So Sonja had seen *Quo Vadis*, *The Queen of Sheba*, *Intolerance*, *The Kiss of Judas*, *The Ten Commandments*, *Judith of Bethulia* and *Ben Hur* and she knew about the grey and ancient Bible lands which were peopled by languorous oriental princesses wearing thick mascara and who were waited upon by slaves wielding ostrich-feather fans. The film barker stood beside the sheet on which the films were projected and he shouted out the plot and supplied some of the dialogue. He had to shout in order to drown out the noise of the projector.

But there were other films she was forbidden to see – for example, the Biograph Company masterpiece: *The Battle of Elderbush Gulch*. The poster showed a white woman lying unconscious in the middle of a prairie. A fierce Red Indian knelt over her and held a screaming baby over his head. Had the woman just been ravished? Or would she surrender herself to the savage in order to save the life of her child? It all looked quite exciting. Then there was the poster for *Cleopatra*, which showed Theda Bara (Arab Death to her anagrammatically knowing fans) standing with arms folded in a hieratic pose in front of a disc covered with hieroglyphics. Hers was the gaze that commanded the destinies of men. She was indeed Death incarnate.

Now Sonja recalled that when she was a child there was always plenty to eat – herrings, black rye bread, split-pea soup, bacon, onions, gherkins, cheese and apples. Not like now. The UFA canteen provided more and better food than could be found in all but a handful of restaurants in Berlin. Even so, for almost two years now Sonja had been eating powdered eggs, bread that was made from something that caused her to fart a lot and ersatz marmalade. It was pleasant then to linger in memory over laden tables and busy restaurants in Dordrecht, so pleasant that Sonja now wondered if her autobiography would ever get any further. Perhaps she and her readers might settle for dining on memories.

But reflecting on restaurants brought Wieland back into the picture. Sonja had found temporary work in a restaurant in Dordrecht, her first job. It was a Saturday lunchtime and they had a dozen customers, which, considering the times, was unusually good business...

But no this was not the right place to start. (Sonja was beginning to understand that the main business of writing was ordering one's material.) So another beginning. This time in Amsterdam. She was seventeen or eighteen then and in a tram that was caught behind a convoy of horse-drawn delivery carts. She was thinking that a funeral cortege would have delivered her to her destination faster. Just then the strange young man sitting beside her gave her a nudge.

'Excuse me, miss,' he said, 'but I have to take some medicine now. I don't suppose you happen to have a glass of water on you of which I could avail myself?'

'No, sorry. I don't.'

But no sooner were the words out of her mouth than she was thinking what the hell am I apologising to this lunatic for?' How am I going to have a glass of water on me while travelling on a tram? Did he think I had one in my coat pocket filled and ready for the emergencies of travelling strangers? If only the tram were not so crowded, I could change seats. Otherwise the next thing he will ask me for is a stethoscope or a bottle of surgical spirits. Or is his silliness the new way of chatting up girls? He must think me a fool! Damn him for his impudence!

Sonja turned back to the window. The young man did not seem put out at being rebuffed by her. Now she could see in the window's reflection that he was tapping the shoulder of an older woman sitting on the seat in front of him and he was repeating his crazy request, adding that it was really rather urgent. His accent was foreign – German probably. Sonja looked to the woman to see how she would deal with the madman.

Although the woman looked alarmed and confused, she started to forage about in her large handbag, in course of which she apparently discovered all sorts of stuff which she had forgotten was in there. But finally, with a triumphant flourish, she did produce a glass of water. This the young man grabbed and, after some fumbling in his coat pockets, he found a large pill which he proceeded to swallow with the aid of that water. Having drained the glass, he returned it to the woman with the most profuse thanks. She just looked confused and embarrassed.

The man, the lunatic, had an extraordinarily long face, in the midst of which was an extraordinarily long nose. His eyes were hooded and he had wispy blond hair. He did not look entirely human. At the next stop along the Amstel the lunatic alighted and Sonja in a daze watched him pull his coat tight around him before he slouched off into the darkness of one of the narrow streets that led to the Rembrandtsplein. So the world was not as Sonja had supposed. There were holes in it through which one could tumble and find oneself in another reality. The tram, still stuck behind those carts, was moving slowly when Sonja rose from her seat, pushed her way to the rear platform and jumped. She landed ankle-deep in slush and hurried back to the little street. She thought that this was the beginning of an adventure and she was right.

Chapter Two

Cigarette break.

Sonja paused in her writing. Should this sort of crazy stuff feature in the beginning of a film star's autobiography? Moreover, she did not want Wieland to take over her book. But she could write it out anyway and perhaps throw it away later. Meanwhile writing about it might function as a kind of exorcism. But first she supposed it was necessary to give a sense of the city in which her first encounter with Wieland took place.

She was last in Amsterdam about twenty years later in the winter of 1941-2 for the filming of *Eternal Rembrandt*, directed by Hans Steinhoff. She was not one of the cast. Steinhoff had told her that, with her glossy dark hair, slightly slanting eyes and dark complexion, she just did not look Dutch enough. He was looking for a flaxen haired Hausfrau – for the film at least. Still, she had been loaned by UFA to Terra productions to serve as interpreter and to advise on props and locations. This was yet another of those films about a towering Germanic genius who faced great obstacles before triumphing over lesser folk, the sub-humans who populated most of Europe. Rembrandt was a perfect example of the 'creative brain' that Hitler had praised in *Mein Kampf*. The plot centred round Rembrandt's painting of *The Night Watch* and the company of burghers-posturing-as-soldiers who had protested that some of their members could hardly be seen in the deep shadows that the great artist had painted them into. And meanwhile his wife, Saskia, was dying. Sonja would have loved that part, but she had to acknowledge that she did not look right for the part.

In some ways that winter in Holland was hard. Of course, there was a blackout. Also food for the actors and film crew had to be brought in from Germany. The locals were unfriendly. Several times Sonja was spat at and, when she ventured to protest that she was Dutch like them that just made it worse. She was judged to be one of those tarts who slept with the enemy in exchange for food and cigarettes. She could understand their response and she even sympathised with it a little, even though, in some cases, she guessed that they were just jealous.

Despite the resentment of the locals, there were good times to be had. At the end of a day's shooting there always seemed to be a limitless supply of Dutch gin. The wonderful thing about being in the film business was the number of parties. And besides, parties were fun that also happened to be work. As Sonja saw it, parties were hiring fairs and, if she was not at the parties, she would be forgotten about and not be hired. So she felt that there was a strange kind of virtue in going to a party, getting very drunk and going to bed with someone afterwards. But none of that was relevant and none of it should appear in her autobiography.

She should now give some picture of Amsterdam as it appeared to her when, as a young woman, she first met Wieland. It was just that she had such a dizzy mind and she was aware that she inclined to wander from subject to subject and from memory to memory. People thought this charming, she was sure. But just now she knew she needed mental discipline. Perhaps she should take up algebra or Sanskrit? But not now. Now she needed to concentrate on Amsterdam and that first meeting with Wieland.

Sonja had ran the length of Pilgrims Paarden Straat. Rembrandtsplein was almost deserted. The lunatic was nowhere in sight. She was back in the world of the familiar and the dull. Soon she would be returning to Dordrecht and that interrupted course on stenography. Just as she was walking past the Café Schiller and thinking about the closure of the magic hole into another world, she caught a glimpse through the café's frosted window of the lunatic sitting at a table with four other young men, lunatics also presumably. They were mostly silent and seemed to be waiting for someone. Then a woman brushed past Sonja and, having entered the café, joined the gathering of lunatics. They were certainly lunatics for, as she arrived at their table, they all burst into manic laughter. The woman turned and gestured, apparently pointing to something that had happened outside the café. She had long black hair and, though her face was ugly, her eyes were bright with wild glee and now Sonja recognised her as the woman with the providential handbag on the tram.

This was too much. Sonja was going to confront these people and demand an explanation. She entered the café, but then stood close by the door uncertain what to do next. The wispy haired man had his back to her, but the woman with the handbag eventually saw Sonja and clearly recognised her. She raised a finger to summon her over. Sonja moved like a sleepwalker towards the group. She had no idea at all what she was going to say.

The lunatic was saying something to the woman, it was impossible to hear what, until, directed by the woman's gaze, he turned at last to look at Sonja.

'Ach! It is the beautiful girl from the tram!'

The table was lit by a candle and the shadows it created made the lunatic's face seem stranger than ever. He might have been an apparition conjured up in a séance.

He sprang to his feet and seized one of Sonja's hands.

'I kiss the hand!' he declared with mock formality and he bowed and clicked his heels as he did so. Then he spoiled the effect by bursting into laughter.

'Please be seated!' he said and dragged another chair over and pressed her into it. 'My name is Wieland. Then he introduced her to the others. They were all Germans and the woman's name was Mechtilde.

'I will get you a schnapps,' said Wieland.

Then they sat in silence, the young men studying Sonja's face intently as if they hoped to learn something from it. Wieland returned with the schnapps.

'Drink up,' he said. 'But, if you have pursued us in the hope of getting any kind of apology, you should put such a thought out of your mind. We never apologise. What is your name please?' Wieland's manner was defiant, yet nervous. With a shaking hand he tried to light a cigarette.

'Sonja Heda.'

'Well, Miss Heda, you should feel flattered. I only chose you for our little drama because I liked your face.'

Sonja did not feel flattered.

25

'Where are you from?' Wieland asked. 'You look foreign. You are not Dutch.'

'I *am* Dutch. I am from Dordrecht,' Sonja replied. (When she was young she was proud of coming from Dordrecht, God knows why.) Then she continued, 'What do you do – apart from play stupid tricks on people?'

'Trickery is an art form and not necessarily such a stupid one either,' Wieland replied slowly. He was having difficulty finding the right words in Dutch. 'I think of the charade this evening as a dramatic performance... why should drama always be crammed onto a tiny stage in a stuffy little arts theatre filled with bourgeois folk intent on improving their cultural understanding? Why should all the parts go to actors? Theatre should be out in the streets and it should be making life more exciting for the people who trudge along those streets. Art is part of life... not an alternative to it.'

Suddenly Wieland looked sad and he continued, 'Just now we, Mechtilde and I, had wanted to give you mystery as a gift. But you have spoilt it all by insisting on following us and discovering the duller reality behind the mystery. So goodbye mystery! And goodbye you! Go now!'

The young men with Wieland continued to stare at her as if they were willing her to go.

And Sonja went. At the door she turned and shouted, 'Grow up!'

Adults playing childish games. If only they had gone no further...

Having written an account of all this, the story of her first encounter with Wieland, she realised that, despite her first intention, she had given her future readers no idea of what

Amsterdam was or is like. The truth was that on that early visit, she had hardly registered her surroundings. She had been thinking about stenography, the Spanish flu, the prospects of enrolling in a dance class and doubtless other stuff which by now she had forgotten. It was really some twenty years later that Richard Angst taught her to look at the city. She thought it was twenty years ago, but really she was hopeless at chronology and it might have been more or less. She even found the order of the days of the week a problem. On waking up in the morning, her default position was that it was Tuesday. It was surprising how often it really was Tuesday. Richard was the lighting cameraman on *Eternal Rembrandt*. As a young man Richard had worked on filming the shadowy and bizarre architecture of *The Cabinet of Dr Caligari* and he was by now at the top of his profession. He and his crew were steeped in the works not just of Rembrandt, but also of Ruysdael, De Hooch and Jan Steen. For them the Rijksmuseum and the Mauritshuis constituted grand manuals of lighting techniques and camera angles and they talked about the paintings constantly. They also studied the canals and took photographs of the play of light on the water and the reflections of sunlight under the bridges. It was Richard in consultation with Hans Steinhof who had decided that in the early scenes featuring Rembrandt the blacks and whites should be in crisp contrast with one another and that, wherever possible, the scenes should be shot in deep focus (as in a De Hooch painting in which the spectator's eye passes from a room, through an open door down a corridor and out into a courtyard). But in the scenes featuring Rembrandt in old age the perspective should be much shortened and everything should take place in a kind of sepia fog.

Richard's team took lots of photographs of Amsterdam's architecture, for, rather than shoot on location and be at the mercy of the weather, they preferred where possible to re-construct the necessary exterior scenes later in lots at Babelsberg where the lighting could be controlled by the gaffer and best boy. The whole city presented streets composed of potential sets and so their houses were examined as possible backcloths to human dramas. Richard and Sonja walked through a city of smoke and fog, out of which rose the great gabled buildings that were built centuries ago by the grand merchants and that now were a testament to Holland's lost grandeur and the empire that Holland had forfeited to the Japanese. It might have been Rembrandt's Amsterdam that they were walking in, since almost all cars had been sequestered by the German authorities and bicycles too and, apart from the trams, what little traffic that passed in the streets was horse-drawn. Because of the blackout, gas lamps were not lit and people used torches as they cautiously felt their way through the night. Accidents were common, for the canals presented a particular hazard in the dark. The city appeared to have been conjured up from the waters and it seemed that it might, when its time was decreed, sink back into those waters.

Sonja knew that it was important for an actress to stay on the right side of the camera and lighting crew. They had it in their power to make her look ravishing or, if they were in the mood, they could make her seem even older than she was. God knows, if they took it into their heads, they could make even someone like Dietrich look ordinary. Sonja's face should be filmed in soft light from the front, rather than in profile and sometimes a back spotlight from the top might be used to give her a halo effect… there now! She was rambling again. And the stuff about being extra friendly with cameramen was not going into her autobiography. She knew that she ought to be describing the architecture of Amsterdam, but she lacked the vocabulary to do so. She had not had that sort of an education. She decided to leave the architecture of Amsterdam till later, when she could copy the details out of some old guide book.

At this point she was for once thankful to be interrupted by Gunther, who was as usual clutching a portfolio of sketches. The lugubrious Gunther haunted the UFA studios, in search of people who were not actually busy and whom he hoped might listen to him for an hour or two. He was a man on a mission. The Nazi cartoon! So far the Nazis had made no cartoon films and only used animation to illustrate certain facts in their documentaries. This was a cultural gap and it was to Germany's shame that it had no great artist who could measure up to Walt Disney. And yet both Hitler and Goebbels were known to be enormous enthusiasts for *Snow White and the Seven Dwarfs*. So Gunther was eternally optimistic, if gloomily so. Sonja was a particular target of his since he had often seen her in the company of Goebbels. Now he wanted Sonja to get the Reichs Minister interested in *Max and Moritz*, a nineteenth-century comic strip about two naughty boys who ended up being eaten by ducks. To hear Gunther talk, a feature-length film based on *Max and Moritz* could turn into something as grand as *Metropolis* or *The Nibelungs*. In fact Sonja had once mentioned the possibility of cartoons to Goebbels, but he had cut her short. He would not contemplate the making of cartoon films, since he associated them with the experiments made by Jewish and Bolshevik artists in the Weimar period. Besides,

29

Germany's cinema screens needed heroes and this cartoons could not deliver. Now Gunther was going on and on about his latest wheeze and Sonja was easily bored and *Max and Moritz* sounded very boring to her and she tried to think of a polite way of telling him so. But she was saved from that necessity when Gunther spotted someone more important to talk to, Fritz Hippler, chief of the film division in the Propaganda Ministry. As Gunther hurried away, Sonja was momentarily offended, but then she realised that she did the same sort of thing herself.

Gunther would never give up. He was a typical Taurus. Then Sonja realised with a start that she had not looked at her horoscope that day. She never bothered with the political and military news. That would only depress her and what would be the point of that? The horoscope was usually more cheerful and certainly more useful, as the horoscope told her what was going to happen, whereas the news only told you what had happened. Since she was finding the autobiography business rather difficult, she was hoping that her horoscope would tell her to give the whole notion up. She was a typical Libra, warm and sociable. Alas, when she consulted the advice for Librans in the coming week, this was what she read: 'Since the new moon four weeks ago, you have been very uncertain about what you should do next and what possibilities are open to you. You are finding it difficult to plan ahead. But you must press on with what you have decided on earlier. Yes, it will be challenging, but that will be good for you and you will find that your way will get easier if you persist.' Damn! So she was stuck with the autobiography. (And she still did not even have a title for the book. She was fed up with thinking about it as 'the autobiography'.)

So now perhaps she must buckle down to write about the strange business in the restaurant in Dordrecht. (She had had no idea that writing could be so difficult. Free association would not do.) Back then, so many years ago, she had found temporary work in a restaurant in the town, her first job. It was a Saturday lunchtime and they had a dozen customers in, which, considering the times, was unusually good business. She was stacking dishes in the kitchen when Katje, the other waitress, came back from the dining room and asked Sonja, 'There is no turbot on the menu is there?'

'No, of course not. We do not do fish dishes. If anyone wants fish, he or she will have to go to another restaurant. The Windjammer does fish.'

Katje could be so stupid at times – well, all of the time really.

Katje persisted, 'But there is a party at the corner table demanding turbot.'

'Katje, they cannot have it. We do not have it. Point out to them that it is not on the menu.'

'But there is a man at the next table who is especially recommending the turbot. He says our turbot is excellent and definitely the best thing on the menu.'

'He is mistaken. We don't serve turbot – excellent or otherwise.'

'But he says it was on his menu and there is turbot on his plate. He is kissing his fingers and going into ecstasies about it.'

'Don't be silly, Katje.'

'It is definitely turbot. He invited me to examine it closely. The fish is rather flat with a greyish back and it seems to have been steamed.'

Katje tugged at Sonja's sleeve. Sonja sighed. But then, as she walked into the dining room, she gave a cry of dismay. It was Wieland who sat with knife and fork poised over the fish.

'Really excellent turbot! Done to perfection!' he shouted as Sonja appeared in the doorway. 'If my friends here cannot have the same, they should be told why.'

He winked at Sonja, before turning to his neighbours to urge them on to demand their rights. Such an excellent dish should be enjoyed by everyone, not just by favoured customers. Did the restaurant have a secret menu? The restaurant's owner had been sitting by his wife's sickbed upstairs, but now drawn by the commotion he came down to see what the matter was. Claus Van Doorn was a big man and he loomed over Wieland who quivered in his seat. Claus insisted that Wieland should leave the restaurant immediately. Wieland defiantly argued that he could not possibly leave without paying for what he had eaten. If he could just have the bill, so that he could pay for the turbot (and compliments to the chef, by the way), then he would be happy to pay up and go. Claus was not having any more of this nonsense. He picked Wieland up off his chair by the scruff of his neck and forced him out of the restaurant.

Two hours later, when the restaurant closed for the afternoon, Sonja found Wieland outside in the street, waiting for her.

'I kiss the hand,' and he managed to do so before she snatched it away.

'What are you doing here?'

'I have come to find you,' he replied.

'How did you find me?'

'There is only one Sonja Heda in Dordrecht. Indeed, there is only one Sonja Heda in the world and I have come for you.'

'What for? Have you come all this way to apologise?'

Wieland looked a little irritated.

'Of course not. I never apologise. I have decided that after all you are the incarnation of mystery and so I have come for you. I have hardly slept since that evening in Amsterdam. You have the face that can lure men to their doom and I have chosen you to lure me to my doom. I will make you great. What is it that you want to do? Who is it that you want to be?'

'I want to work in a restaurant?'

Wieland waved his hand dismissively, 'No, no, no. That sort of thing is for the girl next door and you do not have the look of a girl next door. You are too beautiful to be a waitress. What do you dream of becoming?'

Sonja obstinately insisted that she liked working in a restaurant and she intended to continue doing so. But this was not the truth.

Time for another cigarette... by now stagehands were moving in to dismantle the set of *The Woman of My Dreams* and that was a bit distracting. The truth was that from quite an early age she had wanted to be a film star. Now Sonja's readers would want to know why she had to be in films, rather than be content just to watch them. What was it that set her on the path to stardom? What was it that took her steps towards the Holy Kingdom of Shadows and Silence?

Not what but who. Pola Negri. Sonja had seen Pola Negri in *Madame Dubarry*, *Sumurun*, and *The Eyes of Mummy Ma*. Sonja had seen her as the sultry Madame Du Barry, as she presented a petition to Louis XV before leaping onto the lap of the startled king. And in *Sumurun*, the epic Arabian romance, Pola as Annaia danced herself towards her death in the harem. Sonja had screamed when, in *The Eyes of the Mummy Ma*, the coffin lid was raised to reveal the hypnotic eyes of Radu, Egypt's answer to Rasputin. A few moments later Ma, the maiden played by Negri, was released from captivity in the tiny chamber beyond the coffin. Yet it is of course her ultimate fate to perish with the sinister Radu and Sonja had screamed again when Ma was stabbed and fell backwards down the stairs. In *Gypsy Blood* she had lured her lovers to their deaths with a rose between her teeth. Pola Negri carried her fated doom with her in most of the films Sonja had seen her in – old films lit by lanterns and candles. Pola had gypsy blood. She was rumoured to have been the lover of Valentino. Prudish critics said she was a man-crazy vamp. She had a Roman bath in the middle of her living room. She took a tiger for a walk down Hollywood Boulevard. She was Hitler's favourite actress and she was Sonja's heroine.

So finally Sonja confessed to Wieland, 'I want to be a film star.'

Again he was disappointed.

'That is a shop girl's dream. That is so banal. I want to make you truly great. Listen. With the triumph of America and the establishment of the League of Nations, history has come to an end. No country can think of doing anything except emulate America. Everywhere dull, decent men of bourgeois origins have taken power: Poincaré, Baldwin, Coolidge, my President Ebert and your Prime Minister Charles de Beerenbrouck. The dark shadow of boredom is sweeping over Europe. Germany needs me. Europe needs me. I am the man of destiny who will awaken my country from its somnolence. I will lead my followers (though admittedly they are few so far) from street theatre to total theatre. I will have thousands, no hundreds of thousands marching and performing at my command. Forget the cinematograph. It is a sideshow – like those booths where idiotic punters pay money to gaze at the bearded lady, the Siamese twins or the man who eats coal. The craze for going to see films is part of the end of history. It is a fad like the craze for the diabolo. It has no future. Right now the cinematograph is feted as a novelty, yet it is destined to follow the magic lantern, the praxinoscope and the stereoscopic photograph into obscurity. Anyway, the Dutch don't make films,' he ended bathetically.

Such crazy stuff! But Sonja thought it safer to be polite.

'I am sorry. That is what I really want to do – to be in films.'

'Come away with me, Sonja Heda. Together we will do great things.'

She shook her head.

'Then have dinner with me. I will buy you dinner at The Windjammer and we shall see if I can get you to change your mind.'

But Sonja pointed out that in the evening she would once again be waitressing in the restaurant.

'In that case,' said Wieland, 'I shall return in exactly a year's time. By then perhaps you will have changed your mind – no, I am sure of it. In the meantime I will have done great things. You may even read about me in the newspapers.'

Sonja doubted this as she did not read newspapers, except for the horoscopes, but she said nothing in reply.

Wieland shrugged and started to walk away. Then he turned and shouted at her, 'The eternal in woman draws us on.'

What was he talking about?

Wieland turned out to be right in that he did get into the newspapers and Sonja turned out to be right in that she did not read about him, since she really never read the news.

Chapter Three

She knew she ought to describe her parents, but then that would inevitably lead on to their encounter with the Spanish Lady. The Spanish Lady, with bones clacking like castanets, had walked the streets by day and night. Her head was covered by a black lace mantilla and she was heavily made up in an unsuccessful attempt to conceal from customers that her face was really just a skull. Wielding a large fan with one hand, she kept the other one free to reach out for trade. Dukes, duchesses, bank managers, clerks, maids and porters all embraced the Spanish Lady, and, having done so, they coughed until they died. One saw the Spanish Lady everywhere on warning posters in the streets and in cartoons in the newspapers.

Sonja did not like to think of dead people. It was too depressing and she wanted her book to be a happy one, full of inspirational uplift. So she did not want to dwell on the Spanish flu and the hard times after the end of the Great War. She could write it all up briefly some other time. Meanwhile on to Berlin and the bright lights! Berlin, the city of the future, her future! Now the capital of a Thousand Year Reich!

She had enough money saved from waitressing to keep her going for a few weeks in the new city. Wieland was just about right that no films were being made in Holland, but

Germany was a different matter. Pola Negri had starred in lots of German films. Moreover, Sonja knew that the famous film star had started out as a dancer. So the first thing Sonja was going to do, after she had reached Berlin and found some temporary job, was to take dancing lessons. She certainly was not going to hang around for a year in Dordrecht, waiting for that long-faced, wispy-haired goon to reappear. Wieland was hardly Prince Charming.

She had found a flat above a stamp dealer's shop in the Charottenburg quarter of Berlin. The impact of the city on a small-town girl from Holland was overwhelming. She used to see the city wake up as she woke up. Gates, shutters, windows, doors and sleepy eyes were all opening at more or less the same time. At first the streets she looked upon were mostly empty, and only wind, water and discarded rags flowed through them. But soon they became crowded as workers in cloth caps, students in peaked caps, businessmen in homburgs, dandies in panamas and women in cloche hats streamed by. Policemen in flat-topped shako helmets sought to control the crowds. (At first Sonja had mistaken them for soldiers.) As she walked through the city, she found the criss-crossing of so many roads, railways and human lives exhilarating, for this all seemed to signal that there were so many futures for life, for her life to take. The city seethed with energy and so did she. She remembered those first impressions. At least she thought she did. She is not sure when she saw Ruttman's film *Berlin, Symphony of a Great City*, but, ever since seeing it, the film's images have infected her memories and have made her uncertain of how much of all that she really saw back then.

She had loved to go out early in the morning and watch the

riders in the Tiergarten and their steeds advancing through the mist like ghosts. But the nights were just as good. At night the streetcars and taxis moved along glistening rainswept streets, reflecting the lights from open windows and flashing neon lights. In the evenings there were films, cabaret shows, dance contests and thousands of people danced to the drumbeat of the future and they came out from the halls and cinemas, quite tired, to watch triumphal firework displays, before going home to sleep. Oh, to sleep. Oh the days when she was young and could do that. And no sirens and no flak and no bombs.

Some things that could be seen then were now gone. When she first came to the city she saw many soldiers who had been disabled in the Great War begging and they competed with the able-bodied unemployed who advertised their claims to charity with pitiful scrawls on bits of cardboard. There also used to be lots of Jews in the streets. They were gone. The Reichstag was gone, of course. It was just a burnt-out shell. The pigeon fanciers' cart that used to stop outside the stamp shop no longer did so.

She had loved the displays of stamps in the ground-floor shop window. One week there would be pages of stamps from Imperial China with their delicately intricate designs, and then it would be the turn of the elaborate calligraphy of the issues of Hejaz and Najd and then perhaps the stamps of the British Empire, every one of which bore the head of one of its villainous monarchs. Next it would be pages of the stamps of the German States: Bavaria, Thurn and Taxis, Baden, Mecklenburg, Prussia and others, most of their stamps resembling tiny ancient banknotes. She thought them a bit boring. But then other displays followed which featured utterly unfamiliar countries, whose stamps presented tiny vignettes of unknown mountains and bays, exotic animals and forgotten statesmen.

There were no more displays now and the window was empty. Manasseh turned out to be Jewish and he was gone. She was so bad at spotting who was Jewish and who was not. Similarly she was hopeless at spotting who might be homosexual. And what did freemasons look like? Was there a masonic look? She really must try to be more observant. David used to say that she would be categorised as a scatterbrain, if only she had any brains to scatter. 'We must find you a screwball comedy to star in.' Not that it mattered any more about not recognising Jews, since one never seemed to see them about these days. All the Jews were being taken east to places in Poland (or whatever it was called now) where they could be re-educated and settled. In a way it was a pity and she felt sorry for them. On the other hand, the dismissal of all those Jews from UFA and the smaller studios meant that there was now more work for people like her. Anyway she was not going to write about Jews. Her book was going to be filled with sunshine and romance.

It was unfortunate that the short train journey back from Potsdam to Berlin offered nothing in the way of sunshine or romance. The glass was gone from the windows of the carriage and all the seats were taken. She always dreaded the end of filming and her return to the city and her flat (if she still had a flat, if the building was still standing). Would she get some sleep or will there be another raid? It was sad now to walk through the necropolis of Berlin at night. One had to pick one's way through the rubble and sometimes it was unclear where a street had been and there were so many facades without interiors. Sad and dangerous. Once off the train, she tried to stay in the company of UFA people for as long as possible, since in the blackout women were always in danger of assault by the conscripted foreign labourers.

The Berlin of her youth had vanished in smoke and flame like an enchanted city from *The Arabian Nights*, or, no, like the city of Atlanta as it was engulfed in flames in *Gone with the Wind*. Sonja thought that she was a lot like Scarlet O'Hara. She too had known a life of grace, courtesy and plenty and that life had been ruined, almost annihilated by unscrupulous ideologues and warmongers, but she was going to rebuild her life once more and with it her own version of Tara.

She thought of the Kufurstendam as it once was and how pleasant it was in peacetime days to pass by its shops and cafes on sunny summer afternoons. Then she recalled something else that happened soon after her arrival in Berlin. She had just found a job as a waitress and so she was cheerful as she walked down that street. Then a voice summoned her, 'Sonja Heda.'

Sonja looked round and saw that it was a smartly dressed woman sitting outside a café who was summoning her over. Puzzled, Sonja walked over and sat down at the woman's table. Who was she? She was obviously a Pisces. The typical Pisces was dreamy, mystical sensitive and ever changeable. Beyond that Sonja could not place her.

'We met in Amsterdam,' said the woman. 'My name is Mechtilde, if you remember.'

Sonja looked more closely at her. She was dressed according to what in the Weimar days was regarded as high fashion. (And Sonja, looking back on this, bitterly reflected that it still would be high fashion, if only they could afford it nowadays.) Mechtilde's hair was now short in a pageboy cut and it was under a cloche hat. She wore a loose pale yellow dress that only reached to the knees. Her make-up was immaculate, but no make-up, no matter how copious and how skilfully applied, could compensate for the lopsided and somewhat horse-like face. Still, those glittering eyes…

Mechtilde asked her what she was doing in Berlin and, after some hesitation, Sonja told her about her ambition to get into films. Mechtilde sighed. As Sonja must have guessed, Mechtilde had been an actress and for a while she had been with Max Reinhardt's company. But she was now too old to get the parts. It suddenly struck Sonja that Mechtilde was speaking in Dutch and her Dutch was extremely good (whereas Sonja's German was still minimal). Mechtilde explained that her mother was Dutch and that she had been visiting relatives in the city when Wieland and some of his little troupe had decided to tag along to try out some more theatre in the streets of an unfamiliar place.

Then, seeing Sonja look worried, Mechtilde reassured her. Wieland would not trouble her since he was in prison. Joining Wieland's Theatre of the New Subjectivity had been Mechtilde's attempt to stay in the world of acting. (The Theatre of the New Subjectivity was dedicated to acting in plays that had yet to be written.) Now she was a professional mahjong player. Then Sonja wanted to know what kind of instrument was a mahjong. Mechtilde looked baffled and then gave a silvery laugh. Mahjong turned out not to be a musical instrument. It was a Chinese game which used painted tiles.

(This last remark summoned up inappropriate imagery in Sonja's head.)

'It is all the rage in America and now it is catching on here. Wieland has read about it and is fascinated. Since it is not possible for him to become a mahjong player in the Moabit, he has asked me to master the game on his behalf and I have. In order for an actor to fully understand any role he has to immerse himself fully in it. In order to understand Ophelia I had to become Ophelia. In the same way I have managed to understand the world of mahjong and then I have passed my knowledge on to Wieland.'

'But if it is a game, how can you be professional at it?'

'There are sometimes games with high stakes and, since I am good, I usually win. Also I coach people in how to play the game. I work alternate weeks in Berlin and Munich. It is a craze, but, of course, crazes never last and soon I will have to find something else to do.'

Then Mechtilde set to describing the rules for playing and scoring in mahjong. They were jolly complicated and Sonja thought that Mechtilde must be very clever to master those rules, never mind to win money by playing the game. But the rules were far too complicated for Sonja to follow – and too boring. Sonja was easily bored. She drifted on to asking herself how it was that Wieland was in prison. Tricks involving asking for glasses of water on trams or smuggling turbots into restaurants hardly seemed to merit incarceration.

Then she asked Mechtilde who was surprised that Sonja had not read about it.

'Even the Dutch papers must have covered the story. It ran for days in the German press. Wieland had got a theatrical costumier to rig him up the uniform of a German general and he bought a job lot of medals from a junk shop. He managed to buy or borrow other uniforms from old soldiers and he distributed these to the male members of the Theatre of the New Subjectivity. He also succeeded in borrowing some rifles with bayonets from young men in the Freikorps whom he had known from his days in a student fraternity. Then one Friday he lined his actors up in their military gear and after a quick inspection, he marched them off in the direction of the Town Hall on the corner of König-Strasse and Spandauer Strasse. Since the women members of the Theatre of the New Subjectivity were not given parts in this new drama, I just tagged along as a spectator to see if Wieland's show was going to be a success.'

'Once he arrived at the Town Hall, he posted most of his troupe at the foot of the steps and, accompanied only by the five with rifles, he ran up the steps, brandished a fake but impressive document in the face of the porter and declared that the city's treasurer was under arrest for malversation and fraud. One of the senior clerks then appeared and asked by what authority was the arrest being made. Wieland pointed to his guns and replied that it was by their authority. Then he added that he was declaring a state of emergency in the city. So the terrified treasurer was brought forth and led away under escort by two of the actors. (They bought him a drink in a bar a few streets away.) Next Wieland announced that the funds held in the town hall were to be sequestrated prior to the trial of the treasurer. Slowly sacks of money were brought forth and placed in piles in the hall. Everything was going fine.'

'It was now time for Wieland to make a speech. This he

did from the top of the steps of the town hall:

'People of Berlin, today I address you, but tomorrow I will speak to Germany and the day after tomorrow the world shall surely hear me. Today I have decided to become president of Germany, until that is someone else wants the job. A life that is lived without passion is not a life at all. People of Berlin I lay my passion at your feet. As president I know that my task is to implement the politics of desire. Next, there is far too little drama in Germany and what there is has been confined to pokey little theatres. On the other hand, there are too many dull people on the streets. They must be arrested and sent to re-education camps. Germany is actually much duller than quite a few other countries that have far fewer material resources, for examples Tibet, Madagascar, Mexico and the Congo. Next, too many people suffer from the knowledge that we lost the war. I propose that we decide that we won the war. Our task then is to persuade other countries that we won the war and we must allow ourselves to gloat over the defeat of France and Britain. We shall have victory parades and celebration dances and dinners. The whole country ought to learn the art of impersonation. This great nation of ours just needs a flower in the buttonhole and a cigar in hand and it will take its rightful place in the world. Next, there is too little space in this land of ours to dream in. We need to annexe the land of dreams. We need to sleepwalk across its open plains towards impossible victories. People of Berlin, I tell you that we must learn to dream and to that end I demand of you now to sacrifice some of your time awake in order to spend extra hours in bed...'

It was a very long speech and Mechtilde could not remember it all and much of what she could remember and passed on to Sonja, Sonja forgot. Wieland sounded very silly to her, but then all politicians sounded silly. A lot of men arguing noisily and then, when the argument was not being won, they reached for their guns and coshes. Politics! Was there anything more boring than politics? Except sport, chess and knitting patterns maybe. And now the rules of mahjong. She wished that she were not so easily bored. It was because of her impatience, sitting around during shoots in the studios, waiting for the leading man to turn up, then for the lighting to be adjusted, and then for the actual shooting to begin, because of all this, she had decided to write her autobiography. Or was it a memoir? She was not clear about the difference. Anyway she now had a notebook and soon the great work would take shape.

When she had listened to Mechtilde's account of Wieland's speech, Sonja was briefly worried that she might be one of the dull people on the streets, but then she found reassurance in remembering that Wieland had declared her to be full of mystery. Surely one could not be both mysterious and dull? But then what did she care what Wieland thought of her? She was rambling and hardly heard anything of Mechtilde's account of the last part of the speech on the steps of the town hall. She must learn to concentrate.

Mechtilde continued, 'The Theatre of the New Subjectivity had been short of money and Wieland had at first thought of robbing a bank, but then why stop at that? Two more of his actors made off with as much of the city's treasury as they could carry, while Wieland, on the steps of the town hall and quite carried away by his own eloquence, continued to rant to a small audience until someone, who thought he could recognise a madman when he saw one, fetched the police and that was the end of what was known as the Wieland Lowenfeld putsch. The actors who made off with the sacks of money were never seen again. Perhaps they got away to Switzerland or to France. Now the Theatre of the New Subjectivity is disbanded and Wieland is currently in the Moabit prison where he has started to read some strange books by the Marquis de Sade and he has asked for a mirror to be installed on the ceiling of the cell so that he can watch himself masturbating. Though his jailors love him, they are not going to give him that. He is also writing his memoirs, which he is calling *Tomorrow Belongs to Me.*'

Sonja hoped that he was not thinking of her when he masturbated. Now, looking back on all this, Sonja was jealous that he had a title for his book. Now, if only she had a title, then she would know where she was going with her book.

'When the judge heard what he had done, he roared with laughter and only sentenced him to six months, said Mechtilde. 'The Moabit Prison is enormous and quite frightening. I have been visiting him there. His cell looks down on the execution yard. He has often talked about you and your beauty.'

She laid her hand on Sonja's.

'I am safe, for I know his ways and I love the man. But he was rather struck with you,' she said. 'In Amsterdam he told me that he thought that you might have been promised to him by destiny.'

Sonja shrugged. What right had destiny to promise her to anyone? Besides, she was not afraid of a clown. Or rather, come to think of it, she was afraid of clowns and had been ever since she had been taken to the circus as a small girl. She was

47

afraid of the white mask, the baggy trousers, the giant shoes and the random pranks. Clowns had made her cry with fear when she was a child. But this was not really relevant. The point was that she was not afraid of Wieland.

Seeing Sonja shrug, Mechtilde insisted, 'People find him sinister. He does not wear a hat!' But then, seeing that Sonja was still unimpressed, she added, 'His eyelids are very thin. When he closes them, he can still see through them!'

Now Mechtilde prepared to leave, 'Goodbye Sonja. It is unlikely that we shall meet again.'

But as Mechtilde started to rise, Sonja pulled at her arm, 'Please, I know no one in this city and I should like to have a friend here.'

Now it was Mechtilde's turn to shrug, 'In this city it will not be long before some man comes after you. Just now there have been men in this café who have been looking you up and down. Besides, my shoulders are too pointy for anyone to cry on them. I have my own life and I can carry no passengers. So now once more goodbye.'

Sonja flapped her hand in a feeble gesture of farewell and started to cry.

Mechtilde, exasperated sat down again. Then, having sat down, she asked why Sonja had come to Berlin, a city where she knew no one, but after Sonja reminded her of her ambition to act in films, she was pleased to hear Mechtilde say, 'Well you are young enough and pretty enough. Perhaps you have a chance, though cinema has come too late for me.'

Then it was bizarre. Mechtilde, having fallen silent, immediately started to pull hideous faces. It was as if her head was made of rubber. As she continued to make faces, people at neighbouring tables stopped talking and stared at her. Sonja, embarrassed, had no idea what to do. The first face was lopsided and the eyes seemed to be turned inwards. Then the brow started to furrow in great corrugations. In another instant the head was thrown back, the mouth opened and the eyes widened. It seemed that the face, which had somehow become independent of its owner, was terrified of something. Then the head tipped forward, the upper lip drew back and the tongue shot out. After this the lower lip was also drawn back and the eyebrows contracted. And so the facial phantasmagoria continued for fully a quarter of an hour. Finally Mechtilde's face smoothed and her eyebrows rose. She now looked as though she did not know where she was and she was looking at Sonja as if she had never seen her before.

'That is the first thing you will have to learn,' said Mechtilde. 'Facial control. Especially if you are going to be a film actress, for in films your facial expressions will have to do the work that dialogue can do in the theatre. So your face must acquire its voice.'

There was a small ripple of applause from nearby tables. Mechtilde smiled and ordered coffee for herself and Sonja before continuing to talk about the theatre. Since she had abandoned a career in the theatre, or rather it had abandoned her (for an actress has to sell her youth and beauty and that is an ever-diminishing capital sum) she said that she was happy enough to pass on what she had learnt of the tricks of her former trade. Sonja needed to build up muscle tone in her face. Also, as she walked through the streets, she must observe how other people walk. One could build up a whole character out of a certain way of walking. She would have to learn to walk as a child learns to walk, but again and again in a hundred different ways. As an actress, she will have to perform other people's dreams to order. For this she will need all her resources of relaxation, concentration and emotional memory. In acting the trick is to make the easy look difficult. It is dog eat dog in the acting world. It was no good sitting around and moping. She must behave and talk flamboyantly, so that producers and directors will remember her. She has to project herself and she must be energetic and strong. Through strength she will find joy. That was it. Mechtilde had nothing more to give her.

'Thank you, Mechtilde.'

'Call me Tilde. And give me your address.'

As she finally rose from the table, Tilde admonished her, 'You must never admit to being shy and lonely. You must never let people know that things are not going well for you. Instead you tell everybody that everything in your life is wonderful and that the signs are that it is going to get yet more wonderful. You must always smile. In my experience, losers engineer their own failures. And you must give off energy. Energy always attracts. I will tell Wieland that I have seen you.'

She hurried away and was out of earshot before Sonja could beg her not to mention to Wieland that she was in Berlin. She lit a cigarette and, as she did so, she resolved to become more tempestuous, more flamboyant. But then she wondered how a waitress could be tempestuous and flamboyant and still keep her job. Was this realistic? Now, walking through the blitzed streets of Berlin and looking back on Tilde's advice about acting all those years ago, Sonja thought that she could put a lot of this in her memoir and pass it off as the fruits of her own experience. The general reading public might find it interesting, but, of course, nothing about the source of those acting tips would be in her memoir, or autobiography, or whatever it was. Just as she was probably not going to write about her encounters with a criminal lunatic in Holland, so she was not going to reveal her lonely desperation to have a friend in Berlin back in the 1920s. She will have to find something more cheerful that she can put in her book. She just has to write about all those parties she went to.

A week after her encounter with Tilde, Sonja registered at Helene Grimm-Reiter's Berlin School of Dance. She was told that she was late starting and that she should have taken dance lessons as a child at school. But there had been no such dance lessons in Dordrecht. Berlin, on the other hand, was the centre of modern dance. On alternate afternoons Sonja studied ballet and interpretive dance. Though she could never become a ballet dancer, she was told that the discipline was good for her. She much preferred the interpretive sessions when, like Isadora Duncan, she danced barefoot and there was much more liberty in acting out the music. But even more she liked the shimmy, the Charleston and the black bottom and they were not on the curriculum of the Helene Grimm-Reiter's Berlin School of Dance. On her evening off Sonja usually went to a dance hall.

Chapter Four

A fortnight later she received a note from Tilde, dropped off at her lodgings, proposing that on Sunday they should take a train out to Potsdam and from there go on by bus to Babelsberg and the studios of Universum-Film AG, where they would be able to take a conducted tour. Sonja's first impressions of the UFA studios should certainly go in her memoirs. She would write the experience up as the responses of a young ingénue who was dazzled by the whole experience. The studios were vast glass-roofed hangar-like buildings that seemed more suitable for parking *Zeppelins* than serving as theatres for tragedy and comedy. Then there was the sheer noisiness of silent film-making, with the director shouting instructions to the actors, the actors sometimes choosing to mouth their parts in order to give their gesturing added conviction, a violinist playing mood music, the camera crew making loud comments, many of which were unflattering, and the rumble of the camera as it moved backwards and forwards across the wooden flooring. Then there was the heat given off by the Klieg lights and the smell of melting make-up. Most bizarre were the long sheds used to store props: hat stands, mattresses, umbrellas, chamber pots, uniforms, tutus, stuffed crocodiles, rocking horses, pianos, cigarette holders, wigs, harlequin costumes, scimitars, drums, carpets, clocks, false teeth, tarbushes – everything necessary to sustain the fantasies manufactured in this engine of dreams.

The tour only took one hour and twenty minutes including a brief talk by the Mistress of Make-Up and, as a climax, they were permitted to watch the filming of a scene from *Woman in the Moon*. The vast glass-roofed studio that they had been ushered into housed a moonscape fashioned out of an enormous quantity of bleached sand that had been sculpted into desert dunes in front of a backdrop of painted crags. The bit that they were privileged to witness was the final one when Helius, the brilliant rocket scientist played by Willy Fritsch, finds that he is not alone on the Moon, for Frieda, the no less brilliant astronomer played by Gerda Maurus, has not after all departed back to Earth on the rocket, but has stayed back to be with him. But they are marooned with very little food and water. So death is certain. In the close-up he weeps on her shoulder as she gently strokes his neck and looks up to the stars and a dark future.

To die with the man one loved, Sonja thought that would be the finest of deaths. If only she could find the man she was prepared to die with. Tilde and Sonja stood beside a group of men whom their guide told them were real rocket scientists. They had been advising the director and at the same time they were trying to learn from his simulation of rocket travel. Looking back on that day, Sonja felt wistful. Then rocketry had just seemed a fantasy, like the lost city of Atlantis or the race of supermen in Tibet. But now rockets were real and it was rumoured that some kind of super-rocket was going to be Hitler's secret weapon, though a rival rumour had it that a special drug was going into production that would give German soldiers several times the speed and strength of their Bolshevik antagonists. The rockets seemed more likely. Germany was bound to win because it had the best scientists, whereas its enemies used Jewish scientists who believed in mad things like relativity, whatever that was. And once Germany had won the war, more and bigger rockets would allow the Germans to colonise first the Moon and then the solar system. The country would be served by an underclass of robots, very like the one in that film *Metropolis*, and everyone would live in sky-scraper cities. Sonja looked forward to those future cities with their canyons of glass and metal. In the future skirts would be shiny and very short.

As she watched the final tragic scene of *Woman in the Moon*, Tilde occasionally winced, since, as a trained stage actress, she found the gestures used by film actors to be bizarrely exaggerated. She muttered to Sonja that Gerda Maurus was having an affair with the director of the film, a man called Fritz Lang. Tilde pointed him out to Sonja and added inconsequentially 'He has a Jewish mother.' Gerda was a classically beautiful blue-eyed blonde. That was what Germans thought they ought to desire. But Sonja was pleasantly aware that she too was an object of desire. The looks of the camera crew on this set told her so.

Since the tour of UFA had taken less time than expected, Tilde proposed that they also visit The Brentano Museum of Fairy Stories and Folk Literature in Potsdam. The museum's façade was a mess. It looked a bit ancient Greek and a bit medieval. Sonja decided that she would have to look up the architecture of the museum in some book if she was going to

write about it, and she was. Previously, the only museums she
had been in were in Holland and they were full of paintings,
Delft ware, old furniture and not much else. So she had
anticipated something dull.

Cigarette break.

And it was a bit dull, yet looking back on that visit, Sonja
knew that it was mysteriously important to her. For some
reason, she had kept the leaflet they were given at the entrance
and now she decided that she would reproduce some of it in
her autobiography.

The Brentano Museum of Fairy Stories and Folk Literature

Open 10-4, Tuesdays – Sundays. Closed Christmas and New Year'
Day. (Puppet Theatre performances Saturday and Sunday, 2 and
4.) Entrance five pfennigs; children half price. A quarter of an
hour's drive north of Potsdam. Buses 38 and 42 from the centre
of the town.

The Brentano Museum (originally the Prussian State
Museum for Fairy Stories) is the only museum of its kind in
Europe. Although popular with children, there is also much in it
to interest and inform the adult visitor. Many of the exhibits are
in the grounds of the museum and one should visit these before
proceeding on to the main building. The outside exhibits include
a wishing well, a log cabin on chicken's legs, a giant beanstalk and
the famous gingerbread cottage.

The main building dates from the early eighteenth century
and was originally a hospital. However, in 1877 at the World
Congress of Folklorists in Geneva, a panel of German academics
issued a resolution calling for the establishment of a museum

which should commemorate the achievements of the Brothers Grimm and those who came after them, as well as housing an archive of materials relating to Germany's traditional fairy-lore. At first, the Museum was housed in an apartment block in Berlin, but in 1896 the present site was purchased and a year later opened to the public.

The main reception hall is dominated by a large canvas depicting 'The Marriage of Titania and Oberon', painted by Heinrich Fuseli. The long gallery to the left of the reception hall is devoted to the lives and work of Jacob and Wilhelm Grimm. Many interesting documents as well as portraits are on display here. The glass cabinets contain examples of all the main editions of Kinder- und Hausmärchen, as well as translations of the stories in forty-eight languages. At the far end of the gallery, one comes to The Chamber of The Nibelungen, a small display devoted to Germany's dwarfs and their legendary mining activities. The bust of Richard Wagner is by Ernst Wessler.

Sonja had seen Snow White and the Seven Dwarfs in the private cinema of Goebbels. The dwarfs in that had been miners. One would not have thought that dwarfs had the physique for mining. She said as much to Tilde, but Tilde said that Wagner's dwarfs were not really miners. Instead Alberich, who was a hoarder of treasure and crazed by sex, was a lightly disguised portrait of a Jew.

Retracing one's steps and turning left at the vestibule, one comes to the old operating theatre at the back of the building. This theatre, with its steep-banked tiers of seats, was originally used for teaching, but it has since been converted into a puppet-theatre. The wide ramps with high fences are part of the original design and were used to bring beds and stretchers down to the operating table. The puppeteers' repertoire includes 'Ali Baba and the Forty Thieves', 'Rapunzel', 'Baba Yaga' and 'The Snow Queen'.

The museum was indeed popular with children, they occupied all the seats in the theatre and waited for a performance of 'Rapunzel' to begin. So Tilde and Sonja had moved on to the west wing.

The west wing, which was originally the stable wing, now houses the Brentano galleries. In the main general gallery, the photographs of the Cottingley fairies are of particular interest. These were acquired by Sir Doyle, the British author best-known for his Sherlock Holmes stories. The waxwork tableaux in this gallery are devoted to the themes of The Princess, The Witch, The Trickster and The Talking Animal. Although the museum is primarily devoted to the lore of the Indo-Aryans, two rooms off the main Brentano gallery have been set aside for the fairy-tale culture of the Semites. That on Jewish folklore includes waxwork effigies of Lillith, the Dybbuk and the Golem.

Didn't the Jews go in for frightening folklore! And indeed the leaflet continued:

(This display is not recommended for small children of a sensitive disposition.) The Arabian Nights Chamber is, however, charming. Here the story-telling Sheherezade presides over a motley assembly, including Sinbad carrying the Old Man of the Sea on his

Shoulders, the Bronze Horseman, Prince Ahmed on His Flying Carpet and the giant Roc's Egg. The costume designs on the wall are for a Russian ballet version of Sheherezade and are by Bakst.

Perhaps the visit to the Brentano Museum and its *Arabian Nights* Chamber was something decreed by fate, since it prefigured Sonja's destiny as the star of *Baghdad Capers*, the climax of her career so far. By then, of course, the museum was closed. But, no. There was something else. What was it? She was always conscious of things on the edge of her mind, in the shadows and waiting to come into the full light of her consciousness. Was everybody like that?

Anyway, the leaflet continued:

At the far end of the Brentano Gallery, the door on the left leads to Bluebeard's Chamber. (Again, this is not recommended for small children of a sensitive disposition.) The door on the right leads to The Giant's Breakfast Table. This is one of the most popular exhibits and should on no account be missed. The archive and library on the top floor are open to members of the public who have furnished themselves with suitable letters of recommendation.

The Brentano Museum of Fairy Stories and Folk Literature stands as a fitting memorial to the Brothers Grimm who did so much to lay the seeds of Germany's future greatness by collecting the oral traditions of the Folk. The essence of our sacred Germanic heritage is to be found not in the airless libraries and theatres of the cities, but rather in Germany's fields and forests, as well as in the wise hearts of those who dwell therein. People, pay attention to the lore of the fairy tale! The fairy tale teaches virtue and valour. The Aryan hero is strong, fearless, resolute and straightforward in his thinking. The Aryan heroine is also brave, as well as being chaste and a good mother to her children. The Aryan child loves to hear our ancient fairy tales being retold. In so doing, he is absorbing the blood wisdom of our race.

Maybe she should also include other documents, mementos of her past, in the autobiography. Sonja had found herself moved when she contemplated such reminders of her childhood. If ever she complained about being unable to sleep, her mother used to compare her to the princess in 'The Story of the Princess and the Pea'. Did all small girls dream of becoming princesses? In August her family would stay in a boarding house in Scheveningen. The lodgings were not very comfortable, but that hardly mattered as they spent all day on the beach, sheltering from the fierce wind in the wickerwork basket chairs, or, if the weather turned really bad, then they would take shelter in one of the wheeled changing cabins that had been brought down to the beach by horses. Sonja, who read and reread the stories of Hans Christian Andersen, would spend hours by the water's edge, looking out for mermaids, searching for playmates in the sea.

Looking back on the visit to the museum and knowing what she knew now about Tilde, Sonja realised that Tilde's real purpose in getting her out to Potsdam was not to visit the UFA studios. That was merely a pretext for showing Sonja round the Brentano Museum. For some reason Tilde was obsessed with the tales of the Brothers Grimm. Listening to Tilde, Sonja thought that their stories seemed violent and gruesome, for she preferred tales in which the princess, after facing down certain dangers, finds true happiness and marries the prince. Come to think of it, it would be even better if the princess did not face dangers. But then, as she thought this, she felt a flash of joy, for she had realised something much more important. Now she had a title for her autobiography! *My Life is like a Fairy Tale*. Having got the title, all she needed was a structure for the book. Her story needed to build to a climax and end with a grand flourish and for that she thought that she needed a big part in a big film. But her book would need more planning. Perhaps she needed to talk to a professional writer.

Chapter Five

A week after her visit to Babelsberg and Potsdam she and Tilde went to see *Mandrake*, a film in which Brigitte Helm played the young woman cursed by that unhappy name. Dressed in white and wearing a turban, this blonde vamp, who writhed and undulated seductively on a series of couches, led the men who loved her to their ruin. It was supposed to be a horror film, but Sonja did not find it particularly horrific. Instead, she was tempted by the thought of becoming a demi-mondaine herself. She might enjoy leading men to their doom.

Mandrake was of course an exception. In those days there were too many films that dealt in fear and drew on tales told in the darkness, sinister narratives that overtook old towns of teetering houses with gabled windows and pointed rooftops. Through their narrow streets that sometimes turned into stairways crept men newly awakened from their coffins, master criminals, lunatics on the loose, Jews escaped from their ghettos, shadow creatures. Such films spoke of the obstinacy of the past that ought to vanish but will not. The monsters were old and ugly and the ugliness of old people served as advance warning of the greater horror to come as the world closed in on its victims. *The Hands of Orlac*, *Nosferatu*, *London after Midnight*, *The Golem*, *Waxworks*, *The Student of*

Prague, Lost Shadows, Vampyr, Dr Mabuse; Sonja had seen none of these films, for after all why should she pay money to be made afraid? But later she would hear David and his clever friends discuss them and she had studied the posters. At dinner one evening she had heard crazy speculation from David that on one winter night the monsters might succeed in breaking free from the screen and then they might creep out through the darkened cinema to escape into the world of the everyday, a world which from then on would be subjected to their violence and horror. David said such strange things at times. He spent a lot of time thinking about death, whereas she thought of herself as being one hundred per cent for life. She did see *The Cabinet of Dr Caligari* in most curious circumstances, but she was not sure that she was going to give an account of that event in her book.

She was to experience horror of a more ordinary kind when she went alone to the cinema in the following week. She usually went to films at least once a week and, apart from avoiding horror, she was perfectly indiscriminate in what she saw – comedies, crime films, westerns, musicals, romances. Though she liked to be surprised, she did not like the shock she got when she went to see *Melody of the Heart*. She had been looking forward to a romance, which is what the title suggested, and indeed it was a romance, the tragic love story of a peasant girl and a Hungarian army corporal. But Sonja had to walk out of the film half way through. She was in tears, not about the doomed love of the soldier and his girl, but because they talked and sang. Her first thought had been that this was an amusing little trick – to make the characters on the screen appear to talk and sing and the Hungarian folk songs did sound quite cheerful, but slowly the realisation was borne in upon her that now her ambition of becoming a film star was further away than ever from being realised. Her German was still far too poor to pass muster if she was going to have to master memorising a script and speaking from it and besides she knew that her Dutch accent was quite strong. Thinking the matter through later that evening, she thought that she would have to give up her dance classes. She could not afford that as well as the language lessons that she was now going to have to pay for. The following week two more talkies were released and her mind was made up. The dance classes would have to go.

Meanwhile she had been working towards becoming a flamboyant waitress. She had started to dance out to the tables and, when she got to them, she shimmied seductively, before singing out the extras. It was absurd and, since she was not naturally flamboyant, she was scared stiff. She thought that she would almost certainly attract ridicule. She would probably lose her job. Indeed, Martin, the proprietor, was at first unhappy, but when, he saw how popular this was with some of the patrons, he just scowled and shrugged. Not only did customers return for further performances, but the restaurant soon became a draw for new clients. She even began to forget the original reason for these performances and just looked forward to getting the tips. In retrospect, Sonja was embarrassed by how she had been selling herself. It would have to be downplayed in *My Life is like a Fairy Tale*. It was silly and it was humiliating, but yet it worked.

One evening a noisier party than usual arrived in the restaurant. Apparently they had checked that this was indeed the restaurant with the singing waitress. There were eight of them at table and one of them was supposed to be a famous Swedish film actress. (Sonja could no longer remember her name, but she could make that up. She could claim that it was Garbo and probably get away with it.) The man at the head of the table, who was obviously the host, kept looking at her. His bald head was extraordinary, for with its smooth, gleaming planes, it could almost be the head of a bronze statue. Also, it was scarcely perceptible, and indeed perhaps Sonja imagined it, but the man seemed to vibrate as if he had difficulty in controlling the power within him. So she was fairly sure that he must be a Leo.

At length he summoned her over and after continuing to gaze intently at her for a few minutes, he said that extraordinary sentence, 'Would you like to be in films?'

Sonja just laughed and smiled, but he was impatient with this and repeated the question. She nodded.

'My name is David Rego and I am a film producer.' Then, when Sonja stammered out her name, he handed her his card and said, 'Meet me in the Palm Court of the Adlon Hotel on Sunday at midday and we shall see what we can do with you.'

Then he and his party resumed eating. Sonja had to beg Martin for a few minutes off, so that she could go into the backyard, smoke a cigarette and calm down. Films! Apart from anything else, it was from watching films that she had learnt how to hold a cigarette and smoke it in a way that she thought looked sensual.

Chapter Six

Ah, the Adlon Hotel! Suddenly the golden dream! The description of the luxury of the Adlon on Unter den Linden will be laid on with a trowel, since she is coming to realise that the chief response she wants to provoke in her readers is envy. So first there were the uniformed commissionaires at the top of the entrance steps who respectfully usher her through the door, then the flunkey inside who asks if she is meeting anyone. His eyebrows rise in respect when she gives the film producer's name. She barely has time to contemplate the large reception area with its vaulted and coffered ceiling, stained glass dome and elephant fountain before a bellhop is found to conduct her to the Palm Court. David Rego rises to greet her and kisses her hand, but then he briskly leads her to the Japanese Garden in the middle of the hotel. There a photographer is waiting beside its fountain and a couple of his assistants struggle with the extra lights that are supposed to give the faint sunshine some back-up. The photographic session took three-quarters of an hour and was very tedious. The only good thing about it was that lots of people stopped to watch, convinced that she was already a famous star of some sort. Yes, that was it! How she wanted to be looked at and envied! One of them wore a turban and he must have been a maharaja.

Finally David took her in to lunch. Crabe royale à la mayonnaise was followed by asparagus and then a clear beef soup. The main course consisted of goose with brown potatoes, after which they moved to the hotel's library, where in more comfortable chairs, they were served cakes and liqueurs. Sonja had been listing all the films she had seen and in desperately broken German detailing the plots of the ones she could remember. David had seemed amused. Now in the library, he lit a cigar. Hitherto he had been talking about the hotel and his suite in it, the history of Dutch art, the diamond trade, horse racing and fine wines. Only now did he get down to business.

'The accent is enchanting, but it will have to go. I will arrange for you to have coaching in elocution. You won't be the only one. More than half our people at UFA are going to have to go to classes in order to get rid of their high pitch, their stammer, their lisp, or their provincial accent. But there will be no need for language lessons. You will find that all you will have to do is memorise the scripts that you will be given. Today's photographs will be developed by tomorrow and I will show them to my associates.'

Then…

How does one write about sex, she wondered, but did she have to write about sex at all? Perhaps she should present herself as being like the Snow Queen whom she had read about as a child and whose tableau she had seen in that museum. She could write about all the famous actors who she could claim had made passes at her and then tell her readers how coldly she had rebuffed them. Then the men who saw her films might dream that they might be the first to soften and win her icy heart. But, as she continued to ponder this, she thought that it might be more exciting to present herself as a man-eating vamp. If so, she needed to hint at her numerous sexual conquests, but subtly, so that it was not picked up by some Nazi board of censorship. How did one hint subtly at sex? It would be a hard struggle to get to grips with the dark secret language of this underworld. The meaningful glances, the intimate smells, the tangled bed clothes. Or perhaps just a set of asterisks. No, she really had no idea and so she decided that she would have to read some novels in order to find out how the trick was done, though this was a dismal prospect. She had not read a novel since the one she was forced to read at school, and she could not even remember the book's title. It had knights in armour in it. That book was, of course, jolly boring and she was pretty sure that there was no sex in it, not even of the kind that was subtly hinted at. But then, how did one find out which novels did have subtle hints of sex in them? She could hardly go into a bookshop and ask for a novel, any novel, which had a subtle hint of sex in it. Nor could she ask around. David had vanished and Manasseh had gone too and Tilde these days would be shocked and censorious.

But thinking about sex brought back memories of the first film in which she appeared, though only in a tiny voiceless walk-on part, as her elocution lessons had not then finished. The film was *The Blue Angel*, directed by Josef von Sternberg and starring Emil Jannings and Marlene Dietrich. As Sonja recalled, Jannings was supposed to be the big star and Dietrich was a fairly new discovery, but as the shooting went on and Jannings realised that she was stealing the limelight, he became angrier and angrier, so much so that when he was directed to simulate an attempt to strangle his co-star, he very nearly succeeded in killing her and had to be pulled away. Or so Sonja was told. She was not actually on the set at the time.

Standing in the shadows, Sonja had closely observed every single gesture or word of Dietrich's. Sonja had been like a scientist who studies a new form of life. The languidly arrogant Dietrich, who played Lola-Lola, lolled back on a barrel, revealing her frilly white panties, a garter belt and exquisitely sheathed long legs and, as she sang 'Falling in Love Again' in a low smoky voice, the doom of the pompous and bullying Professor Rath (played by Jannings) was assured, for he has fallen for an insolent slut who will conduct him to the lowest possible point of degradation.

Von Sternberg's set design for the interior of the Blue Angel nightclub was elaborate and cluttered. In front of the backcloth of a painted harbour, mirrors, birdcages, caryatids and sordid fripperies were suspended from the ceiling. The floor was sticky from spilled beer and the set was filled with smoke and there were quite a few retakes because of the coughing. Von Sternberg had encased the cameras and cameramen in large wooden crates in order to silence the cranking of the machines. Moving these crates for new shots was an extraordinarily elaborate and slow business. And everything was made slower yet by the fact that each scene was being shot first in German and then in English. All sound had to be recorded live, simultaneously on a single track. Every time there was coughing they had to start again. Sonja's excitement soon shaded into boredom.

Lola-Lola sang from a stage and behind her sat a line of fat and extraordinarily ugly women who clutched beer steins and who looked a little like badly sculpted Polynesian statues. Of course Sonja had wanted to be on the stage too, but von Sternberg had been abruptly dismissive. David had explained that the director needed only fat ugly women on the stage in order to set off the slender beauty of Dietrich. The truth was that von Sternberg had not wanted Sonja in his film at all, but David had forced her on him and she had to be content with her momentary appearance as a waitress bringing beer to a table. It was ironic of course, but at least this was something she knew about. If she had had to play a brilliant astronomer, pretending to be that might have been a bit more difficult. Anyway, as that man with the foreign name said, 'There is no such thing as a small part.'

The reason that she thought back on all this now was that she remembered that there had been someone else standing in the shadows with her and watching the shooting. This was the person who had written the novel on which the film was based. He was a young man in his twenties and he was called Heinrich Mann. He had muttered to her that 'The success of this film will be found between the naked thighs of Miss Dietrich'. Sonja did not know that, young though Mann was, he was already famous and they did not have much to say to one another, but she thought that Tilde would be impressed to learn that she had met an actual novelist. This was not the case. When much later his name came up in some context, Tilde, who was in her Nazi phase, said that she knew of him, but she described him as a culturally poisonous degenerate who mixed up left-wing polemic with something dangerously close to pornography. And then Tilde had asked Sonja not to smoke in her presence in future.

But, despite what Tilde said, Heinrich had not looked like a degenerate. Sonja had seen all sorts of films in which degenerates featured and thought that she knew what they should look like. They were loose-lipped and inclined to drool. They were not good at shaving and their hands trembled from relentless self-abuse. They might have English accents. They often had hooked noses. But Heinrich Mann had looked quite normal and besides Sonja had liked to stay close to him as she was afraid of Reinhold Bernt, who had the role of the clown and shambled about the set in his sinister clown's outfit. As the clown who appeared in a series of scenes within the nightclub, he was supposed to presage the evil fate awaiting the Professor who, enslaved by his love for Lola-Lola, would end up donning a clown's outfit himself. As Sonja gazed on Reinhold's horrid white mask, she thought that it was more that his appearance on the film might presage an evil fate for everyone associated with it and maybe this was not silly superstition, for, as Tilde later pointed out, von Sternberg, Dietrich and Mann all betrayed their country by fleeing to America and putting themselves in the hands of Hollywood's Jewish plutocrats. Well, good riddance to Dietrich. There had been a time when Sonja had thought that she might like to go to Hollywood... but no, she must stop rambling.

Cigarette break.

What had now occurred to her was that when people picked up a copy of *My Life is like a Fairy Tale* and discovered that she had been in such famous films as *The Blue Angel*, *The Gypsy Baron* and *Munchausen*, they would not want just to read about her, they would expect anecdotes about the other stars: Jannings, Negri, Albers, Baarova, Fritsch, Rökk and the rest of them. Also they would want to hear about temperamental and dictatorial directors. The trouble was that during the shooting of *Blue Angel*, von Sternberg had hardly said a single word to Sonja and Dietrich did not even seem to be aware of her presence. So Sonja was jolly well going to have to make stuff up. Perhaps she could pretend to have been present at some kind of sinister Svengali and Trilby scene between von Sternberg and Dietrich. She would have to think about that. As she reflected back on hearing Tilde denounce Heinrich Mann for his decadence, Sonja wondered if his novel about the tart and the professor may not be exactly the book she needs to look at for guidance on how to write subtly about sex. The novel was not called *The Blue Angel*. It had another title. But then she remembered another meeting with Tilde. Tilde had entered the restaurant looking stern yet pleased. She was late. By way of an apology, she explained that she had been attending a book burning at Opernplatz and she continued, 'Your friend, the one who wrote a book about a prostitute and a professor in a cabaret, his book was on the bonfire.'

'He was never my friend,' Sonja protested anxiously. 'I barely exchanged a few words with him.'

By now Sonja was wondering if she and Tilde should remain friends. After all Sonja knew plenty of more comfortable and entertaining people. Perhaps she did not need Tilde. This incarnation of Tilde had grown her hair long and put it up in braids. Her skirt looked as though it was made of horsehair and she wore a white blouse and tie, and the tie carried an enamelled tiepin in the shape of a broken cross. So very different from the Tilde she had met all those years ago on the Kufurstendam. But that was Pisces for you. In the end Sonja decided to stay 'friends' with her. It might after all be useful to have a contact with someone so high up in the National Socialist Women's League. Tilde even nourished hopes of succeeding Gertrud Scholtz-Klink as National Socialist Women's League 'Fuehrer'. In the meantime Tilde had become a leading campaigner against women smoking cigarettes. Smoking was not properly feminine. Also make-up was bad. 'Make-up is make-believe and your red talons like a bird of prey. Your face like butcher's shop. All your face needs is water and fresh air. Painting the face is decadent.'

Why had Tilde been so down on decadence? Sonja had always thought of decadence as a good thing. Well, obviously, now Sonja thought about it, there was not going to be any point in going around asking for a novel by Heinrich Mann. That could only get her into trouble. But then she remembered that film *Mandrake* about a man-eating vamp who was played by Brigitte Helm. That had lots of sex in it and it was based on a novel. She knew that, because later she met the author, Hans Heinz Ewers. Well, naturally she had, since she had met just about every famous person in Germany from Hitler downwards: Goebbels, Goering, Leni Riefenstahl, Hans Albers, Putzi Hanfstaengel, Richard Strauss, Herbert von Karajan, Sepp Dietrich, Veit Harlan, Admiral Canaris, Prince Willi, her special friend Eva Braun, and so on and so on. That was why *My Life is like a Fairy Tale* was going to be such a fascinating book, as it let ordinary people get a glimpse of what life was like among Germany's elite.

If she remembered rightly it was around this time that it occurred to her to ask Tilde about the autobiography that Wieland had been writing in prison. *Tomorrow Belongs to Me* turned out to be a very peculiar sort of autobiography, since it was about what was going to happen to him. It was all based on the dreams he had. Those dreams promised him a golden future, after, that is, a hard stint in the Foreign Legion.

'He says that if the future had not already happened the present could not exist. He will turn out not to have the physique to be a soldier and his time in the Legion will be short. But beyond that he hears his future selves calling to him and promising him wonderful things. There are so many plays, as yet unwritten, which are waiting for him to write and, of course, his time in the Legion will provide him with lots of material to draw on. But there are odd gaps in what he sees and he found it difficult to get his future experiences in the right order.'

(Sonja was glad that he too had had that problem.)

Tilde continued, 'I smuggled the manuscript out of Moabit and took it to various publishers. But you would not believe it! Publishers are such second nighters! They want all those marvellous things he has described to actually happen before they are prepared to publish his account of them. What would be the point of that? That would be missing the whole point of the book, and by then, after his adventures in North Africa and as Germany's leading dramatist, as well as the pioneer of future-life-writing, publishers will be queuing up to publish him, but he will have no need of them. Publishers!'

Then seeing the apprehensive look on Sonja's face, Tilde laughed bitterly and said, 'Oh yes, you do feature prominently in his book. You will be beside him as he receives the nation's acclaim.'

But now Sonja must not let Wieland take over her

thoughts, still less her hypothetical future. All of this was just wool gathering. She must get back to the point. What was the point? Yes, writing about sex. She realised with a cold start that she dared not write about sex at all, not even in a most subtle fashion, for surely Joseph would be furious if *My Life is like a Fairy Tale* revealed how many men she had slept with and the reasons for her doing so. Therefore, for the time being at least, she would skip what happened at the Adlon Hotel after lunch. Not even asterisks would serve. It was going to be the Snow Queen after all. So how dull her memoir was going to be, with no sex, no mention of smoking and only an occasional and polite glass of champagne. She will stop thinking about sex. It was cold in her flat and the electricity supply had not been repaired yet, but at least the sirens were quiet tonight.

Chapter Seven

The following morning Sonja clocked in once more at the UFA studios where she found men still working on demolishing the closing set of *The Woman of My Dreams*, while some of the chorines were helping the wardrobe mistress put away costumes, but there was nothing for Sonja to do. Perhaps there would be news later in the day, but who could tell whether it would be good or bad? Only the horoscope. Sonja borrowed a newspaper and found her star sign. 'The alliance between your ruler, Venus, the Sun and Neptune which accentuates both transformation and illusion during the coming week, will bring back many memories and these in turn will stimulate strange ideas. However good these ideas seem to you, proceed with caution.' Not very useful. So anyway Sonja settled in a quiet corner of the canteen and took out her notebook once again. She was going to write about parties: the Press Balls, the reception of Prince Paul of Yugoslavia, the Night of the Amazons in the grounds of Nymphenburg Castle, Goering's birthday at the Opera, the fateful Peacock Island party, the UFA anniversary celebration, the premiere of *Baghdad Capers*, the harlequinade in Venice, Eva Braun's birthday… so many parties! No, not the party on Peacock Island.

But the first party she went to was a relatively small-scale affair – the first that is apart from children's parties in Dordrecht. Not that her first party felt small-scale then. This was the party thrown after the first showing of *The Blue Angel* at the Gloria-Palace cinema, April 1st, 1930. She smiled to remember how terrified she had been as she entered the foyer of the cinema where it was taking place. She might have been entering a cage full of wild beasts, but yet she was aware that her terror of the wild beasts was less than her fear of the deathly boredom she would experience if she spent that evening alone in her flat. In an odd sort of way, in a way that she could not understand, fear was her friend. She had to be at the party. David would be there. And, of course, going to a party was good practice for going to more parties. As it turned out, though the party was not the sort of ordeal she had been anticipating, something awful did indeed happen.

She wore a heavy black silk dress, close-fitting at the waist, with a wide bell-shaped skirt, with a short bolero jacket. It was her armour, but was it strong enough? At first she could not see David. So who on earth was going to talk to her? She need not have worried. It seemed that lots of men wanted to talk to her and lecture her about the Austrian banking crisis, international yachting competitions, duelling fraternities, Rosicrucianism, cross-country walks, psychoanalysis, the Rhineland, rent increases, the novels of a certain Herman Hesse. God they were boring, but she hardly had to say anything. All she had to do was smile while they talked. Alcohol was rather wonderful. But so many of these people were fat! It was not just the fat ladies who had sat behind Dietrich in *The Blue Angel*. Most of the money-men behind the films were fat too. Eventually she was introduced to Alfred Hugenberg, the fabulously wealthy industrialist who had recently bought UFA. He was very fat, moustachioed and, as she learnt at wearisome length, he hoped for the restoration of a Hohenzollern emperor. Having established that she was from Holland, Hugenberg went on to praise the Dutch for giving Kaiser Wilhelm refuge in Doorn. The Kaiser was a martyr to the vindictiveness of the French and British. Did she not agree?

Well, she was about to agree, just as she had agreed that duelling scars were sexy and that the Rhineland would benefit from being remilitarised. But at this point, David joined them. Where had he come from? She stood there listening to the two men politely chatting about the reduced circumstances of Germany's imperial and princely families, but by God she could see how they hated each other. So anyway, was this all that a party was, people standing about drinking and talking? Perhaps things might perk up with Pass the Parcel or Pin the Tail on the Donkey.

Dietrich was, of course, not there. She was already on her way to the United States – and von Sternberg was also not at the party. He was probably busy packing and preparing to follow her there. So the only real star holding forth in the foyer of the Gloria-Palace was Emil Jannings. He did so with his mouth full and there was something rather panicky in the way he kept grabbing at the canapés. He was even fatter than Hugenberg. A few years later Sonja saw Jannings play the President of the Boer Republic in *Uncle Krüger*. He led the Dutch-speaking farmers in their valiant but doomed attempt to fight off the English who were lusting for the Transvaal's gold. The film ended up with Krüger old, blind and in exile in Switzerland. Though he had been defeated, he was defiant in defeat, 'That

77

was how England subdued our small nation by the cruellest of means, but eventually the day of retribution will come!' he had declared. 'I don't know when, but all that blood could not have been spilt in vain. We are just a small, weak nation. But great and powerful nations will revolt against the British tyranny. They will knock England to the ground. God will be with them and this will clear the way for a better world.'

Sonja was as anti-English as the next person and this was supposed to be a moving moment, but all she could see on the screen was the fat, grumpy man who was obsessed with stuffing his face. Anyway, back to the party. Hugenberg was saying that what Germany needed to lead it out of the current crisis was a strong man at the helm. David, who enthusiastically agreed, said that General Schleicher was just the man. Hugenberg was stony faced and even Sonja could see that he thought that *he* was just the man.

But then she was distracted by the sight of the clown pushing past the commissionaire at the doorway. How extraordinary and how tasteless on the part of Reinhold Bernt to turn up at the party in his clown's outfit! Now the clown – white face, a long nose and red hair shooting out from the sides of an otherwise bald white head – seemed to be making his way towards them and then Sonja spotted Reinhold who was in a dinner jacket and who was also looking at the clown in some consternation. Sonja shrank back against David, while Hugenberg turned to look at what or who was troubling her.

The clown seemed to ignore her and addressed the two men, 'You see me here dressed in motley, for I am come as a warning, Mr Rego. I was once as steady and sober as you two gentlemen, but look at me now! I am merely a clown, for I am become a slave to beauty. Beware of Fraulein Heda's beauty, Mr Rego! She is a fatal woman and she has me in her chains. Don't follow me into her trap, I beg you. Beware, Mr Rego! If you let her, she will saddle and ride you as if you were her donkey, Mr Rego. Mr Rego, I am come here as a friend to warn you. Let me take you away from here and buy you a drink and together we can drown our sorrows as we discuss Fraulein Heda's undeniable yet dangerous charms.'

This terrifying madness in what had hitherto been a sedate party! It must be Wieland! It was Wieland. And yet he did not look at all like Wieland.

Hugenberg was gesturing to the commissionaire to come over and deal with this intruder, but David did not wait for assistance. His fist shot out and he punched the clown on the nose. Sonja, looking down on the man sprawled on the floor, saw that his nose had been squashed sideways and flattened across his cheek. It was like an episode from a nightmare.

'That is right. Humiliate me. I deserve it,' Wieland mumbled.

Yes, it was Wieland and he removed the rest of the false nose from his face before coughing experimentally and spitting some blood onto his hand. Then he wiped the bloody hand on his clown's skullcap which was now tilted at an odd angle. Now at last the commissionaire backed up by one of the wine waiters came bustling up and dragged Wieland away. As he was being pulled through the doors, Wieland shouted, this time to Sonja, 'You are a creature of light and I am your dark shadow. We are two sides of the same story.'

David looked enquiringly at Sonja. Indeed, everyone was looking at her.

'I have never seen that man before in my life.' Well, lying is what actresses do. Sonja, looking back on the incident, thought that she was a good liar. That was one party she was not going to tell the whole truth about. But the same was true about the night on Peacock Island. She must include an account of it in *My Life is like a Fairy Tale*. But only part of the story could be told, or even thought about.

Cigarette break.

No need to face the event on Peacock Island quite yet. Back to the premiere of *The Blue Angel*. As Wieland was being dragged away, Sonja heard a woman behind her comment, 'You really have made a good start. Men fighting over you at the premiere of the season's major film. That will rate a paragraph in next week's *Film Courier*.'

Sonja turned and, while David and Hugenburg continued to argue about politics, she found herself talking films with a youngish blonde woman who had introduced herself as Lilian. She looked vaguely familiar. Sonja guessed that she might be the wife of one of the film executives. They often hung around the set during shooting. Anyway Sonja and Lilian exchanged gossip about the next big film which was said to be a costume musical with the working title *The Congress Dances*.

What happened thereafter was again a bit embarrassing and so Sonja was relieved to be interrupted in her writing by a gofer who informed her that one of the casting directors wanted to see her the following week. This might be her big chance. An account of how she secured a starring role in *Kolberg* would make a wonderful climax to *My Life is like a Fairy Story*. Tomorrow. It was now impossible for her to concentrate on any one thing. Perhaps Wieland was right to warn David.

Perhaps she was bad news to men. Certainly she was not lucky for David. She could not remember how Wieland had tracked her down at that premiere. Her memory was getting worse. Perhaps it was due to the barbiturate sedatives that she had started to take on Joseph's recommendation? Surely Joseph was a Jewish name? Would there be lots of dancing in *Kolberg*? Was it Sonja's destiny to bring fame to Dordrecht? Everybody knows about the Peacock Island party, but Sonja's book will try to give a sense of what it was like to actually be there, though not, of course, the real truth of the matter. Cigarette break again? No, she better not. God, she was running short and would have to cadge some to see her through the rest of the day. The second embarrassment produced by the party for the premiere of *The Blue Angel* was a delayed one. A few weeks after the premiere, she discovered that the Lilian she had been talking to was Lilian Harvey, the famous Lilian Harvey. That was why she was so familiar. Sonja had seen her in *Three from the Filling Station* as well as several earlier films. Moreover, though Lilian had been too discreet or modest to say so, she must have already known that she had got the star part in *The Congress Dances*.

If only Sonja could give up smoking. Tilde had told her that she did not have the right to poison her body in this way. Women who smoked aged prematurely and lost their attractiveness to men. The Fuehrer never smokes and he has denounced cigarettes as a decadent Jewish import. But David had thought her attractive when she smoked, but perhaps he would... but also Eva smoked and she and Sonja sometimes shared cigarettes. Anyway, though the government condemned smoking, she was sure that she would not have a need for cigarettes, if there was not a war on. So it was really the government's fault. Barbiturates worked up to a point, but what she really needed was anti-boredom pills.

This is no good, skittering from subject to subject. She must write something. *The Congress Dances* then. That was such an innocent musical, so full of laughter, dancing, singing and romance. Set against the background of the Congress of Vienna in 1814, it was the story of a brief flirtation between Tsar Alexander and a glove seller called Christel. Sonja thought that she was a bit like Christel, for she too was bubbly, frothy and simple-hearted and yet she had been taken up by a great man of state. But, though Sonja did secure a role in *The Congress Dances*, it was only as the lead female dancer in a version of the Polovtsian Dances which was being performed at the Vienna Opera House in honour of the Tsar. Seductively veiled and crowned, she had arched away from a Polovtsian archer before yielding to his embrace. She was also one of the hundreds of dancers who waltzed at the Grand Charity Ball, but that *was* fun.

She had loved being part of that film – the dances, the bonnets, the satin dresses, the landaus, the uniforms, above all the uniforms. Were people happier in those days? They ought to have been. What a pity that the film had not been made in colour. (If only they could have also made *Baghdad Capers* in colour.) Even a few years ago films were never in colour. But those shakos and the tunics with gilded epaulettes and the swinging scabbards in *The Congress Dances*! She loved uniforms and, even though today's uniforms were drabber in colour, still Sonja thought that one had to admit that they were much better cut than in olden days. She particularly admired the swooping long grey greatcoats of the generals with those wide red lapels, as well as the flare of the long black leather dress coats of the senior SS with the jodhpurs and the riding boots. These things made her heart sing. She thought it most unfair that there was not an SS costume for women. And then the officers sported badges of rank and maybe SS runes and silver chains, all things that caught the torchlight so well in the night-time processions. But as for women, the sort of costumes worn by Tilde and her sisters in the Nazi Women's League, or whatever it was called, were just monstrously frumpish.

If there was a party for the premiere of *The Congress Dances*, she did not remember it. So many parties and perhaps also so much drink. She does remember the scene in the film in which Christel/Lilian triumphantly rides through Vienna in an open carriage and sings: 'Today all fairy tales come true.' Yes, that should be so. But one day, maybe soon, everyone who had taken part in that film would be dead – so many silver ghosts. Perhaps that was why Sonja was writing *My Life is like a Fairy Tale*. As a kind of memorial to be set over a mass grave. Anyway Lilian Harvey was now back in England and good riddance to her. She had been perfectly pleasant, but annoyingly in the way. Sonja also remembers Conrad Veidt, the star who had played Metternich in the film. He was so handsome. Why did he have to leave Germany? Was he Jewish? Even if so, she had really fancied him, just as she had desired David. But it was no longer correct to have such desires and her thoughts were taking her once again to places where she ought not to want to go.

Chapter Eight

In the corner of the canteen someone has put a record on. Zarah Leander was singing 'The Wind Has Told Me a Song' from *Habanera*.

> The wind has told me a song
> Of fortune indescribably beautiful.
> He knows what my heart is lacking,
> For whom it beats and glows.
> He knows for whom.

Habanera had been Sonja's first credited role. That was in 1937. Even as recently as then she was still able to fool herself and think that she was still young. Now the song made her heart ache, not for any man, but for the woman she was then who did yearn for a certain man. Though part of her wanted to rush on to the good bits in her story, like being chosen for the starring role in *Baghdad Capers* or her time in Venice during the shooting of *Munchausen*, or perhaps her visits to the Berghof, nevertheless the more sensible part of her had decided that she should be more disciplined and put things down in chronological order. The trouble was that she was no good at chronology. Getting things in the right order was all but impossible. Still she was a little surprised to find that part of her was sensible, surprised and saddened, for that just made her feel middle-aged when she only wanted to be young and silly again. As for Zarah Leander, Sonja knew her well, but she would write about her and *Habanera* later.

For now she wanted to give her readers an impression of how it was when she was a young aspiring actress. Her readers needed to be told that it was not all easy, by no means just a matter of luck. She had thought that *The Congress Dances*, which had been her biggest part so far, would soon lead on to bigger things. It was not so. Over the next few years she was given a few walk-on or dance-on parts in small films, but mostly she was unemployed. The opening years of the thirties were hard for her – and for most people. The collapse of the Credit Anstalt Bank in Austria led on to the bankruptcy of several German banks. Money was tight in the film business and elsewhere. David bored her with his ruminations about the country's continuing need to pay or not to pay reparations and the analyses that he made of one inconclusive election after another. What was the point of political analysis? What will be, will be. But there was also all that marching in the streets and sometimes fights too. Then Hitler came to power. At least there were no more elections after that, but it did become difficult to buy things in Jewish shops.

At this point she was going to pile it on. Stuff about trooping along to cold audition halls. Friends and rivals but all gals together in the dressing rooms. 'If it's not me they choose, I hope it's you.' The shared laughter and the shared hopes too. But that was all rubbish of course. First, the competition was too fierce and the times too hard for any genuine camaraderie.

Secondly, Sonja was disliked because she was a foreigner who had come to Germany to steal parts that ought to go to German actresses. The country's film industry harboured too many of these parasitic foreign harpies: Pola Negri and Marika Rökk were Hungarian; Zarah Leander and Kristina Söderbaum were Swedish; Olga Chekhova was Russian; Lillian Harvey was English; Lida Baarova was Czech; Rosita Serrano was Chilean. Then and in the years that followed Sonja had heard a lot of that sort of thing. And sometimes it was insinuated that she looked awfully like an oriental Jewess... but she was drifting again.

She was never really on the breadline, for not only did she have a small retainer from UFA, but David looked after her, sort of. But she thought that he was not trying hard enough for her and that he was secretly happy enough to keep her for himself, only bringing her out for parties. He was often inattentive and more and more preoccupied with moving money around in various foreign banks. One morning the post brought her something interesting. The envelope was in an unfamiliar hand. Inside was a postcard of Goethe's house in Frankfurt and on the other side was scrawled, 'This might interest you'. The signature was indecipherable. Attached to the card was a small ad from *Film Artists and Film Art* which announced auditions for a female lead in a feature film that was shortly scheduled to go into production. A young woman was wanted and exotic looks would be an advantage. Sonja was not excited to read this. She'd had her hopes raised too often. But David was away in Switzerland doing something complicated and financial and he had refused to take her with him. So she thought that she might do something on her own initiative and go to the audition.

The audition was held in a community hall in Wilmersdorf. Four other women had turned up for the audition and only one of them looked at all exotic. First they were given a text from Schiller's *William Tell* to read from and after this they were asked to extemporise and give their impression of a woman mad with grief because she had lost her baby. They were all very nervous, but Sonja judged that she was far and away the least nervous. After all, what was at stake? Wilmersdorf community hall was hardly likely to be the portal to stardom. They were asked to sit outside in a draughty anteroom, while the three men briefly deliberated. Somehow Sonja was not surprised to be called in and told that she had got the part. She actually shrugged. 'What part?'

Now the young man who was clearly in charge of the audition was in a hurry to reassure her. This was the leading female role in what would certainly be a major film, the remake of *The Cabinet of Dr Caligari* as a talkie. Sonja would play the part of Jane. Was she familiar with the film? She had to confess that she had heard of it, but never seen it. (She was sure that it was not the sort of film that her parents would have allowed her to watch.) The young man – his name was Hans Becker, by the way, and he would be directing the film – assured her that this was not a problem and that he would arrange a screening for her before shooting began. If she was available, filming would begin the week after next. A car would come for her on the Thursday and she should have a bag packed for a week away as they would be shooting on location. Of course, she did not believe a word of it, but the young man with thick curly black hair and heavy-rimmed glasses had such a disarming grin. So she crossed her fingers, smiled back and said that would be fine with her. He smiled too. There was one final thing. He wanted to check that her name was Sonja Heda.

She stayed in that Thursday with a bag packed, just in case, and the hours passed and no car came. Around midday she was feeling a fool and thinking that she really ought to go out and get some air. She should have guessed that it was just some amateur outfit that was incapable of getting anything serious off the ground, or even perhaps a practical joke. Wieland had taught her to be wary of practical jokes. Still she took comfort from the fact she had been a bit suspicious from the start. She began to unpack, but then as she passed by the window she saw that a Mercedes was pulling up outside her flat. Manasseh went out to talk to the chauffeur while Sonja hastily threw things back in the case before hurrying down. Manasseh made a face as if to say 'What is this?' Sonja smiled brightly back at him. She was feeling very smiley. The chauffeur opened a door for her and, when she was seated, presented her with an enormous bouquet of flowers. Then they were off.

They drove for hours. The chauffeur had no conversation. All he could tell her was that his instructions were to drive her to a place outside Rosenheim. Rosenheim, that was in southern Bavaria! It was dark when they arrived and there was little she could see. Heavy ornamental iron gates swung open and the car swept up the gravelled driveway. An old woman, presumably the housekeeper, stood on the steps of a great house whose wings vanished into the darkness.

'Welcome Miss Heda. Herr Becker sends his apologies. Though he cannot be here tonight, he expects to be with us tomorrow. You must be very tired. I will conduct you to your bedroom.'

Sonja had wanted to say that she was actually starving, but she need not have worried. Sandwiches, fruit and a bottle of wine had been laid out on a table in her suite. She fell asleep listening to the cries of what must have been peacocks.

She awoke to late autumn sunshine. Her first starring role. Would she be up to it? Hans Becker was at the foot of the stairs as if he had been waiting for her.

'Good morning. Follow me if you will. Breakfast is in the ballroom.'

The breakfast was laid out on a trestle table towards the far end of the ballroom. Canvases of famous Germans lined the walls, like a giant's collection of cigarette cards: Wolfram von Eschenbach, Paracelsus, Frederick the Great, Goethe, Bismarck, Wagner. The most recent addition was General Ludendorff.

'Yes, isn't it marvellous?' said Hans gesturing round him. 'We shall be doing everything on location. No painted backdrops, no studio stuff.' Then, 'You look rather nervous.'

He leaned across the table and continued, 'Do please relax Sonja. I know what it is. You must be wondering how we chose you and why we did not recruit Olga Chekhova, Christina Söderbaum or some other big name. Why? Because we want to defamiliarise the familiar. So we do not want a big star – or rather we do, but someone who is made a big star by just this film. Actresses who are already famous just play themselves. The only part that Söderbaum seems to be equipped to play is that of Söderbaum. Whereas we do not want the viewers to experience the comfort of recognition, for this is going to be no ordinary film.'

Sonja wondered what Hans' star sign was. He was

young enough to be a student. Now she registered that a large white sheet had been hung on the wall beyond the table. The projectionist stood ready beside his machine and, as Hans poured out the coffee, the curtains were drawn, the projectionist started his cranking and the showing of Robert Wiene's version of *The Cabinet of Doctor Caligari* began. Hans kept up a running commentary throughout the showing.

'This is the film we have to destroy. The film you are about to watch is destined to be consigned to the dustbin of cinema history. This is likely to be one of its last showings. I think I can promise you, Sonja, Wiene's tawdry gothic fantasy will soon be quite forgotten and in future, when people mention The *Cabinet of Doctor Caligari* in conversation, it will be taken for granted that they are referring to the Becker masterpiece starring Sonja Heda.'

Sonja, who preferred musicals and romances, had seen nothing like the old film of *Caligari* before. In it, a hypnotist with that name used Cesare, a somnambulist who was under Caligari's hypnotic powers, to commit murders and terrorise the small town of Holstenwall. It was Hans who pointed to the screen and identified the actor playing the murderously sinister somnambulist as Conrad Veidt, the same actor whom Sonja had half fallen in love with when he had appeared as Metternich in *The Congress Dances*. She could never have guessed that one actor could play such different parts. Anyway Cesare killed Francis' best friend Allan and carried off Francis' girl.

'That is Jane,' said Hans when the young woman first appeared. 'That is your part. Watch her closely. I shall be playing Francis by the way.'

Sonja had no difficulty in recognising the actress as Lil Dagover, since she had even shared a changing room with her, as Dagover had been the supporting actress in *The Congress Dances* in which she had featured as the glamorous countess who has been detailed by Metternich to distract the Tsar. Dagover's milk-white skin was set off by her black-rimmed eyes and thickly applied lipstick. Sonja's Jane would obviously look rather different. But all the cast of the Wiene film were heavily made up. That was why she had not recognised Veidt with that ghastly white face and those dark shadows painted under his eyes. When Veidt as Cesare lifted Jane up in his arms, Dagover swooned beautifully and Sonja wondered whether she in her turn was going to be any good at swooning.

There was a change of spools and at that point Sonja allowed herself a cigarette and Hans launched into a diatribe about the sets used in the old film. These were painted flats set against one another at crazy angles with jagged shadows daubed on them. Pools of light were created by lanterns that teetered at unnatural angles. Sonja thought that if she had lived in such a town as Holstenwall she would have continually suffered from sea sickness. There had been no attempt at realism on the part of the designers and it was as if the whole gruesome drama was taking place in a badly damaged dolls house. Hans said that the designs were what was called Expressionist, but Expressionism had had its day. Now he was proposing a starkly realistic remake of the story. 'It will speak to our times and those times are too grim for fantasy. The whole country, in prey to demagogues, is sleepwalking into disaster.'

The projectionist resumed his cranking. Cesare abducted the swooning Jane and struggled under her weight as he sought to escape over the rooftops. In the end Francis not only rescued her, but he seemed to succeed in exposing Caligari as the crazed master brain behind the murders, but then it transpired that the whole thing was a fantasy and that Francis was really a patient in a lunatic asylum where Caligari was superintendent. Finally Caligari declared that he now had hopes of finding a cure for Francis' madness.

The end of the film flapped round and round on its spool.

'And then he awoke and found that it had all been a dream… and so it is and must be,' said Hans and he laughed. 'The whole film is a nightmare from which Germany's collective soul must awake.'

Though Sonja did not judge the film as harshly as Hans did, she did find it decidedly old-fashioned with so much overacting, garish make-up and quaint costumes, and having to read so many subtitles was a strain too. Moreover, although as Jane she did have the leading female role, she was disappointed to find that it was still quite a small one.

The curtains were pulled back.

'We have been lucky with the weather,' said Hans. 'The sun is up. We cannot afford to waste a moment of the light.'

At this point Sonja gave a little scream as, with the opening of the curtains, she became aware of a great shadow cast over her and, glancing back over her shoulder, she saw that a vast gorilla of a man stood behind her chair, towering over her.

'This is Joachim. He will make a fine Cesare.'

Sonja half rose and tried to shake the man's hand, but the man (or was he a creature?) just gazed at her. There was something odd about his eyes.

'In the storyline Caligari will send Cesare to kill you, but monsters love beauty and he will be smitten by your beauty and so he will abduct you instead. But right now the camera and recording equipment are being set up in the conservatory where we will shoot our first scene,' said Hans. 'Shall I give you a quick tour of the grounds while they get ready?'

They stepped down into the sunshine and onto the grass. Looking back, Sonja saw that two barrack-like wings of red brick with steeply slated roofs flanked the classically marbled portico. The grounds were extensive and men and women shambled around the lawns. Hans and Sonja passed a dilapidated tennis court that obviously had not been played on for years and then a swimming pool that contained nothing but a shallow, muddy puddle of rainwater. Some of the people they encountered saluted them or muttered some kind of greeting, yet none of them could meet Sonja's gaze. In the distance she could just make out that the grounds were enclosed by high walls which were topped with barbed wire.

'What is this place?'

'It is a lunatic asylum.' Hans was obviously amused that it had taken her so long to work this out.

'But the ballroom?'

'Up to the outbreak of the Great War the Lunatics' Ball was one of the highlights of the Bavarian social year. Cars and carriages would come from miles around. The cream of society came to dance with the lunatics and there was a madmen's orchestra that could just about manage to play a few waltzes and polkas. I wish I could have been there to see it. But, as you can see, the place has fallen on hard times.'

'And these people?' Sonja gestured. 'They are all lunatics?'

'Most of them, yes, but a few are actors.'

'But they all walk so weirdly and look strange.'

'That is because our actors have been hypnotised and under the influence of hypnosis, they have been told that they are mad. On the other hand, when the mad people are put under hypnosis they are told that they are sane.'

Hans laughed again, 'Please don't look so horrified, Sonja. I told you that we would be aiming for absolute authenticity. Gritty realism is what we must have.'

Sonja did not dare tell Hans that she was afraid of mad people. She always had been. They were, like clowns, capable of saying and doing unpredictable things. Besides, though she knew it was a kind of madness for her to think it, she nourished the irrational fear that lunacy might be contagious. How else could madness spread? She had once confided her fear to Tilde who had told her that she was suffering from dementophobia and seemed to expect Sonja to find reassurance in the fact that what she feared had a name. Still Tilde had been sympathetic, though she took a larger view: the mad and the moronic were contaminating Germany's genetic pool. Not only did lunatics not contribute to the nation's wellbeing, they were also unhappy individuals. So it would be a mercy to kill them. But, of course, that was not going to happen. That was Tilde. But Sonja had to stop thinking about that, as another of her ideas was that the contagion of madness was spread precisely by the act of thinking about it. She should concentrate on the reality of a walk across the lawns in the sunshine. But this would be difficult, as her path kept crossing those of people who stumbled and slowly felt their way around as if they were underwater. Where were the doctors and nurses?

Once inside the conservatory she was given a piece of paper with her lines for the coming scene. Fortunately she did not have much to say. She was still going over the lines, when she was interrupted by Hans and introduced to a pudgy man in a cape and plus fours.

'This is Markus who will play Caligari. As it happens, he is also a doctor and our hypnotist... but we don't need to hypnotise you for this scene... probably just for rooftop shots when you are in the arms of Cesare. That can wait until the light is about to fade.'

Sonja, still distracted by the task of learning her lines at short notice, hardly took this in. Hans squatted down in front of her and then declared that no make-up would be needed, as gritty realism was indeed the order of the day. She had been hoping that she would wear a lovely long period dress of the kind that Dagover had worn in the version that was going to be superseded, but no. What she was wearing would be fine. They could proceed to filming.

In this, one of the opening scenes, Jane serves Francis and his friend Allan with tea and it is briskly established that they are both in love with her.

'Allan fancies you, though he dare not even hint at this in the presence of his best friend. As for you, though you do not know it yet, the oh-so bourgeois Francis and his oh-so virtuous friend Allan are not enough for your needs. You will discover that your deepest wish is to be carried off by Cesare.'

Though Sonja smiled brightly, she was not at all happy with the shooting of this scene. It was a tiny crew compared to the battalion of technicians who had worked on the filming of *The Congress Dances* and the men behind the camera in the conservatory did not seem quite sure of what they were doing and so they were lighting her face in the wrong way. The sunlight that streamed through the glass was too harsh for her features and the camera was soon moved in far too close, with the result that not all of Francis or Allan would be in the picture.

Yet Hans professed himself pleased. Sandwiches were brought to the actors and camera crew in the conservatory. There was little in the way of conversation. Indeed the actor who was playing Allan seemed incapable of coherent speech and Sonja suspected that this might be the effect of hypnosis. Hans told her that she would not be needed in the next scene they were going to shoot as this simply involved Cesare lying in a coffin-shaped box and Francis and Allan looking down on him and deducing that he was in a deep hypnotic sleep and hence could not have committed the murder he was suspected of. But, as Hans explained, what they were looking at was actually a lifelike waxwork of Cesare which the cunning Caligari had placed in the box in order to create an alibi for his murderous monster – so those who see the film will be given to understand. But of course there is no need to film an actual waxwork since Cesare will impersonate it.

'That way everybody is fooled,' said Hans laughing. Then he dropped his voice. 'Sadly Joachim is not very bright. Playing a waxwork stretches his acting ability to the limit. After that scene is in the can, (and it will only take a few minutes) I will join you at the front steps and we will take a shot of you in the grounds.'

Sonja had time for another cigarette before Hans came bustling out followed by his crew. Now he wanted a kind of group photograph to be filmed with him and Sonja sitting together on a bench surrounded by assorted lunatics and, she supposed, actors. One man indeed stretched himself out in front of their feet, rather as if he was a tiger that had been bagged during a successful shoot. Hans held her hand and looked soulfully at her. There were a few delays as some of those who were supposed to be in the picture kept wandering off and had to be fetched back. Even so, the scene was soon over.

Then Hans said, 'The next thing is that I shall be filmed raving away in the grounds of the asylum and for my perform-ance to look convincing I shall need to be put under hypnosis. All this will take time. So I suggest that you go to your room and rest. We shall call for you when we need you.'

Though she was uneasy she did as she was told. At least she tried to rest, but she found that she could not. Something was wrong, but no, rather it was that everything was wrong. What was going on? Where were the doctors and nurses? If she walked out of the filming, could they stop her? Come to think of it, she had no contract. She should ask Hans about that. But not while he was under hypnosis. It was still bright outside. They would come for her only when the light was about to fade. She should try to not think about that, but how did one not think about things? There were so many things not to think about: mutilated animals, rape, car crashes, the Jewish Conspiracy, clowns, rats, ghosts, the contagion of madness, old age and death. How could she now turn her eyes away from what was coming? Learning not to think about certain things was a skill that she tried to master. She supposed that the trick was not to think the thoughts that led on to the thoughts that one did not want to think. She should think only pleasant thoughts, such as the fact that she was going to be a star and as famous as Dagover. David would marvel at her success. She would move in to join him permanently in the Adlon Hotel.

She was roused from this pleasant reverie, by hammering at the door. It was Hans with Markus close behind him.

'There is not a moment to lose,' Hans' voice was hoarse and urgent. 'We must get you upstairs and then get you hypnotised before you go out on the roof. We should just be able to catch the light before the sun goes down. You don't need to bother with your shoes. Come as you are.'

Joachim, who was waiting on the landing, set off up ahead of them taking several steps at a time. By the time they reached the attic which doubled as a vast dormitory, Sonja was quite out of breath. Hans gestured that she should sit on one of the beds. Joachim stood on another bed and struggled to open one of the large dormer windows. He was having difficulties with its catch. Francis looked on in exasperation. Then he turned to Sonja.

'Now it is time for Markus to hypnotise you.' And Markus came and sat beside Sonja who screamed and shouted, 'But I don't want to be hypnotised! I won't be hypnotised! Stop looking at me!'

'Of course you must be hypnotised. Otherwise you will not be able to bear the terror of being carried across the roof in the arms of Joachim.'

Sonja said nothing to this but shook her head.

'Joachim has been hypnotised. That is why he is finding it so difficult to open that window. But under hypnosis he has no fear. Markus' mesmeric power never fails. You have no reason to fear Joachim. He thinks that you are wonderful. You will be in good hands.'

Sonja just closed her eyes and continued shaking her head. Then she felt a breeze on her face. The window must be open.

'Very well then!' cried Hans. 'Without hypnosis. Take her Joachim!'

Sonja felt herself being lifted off the bed. She opened her eyes and found herself looking up at Joachim. Grim determination warred with lust on the man's face. He would do whatever Hans told him. Those bulging eyes were the last thing she saw before she swooned.

It was a strange sort of bedroom with mattresses attached to the walls. Sonja lay in it feeling dizzy and slightly sick. It took her a while for her to recognise the room for what it was – a padded cell. And it took her a little longer to register that she was in a straitjacket. While she was unconscious she had been stripped of her blouse and bra and the coarseness of the straitjacket's fabric was making her skin itch. A single unshaded lightbulb hung above her. She closed her eyes against its pitiless light. If only she was in a movie about a flower girl who wins the love of a prince...

There was a scuffling sound. Sonja thought that it might be a rat, but then it was Hans' voice that spoke, 'I had hoped to have everything set up before you came round. I wonder why they are taking so long. But it is a big building with several staircases and I suppose that they have got lost again. They were the best I could find at short notice, but even so...'

Sonja gathered that he was talking about the cameraman and his lighting assistants. With some difficulty she twisted round and saw that Hans too was confined in a straitjacket.

'That was an excellent faint. We might try and get a few extra shots tomorrow. But Joachim has tied my straps awfully tight. I hope you are not too uncomfortable, though of course some discomfort will assist in simulating the realistic effect that we are striving for.'

He attempted what was probably intended as an apologetic smile, but the smile she had previously thought so charming, now looked more like a rictus.

'In the scene we are going to shoot in here...' Hans never finished his sentence, for suddenly the light was switched off.

'That was not supposed to happen.' Now he was sounding panicky. 'That is most peculiar. A power cut perhaps...' Clearly he did not believe in a power cut, for he immediately started shouting for help.

Though a little light still came in from a high window, the evening was coming on fast. Sonja was too terrified to speak. She was in despair to find herself so trapped, trapped within a straitjacket, trapped within a padded cell and trapped within a lunatic asylum whose walls were crowned with barbed wire. It was like a nasty dream over which she had no control. Yet what really terrified her was that she found herself in a confined space with a lunatic, for that was surely what this young man was, and Sonja feared to catch his madness and so she wriggled away to put as much space as possible between her and him. There was no possibility of rescue, since David would have no idea where she was.

Eventually Hans gave up shouting. After a long silence he spoke again, 'Do you like Dostoevsky?'

Sonja did not know what to reply to this. She thought she had heard the name before, but she did not know who he or she was, always assuming Dostoevsky was a who rather than a what.

'You must have read some of his novels,' Hans persisted.

But Sonja replied, 'I never read novels.'

Hans was evidently impressed, 'My God! How serious minded you are! If only I could confine myself to non-fiction. Yet I love novels too much and I devour them like chocolates, especially Dostoevsky. You are missing so much if you do not read Dostoevsky. I especially love *Crime and Punishment* and I especially love Raskolnikov and the way he philosophises about how he is not bound by common morality, so this means that he can murder an old woman for her money. Then I like to think of Raskolnikov's solicitude for his poor old mother that Dostoevsky portrays with such exquisite sentimentality. And the murder scene is so well done! You should read it. How the young man sets about the little old woman with a hatchet! Whack! Whack! And the blood comes spurting out. The detail in it all… the greasy thinning locks on a head which is about to be split open is very well observed… and the dead eyes that seem about to spring from their sockets… blood everywhere and Raskolnikov's shuddering re-examination of the corpse. Oh, it is terrible to think of this scene! And the struggle cut the cord with the key that hangs round the corpse's scraggy old neck. And then, when one thinks one can tolerate no more and that one really should close the book and allow oneself some time to recover oneself, well then the sister, Elizabeth walks in and Raskolnikov has to wield his glory hatchet once more. Whack! Whack! Oh, it is the very height of theatricality! And how good Dostoevsky is at depicting pangs of conscience! We all have bad consciences about something or other, even if we have not actually committed murder. I think it could be said that there is murder somewhere in the hearts of everyone, no matter how blameless they are in their actions, and Dostoevsky, with his great soul, has divined this. He writes about murderers and saints, but really it is us, ordinary old us, that he is writing about, for Dostoevsky sees into the heart of Everyman. We all have a bloody axe somewhere about our persons. And finally, the way Sonja, the saintly prostitute with a heart of gold, brings Raskolnikov to Christian repentance! So affecting! One weeps when one reads about it, but one does feel so much better when one has shed those tears. When I first read about Raskolnikov and his crazed slaughter of the little old woman, my life was changed forever and for the better. *Crime and Punishment* made me the man I am today. But you, Sonja, have the same name as the sainted prostitute who is destined to bring Raskolnikov salvation. It was this that made me feel that our meeting at the audition was fated.'

Sonja would have clapped her hands over her ears if she could. She wondered if she dared ask him to shut up, or would that make him worse. Hans carried on regardless.

'Our plight seems black indeed for both of us. Yet things are not always what they seem… I am reminded of a terrifying night I once endured a few years ago when I went walking in the Tyrol and, late in the day, lost my way. You must listen to this. Don't go to sleep on me.'

(How could she possibly go to sleep? She was sick with terror.)

That night all those years ago when I had no hope of becoming a film director, that night the darkness was coming on fast and I had no hope of finding the hostel that had been my original destination. I walked for hours without coming across any sign of human habitation. I came to fear that I might be walking round and round in circles. In that upland wilderness. So I was greatly relieved when I saw some lights twinkling below me. How providential that there should be an inn in the middle of nowhere! I hurried down the slope and knocked on the door. Was it possible to have a bed for the night? Indeed it was for there were no other people staying there that night and I was the only person to sup there that evening. I was the only person in the place apart from the innkeeper and his daughter, and I thought it curious that the place had so little custom. The tavern used to be more popular, but trade had fallen off since a great tragedy had occurred. Though the innkeeper was not a great talker and he was eager to drop the topic, I gathered that it was something to do with his wife who was now dead. I was a little curious and might have pressed my enquiries further, only I was distracted by the girl herself. It was she who brought the tankard of beer and the plate of boiled ham, potatoes and sauerkraut to my table. Her eyes were – they are hard to describe – like anemones under water. And it wasn't just the eyes. There was something odd about the way the girl moved, odd, but seductive. The way she leant over my table and the sway of her breasts as she did so, might have been sending me a message. I do not think that the innkeeper liked the way I was looking at his daughter and he interrupted my sensual meditation. What did I want for breakfast the following morning? Would fried eggs and slices of smoked sausage be acceptable? Yes, of course. Anything whatsoever would be acceptable, if only the girl with those extraordinary eyes was going to bring it to me. So I thought.'

It was clear to Sonja that this tale could have no good end. What she could not understand was why it was being told to her. If her arms had been free she would have clapped her hands over her ears. She only hoped that Hans was indeed tightly secured within his straitjacket.

'The tavern was very small. There was only one guest bedroom and it was just over the dining room and bar. The innkeeper escorted me up to my bed and made a great point of showing me that his bedroom and his daughter's bedroom were just across the landing. If I was troubled by anything in the middle of the night, I had only to cry out. He stood by the door with a candle to show me where my bed was. He was not prepared to let me have a candle of my own, as he and his daughter had a pathological fear of fires. With that he bade me goodnight. I groped my way to the bed and undressed. Yet it was a long time before I could get to sleep, for I was haunted by a strange smell. Strange yet familiar. I could not quite place it. The smell and thoughts of the innkeeper's daughter combined to keep me awake for hours. Was she too lying awake just across the landing, waiting for me to visit? Or should I expect her to come to me? How had her mother met her end? How could an inn in such an isolated place as this possibly make any money? Why had I not spotted this place on my map? My thoughts raged, so that I should have liked to pace about the room, only I was uncertain of its dimensions and of the disposition of the furniture in the room. Eventually I did drift off to sleep, though my slumber was fitful and shallow. Suddenly I was jerked awake. I must have been asleep for longer than it had felt like, for a narrow beam of sunlight had pierced the shutters. Thank God for the coming of the day,

I rejoiced.'

Hans laughed mirthlessly.

'But what was it that had woken me? At first I thought it must have been the smell, which now seemed more overpowering than ever. But then I heard a floorboard creak. Fool that I was! The moment that I heard that creaking, my heart rejoiced, for I instantly entertained the wild hope that it was the girl with the anemone eyes who was now cautiously feeling her way towards the warmth of my bed and my embrace. An instant later I knew my mistake, as I saw the glint of a large butcher's knife caught in the beam of sunlight. The hand that wielded the knife was large and hairy and I knew then that I was confronted not by the girl but by her father. I would have cried out if I had dared. The innkeeper leant across my bed and the knife flashed over me. He grunted and then, seeing I was awake, spoke, "I am sorry to trouble you, sir. I hope I did not wake you, only it is nearly breakfast time and you did say that you were partial to smoked sausages."

And with that he cut down one of the smoked sausages that hung on long hooks over my bed. It was the smell of these that had been giving me such a troubled sleep. The message of all this is that things are not as grim as they seem and I have told you this story to put you at your ease. Perhaps you could put me at my ease by singing for me.'

Sonja did not reply. An hour might have passed before the light was switched on again and Joachim came through the door, closely followed by Wieland who was wearing a white coat. What was he doing here? Joachim appeared to be weeping and Wieland (who was smiling) carried a gun, the sort that she had seen cowboys wear in films. She thought that it would be called a Colt.

'I have come for you, Sonja,' said Wieland. 'You will soon be free of these villains and their machinations.' He gestured with his gun to signal that Joachim should retreat to a corner with his hands up.

'What about me? What about the film I am making?' asked Hans, but Wieland ignored him.

'My eyes hurt,' said Joachim. 'I have to do something about them or they will soon start bleeding.'

Wieland, who was struggling with the straps of Sonja's straitjacket, nodded impatiently. Joachim brought his hands down and started feeling round his eyes with his fingers. Slowly and carefully he removed the thin wires that had been tightly drawn round his eyeballs and, now that his eyes no longer bulged, he looked almost normal for a giant. Wieland, having dragged the straitjacket off Sonja, was taking off his white coat so that Sonja could cover herself up with it and at this point Joachim lunged at Wieland, who fired at him. Almost immediately a red stain started to spread across one of Joachim's shirtsleeves. He staggered back clutching his arm and slowly slid down one of the padded walls onto the floor.

'We must hurry,' said Wieland as he helped Sonja to her feet. He led her swiftly back up to the ground floor and then to a Cabriolet he had parked at the entrance of the asylum. The car skidded on the gravel as he took the final corner of the driveway at speed. The gates were open and they hurtled through them into the darkness.

She needed a smoke. But then she realised that her cigarettes were in her handbag and that must still be in the bedroom in the asylum. Not that she would have been able to get it alight in the speeding car anyway for the hood was pulled back and the wind streamed through her hair. The night was clear, the stars were bright above and for a moment she allowed herself to fantasise that she was the barefoot heroine of a romance who was being rescued from danger. If only she had been able to swoon in the arms of Conrad Veidt... but it was not a romance. It was real and she had just escaped from a horror film, or rather something that only seemed like a horror film. Some adventure! But at this point she fell asleep. Looking back on it, this may have been a response to shock. She had heard of soldiers in the trenches of the Great War who, the instant they were not actually engaged in battle, used to drop off to sleep.

When she awoke, they were at a filling station just beyond Munich. Seeing that she was awake, Wieland spoke, 'I hate melodramas,' he said. 'Hans is obsessed with –'

But Sonja interrupted, 'Wieland, what is going on? How did you find me?'

'Be patient. Everything has a rational explanation, though perhaps it is sad that everything always does have a rational explanation. It is as I proclaimed to the world in the foyer of that cinema. You are a creature of light and I am your dark shadow. Ever since then I have been watching over you and following you wherever you went. After you allowed yourself to be deceived by that absurd charade in the Wilmersdorf Community Hall, I took pains to research the background of this Herr Becker. As I was about to say, he is obsessed with melodramas. One could say that he is mad on films, or one could go further and say that he is mad and that it is films that have driven him mad. In particular, he is mad for those old films of Robert Wiene: *The Cabinet of Dr Caligari, Raskolnikow, Orlac's Hands* and suchlike horrors performed within the architecture of nightmare, and full of mad melodramas and exaggerated passions.'

'There are dangerous people in the film business,' Wieland continued. 'That is what I have been trying to warn you about. Let this be an object lesson to you. Film directors assume despotic powers and, because they can boss their actors about in any way they like, this power goes to their heads and in some cases it makes them crazy. They come to believe that they can also control the destinies of ordinary people who are not on their film sets. Also a lot of the actors are on drugs. They think that cocaine is a kind of magic that helps them act better and they hold film parties that are really orgies. Wealthy men like the decadent Jew David Rego invest in films not for the financial returns, but because they like to be invited to such parties.'

'But what about the *Caligari* film and the asylum?'

'As I was saying, Hans is obsessed with *Caligari*. He really is an amateur with not much idea about the practicalities of filmmaking, but his father indulges him and gives him full range of the asylum.'

'Hans' father?'

'Yes, his father is boss of the asylum. Oh, did you not understand? Markus Becker is Hans' father and he has indulged his son to the point that he has driven him mad. Father and son both have a crazy belief in the creative possibilities offered by hypnosis. According to the enquiries I have been making, this version of *Caligari* is only one of a series of strange films that have been shot within the walls of that place. It is what happens when madmen take control of the asylum. Since I knew the place was dangerous, I had the forethought to bring a gun with me. In order to find out where they were keeping you, I had to question Joachim at gunpoint. He is a real lunatic and he has become quite obsessed with you after he saw you in *The Congress Dances*. Monsters love beauty. Fortunately my aim was good, I think, and he will not die of his wound.'

'Monsters love beauty.' That was something Hans had also said. Sonja closed her eyes and, as she drifted in and out of sleep, she only caught snatches of Wieland's monologue. He talked about his years in the Moabit Prison and how the experience had changed him and knocked the nonsense out of him. He compared his time in the Moabit to the sojourn of St John on the Island of Patmos and to the revelations received by St Francis on Mount Alverna. Prison was a blessed place in which Wieland had visions and these he had put down in *The Future Belongs to Me*, the publication of which was imminent.

Sonja was not required to respond. Nor did she say thank you when Wieland's car delivered her to the door of her lodgings. Instead, desperate for a cigarette, she rushed inside. She was angry, but too tired to be very angry. It was obvious that all that had happened was like a series of scenes from a badly written plot and she did not believe a word of what had been scripted. Moreover she had seen stage blood before. The special effects workshop at UFA had vats of it. She guessed that Joachim had a little balloon filled with tomato ketchup concealed under his shirt. The whole thing had been an extended practical joke orchestrated by Wieland, the convict turned *soi-disant* mystic. Monsters love beauty, yes, and Wieland was the real monster.

How should this ill-starred adventure feature in *My Life is like a Fairy Tale*? Perhaps she could present it as a kind of kidnapping? But maybe it would be better if she wrote about it as one of cinema history's might-have-beens. The remake of *The Cabinet of Dr Caligari* could be written about as a brilliant project that had been tragically doomed from the beginning by its very brilliance and by the fiery temperaments of its protagonists, as the producer, the director, the cameraman and the cast fell out with one another. But come to think of it, there was also the later reappearance of Hans Becker. It would be best not to write about that, as she wanted no anti-climaxes in her story.

Chapter Nine

Meanwhile Sonja wanted a part in a real film. The forthcoming production of a film called *Vampyr* was announced in *Film Artists and Film Art* and Sonja had thought of trying to audition for it, but when she mentioned the possibility to Manasseh, he told her that a vampire was supposed to be a kind of blood-sucking monster. 'Vampires come back from the land of the dead, they make death seem attractive and they seek to lure others to join them.' So Sonja guessed that this might be another of Hans Becker's mad projects and she thought no more of it. In the past she had read a lot about vamps, but she had hitherto just thought of them as seductive and exotic looking women. Goebbels had decreed that only foreign actresses should play vamps on the screen, since the honour of German women should not be besmirched. Though she had even fancied that she might be a vamp herself, she had never tried imagining herself as some kind of sales representative for the dead. In those days she never thought about the dead or dying. But Manasseh seemed to be frightened of everything and saw monsters everywhere.

At last David returned from Switzerland. He said that he had done good business and he was in a good humour. Soon things were going to change. It was somewhat mysterious why he was so cheerful, since he was emphatic that Germany was going to the dogs. Hindenburg was losing his grip and, according to David, Hugenburg was poised to take over with the support of a minor aristocrat called von Papen and a street-corner thug called Hitler. It was better not to tell him anything about the so-called remake of *The Cabinet of Dr Caligari*.

She learned about the next possible film from an unexpected source. One Sunday morning she had a visitor. She gave a little scream when she opened the door of her flat and found Hans Becker standing there. But he gave her one of his devastating smiles and then she saw that he had brought with him her suitcase, with her clothes, handbag and shoes.

'I have come to apologise,' he said. 'Can you possibly forgive me? When I saw you, I wished that it was not you who was chosen to be the victim of our masquerade. I would not have let you come to any harm. But really I had no choice. Please let me hope that you will forgive me.'

'Of course you had a choice. What do you mean you had no choice?'

'No. I was only following orders.'

'Who then gave you the order to lead me on and then terrorise me?'

As Sonja asked this, she feared that answer might be invisible voices coming from leaking pipes, or cowled, spectral figures who gathered on barren hillsides and issued directives for the torment of mankind, or Hans' dead mother who from the grave was determined that her son should never enjoy normal relations with any other woman, or...

She was relieved that Hans' answer was less weird than any of these possibilities, though the answer was still strange.

112

'Markus and Wieland told me what I must do. But things sometimes get out of hand. Well, to be honest, they often do.'

'And do you have to do what they tell you to do?'

'Of course. Wieland is my brother, half-brother rather, and Markus is my stepfather. Did you not know that? Wieland is very brilliant. Do you not find him so? His father favours him greatly and will do anything for him. Wieland is oh so brilliant, but perhaps a little spoilt and so he is allowed to produce films in the asylum. He got the idea while he was in prison when he read about the Marquis de Sade and how the Divine Marquis used to put on plays during his incarceration in the Charenton Lunatic Asylum.'

Then seeing the baffled expression on Sonja's face, Hans explained that the Marquis de Sade was a famous or notorious writer who lived around the time of the French Revolution and who wrote pornographic books. The word sadism derived from his title. Sonja had never heard of him and she supposed that this was what came from not reading books, but surely she was better off not reading about such unpleasant things? And what was it about De Sade that was divine?

'I love films, as I think you do. Wieland knows this and so he uses me. But let me buy you coffee round the corner,' Hans concluded.

Sonja warily agreed, as she thought that for her own safety she needed to know more about Wieland. But at the coffeehouse, Hans mostly talked about himself. Wieland had been right in saying that Hans was obsessed with films. He spoke at length about Robert Wiene's silent film *Raskolnikow*, which he claimed was a brilliant adaptation of a novel by Dostoevsky and he had started to explain exactly how this was so when she cut him short. She wanted to know why she had been lured to the asylum and what had really been going on there. Hans shamefacedly confessed that the whole business was the result of a pact between him and Wieland – a kind of marriage of obsessions. Wieland, who was obsessed with Sonja's beauty, wanted a filmed record of her that he could watch night after night, whereas Hans, who was as Wieland had claimed, mad about the cinema, was desperate to try his hand at filmmaking and in particular to produce and direct an improved version of *The Cabinet of Dr Caligari*. Hans was doubtful whether he had succeeded. Apart from anything else, it was difficult to work with a camera crew composed of madmen. As Hans talked on, Sonja realised that he was somewhat in awe of her.

'But you are a real film actress. You have been in some big films.'

And he wanted to know what it was like to have been on the sets of *The Blue Angel* and *The Congress Dances*. Sonja started to describe the filming of *The Blue Angel* when Hans interrupted her, 'Such a film could not be made any more. The times are changing and with them the taste of the people. What cinema audiences want now are films featuring strong and healthy people who will invariably succeed in finding the happiness they deserve. Anything else is decadent. Sadly, people will no longer want to see films like *Caligari*. It will become a lost film. People nowadays have no wish to see films with monsters in them and besides Wiene's film was silent and nobody watches silent films any more. Much of the old film stock has been recycled for its silver content. Storage of anything is expensive. Even those films that someone has thought to preserve and save in metal canisters will in time crumble into dust or even spontaneously combust. Where is Theda Bara's *Cleopatra*? Or *For the Queen's Honour* starring Mary Pickford? And Murnau's *Desire*, and *Maria Marten, or The Mystery of the Red Barn*, and *The Caravan of Death* with Conrad Veidt, and Wegener's *The Golem and the Dancing Girl* and *The Night of Queen Isabeau*? I fear they are all lost and gone forever. It is as if they had never been made. All that beauty, romance, danger and laughter gone for nothing. Why keep silent films, the philistines want to know. Those old stories are obsolete and it would be as if the Berlin municipality were to maintain a fleet of horse-drawn chariots.'

Sonja found this all very boring. She was in talkies and only their immediate future was of interest to her. Anyway it struck her that it was not quite true that films about monsters were no longer being made.

'Did you make *Vampyr*, the film that is showing now?'

Hans shook his head impatiently.

'*The Cabinet of Dr Caligari* is my only production so far. But *Vampyr* is quite marvellous. You should see it. It may be the last horror film ever to be made. As I was about to say, from now on manias, phobias and homicidal possession will no longer feature as suitable subjects for films.'

Sonja said nothing, but she thought that she definitely preferred films about strong healthy people who found the happiness they deserved. Every film should have a happy ending. She was definitely not going to see *Vampyr*. She liked to come out of the cinema humming.

'Mountain films are the latest thing,' Hans continued. 'Films in which men pit their courage and their strength against the elements. Luis Trenker is known to be planning his next mountain film and I am hoping to get a job on it as a grip.'

Then seeing Sonja's blank expression again, Hans saw that he had to do some more explaining,

'A grip is the member of a production team who is responsible for laying the tracks on which the cameras move and for heaving the cameras into position. No brains are needed, only physical strength. But it may be a way into filmmaking for me.'

Then, though he offered to take Sonja to see *Vampyr*, she refused.

'No? You are still angry with me and I don't blame you. Another time then, for I am sure that we will meet again,' and with that he was gone.

As soon as he had left, Sonja foraged for a cigarette in her handbag. She thought that she too might try for something on Trenker's film. Asking around, she discovered that it was going to be a costume film set in 1806 about the revolt of the Tyrol against the tyrant Napoleon. What was more, there was going to be a big ballroom scene in it, featuring hussars in uniform and ladies in crinolines. The film, which was about to go into production under the working title of *The Rebel*, sounded perfect for her.

When she saw David later that week she tried to tell him about it. Surely he could get her a part in Trenker's film? But he was not listening. She repeated all that she had just said about it being just the sort of film that could advance her career. David said that he did not know this man Trenker and that he would have no influence on whom his production would be taking on. Besides, he had something more important to tell her.

'We are getting out of Germany while we can. I have paid the bill at the Adlon till the end of the week. I have transferred all but a residue of my capital to French banks. On Saturday we move to a hotel in the South of France. I am negotiating to buy a villa just outside Carpentras, conveniently close to Les Baux and therefore to the Bauxite mines. There is not all that much ore left there, but it will be a start.'

What on earth was David talking about? Had he gone mad?

He explained, 'Filmmaking in Germany is finished. The political climate is changing and other countries are soon going to stop buying German films. The future of the cinema, if it has any, which I doubt, will be in Hollywood and it is too late for me to set up anything over there that would be financially viable. The big studios would run me out of town. Bauxite ore is the future. I have told you about it before but you just weren't listening. Bauxite is a clay-like compound. The thing about it is that it is the main ore of aluminium and aluminium will be needed for the construction of aircraft and shipping, especially aircraft. War is coming and, whereas films will be a senseless luxury in wartime, bauxite will be like gold dust.'

'And what would I do stuck in the South of France while you are busy mining aluminium? I would be nobody and my career in ruins.'

David looked hard at her, 'You will be my wife. I am asking you to marry me. We can honeymoon in Monte Carlo.'

Sonja faltered, 'But what about my career?'

Then it was like a thunderstorm on a summer's day.

'Your career! What career?'

Sonja looked pleadingly at him but he continued relentlessly, 'God knows I have tried to get you parts, but again and again the people doing the casting have found no signs of acting ability in you. You want to be a film star, God yes, but you do not want to actually do the acting that is necessary to become that star. Though I have paid for acting classes, they have borne no fruit. I conjured you up from nothing. You were a nobody when I found you and without me you will be a nobody once more. It will be as if you have never been and you will leave not a ripple behind you. I think that I can promise you that when they come to write the history of cinema in the twentieth century, you will not be in it. You are like a cat and with a cat's cupboard love. I am just the person that puts a bowl of food out for you in the evening.'

As he looked at her, he seemed to be hoping that she would deny this. If so, he found nothing for his comfort.

'So why did you waste your time telling your friends in the business that I would be good in films? At least I value something more than making money.

Films are my life and they always will be. And I like it here in Berlin. I don't speak French. And though it is true that I am not yet a successful star, as you have so kindly pointed out, it is you who have stopped me having a career. I am just your doll, your fetish doll, someone, no, something that has to be around for your amusement in the evenings.'

'How can anyone so beautiful be so evil?... no, you are not really evil. You are just nothing. Not so very beautiful either. Age is catching up with you. There are the beginnings of crow's feet at the corners of your eyes. I have loved you even though you are not a very good actress. But now get dressed and get out.'

God! That was dramatic. Looking back on it, it was just like one of the closing scenes in *Gone with the Wind* when Scarlet O'Hara and Rhett Butler were breaking up. Scarlet, who sat weeping on the staircase, vowed to win back Rhett's love. Though *Gone with the Wind* had been banned by the Nazis as soon as it was released, Sonja had been privileged to see the film in the little private cinema in the Goebbels' house at Schwanenwerder. 'They make these sort of films so well,' had been Joseph's verdict. It is so lovely on Schwanenwerder, an island on the Wannsee. The lawn stretches down to the jetty where the motorised yacht, the *Baldur* is moored. And the doors that led out to the lawn! She thought that they were something supernatural when she first saw them, as they opened as if by magic whenever she approached them. But, as Joseph showed her, they were operated by electricity. He delights in showing his guests how they work… she was drifting again.

No the scene with David wasn't like *Gone with the Wind*. Not really. She had never vowed to win back his love and the scene, though dramatic was also somewhat weird, as his proposal of marriage had been followed so swiftly by a tirade of hate. Perhaps she had made a mistake. He had had such strength of purpose. She had to admit that was attractive. Perhaps she should have gone with him, for, even though he hated her, he had still desired her. Where was he now? Was he even still alive? But really it had just been a liaison of convenience for both of them. Sadly it was to be years before she set foot in the Adlon again. Now she thought of it, David had been one of many in the business to leave Germany. Soon other producers and directors, many of them his friends, also fled Germany, mostly heading for Hollywood, including

Pressburger, Siodmak, Pabst, Wiene, Wilder and Lang.

If they ever made a film about Sonja's life and her rise to stardom, David should feature as a megalomaniac tyrant. The hotel room's ceiling should be artificially low and the filming of him in a rage should be done by a camera placed at floor level and tilted upwards, so that he seemed to dominate the cinematic frame in the way that he sought to dominate her, and though in reality David had been perfectly controlled, in the film he should be shown as throwing a vase at the wall, knocking over a bedside light and things like that and, as the bedside light was knocked over, it would cast strange shadows that signified mad passions. Clever lighting would be needed to show David's face, distorted with rage, emerging from the darkness. Meanwhile she would be on her knees looking pleadingly up at him. She should be back-lit, so that a kind of halo effect was created over her hair and the whole scene should be shot in deep focus. These days Sonja knew all about camera angles, golden frames and travelling matte. Of course, in the film version they would both be fully dressed.

But for the time being, the stuff about David finding her in that little restaurant and summoning her to the Adlon Hotel and everything that happened with him thereafter was yet more stuff that would have to be kept out of *My Life is like a Fairy Tale*. These days Jews only featured in horrid films. It was a bit annoying. As soon as she had started planning her autobiography, all sorts of unwanted memory had started to flood in. Unwanted memory was her shadow. It followed her wherever she went. If only she could sell her memory to the Devil and trade it in perhaps for a starring part in a major movie.

As soon as she returned to her flat after the breakup with David, she had consulted her horoscope: 'You are not alone in being battered by the unsettling events triggered by the ascendance of Saturn and retrograde Mercury. It will not be easy and you must be patient, but eventually things will come together in a way that you do not expect.'

It certainly was not easy. The following week she went along to the auditions for *The Rebel*, but at the door of the theatre where the auditions were being held she was turned away by a big man in a suit. 'Go home, miss. You will be wasting your time. You just don't look German enough.' Though many disappointments were to follow, few were quite as peremptory as this.

Early the following year she attended *The Rebel*'s premiere. As she was without David, she had to gatecrash the event, but since her face was familiar and she could wave to acquaintances in the foyer they let her through without an invitation card. (She gatecrashed as many parties as she could as a way of saving on food and cigarettes.) All sorts of grandees were in attendance for the showing of this film. This was her first sight of Herr Hitler, the coming man, and with him was Dr Joseph Goebbels. That evening Sonja did not even bother to look at Goebbels twice. As far as she was concerned, he was just another politician and not at all a prepossessing one.

The film was, as Hans had said it would be, about man pitting himself against the elements – precipitous heights, precarious handholds, glaciers, clouds. Why do men have to pit themselves against nature? Why can't they just leave nature alone? Anyway she was to understand that the film was an expression of the heroic German soul. Toward its end there was a great avalanche engineered by the rebel and his friends. The snow and rock thundered down and buried the French regiment who had been marching below. The avalanche was a kind of metaphor for the unleashing of a popular uprising against the alien tyranny. Sonja thought that she was well out of this film, since there was not much dancing in it and besides she did hate films with lots of snow in them. Snowy scenes always depressed her. Moreover, in the final scene the captured rebels were executed. Why did people keep making films with unhappy endings? But then in reality perhaps everybody's life has an unhappy ending? Forget that thought. At the reception afterwards she had noticed that the Nazi politicians were enthusiastically congratulating Luis Trenker. Hans had not been listed in the credits and, thank goodness, he was not at the celebration afterwards.

It must have been at the reception for *The Rebel* that she first met that horrible woman, Leni Riefenstahl. Though Leni was not then as grand as she became after the releases of *Triumph of the Will* and *Olympia*, she behaved as though she was. Not knowing who she was and for want of anything else to say, Sonja had begun to talk about how she hated mountain films because of all the snow in them. That was a bad start and Leni, the star of *The White Hell of Piz Palü*, let her know that this was so. But Leni would have to be presented favourably in *My Life is like a Fairy Tale*. She was after all a power to be reckoned with. Perhaps Sonja could claim that Leni's career had been an inspiration to her. She would have to work on the necessary inspirational dialogue. She could have Leni spouting stuff about how she was totally dedicated to creating visions of strength and beauty. God knows, Sonja had subsequently heard enough from her of that sort of high-flown rubbish. In actual fact, at the premiere of *The Rebel*, Leni had grilled her about what she was doing and whom she knew. Sonja, who these days was always careful to present herself as being on the cusp of something, had burbled on about taking a break between films and what a relief that was, because (didn't Leni know it?) the pace at Babelsberg was so hectic. But Leni was a relentless interrogator and, as soon as she had worked out that Sonja was just an unemployed starlet, she walked away and vanished into the assembled crowd.

At this point Sonja paused and lit another cigarette. She was wondering if there was anyone in the world that she hated more than that flinty-eyed bitch, Leni Riefenstahl. True, Sonja also hated Wieland, Veit Harlan, Magda Goebbels, Winston Churchill and Marika Rökk, but there was no one she hated so much as Leni. How had that woman become so successful? Though some whispered that Leni's Nordic looks had attracted Hitler and consequently he had taken her to bed, Sonja did not believe this, for surely one would need nerves of steel to contemplate taking Leni to bed and Hitler... but no. Stop that thought right now.

Instead she should make a big list of things that she does not like, apart from snow in films and sad endings to stories: Beethoven, books, air-raid sirens, ersatz wartime food, horror films, arithmetic, politics, knitting, card games, large dogs, cripples, sport, sauerkraut, folkloric peasant costumes, and above all the war.

Chapter Ten

Sonja did not know quite how it had happened, but suddenly Hitler and the Nazis were in power. At which point things that had been legal became illegal, while things that had been illegal, became legal. It was all very confusing, if also exciting. She had loved the torch-lit processions, the singing and displays of flags and weaponry – and, of course, those uniforms. Germany was on the move once more. It must have been as exhilarating as this, she thought, when the Roman Empire was just beginning.

But an instant later she was sad to think that the last faint echoes of the twenties, and with them her youth, were gone. There was a sweet sadness in looking back on those years. At the time she had thought that she was in a party that was never going to end. The brassy jazz music would go on forever and she and her friends could shimmy their lives away. One never notices when something vanishes. She could not remember when she had last heard jazz being played. Nowadays she often met people, mostly Nazis, who denounced those years as a time of decadence. Tilde was particularly vehement and Sonja thought that this was mostly because Tilde was embarrassed by her raffish start as an actress with the New Subjectivity gang. But when Sonja thought about it, she thought that she actually liked decadence. It had suited her and the way she looked and dressed. After all, she was never going to look good in a dirndl. She supposed that she was really a twenties girl whose misfortune it was to have lived on into the forties and by now the twenties were long gone in a swirl of cigarette smoke and the Nazis had closed the jazz clubs.

A couple of years after the Nazis came to power, two policemen came for Manasseh. They grudgingly gave him a few minutes in order to arrange his affairs and pack. They told Sonja that they were taking him to some new settlement in the East where work would be found for him. Manasseh's suitcase was tied up with string since the lock did not work. As he was leaving, he turned to Sonja and said, 'You have been a good girl and you always paid your rent promptly. I want you to have this,' and he pressed a large volume into her hands.

She told him to write. Manasseh was not very practical. She hoped that he was going to manage in Ostland. Perhaps this was all a bit like the departure of the Jews from Egypt in the Bible? When she went back up to her flat and examined the large volume, she was disappointed to find that it was a stamp album and it was full of those very old and dull stamps issued by the princely German states – the ox heads of Mecklenburg-Schwerin, the embossed numbers in squares of Bavaria, the heraldic shields of Oldenburg and Saxony, the post horn of Hanover and so on. Some of the stamps had been misprinted, so that for example, the head of the King of Bavaria, or whoever he was, appeared upside down. Old stamps and misprinted stamps would be pretty worthless. She preferred the stamps with proper pictures on them that the Nazis would issue which showed *Zeppelins*, racehorses, gymnasts and scenes from operas. But it was all stuff for schoolboys. A few days later she remembered to put the album in the bin. Manasseh really should have taken the album with him as rearranging the stamps might have given him something to do in the new settlement to which they were taking him.

A few days later some Nazi official arrived to confiscate the rest of the philatelic stuff and a new landlord took over, a Dr Giselius who was an optician and who changed the ground floor into his workplace.

Sonja was used to politics as being something that happened elsewhere and which had no effect on her daily life. But she found that things did change at UFA as the Nazis established control over it and the other smaller studios. In future only certain kinds of film could be made. In *Film Courier* Sonja read the text of a speech which Joseph Goebbels, the new Minister for Propaganda, had delivered to filmmakers assembled at the Hotel Kaiserhof:

'Gentlemen, we must rid ourselves of the idea that the present crisis is a material one: it is more a spiritual crisis, and it will go on until we are courageous enough to radically reform German films. For the past two weeks, I have been having long discussions with representatives from every branch of the German film industry with very amusing results. These film gentlemen have the same picture of National Socialism as that given in the hostile press. These people have no real idea of the National Socialist movement and its supporters. Not even in their own minds. In every discussion, fears of an uncertain future were expressed again and again. They thought that the future of film production was uncertain. In fact, the exact opposite is the case. Now we have arrived. That which is here remains – we shall not leave!'

Then Goebbels had listed his three favourite films, before returning to a lengthy discourse about the politics and economics of filmmaking, all of which Sonja skipped. The speech concluded:

'You must not believe that we feel ourselves compelled to make life difficult for you. The young men who are now in government feel very sympathetic to the problems of the German film artist. I myself have watched films on many evenings with the Reich Chancellor and have found relaxation after the trying battles of the day. Believe me that we are grateful for this. I ask for trustworthy cooperation, so that it will be possible to say of German films, as in other fields, Germany will lead the world.'

In his speech Goebbels had listed his three favourite films: *Battleship Potemkin*, *Anna Karenina* and *The Nibelungen*. But Sonja had also later heard him express admiration for *Snow White and the Seven Dwarfs*. Hitler, she knew, was a big fan of Mickey Mouse. But for some mysterious reason he hated the Tarzan films. Now that the war was under way, Hitler had stopped watching them for its duration. But Eva liked to watch films in the bowling alley in the basement of the Berghof and Sonja often kept her company. On such evenings she could brief Eva with gossip about the stars featuring in whichever film they happened to be watching. But she was getting ahead of herself. She had an image of herself struggling up a hill. But ahead of her and near the summit there was another Sonja who was impatiently beckoning her to catch up. And then looking backwards she saw other slower Sonjas toiling behind her. She found her lack of grip on who she was and what she was disturbing.

What were Sonja's favourite films? It was time for another list. *Snow White and the Seven Dwarfs* certainly. Then *Gone with the Wind, The Hound of the Baskervilles, Ben Hur, The Broken Jug, Sumurun, The Four Horsemen of the Apocalypse, Singing Fool, Bolero, The Thief of Baghdad* and *White Shoulders*. Of course she was not counting the films that she had been in herself. Eva was mad for Clark Gable in *Gone with the Wind*.

Sonja did not bother to try for a part in *Hans Westmar*, as she gathered that the film was all about men fighting in the streets – Nazis against Communists. Also it ended unhappily with the young Hans Westmar dying after having been beaten up by the Communists. Nor did she attend its premiere, but of course, she did go to the party afterwards and it was there that she met the writer, Hans Heinz Ewers. Now, her narrative must not be entirely composed of long shots. She would need a few close ups. So she might as well start with Ewers. They had got to talking after she cadged a cigarette off him. Not only did he have lots of expensive Turkish cigarettes in a silver cigarette case, but he was wearing a black and gold smoking jacket, which seemed not the right thing at an event like this. He also sported a floppy bow tie. Quite a few of the other guests were wearing brown uniforms and they looked at Ewers curiously. He was slightly plump with a jutting brow and deep-set eyes, one of which sported a monocle. The regulation duelling scar was vivid on his ash-white face. Had the man been living under a stone? His manner was languid and quizzical. Also rather drunk. So he was not at all Nordic looking and he did not hold himself like a Nazi. But then, when one thought about it, so few of the Nazi leadership did look the part. Dear Joseph could hardly be taken for a latter-day Siegfried. There was that joke which was being whispered around Berlin: 'The ideal German must be blonde like Hitler, slim like Goering and tall like Goebbels.'

Seeing her eyeing the smoking jacket, Ewers smiled and told her that he could wear what he liked, as he was the most important person in the room. When younger he had been in the same student fraternity as Hans Westmar and he had written the biography on which this film was based. Also, he had scripted a horror film, *The Student of Prague*, and he had written several novels. Moreover, in the Great War he had operated as a German agent in the United States and Mexico.

'I joined the Nazi Party early – not like so many of these April Violets who have suddenly sprung up to support the cause. The Party needed people like me. I am no ordinary person, for when I think of something that I would like to do, then I just do it, since I am never deterred by fear, by convention, by the law or by sheer difficulty, or, come to think of it, even by common sense. Morality today is just herd morality and common sense is for the ordinary man, whereas I take what I want from life, since the ordinary man is something that has to be surpassed. Now what did you think of my film?'

Sonja told him that it was quite wonderful and that it had opened her eyes to what was happening in Germany today. She was praying that he would not ask her what was happening in Germany today as she had not a clue. She was lucky.

'Yes, Germany awake! As you saw, the final burial scene was a holy ritual. The drums roll, the drums roll dully and glowing-red torches light up the graveyard. At least that is how it is in my book. It is unfortunate that the film is in black and white. I intended there to be something Christlike about Westmar's struggle against the swindlers, Jews and pimps of Berlin. I have made him just like Jesus when he drove the moneylenders out of the Temple of Jerusalem.' Ewers paused. 'In reality, of course, the man I knew was a pimp himself and a little shit. Nevertheless, at the end of my story, he comes to resemble Saint Sebastian. That dear blond could fill a canvas by Guido Reni in which he would be struck down by the arrows of desire. Do you not think so? Did you not spot the resemblance? The pink flush of youth and the graceful acceptance of pain… grace in suffering… it is so very German. I dream that I might drink from the blood that flows from his wounds at night time when its hot fluid might mingle with my own blood. But you! You, with all those curls and curves, might have stepped out of a poster by Alphonse Mucha.' He paused again. 'No, that is not right. Not Mucha at all… but, let me see, you could have sat for Gauguin and he would have loved you. Your face is like a primitive mask which conceals an ancient wisdom. You are an exotic enigma and should be living in an island paradise. You are not German at all, I think.'

'I am Dutch.'

'Oh.'

He could not think what to say in response to this, but he gravely presented her with his card and told her that she would be welcome to visit him at any time.

'You may have need of me. I have some influence with those who are coming into power.'

Now looking back on that encounter, it was obvious. Ewers was a professional writer and he had written that biography of Westmar and he had obviously found her attractive. Though their only meeting had been some years ago, she still had his card. She should seek him out and get his advice on how to write her autobiography. Maybe he could look at what she has already written and help her with it. Also, another thought had just struck her. Maybe he could use his influence to persuade Goebbels to give her a major part in *Kolberg*.

An old woman, the housekeeper presumably, let her in and led her up to Ewers' bedroom. The man seemed to have shrunk and he was dwarfed by the immense canopy bed, standing on low baroque columns. At the end of the bed two small tables supported shallow vessels in which burnt golden flames. The sides of the bed were carved with erotic scenes which she guessed were taken from Classical mythology. Winged boys and doves sported amongst scrolls of acanthus. Ewers tried to sit up and failed. Then he addressed her in a quavering voice, 'Ah a wild sinful dream sister of my feverish days and nights, a phantom of delight. Dear flower of death, art thou come as presage of my end?'

Sonja did not know how to reply to this and instead continued to look round the room. This was just like a film set. A tiger-skin rug lay at the foot of the bed. Perfumed smoke issued from bronze censers placed on pedestals in the corners of the room. Monkey arms served as candelabras. There were two vast cabinets of majolica and Chinese porcelain. The walls were covered with framed stills from old movies and a large portrait of Hitler hung over the fireplace.

Seeing the direction of her gaze, Ewers said, 'I have to have it, but it is a pity that he is such an ugly little fellow. But now dear flower of death, do you have a name?'

There was no window and the air was heavy with incense. It was dark and her head swam, but Sonja managed to give her name and remind him of how they had met. Then she told him that she had come to seek his advice on how to write her autobiography. The problem was that the early part of her life, from her infancy in Holland up to and including her taking bit parts in mostly forgotten films, lacked interest, and it would be hundreds of pages before she got to the chapters that would really engage her readers. Also she kept getting the chronology muddled.

'Ah, but this is a three-pipe problem!' he declared with some faint animation and with that he reached for what he said was a Tibetan exorcist's bell which he kept beside the bed. The housekeeper appeared in answer to its ringing and a few minutes later brought him a long-stemmed opium pipe and, having filled and lit the bowl, she disappeared. Ewers offered Sonja the first puff and, when she refused, he drew hungrily on the pipe before saying, 'I used to take this for the pleasure. Now I take it for the pain. Come and lie beside me and we will put our heads together and consider what should be done.'

Rather hesitantly, Sonja did as she was told. Observing how stiff and cautious she was as she lay beside him, Ewers laughed.

'Ten years ago, when I would have seen you enter, then I would have knelt at your feet and kissed your pretty red shoes and that would have only been the beginning of my kissing. This afternoon, it is true, my eyes desire you, but only my eyes. The rest of me is quite unmoved.'

Suddenly he put down the pipe and cast aside some of the blanket that covered him and, seizing one of Sonja's hands with surprising strength, he forced it down and into his pyjama trousers until it covered his flaccid penis.

'You see! Nothing stirs! I have passed beyond the common rut of desire and so I exult! For most of my life I have been the abject slave of the flesh of other men and women. I was like a lunatic led in chains by people whom often I did not even like. But now I am free! Free at last!'

The unwonted effort brought on a fit of coughing. Meanwhile Sonja hastily removed her hand. It was a while before he could speak again.

'First, you must ask yourself, why are you writing your book at all? Does the world really need it? Why? Why? Everybody thinks that they have a story in them, like a jinni trapped in a flask that has been cast upon the seashore. So one only has to remove the stopper and the jinni comes billowing out until its mighty presence shuts out the sun and it announces in a thunderous voice that it is ready to fulfil all wishes. But the truth is, as any beachcomber can tell you, that such flasks generally contain only seawater and a little sand. Writing self-revelation is not the easy business of removing the stopper from a flask. It is rather the dirty business of selling your soul to the Devil. Oh, not literally, but in order to write a successful autobiography, you will need to betray your friends and relatives and ultimately, yourself. You will have to lie and cheat and you will have to expose your private parts. So why do you want to do this?'

It was an obvious question and yet Sonja was quite unprepared for it. For want of anything better to say, she said, 'I want to be famous.'

Ewers tried to laugh, though it came out as wheezing.

'But if you are not already famous, why on earth would anyone want to read your autobiography?'

'I am quite famous,' she said. 'I have appeared in quite a lot of films.'

Ewers closed his eyes and Sonja feared that he might have drifted off into an opium-fuelled sleep and so she was about to edge off the bed when he opened his eyes again.

'Yes, dear flower of death, I knew you were familiar to me. I have seen one of the films which you so beautifully graced. It was *The Gypsy Baron*.'

Sonja was always flattered when someone said that they had seen her in one of the films she had appeared in. *The Gypsy Baron* had been one of her few breaks in those difficult years. It must have been released in 1935, the same year that *Lives of a Bengal Lancer* and *Anna Karenina* came out. These days Sonja identified a lot with Anna Karenina. Just as Anna had despairingly taken to morphine, so Sonja was on barbiturates. Moreover, just like Anna, she faced diminishing options and sometimes she even thought of suicide. No! Stop that thought!

Things were so much better in 1935. Hitler and his party were riding high. They were repudiating lots of treaties and the rest of the world dared not stop them. There were lots of processions and there was cheering in the streets.

Anton Walbrook was the big star in *The Gypsy Baron* and Hansi Knoteck had played Saffi, the gypsy heroine. (Whatever became of her?) Walbrook was half-Jewish and had to leave the country a little later. Unlike Conrad Veidt, Walbrook had not really been Sonja's type. The film was based on one of Johann Strauss' operettas and it was notionally set in the province of Temeşvar. But, of course, the ruined Hungarian castle and the half-derelict village had been built on a vast lot at UFA. In the film those ramshackle houses that were still lived in were inhabited by gypsies. For once Sonja had no difficulty in securing a part and she was appointed the leader of the chorus of the gypsy women who lined up behind the heroine. None of them were real gypsies of course and most of the actresses, though not Sonja, had recourse to walnut juice.

The making of the film took months and, like most of the cast, she had gone through it all without having any idea what the plot was. It was something to do with mistaken identities, thwarted passions and buried treasure, but what exactly she could not say.

As leader of the female chorus, Sonja had consequently been among the favoured few to be presented to Herman Goering when he visited the UFA sets and she had the honour of presenting him with a bouquet of flowers. Then the former air ace still had something of the aura of a hero and, though he was already fat, he was not yet grotesquely so. These days nobody thought him much of a hero. A few years ago, boasting of Germany's air defences, he had declared that 'if a single British bomber reaches the Ruhr, you can call me Meyer'. So now, of course, almost everybody did call him Meyer. Not even fear of the Gestapo could deter them. But all that was in the future and in 1935 the sun had shone on Goering and Sonja.

'It was a terrible film,' said Ewers breaking into her reverie, 'but you were very pretty my dear. Of course, one could not make such a film nowadays. I am surprised that they could do so even then.'

What was Ewers talking about? Surely there had not been a Nazi law that banned the filming of operettas, even inferior ones? What Ewers said next only increased her confusion.

'If I remember rightly it was just a few years later that Himmler issued his decree: 'Combatting the Gypsy Plague' and now they are being sent to the camps.'

Don't gypsies camp anyway? What were the camps? Sonja decided not to ask. But she had another question, 'What day is your birthday?'

'Now it was Ewers' turn to look surprised.

'November the third,' he said. 'But nobody ever gives me presents and I do not expect one from you.'

So Ewers was a Scorpio! That all made sense. Scorpios were characteristically moody, obsessive, highly observant and independent minded. It was wonderful the way the stars could be used to unlock the secrets of a person's character. Perhaps it was because he was obsessive that he was insisting on talking about gypsies and 'the camps'.

'Once the war started the gypsies got themselves into serious trouble, as they used palm readings and tarot cards to predict the end of the war and so they were responsible for spreading false hopes among the German people. The camps are the right place for the Bolsheviks, the mentally deficient, Negroes and gypsies, but not the Jews. The last was the big mistake...'

Sonja, of course, did not want to hear about camps,

136

gypsies or Jews (and she did wonder momentarily what kind of Nazi was this man?) But Ewers persisted.

'Come to think of it, I may be wrong in thinking that it is no longer possible to make films featuring gypsies. I did hear that awful woman, Leni Riefenstahl has got money from Hitler to make a film based on a Spanish opera called *Lowlands* and that she has been using gypsies from the collection camps to impersonate Spanish peasants. But then they are supposed to be Spanish and not gypsy and I suppose that makes a difference.'

(Another person who hated la Riefenstahl!)

'Let me show you something,' Ewers continued. 'Do you see over there in the cabinet full of porcelain, on the bottom shelf there is an egg in an eggcup? Bring it over here and I will show you the face of fear. Be careful with it.'

Reluctantly, Sonja did as she was told and then resumed her place on the bed. Ewers reached for a paper knife that was lying beside the exorcist's bell and he expertly sliced off the top of the egg and then tipped up the egg in its cup and Sonja gave a little scream as a tiny skull rolled out. She had seen shrunken heads before, but this was smaller yet. She was in bed with a mad sorcerer. Well, not quite in bed.

Ewers laughed and coughed, before launching into a lecture about gypsies in film and literature. Had she seen Pola Negri with a rose between her teeth as Carmen? What about the gypsy Esmeralda in *The Hunchback of Notre Dame*? Then there were the gypsies in the service of Count Dracula (though Dracula himself might possibly have been Jewish). This was hopeless. Clearly Ewers had a disorganised opium-soaked mind and was going to be of no help at all in sorting out the chronology of *My Life is like a Fairy Tale*. At last Ewers' rambling discourse on the gypsy in Western culture petered out. The romance of the gypsies was over and he looked curiously at Sonja.

'What are you doing here, dark angel? Have you been sent to collect my soul?'

'I thought that you might be able to advise me on how to write my autobiography.' Sonja was unable to keep the hopelessness out of her voice. But he did not notice.

'Ah yes, I am with you now. Yes, you were worrying about the early years. Those years will be so very tedious and all those details about aunts and grandmothers and what you did at school will be incredibly boring. And you are Dutch, I do now remember that, and the Dutch are intrinsically boring too. I suggest that your problem is that, like most ordinary people, you think of life as a journey. As an infant you set out on it, you plod on in middle age and then, when you reach your deathbed, your journey is ended. But this is a delusion. There is no journey and you never leave home. Every day you live is the same day. It is just that different things happen in it. So you can forget about chronology and we can all be spared your aunts and what you learnt in the schoolroom. Only fools believe in the linear progression of time. But I see that you are looking worried and not paying proper attention...'

When Sonja pointed to the tiny skull, Ewers cackled gleefully, 'Fear in an eggcup! It is an old gypsy trick which they use to impress those who come to have their fortunes told. The gypsy tells the inquirer that it is the sign of a curse which can only be lifted if a large sum of money is placed in a cloth and the gypsy will sleep with that cloth overnight. But by morning the gypsy and the money will be gone. The skull was inserted through a hole in the bottom of the eggshell. You didn't think it was a human skull did you? You silly! It is of course a pigeon's skull. Now back to the story of your life. In these difficult times you must tell a story that will be an inspiration to others. Your life must be shaped into a narrative that will offer the German people hope, even though their situation is hopeless. As I see it, you will be like a gypsy fortune teller who sees death in the play of the cards, but who is careful to tell the client that there will soon be a wedding.'

Ewers was mad. How could the German situation be hopeless? Most of Fortress Europe continued to be garrisoned by German soldiers. Sonja had listened to the Christmas broadcast in which German troops stationed in La Rochelle and then more soldiers in Crimea sang carols and they all sounded in good heart. Ultimate victory was assured. And besides, there was the secret weapon.

'You must think of others and your book should tell them that miracles can happen,' Ewers continued. 'I think that your book must do two things. First, it must conjure up memories of better times in peace: of walking down Unter den Linden on a spring day, of sunbathing by the Wannsee, of slicing up a fat carp for Christmas dinner, that kind of thing. Secondly, when the reader closes your book, he must be ready to die. Your book must prepare the readers to be raped and then killed, since that is what is going to happen to most of them quite soon.'

Sonja did not like to think of *My Life is like a Fairy Tale* as something that should prepare its readers to be raped and killed.

'We are all doomed,' Ewers continued. I tried to warn Hitler and Streicher and Goebbels – anyone who would listen to me. It was a terrible mistake to take on the Jews, for the Jews and the Germans are the two natural master races of Europe and an alliance of German strength and Jewish cunning would inevitably have triumphed over the lesser races of Europe. But none of my fellow Nazis would listen to me. My party membership has been revoked and I am cast into outer darkness and soon, very soon now, our great drama will be over. They should have listened to me.'

So it was obviously no use hoping that Ewers could use his influence to get her a part in *Kolberg*.

'But you must lead your reader back to memories of the days of hope,' Ewers continued remorselessly. 'You should try to make them glad that they have seen you in your films, so that memories of your beauty and glamour may make their ordinary little lives seem worthwhile and that will prepare them to behave like heroes as they face their end.' Ewers paused. 'I can see from your face that you do not like what I am saying and I guess that you want your life story to have a happy ending, but the best books do not have happy endings.'

He rang the bell again and muttered to the housekeeper who disappeared and then reappeared with a book.

'This is my great novel, *Mandrake*. It was published a long time ago. I will read from its finale and you will see how this sort of thing should be done.' His hands shook, so that he had difficulty in reading what was before him: *"The shadows fell. And in the dark of night eternal, sin rose out of the sea, having ripened in the glowing deserts of sand in the South. Her pestilential breath preceded her and she strewed my garden with the veils that covered her sensual beauty. Then, my wild sister, your hot soul was aroused and filled with poison, it gloried in utter shamelessness. You drank my blood, and screamed and exulted amid the torture of kisses and the pangs of desire. The sweet wonder of your rosy nails, so sharply trimmed by your maid Fanny lengthened into wild claws. And the gleaming milk opals of your white teeth thickened into mighty fangs. While your sweet snow-white breasts, so like newborn kittens, stiffened into the terrible paps of a whore. "* Now that is fine writing! God, I had genius when I wrote that! Do you think that you can do as well? If not, you should abandon all thoughts of becoming a writer.'

Sonja was despondent. She was never going to be able to write like that. Ewers did not seem to expect an answer from her, but painfully rolled over to reach for the paper knife from the bedside table and he handed the knife over to her.

'I read that passage for a particular purpose,' he said. 'I have tuberculosis and I don't want to die of tuberculosis, for that would be so commonplace. But now Destiny has brought you to my bed. It would be so much better if you, fair emissary of death, sank your teeth into my scrawny old neck and drank my blood until I drifted off into the sweetest oblivion. If you think that your teeth may not be sharp enough to make the initial incision, you may use this knife. Here is the carotid artery,' he said, pointing.

But Sonja threw the knife away and leapt from the bed. She ran out of the room, down the stairs and out into the street and the fresh air. Maybe he could persuade that old housekeeper to drink his blood.

Perhaps the housekeeper did, for a little later she learnt that Ewers had died.

Chapter Eleven

It was pleasant to be reminded of *The Gypsy Baron* and that time when Goering came to watch some of the filming, for it also happened to be the day when Eva turned up on the set. Eva was not one of Goering's party and Sonja was not clear why she too was being treated as an honoured guest by UFA officials. Anyway, they got to chatting and it turned out that Eva was mad on films. Indeed, she seemed to have seen so many films that she must have gone out to the cinema almost every night. What really won Sonja's heart was that Eva not only praised her dancing on the day's shoot, but she actually remembered seeing her in *Congress Dances*. What a pleasant young woman she was. Not only was she mad about films, but she loved dancing. Sonja took her to an empty studio where they were joined by a member of the male chorus and Sonja showed them the steps for a Hungarian gypsy dance; lots of high kicks, hand clapping, slapping of the thighs and fanning out of the skirts. Such fun! Sonja still felt young. And Eva was, like Sonja, a dedicated smoker. Also, since neither Eva nor Sonja were blonde, they agreed that they should form The German League against Blondes. They must meet again soon. Eva agreed, but there was a problem. She was not from Berlin. She was only visiting and she lived in a place called

Berchtesgaden in the Bavarian Alps. She took Sonja's address and said that she would be in touch. That was one of the good days, the sort that did not happen any more.

But in 1935 good things kept happening. Four weeks later Sonja received an envelope by special delivery. In it there was a scrawled message from Eva Braun imploring her to come in six weeks and with it was a formally printed invitation on a stiff card. It was an invitation to the Berghof and it was signed by Hitler's adjutant. There was also an accompanying document instructing her what train she should catch, what sorts of clothes she should bring, how she should address the Fuehrer when she was spoken to, what time breakfast was served and stuff like that.

Six weeks later when she got off the train at Munich she was met by a junior officer of the *Leibestandart SS Adolf Hitler* who carried her case and conducted her to the chauffeur-driven Daimler which took her on to the Berghof. High on the mountain, the place was like a chalet that had become bloated and metamorphosed into a palace. That evening she was presented to Hitler. God knows how she was going to write that up, because actually she was quite disappointed. She had never cared for the snot-break moustache in photos and when she was facing him she found his eyes disappointing too. She had heard so much about those piercing, mesmeric eyes that gazed into one's soul, but actually Hans Albers' brilliant blue eyes were much more piercing. The broader truth was that none of the Nazi leadership was good-looking except that charming Mr Speer. (Though she liked Speer, the trouble was that she suspected that he found her a bit boring.) Anyway, Hitler paid little attention to her and Eva soon hurried her away.

Though Eva told her that she was Hitler's private secretary, she had no typing or shorthand and it soon became obvious that Eva's main daytime job was to keep Hitler cheerful with lots of chatter. But she was also usually responsible for choosing the films that were shown most evenings. Sonja was there as Eva's guest to sit beside her and entertain her with gossip about film stars and all sorts of behind-the-scenes stuff. In those early years Hitler often joined them. He was a big fan of an adventure film called *Lives of a Bengal Lancer*. Later, once France and Britain had declared war, he would take the heavy decision to give up watching feature films. It would be his sacrifice for the nation. Besides, he said that he needed to preserve his eyes for reading reports from the front and studying maps.

After dinner on Sonja's first evening, the great hall was cleared and the chairs were arranged, before a panel on the far wall was pulled back to reveal a projector and a showing began of *The Scarlet Empress*, directed by Josef von Sternberg and starring Marlene Dietrich as Catherine the Great. The film was not dubbed and most people kept talking during the screening. So then Sonja felt inspired to tell Eva about what a friendship she and Marlene had struck up during the filming of *The Blue Angel*. Sonja, improvising madly, told Eva, how after the final shoot, she had walked in on Marlene who was supervising the packing of her trunks.

'Marlene, what are you doing?'

Marlene had looked shamefaced and kept on packing while she considered how to reply. Finally, 'I have a boat to catch. Tomorrow night there is a liner leaving from Hamburg for New York. In two weeks' time I shall be in Hollywood.'

'But why, darling Marlene? Why?'

'You are too young to understand.'

Actually Sonja was only a few years younger than Marlene, but in the story she was telling Eva she persisted, 'Why, darling, must you go to Hollywood? We want you here. The German people love you.'

'You cannot understand. You are young and I can foresee that you have a great future ahead of you in films, whereas I, though I am not so very old… I know that I can never perform better than I have done in these last few months. For German audiences I shall never be more than the actress who played Lola Lola. German producers and directors will spot that I am past my peak. I am hoping that the Americans will be easier to fool and I may be able to get away with hamming it up in Hollywood films.'

Marlene's low husky laugh was full of regret. Sonja said that she made one last try.

'Germany needs you. There is no one who can replace you.'

Marlene's eyes rested thoughtfully on Sonja.

'I am not so sure about that.'

As Sonja talked, she realised that spinning out this fantasy to Eva would be a prelude to writing it up in a more elaborate form in *My Life is like a Fairy Tale*. After all, it was not as if Dietrich was ever going to return to Germany and contradict Sonja's version of events. Of course, some people would say that it was a wicked thing to tell such lies and she was half inclined to agree with them. On the other hand, she had been saying the sorts of things that Eva wanted to hear and really she only wanted to make Eva happy.

As for the film that they were watching, *The Scarlet Empress*, showed how a wide-eyed, innocent foreigner had come to a strange land, but how she had soon learnt sophistication and found sexual fulfilment there. It was just the sort of story with which Sonja could identify. And wasn't she herself, a foreigner, at this very moment seated in the centre of all power in Germany – no, in all Europe? It was exciting. Was it the best day of her life or were there yet to be even better ones?

When in the mornings she looked down from the height of the Berghof, the events of the world below seemed as distant to her as the comings and goings of ants – the occupation of the Rhineland by German troops, the outbreak of the Spanish Civil War, the Japanese sack of Shanghai, the Anschluss with Austria, the occupation of the Sudetenland, Polish aggression against Germany and the consequent war with Britain and France – all so distant and perceived through the wrong end of a telescope. Up in the Berghof, Sonja liked to fancy herself as an Olympian goddess contemplating the ludicrous affairs of the mortals below her. That ludicrous mortal, Wieland could not reach her here.

She and Eva spent a lot of the time on the terrace, as that was the only place where Hitler allowed people to smoke. The terrace was where Eva practised her callisthenics. Sonja taught her dance steps. They played with Hitler's beloved Alsatian, Blondi. They mastered the words of 'Ah, Sweet Mystery of Life', as sung by Jeanette MacDonald in the film *Naughty Marietta*. They watered the cacti. And usually they kept out of the way of the Nazi bigwigs, or 'Paladins' as the inner ring liked to be called.

But on Sonja's first afternoon at the Berghof she was out on the terrace admiring the mountains across the valley, when she was joined by Albert Speer. She turned to him and said brightly, 'Isn't this a marvellous place?'

'Well the view is lovely,' he said smiling and squinting in the sunshine. Then suddenly he was serious and, turning round, he gestured to the building behind them, 'But this building is so ugly. It has nothing of heroism about it. It has no more romance than a church hall or an ice cream parlour. So I ask myself what will this place look like when it has become a ruin. It will just fall to pieces and leave nothing noteworthy behind, whereas men still marvel at the Coliseum, the Parthenon and the walls of Constantinople. So what kind of legacy for the Germany of the future are we leaving here in the Berghof? Its walls should have been made of stone and in centuries to come ivy should embrace its crumbling masonry and people from the valley should climb up here on summer nights and by the light of their torches contemplate all the history that was once contained within its broken masonry.'

What a strange man to be envisaging the ruin of the Berghof! Were they not all living in a Thousand-Year Reich?

And Speer continued, 'Though people call me the Fuehrer's architect, I do not build for the Fuehrer. I prefer to build for Eternity.'

What was one supposed to say to that? Sonja guessed that this man was not going to be easy to chat to. And then Speer appeared to come to a similar decision and he changed the subject abruptly.

'It is good that you are here. Eva is lonely. Of course she would like to be Mrs Hitler, but Hitler is wedded to Germany.'

And after a few more inconsequential remarks about the weather, he walked away.

Speer was a frequent visitor and he and Hitler spent many contented hours together planning the remodelling of Berlin, most of which was going to be totally rebuilt and then renamed Germania when it became the capital of Europe. The other frequent visitors during Sonja's early stays at the Berghof were Joseph Goebbels and Leni Riefenstahl. They came to present the plans for Leni's filming of the Olympic Games later in 1936. Naturally, Sonja was introduced to Leni, as one film person to another. It was plain that Leni did not remember her previous encounter with Sonja and plain also that, once Leni had re-established Sonja's relatively minor status in the UFA hierarchy, she had no interest in talking to her. This was the occasion on which Leni turned to Goebbels and said, 'Don't you think she might be good at playing Jewesses? She could easily pass for a Jewess.'

Goebbels stared hard at Sonja, but said nothing.

When, a few minutes later, Hitler and Eva joined them outside, Leni led them to the edge of the terrace and, gesturing at the mountains across the valley, started to lecture them and everyone else in earshot, 'See how peaceful it is! So it should be. The mountains are sacred and do not like their peace disturbed. They and the majestic clouds above, with which the mountains commune, bear eternal testimony to the littleness of human existence. Winter is when the mountains are most alive and then their glaciers speak in deep booming noises, delivering messages that cannot be read, but which are full of menace. But those who know and love the mountains will not be deterred from making the ascent over savage ice falls and inching up those perpendicular rock faces. We who dare to disturb the deep silence of those heights will find ourselves first threatened but ultimately rewarded with visions of ghost marchers in the sky and caverns filled with sparkling crystals of ice and then, when we arrive on a sun-drenched summit, we come to know what our destiny is.'

Though Leni kept pointing to the mountains, Hitler hardly had eyes for them. He stroked his chin as, not for the first time, he gazed in wonder at this noisily confident and handsome woman, the epitome of Aryan womanhood indeed.

Finally he muttered that he did not think that mountaineering was for him and that he did not have the time for it and he thought that just a daily walk on a lower slope would suffice. But then, as they turned to go inside, Leni started to reassure him, declaring that there was also magic to be found on the lower slopes, for the thick pine forests that covered those slopes were the true home of fairy stories. Did he not love fairy stories as she did? Forests that have existed for so long contain creatures and spirits from the dawn of time...'

Sonja and Eva, who were left outside, looked at one another. Sonja was only a little irritated at Leni's annexation of the fairy tale as her province, as well as by her show-off excess of verbiage, whereas Eva was unable to conceal her distress and jealousy. In an attempt to cheer her up, Sonja told Eva about Leni's bitterness at not getting the part of Lola Lola in *The Blue Angel*. She had not sought an audition, but had simply assumed that Sternberg was going to give her the part. Then, after Sternberg assigned the role to Marlene Dietrich, Leni visited the set and, after watching Marlene act, she declared that Marlene's performance was 'vulgar', whereupon Sternberg told her off, while Marlene in a rage declared that she would walk out of the studio, if this 'well-poisoner' ever showed up again. Sonja had much enjoyed the drama of that morning and Eva seemed to draw some little comfort from Sonja's account of it, but she did not really cheer up until dinner that evening.

At the beginning of that dinner Leni had monopolised the conversation as she held forth on the upcoming Olympic Games and the glory of sport: strength... swiftness... beauty of the body... courage... leadership... the struggle and the will to win in the service of the Volk and the racial heritage.

Sonja tried to switch off and not listen to all that nonsense. She hated sport. Such a sweaty, aggressive, noisy activity. It was really only for men – and strange, rather monstrous women like Leni. Hitler was looking somewhat annoyed, since monopolising table talk was strictly his prerogative and so he soon got the subject of sport dropped and then he held forth, as he often did, on the subject of human psychology, 'A highly intelligent man should take a primitive and stupid woman. Imagine if on top of everything else I had a woman who interfered with my work! In my leisure time I want peace.'

Sonja wondered if he was talking about Eva. How awful! Hitler continued, 'Lots of women are attracted to me because I am unmarried. It's the same as with a movie actor; when he marries he loses a certain something for the women who adore him. Then he is no longer their idol as he was before.'

Eva did not think it awful at all. She was smiling. And Goebbels was nodding emphatically. Though Leni looked as though she dearly wanted to change the Fuehrer's mind, she kept silent.

A film show would have followed the dinner. Sonja could not be sure, but she thought that it was probably one of the many evenings on which *The Lives of a Bengal Lancer* was shown, for Hitler loved that film. *The Lives of a Bengal Lancer* showed how a handful of brave, resourceful British officers of 41st Bengal Lancers defended the province from a native uprising. Gary Cooper was Lieutenant Alan McGregor and Kathleen Burke played the seductress Tania Volkonskaya. Again this was mostly men's stuff. They galloped about. When captured, they refused to speak under torture. Then they blew things up and received awards for all of this – except that near the end Lieutenant Alan MacGregor got killed. So it was his horse that received the Victoria Cross in his place.

Hitler watched thousands of films. He was a man who was made by the films he had watched. He lived in a dream in which he was an officer in the Bengal Lancers, or Frederick the Great, Paul Kruger, an Irish patriot, a pilot in the Luftwaffe, a heroic Swedish scientist and a hundred other black-and-white phantoms.

At the end of the showing of *The Lives of a Bengal Lancer* Hitler delivered his verdict, 'This film is good because it depicts a handful of Britons holding a continent in thrall. That is how a superior race must behave and this film must become compulsory viewing for the SS.'

Then he became boring again as he drifted on to lecture about his plans for the German domination of the Slavic East. Sonja wondered if Hitler fancied himself as the Gary Cooper character. It was fair enough she supposed, as she fancied herself as Tania Volkonskaya, the irresistible man-eater, who seduced Englishmen in order to lure them into becoming the prisoners of the villainous Mohammed Khan, who would then tell his prisoners 'We have ways of making you talk'. Watching films was a way of dreaming while you were awake.

For some reason she was apprehensive when she arrived at the Berghof a few weeks later for her second visit. She became even more nervous, when on the evening of her arrival, she was introduced to Magda Goebbels. Her husband was not present as he had been detained on business in Berlin. Sonja's first thought was what a truly brave man Joseph Goebbels must be to have courted and married Magda. She was terrifying. She loomed over Sonja, a statuesque blonde Nordic goddess with cold grey eyes. Hitler adored her, even though he was somewhat in awe of her. Eva hated her and Sonja gathered that the feeling was mutual.

On the second day of this visit to the Berghof there was the usual afternoon walk. Eva had a headache, or so she said. But Sonja was obliged to join the party that set off from the Berghof heading to the teahouse higher up the mountain. It was a sedate affair. Hitler led the way with Magda and they were followed by Sonja, Joachim von Ribbentrop who was Foreign Minister, Ernst Udets from the Air Ministry and various other officials and officers whose names she did not know. The men did not talk to her and she was enjoying the stroll in the sunshine. If only she had dared have a smoke, it would have been perfect.

But then Ribbentrop remembered that there was a confidential matter that he really needed to raise with the Fuehrer. Hitler was not pleased to be ambushed in this manner. But Magda, who also did not conceal her ill humour, had to drop back. Since Sonja was the only other woman on the expedition, she elected to walk and talk with her. What started was not so much a conversation as an interrogation. So Sonja was not German but Dutch. Sonja was a friend of Eva's. Sonja was not married and had no children. Sonja was some kind of film actress. She knew that she was comprehensively failing Magda's exam. Then Magda added, 'I dare say that you have met my husband. But you are not his type.'

(Though Sonja did not want to be that man's type, she nevertheless felt mysteriously insulted.)

Then Magda wanted to know what had led Sonja to try for films?

'I suppose it is because I am a Sagittarian. Sagittarians are supposed to be natural performers.'

'Ah, so you study starlore! I am fanatical about the stars!' At last there was some warmth in Magda's voice and she went on to confide that she was a Scorpio.

'So I am shy, compassionate and I naturally have artistic interests.'

(Sonja did not think that this was the moment to say what she thought of Scorpios.)

'We cannot see the stars on this sunny day,' Magda continued. 'But they are eternally up there, benignly and invisibly directing our destinies. The earth is the mirror of the sky and the star-strewn heavens likewise reflect the earth and so we find ourselves embodied in the stars. They speak to us and we respond to them. Men's destinies are directed by an invisible astral web. Here at the Berghof we are under the sceptre of Jupiter. Have you not sensed it?'

Magda paused. Perhaps she was wondering whether

it was really worth giving Sonja the benefit of any more of her insights and beliefs. But then she continued, 'While the lives of the unenlightened majority here on earth are bound by invisible astrological chains, followers of the rightful way may hope to be delivered from the never-ending cycle of birth and death.'

Again Magda paused. So Sonja felt obliged to ask what the 'rightful way' was.

Magda smiled, 'People who do not know me well think that I live for clothes-shopping, tea parties, collecting for charity, flower arranging and such matters. Well, these things have to be dealt with. That is all part of samsara. But I have a spiritual side. I practise pure mindfulness and I meditate in order to free the mind of doubt and fear. Pure mindfulness is like a samurai's sword. It cuts through everything.'

Then, seeing that Sonja was looking more and more puzzled, Magda explained, 'I am a Buddhist. Unlike Christianity, Buddhism is Indo-Aryan and utterly uncontaminated by Judaism. Also, unlike Christianity, Buddhism is not a religion; it is a way of being for an enlightened elite. Not many people know this, but our swastika is a Buddhist symbol. Nothing earthly can sway a Buddha, for he has risen beyond the world of samsara and is beyond joy and grief, good and evil.'

This was strange stuff. Was Hitler a Buddha, Sonja wanted to know.

Magda laughed at her naivety, though there was sadness in her laughter.

'Hitler is not a Buddha, not in this incarnation, for we live in dreadful times and horrible things will have to be done. A dangerous configuration of the stars is looming and the tenth conjunction of Mars and Saturn in the trigon will occur in four years' time. We must be ready for that. The Fuehrer will know what to do.'

Sonja had always fancied herself as an expert on astrology, but now, listening to Magda, she realised that she was completely out of her depth. Where did Magda get her 'starlore' and her trigons from? Not from women's magazines, that was for sure.

Magda continued, 'Hitler is a Taurus, very obstinate, even too obstinate for his own good. Still, we need a man who is strong and determined and who will not stop until he has finished what needs to be done.'

Then Magda wanted to know if she knew a Czech film actress called Lida Baarova?

No. People who did not work at UFA did not realise how big it was. Thousands of people worked there. It was a world of its own, an empire. A great army of people toiled in that empire to make stories for the German nation.

But then Magda switched to talking about her daughters Helga and Hildegard. How good they were! But how they really needed a little brother. But they were really sweet. And so on and so on. Once they arrived at the teahouse, Magda left Sonja abruptly and hurried over to sit beside Hitler. Sonja sat alone with her cup of tea and slice of fruit cake.

After tea Hitler and Magda were ready to return to the Berghof and the chauffeur was holding open the door of the car when they were detained by the arrival of Heinrich Hoffmann who wanted to take a few photographs. Well, he said 'a few', but, like all professional photographers, he insisted on scores of snaps. It was while she was standing in the line-up under the sun that Sonja had the first of what she later came to regard as one of her 'turns'. Not that she felt faint or in any way physically unwell. It was rather as if she had left her ordinary brain and was seeing things differently. One day, soon, this sunlight, like the sunlight of previous centuries, would be ancient sunlight. Herr Hoffmann was here to make a record of their deaths and he had them lined up for his firing squad. It was as if Sonja was already part of her past. It was as if... what was the word for it? Then she snapped out of it and was smiling in the present sunshine. Had that been a Buddhist insight? She had no idea.

Back at the Berghof, Eva admitted that she had faked the headache because she did not want to spend any time with Magda.

'She thinks I am an idiot. That is because she reads books.'

Then Sonja wanted to know who Baarova was.

'But you know who she is,' Eva replied. 'We saw her in *Lieutenant Bobby, the Devil-May-Care Guy*.'

So many films. How did Eva remember them all?

'You should get to know her, as she is a rising star. She is the one with those fantastic eyes and cheek bones. She is very slinky. It is said that the Propaganda Minister has commented favourably on her acting.' And Eva winked.

Before they went down to dinner and the film, they reaffirmed their loyalty to the League against Blondes. Magda should be its first target. The film that evening was *Bolero* starring George Raft. 'His dancing partners were but stepping stones to fame!' Carole Lombard (another of those beastly blondes) co-starred. But Lombard played Helen Hathaway, a professional dancer. So of course, Sonja had to identify with her, despite the blondeness. In a tight-fitting glittery dress Lombard/Helen danced to the slowly accelerating rhythm of the bolero, pressed hard against Raft/Raoul DeBaere. It was like watching a couple having sex while yet fully dressed. But then the Great War intervened and Helen, spurning her former dancing partner, married an English peer, Lord Robert Coray (played by Ray Milland). Sonja thought that 'Robert' was such a glamorous name. Five years passed. Lord Robert bought a nightclub and there the heroine re-encountered her former dancing partner. There was a crisis that evening in the club and Raoul had to perform the bolero, but had no partner. Impetuously Helen volunteered to perform one final dance with him. Though five years had passed since she had last danced, night after night she had been rehearsing the bolero in her dreams. So, in the low-lit nightclub to the steady rhythm of the massed drums, they clinched and he could be seen voluptuously sniffing her as they swayed to that rhythm. But it was a dance of death, for Raoul had a fatally weak heart and he died as the music died and so it all ends.

How was it that sad films could be so satisfying? Sonja rather wished that she could present her own life as a tragedy, though she could not think of anything particularly tragic about it. She needed to have an affair. An affair was the necessary precondition for things going romantically wrong. Meanwhile she and Eva were going to learn the steps of the bolero.

Chapter Twelve

Back to *My Life is like a Fairy Tale*. The following year, 1936, was the year *Broadway Melody* was released. Also *The General Died at Dawn*, *Mayerling*, *White Slaves*, *The Charge of the Light Brigade*, *Top Hat*, *Dancing Pirate*, *The Garden of Allah*, *Ferry Boat Pilot Maria* and *Under Two Flags*. It was also the year of the Berlin Olympics, the year then of boring men getting all sweaty. Though Sonja was bored by sport, Eva was keen and it was a grief to her that she was not allowed to attend the Olympics with Hitler, who made a point of attending all the events at which the Germans had a chance of winning. So he was often away from the Berghof. But then Eva made Sonja watch the events on the weekly newsreel. Much later, in 1938, Sonja would attend the premiere of the cow Riefenstahl's *Olympia*, supposedly a 'hymn to the beauty and power of Man'. *Olympia* teaches us that there are no easy victories. But an account of that could wait. Sonja must stick to chronology. She was so bad at getting things in the right order and she was so vague that she had difficulty in remembering what she had actually written as opposed to merely thinking about writing. She was always wanting to rush ahead to the next big thing.

Though the sports would not feature in *My Life is like*

a Fairy Tale, the parties held to mark the opening of the Games were a different matter. Her readers would want to know about the glamorous parties. Looking back from present circumstances, the opulence of those grand receptions seemed like a golden dream. After much dithering, she had decided to describe the party on Peacock Island, but she would present herself as a guest at that party rather than relate how she really came to be present. Also she would not give an account of how the party ended. Of course not. She was not actually going to lie. Only there were just a few things she was going to leave out. Her readers would not want to know about these things and she did not even want to think about them. Everybody left things out of their autobiographies. Otherwise their autobiographies would be as long as their actual lives, which would be ridiculous. Writers have to leave things out. Sonja was beginning to think of herself as a writer.

But before the party on Peacock Island, there was the dinner given by Goering at the Opera House. That was a grand affair. Periwigged footmen in pink coats and knee-breeches lined the stairway. There were red and white banners everywhere. The diners, two thousand of them, were entertained by the Opera's singers and dancers. Unfortunately Sonja was not one of those two thousand diners. But she could write about it as if she had been there without actually making it clear that she had not been invited.

So, finally, it was time to write about Peacock Island. This was in a way easier to write about as she had actually been there, but in another way it was horribly difficult. The party, given by Goebbels on the last evening of the Olympics, was intended to outdo the reception given by Goering. The three thousand guests included the King of Bulgaria, the Greek King and Queen, the Prince of the Netherlands, numerous diplomats, the famous aviator Charles Lindbergh, the famous journalist William Shirer and the film stars Gustav Fröhlich and Lida Baarova. Peacock Island was in the River Havel and for most of the year its only inhabitants were peacocks and pheasants, the last residue of the Imperial Menagerie. Normally the island could only be reached by boat, but Wehrmacht engineers had been drafted in to build a pontoon bridge for the guests. Even so, some preferred to arrive by sailboats or canoes whose lanterns were reflected in the dark waters of the Havel. A chain of girls, dressed as Renaissance pages in tabards and tights, white breeches and white satin blouses, waited to welcome the guests to the fairyland island.

Butterfly-shaped lamps hung from monumental trees guided the guests along winding paths to dance floors, marquees and dinner tables... this was all very grand, but it was also quite boring and she was not going to describe what actually happened. If only she was writing a novel or a film script, things would be easier. In the film scenario that she now envisaged she would be an actress who, down on her luck, would try to earn some money by serving as a waitress at the grand party. It would be while she was waitressing that she would overhear a gang of men plotting to assassinate the Fuehrer. But then they spot that they have been overheard and she has to run for her life under the gaily lit monumental trees, forcing her way past cheerful revellers. The island's bridge is blocked by two of the conspirators. She must disguise herself, but how? Then she comes across a party of guests who have decided to go for a swim on this balmy evening. They have left their clothes on the edge of the water. She strips off her waitress' costume and dons a sumptuous ballroom gown and, with as much composure as she can muster, she goes to mingle with other guests. The dance sequence will be like the opening ball in *Gone with the Wind*, only in the open air. Now her skill as an actress comes in handy and it is while she masquerades as a Ruritanian countess that she meets the handsome prince of Illyria. He looks like Hans Albers or Conrad Veidt. She will decide which later. They are mutually smitten. He is flanked by a handsome, but unpleasant woman. (Leni Riefenstahl could play that part.) The Prince, who only has eyes for Sonja, finds a way of ditching his companion. They dance. It will be the waltz from *La Traviata*. But then Sonja is recognised by one of the plotters as the dangerous waitress and without a word of explanation to the prince she has to gather up her skirt and run for her life once more. The ensuing chase scene with the butterfly-shaped lamps crazily swinging around and fireworks exploding overhead, should be shot like one of those Fritz Lang thrillers. Somehow she escapes the island, but ends up in a sinister basement cornered by the plotters. The plotters, who had impersonated Canadian diplomats at the party, turn out to be British Jews working in the pay of Rothschild and the Bolsheviks. In the nick of time she is rescued by the Illyrian prince who turns out not to be a prince at all, but an officer of the Gestapo working under cover. So nobody was what they seemed. A marriage is surely imminent.

It was all utter rubbish. She knew that. It was just as well that she was not trying to become a novelist or a scriptwriter. But it could serve as her latest daydream, somewhere within which she could take refuge from the present nightmare of gnawing hunger pains, sirens, broken glass, looting, hanged men at street corners and lavatories blocked with excrement. She had to be her own cinema now. Almost all the real ones had been bombed.

1937 was the year of *Snow White and the Seven Dwarfs*, *The Stars Shine, Pépé-le Moko, The Man Who Was Sherlock Holmes, Fire over England, Lost Horizon* and *Broadway Melody*. Above all it was the year of *Habanera*. In this ever-so-romantic film Astrée, a beautiful and impetuous young Swedish woman (played by Zarah Leander), visits Puerto Rico as a tourist where she is swept off her feet by Don Pedro de Avila, a proud and wealthy grandee (played by Ferdinand Marion). He demonstrates to her both his courtliness and his courage in the bullring. She marries and has a son by him. They live in tropical splendour. But, though Don Pedro is passionately devoted to her, he is fiercely possessive and is even jealous of Astrée's love for her beautiful blond-haired boy. She pines for Sweden and sings to her boy about how wonderful the snow is. (Of course, Sonja found this scene repellent as she hated snow and had no intention of ever visiting chilly Sweden.)

Then 'Puerto Rico fever' afflicts the island and all sorts of political skulduggery ensues which Sonja could not at first be bothered to follow. (Only on the third time of watching did she get some idea.) Two Swedish scientists arrive in the island determined to find the antidote to combat the lethal virus and Don Pedro is equally determined to thwart them, since any publicity about the fever might affect his trade in tropical fruit. Then there is a great scene in his palatial mansion where Don Pedro is holding a party. Not only has Astrée decided to return to her beloved, chilly and thoroughly Aryan Sweden, but she realises that she has fallen in love with one of the Swedish scientists who is one of Don Pedro's guests. (Dr Sven Nagel was played by Carl Martell.) Astrée gets Don Pedro's permission to entertain the assembled guests by singing the *Habanera*. Dressed in a mantilla and traditional Spanish dress, she sways gently as she sings in slow 2/4 time:

'The wind has sung me a song
Of the heart for whom I long…'

Her voice is smoky. The cameraman under the direction of Detlef Sierck focussed closely on her beautiful face and the violins in the background served to articulate the director's visual concerto of brilliant light and deep shadow. That song is the climax of the film. The arrogant Don Pedro believes that she is singing for him, but her song is addressed to the Nordic doctor and the yearning in her voice is apparently a yearning for her native Sweden. Moments later Don Pedro, who had plans to have the two doctors arrested on trumped up charges, sinks to the floor, mortally stricken by Puerto Rican fever.

There was a lot of location shooting, not in Puerto Rico, but in Tenerife. Sonja had loved the heat and the bright colours. Though she only appeared in the last scene of the film, this had been her best role so far. In this scene Astrée, her ghastly Nordic son and the two doctors are assembled at the rail of the promenade deck of the liner that is preparing to take them back to Europe. They look down on a lighter on which an informal orchestra of men with guitars and marimbas give the rhythm of the habanera to which Sonja writhes seductively as she dances and sings. Leander (who even then was a little bit portly) had only swayed gently as she sang, but Sonja's dance was meant to embody the full seductive appeal of the South: the warmth, colour, sensuality, fruitfulness, easy living and dancing.

Sonja has seen her film six times. It was on the second time of watching that she noticed that Astrée's face does not show her to be exultant or even faintly relieved as she gazes down at Sonja on the lighter. There was something else there. On the third showing Sonja realised that Astrée's expression signified regret and yearning for the years of passion and heat from which the ship was about to take her away. Sierck had dictated this sadness and he had intended Sonja's dance to embody all that Astrée was about to lose. Dressed in black and dabbing away a tear, Astrée was saying goodbye to her impetuous youth. As Sonja watched *Habanera* again and again she came to realise that the plot said one thing, but the film's message was quite another. Films are treacherous messengers. The sixth time Sonja watched it she cried for by then she too was saying goodbye to her impetuous youth.

As far as she could remember, not much happened in 1937 or 1938. She had a few bit parts, but no major roles. 1938 was the year Leni Riefenstahl's *Olympia* was released. She had hoped that the Olympic film would fail, since not only was Leni a bitch, but her film was immensely long and it was silly watching men running after a ball or after each other. A dog could do these things. Had she remembered to add sport to her list of boring things? Yes! It was annoying that, when it came out, everybody said that Leni's film of the Games was wonderful. Well, if nasty people like Leni can produce great art, what is so great about art? Even so Sonja had to admit that she had enjoyed Leni's earlier film, *Triumph of the Will*. She had expected to be bored, because politics is boring, but there was something elating about all those strong-jawed Stormtroopers and soldiers with their flags and torches who paraded in perfectly drilled unison and those searchlights which soared into the night sky to create a cathedral of light. One would have to be a zombie not to delight in the power and majesty of it all. She had said as much to David Rego.

Oh, but she was forgetting that 1938 was the year she re-encountered David. One morning when she was on her way into the UFA compound, the man at the gate pointed to an envelope pinned on the bulletin board which was addressed to her.

If you are free for lunch tomorrow, do please join me at the Adlon at 1.30.

David.

It felt so wonderful to be stepping into the Adlon Hotel once more. So many memories of good food and sex. He was sitting, waiting for her in the foyer and they kissed formally before he took her into lunch. He had grown a little fatter, but then so had she. They toasted one another in cocktails. 'To old times!' In the past few days David had been enjoying himself touring Berlin, visiting old haunts and meeting up with friends and former business partners. Sonja wondered if he was safe in Germany the way things were these days.

'Oh yes, quite safe. I have a French passport now. Besides the Nazis badly want what I have got. War is coming and the

Luftwaffe is expanding rapidly, but it is very difficult indeed to make warplanes without bauxite. Goering and I are going to do business. Then I will be out of the business, for I am selling up my holdings in the mines of Les Baux. It is just a matter of setting up a shell company in order to avoid the scrutiny of the French authorities. That is what I am here for, that and I need to get in touch with whoever is managing the literary estate of Hugo von Hofmannstahl.'

There was no reference back to the bitterness of their breakup all those years ago. Sonja spoke a little about the few films she had been in, especially *The Gypsy Baron* and *Habanera*. David nodded patiently. He had been going to the cinema a lot, but the films he wanted to talk about were French films and he enthused about the poetry and inventiveness of such films as *Le Sang d'un poète*, *La Grande illusion*, *Méphisto* and *Quai des brumes*.

'You have to see *Quai des brumes*. The mist-shrouded port of Le Havre, the wet cobblestones and funereal cypresses furnish a wonderfully dark setting for a tale of grand and murderous passions.'

French cinema had reignited his enthusiasm for film-making and he was going to take his money and move to Hollywood where he would start up a new production company.

'I could take you with me,' he said. 'There would be no strings. Separate cabins.'

Sonja was stung by this. But Hollywood! Conrad Veidt, Ingrid Bergman and Marlene Dietrich were in Hollywood.

'I now have a French... er, companion. But, once I am set up in America, I might have a film role for you. Do you know Richard Strauss' opera *Rosenkavalier* with a libretto by

Hugo von Hofmannstahl? No? Well, I only saw it a few nights ago at the Berlin Opera House. The music is good, as far as I can judge, and it has a terrific plot. It is a bit complicated, too complicated to go into here, and anyway I will probably make some changes, but the essence of the story is about a Marschallin, the wife of a Field Marshal who is away on campaign. She is thirty-two and she is having an affair with Octavian, the seventeen-year-old 'Rose Knight'. As I say, never mind the plot. Their affair is tender and beautiful, but even while she delights in it, she becomes aware of the passage of time. 'Suddenly one is aware of nothing else.' It is with a sad resignation that she realises that soon she will have to surrender Octavian to a younger woman and she sings to him, 'One must be light, light of heart, light of hand, holding and taking, holding and letting go. Life punishes those who are not so and God has no mercy upon them.' It is a great theme and once I am set up in Hollywood, I am going to turn Hofmannstahl's libretto into a film script. It will be the basis for a drama rather than an opera and it struck me that you might be perfect in the role of the Marschallin.'

That was a second sting! David did not notice.

'The story is set in late eighteenth-century Vienna, so lots of silks, satins, wigs and swords. Maybe I can do it in colour. Well, think about it. What else is news? What about your strange friend, the mahjong player?'

Sonja told him that Tilde, having dropped mahjong, had become a fanatical member of the National Socialist Women's League and had consequently renounced smoking, lipstick and looking pretty. What she did not tell him was that Tilde had only done this at Wieland's request, because he wanted to know what it felt like to be a Nazi. Wieland could not currently become a Nazi himself because he was once again in prison. This time he had been found guilty of impersonating a high-ranking state official. He had rigged himself up a uniform which included the shoulder straps of a major, the silver fourragère of a staff officer, a swastika armband with a silver edge and a cap with a silver trimming. He also faked letters from the Transport Ministry in Berlin and the State Railroad confirming that the Fuehrer had appointed him Engineer *honoris causa* and that Wieland's project to produce a diesel car two or three times as fast as the ones used in Hungary should be given every possible assistance. It had all been immensely enjoyable. Eventually Wieland came up against the same judge as last time, but this time the judge was less amused and sentenced him to two years. Two Wieland-free years was a blessing for Sonja.

As she was about to leave the hotel, David said, 'Think it over. I'll tell you what, if you are free tomorrow come to lunch again and I will give you a ticket to tomorrow night's performance of *Rosenkavalier*. Then you can see what a great role the Marschallin will be.'

Back at the flat she wondered about Hollywood. Could Hollywood be an option for her? From what she had heard, Hollywood was no Shangri-La. Instead it was the Babylon of the West and its Jewish-run film studios were synagogues of fornication, sodomy, opium-smoking and champagne baths. It was a factory where dreams were made only to be broken. The sunglasses had diamond-studded frames, dildos were made of gold and chastity belts had heart-shaped padlocks. Life out there was one long Belshazzar's feast. Still, when she had spent some more time thinking about all this, she thought that she might actually prefer Babylon to Shangri-La. And Dietrich was even older than she was and yet she was still getting parts as the mysterious and dangerous woman. Dietrich was a Capricorn, cold and decisive. Sonja had heard Hitler describe her as 'a hyena, but with good legs'.

But how could she get there? She would have to bribe her way out of Germany and where would she find the money? David perhaps. But then she would have to learn English. Learning German had been hard enough and perhaps she was now too old to learn another language. They had tried to make her learn English at school, but it had never really sunk in. She had been made to read *Ivanhoe*, or rather, try to. Come to think of it, that was the last novel she had ever read, though not all of it, just a few chapters. She had found the book boring and difficult. If she went to Hollywood she would have to face many hours of English language and elocution classes. It was difficult. Still a free ticket to the opera should not be turned down.

The following day she went back to the Adlon. David was not in the foyer and when she asked the concierge, he leant over the desk so as not to be heard and muttered that the Gestapo had come for Mr Rego at six that morning. That was the last she ever heard of him.

Chapter Thirteen

1939 was the year *Hallo Janine* was released. Of course, it was also the year that war broke out, but by the time *My Life is like a Fairy Tale* should be published its readers would not be interested in being told about the war. Sonja happened to be at the Berghof on August 23rd, the day that the Nazi-Soviet pact was announced. She had been on the terrace with Eva. Hitler was also there with a Hungarian visitor. They were all gazing at the clouds that seemed to boil above the mountains across the valley of the Obersalzberg. Those extraordinary clouds were jagged yellow, sulphur grey, green, black and red, and there was a strange polar light under them.

Hitler said, 'One sometimes gets these effects in the mountains.'

But the Hungarian woman turned to him and raised a hand in warning,

'My Fuehrer, this betokens nothing good. It means blood, blood, blood and nothing but blood. This time it won't come off without much blood.'

Hitler replied, 'If it has to be, let it be now,' and then he went indoors.

Sonja remembered this incident because that was the evening she saw *Hallo Janine*. As usual, the screening took place in the dining hall after the plates and glasses had been cleared away. At the back of the hall the projection booth was partially concealed by a Gobelin tapestry. She had sat between Eva and Joseph Goebbels. *Hallo Janine* starred Marika Rökk in the title role. Janine was a would-be star and she pouted, sulked and simpered through the early scenes until she got her way and, thanks to a wildly implausible set of circumstances, became the star dancer and singer who performed to huge acclaim at Paris' Moulin Bleu. Attentive men in top hats and leggy chorus girls backed her up. She had curly hair and a childlike plump face. Sonja thought that she looked like a Shirley Temple who had been inflated to a grown-up size. Also her singing was syrupy sweet. The Hungarian Rökk was new to German films and Sonja could see that she was going to be competition. Somehow those strange clouds and the Hungarian visitor's reading of them seemed to be a portent of what befell Sonja as a consequence of her watching that other Hungarian dancing in *Hallo Janine* that evening.

Goebbels had been visibly stirred by Rökk's performance and kept licking his lips. After the film had finished, Sonja found herself for the first time actually having a conversation with the great man and she was able to talk him through the various dance steps that they had seen in the big concluding number, 'Music, Music'. Then he asked about her employment at UFA. Was she happy there? What films had she been in? He seemed so interested in her. Finally, before they retired for the night, he told her to come and see him at the Ministry for Popular Enlightenment and Propaganda at the Schwerin Palace on Wilhelmstrasse and he gave her a number to ring to make an appointment and he added, 'The cinema is me dreaming. Sometimes I have nightmares, sometimes I dream of beautiful women.'

Sonja could hardly sleep for excitement. The film industry was part of his empire and two major films, *The Jew Süss* and *Mary Queen of Scots*, were rumoured to be going into production soon. They would be costume dramas and there would be dancing.

At the end of the following week she arrived at the Ministry of Enlightenment Propaganda and, after a twenty-minute wait, she was ushered into his office which was vast and Goebbels, who was not a big man, appeared smaller than ever as he sat behind such a vast desk. He rose, somewhat painfully to greet her and then retreated to his chair behind the desk. She was going to take the seat on the other side, but, no, he suggested that she sit on the edge of the desk. Did she not remember the scene in *Hallo Janine* where Janine sits comfortably on the desk while she talks to the producer of the show at the *Moulin Bleu*? No, she did not. But, somewhat warily, she hoisted herself onto the desk. Now he was at pains to put her at her ease. He was sorry that she had been kept waiting. It was a busy time in the office, but the current political crisis would soon be over. She must call him Joseph. Had she come from far? 'Hitler weather' was what they called it when it was as sunny as this. Her German was very good.

Then he came round the desk and with some difficulty hoisted himself up, so that he was sitting beside her.

'You are very beautiful Sonja. But you know that. Men must always be telling you that. Your legs are very fine. So plump and adorable. You should sit like Janine and show a bit more leg. It is what men like to see.'

Sonja shifted uneasily, but this was not what Goebbels liked to see and he placed his hand on one of her legs and started to push her skirt up. Though Sonja tried to gently push his hand away, she was too frightened to mount any real resistance and her feebleness increased his ardour. She was being hungrily kissed. 'Hungrily' was the word. As she came to know him better, she found that he needed sex more than food.

Now he pulled her onto the thick carpet, her panties were down and the Minister of Propaganda was sprawled all over her and heaving away with fanatical energy. 'Fanatical' was the word. He was fanatical in everything he did. Films showed people how to kiss, but sadly not how to have sex – not the ones she had seen anyway. Thank goodness there was not a mirror on the ceiling. But then why would there be a mirror on any of the ceilings in the Ministry of Propaganda? It would definitely not be appropriate. It came into her mind that she did not actually know what propaganda was. The eyes burned in that rat-like face. He jerked and slithered over her, muttering things she did not understand. It was perhaps a bit like 'Beauty and the Beast', though she could not exactly remember how that story went. He was briefly fondling her breasts as if he was bent on checking that she was not the same sex as he was. What would it be like not to be a beautiful woman? She simply could not imagine how it would be not to be desired by men. Men look at her and think that she is exotic and alluringly mysterious, but the truth is that inside she just feels ordinary. When this was all over perhaps she could ask him what propaganda was. His climax might now be over, but he continued to paw her flesh as if he could bury himself in her. Suppose someone came in? Was that Nazi goddess Magda in the habit of visiting her husband in his office? That really would be terrifying. Think of something different, as Sonja used to do when she was in the dentist's chair.

Now that she was such a frequent visitor at the Berghof she had often found herself listening to conversations that she did not understand. Besides propaganda there were so many other words and phrases being bandied about these days that she did not know the meaning of, including forcible coordination, Aryanisation, special treatment, world view and Final Solution. Final Solution to what? The Jews presumably, but what was ever final? There was so much she did not understand. The world was changing and leaving her behind. There had certainly been no mention of propaganda in Dordrecht in the 1920s. But now that the ordeal was over she had to concentrate on looking satisfied. His technique, if one could call it that, had been very different from David's. (What had happened to David?) David had been more assured and much calmer. Joseph's mouth was like a scar. Did she dare have a cigarette now? She could not remember if there was an ashtray on the desk. Probably not. It came to her that he hated smoking. In the fairy story the beast turned out to be a prince. Well, Goebbels was a sort of Prince of the Reich. That Czech movie *Extase* with Hedy Lamarr came closest to being a how-to-have-sex film with its erotic nude shots, but that had been all slow and soft focus, whereas there was nothing slow or soft focus in what had just happened in Goebbels' office.

So then they were lying peacefully on the floor and he nearly jumped out of his skin when she asked him what propaganda was.

'Propaganda is the organised spreading of information in order to bring about change and reform,' he snapped. 'It is vital to Germany's future.'

Now she knew what propaganda was she would be able to use it in conversation! 'That looks very like propaganda to me.' 'Have you seen or heard any good propaganda recently?' 'If you ask me what propaganda is, I should say that it was the organised spreading of information in order to bring about change and reform.' Then she found herself thinking about 'Beauty and the Beast' again, and when she thought about it a bit more, she wondered if that particular story was all that nice. Perhaps its moral was that all men were beasts and women just had to put up with it.

Later, as he was pulling up his trousers, he started to explain a bit more about propaganda. It was very like advertising in America, he said, only his propaganda was advertising for Germany. For centuries Germany's curse had been that there were too many intellectuals and intellectuals were always finding fault with things. Damn them. But propaganda spoke in short, simple sentences to the great mass of the people. The people needed to be taught how to hate intellectuals, Jews and communists. Though Christians, Weimar-style politicians and pacifists were all against hate, hate was actually a force for change and that was good. And, if one told lies for Germany, then by that very fact those lies became the truth. Here at the Ministry his task was to forge once more the pure German soul. This was a truly great undertaking.

As she was leaving, he pressed on her his novel, *Michael*, so that she could understand him better by reading it. He wrote it a long time ago and if he had time to rewrite it now, it would look very different, but still…

In the middle of the night that followed she thought that she opened her eyes to find a very strange man leaning over her. He had been trying to wake her up. He was bald with ears that stuck out, teeth that were sharp, fingernails that were long. His face was simultaneously rat-like and yet aristocratic. The thin body was encased in an old-fashioned frock coat. He might have stepped out of a fairy tale, but surely a nasty one. He wanted something that she had. She wanted to scream or perhaps to pray for mercy, but she was paralysed and voiceless. Finally she managed to blurt out 'This is a dream' and with that she did indeed awake and found herself alone in her bedroom. Now there was another phrase running round in her head. 'Monsters love beauty.' Where had she heard those words before?

The following day Goebbels sent her flowers. Of course none of the business on the desk and the carpet was going to be in *My Life is like a Fairy Tale* – not in the first edition at least. There was no need to describe how it had been. She thought that she would present Goebbels' future benevolence to her as being the result of how impressed he had been with her performance in *The Gypsy Baron*. At least she hoped he was going to be benevolent. Surely she must now get a major part in either *Jew Suss* or *Mary Queen of Scots*?

Since she had never got round to reading Ewers' *Mandrake*, *Michael* was the first novel she had read since schooldays. It was a strange experience and rather hard work. Part of the problem was all the 'he saids' and 'she saids'. She kept having to backtrack to work out which character was speaking. Also, since she could not actually see the faces of the speakers, it was often difficult to work out how any particular remark was intended. The same words might be said sarcastically, jokingly or threateningly. She just could not tell. In those respects films were better than novels and she was surprised that they had not yet made novels obsolete.

Michael, which was cast in the form of a diary, told the story of a young veteran of the trenches, one of the millions wrecked by the war, who after his return from the front begins a love affair with a young woman called Hertha. But he is searching for something more, something that will give meaning to his life. The novel describes their encounter with a prophet figure in a beer hall. Hertha says that this charismatic orator will lead the next generation of young men to their deaths, but Michael's reply is, 'Geniuses use up people. That's just how it is. But the consolation is that they don't do so for themselves but for their task. It is permissible to use up one youthful generation as long as you open paths for a new one.' God, this was boring. Sonja had thought that novels were supposed to be fun. So far she had seen no evidence for this.

A little later Michael renounces both his mistress and his former way of life as an intellectual member of the middle class and becomes a miner. In the pits he finds a kind of psychological salvation through manual labour. The book was very preachy and full of stuff about love of the Folk and hatred of the Jews. As she closed the book she wondered if Michael had a club foot.

The book had ended with Michael dying in a mining accident. Sonja wondered why anyone who had taken the trouble to write a whole novel should make it end unhappily. Why was Joseph so cruel to Michael? Where was the pleasure in that? And surely it was going to annoy the book's readers? Also there was no actual sex in the novel. All sorts of things do not get published in novels, like washing up, applying cosmetics, going to the lavatory. It did not help her to understand him better. What were novels for?

A few days later she was summoned back to the Ministry. There were few preliminaries and, at this stage, not much talk afterwards. She would have liked to have thought of herself as *maîtresse en titre*. But this was not really true as too few people knew about their relationship. Some people at UFA came to know, including Goebbels' deputy for film, Fritz Hippler (and consequently they treated her with respect). Then a few people at the Ministry and some of the staff at the villa at Schwanenwerder. Also Sonja had confided in Tilde who quietly congratulated her. But this was not like Joseph's grand affair with Lida Baarova. Baarova really had been *maîtresse en titre*. Anybody who was anybody knew about that scandal and Joseph had even authorised the making of *A Prussian Love Story*, a film which gave a thinly disguised account of their passionate romance.

Baarova was a Czech actress whom Joseph had first seen in Paul Wegener's film *Hour of Temptation* which was released in 1936. She had a beautifully sculpted face with its Slavic cheekbones and she was about ten years younger than Sonja. Like Sonja, she was perfectly formed for the role of seductress and Joseph was willing to sacrifice everything for her. By 1938 he was ready to resign from the Ministry of Propaganda and he was seeking a divorce from Magda. But Magda appealed to Hitler who put his foot down. He harangued Joseph. There was to be no divorce. Baarova was escorted out of Germany and *A Prussian Love Story* was never released. For a while the Gestapo was ordered by Hitler to watch Joseph to ensure that he did not attempt to get in touch with her.

Though Baarova was still alive as far as she knew, Sonja felt Baarova's ghostly presence in the Ministry and later again during her visits to Schwanenwerder. It was Joseph that Baarova haunted and no one could ever replace her in his heart and sometimes he would weep for what was lost.

'You are my consolation prize,' he told Sonja.

Of course Sonja was jealous of her predecessor, not so much for the hold she still had on his heart, but more for her having been assigned more and better films to star in. They had included *Patriots*, *Der Fledermaus* and *The Gambler*. Whereas for a long time Sonja was unable to persuade him to see her as a star.

Chapter Fourteen

Joseph gave better advice than that Ewers… though the war had started, the fighting was still in unimportant places like Poland and Norway. So these were the good times. They had been lying in bed, after coming up from the private cinema where the two of them had watched *Broadway Melody of 1938*, one of those big budget Metro-Goldwyn-Mayer musicals. (Quite a few of the films they used to watch were American or English and were banned from general distribution in Germany, including *The Wizard of Oz*, *Snow White and the Seven Dwarfs* and *Rebecca*.) Magda, who had taken to heavy drinking during the Baarova affair, was away on one of her eternal health cures and then Bruno, the projectionist, had been told to go home. So they were alone in the villa. After the sex, Sonja told Joseph how she had loved those high-kicking dance sequences in which massed lines of lovely smiling girls with plump legs rotated, broke up and reformed. They marched, advanced and retreated and, though their drilling was softly sweet, their discipline reminded her of those sequences in *Triumph of the Will* in which huge formations of the Wehrmacht, the SS and SA had paraded before Hitler and his henchfolk. The speeches from the great podium had been tedious (she did not say this to Joseph), yet the parades below were quite marvellous. Joseph had been more struck by Eleanor Powell and her wonderful tap dancing. So Sonja told him that she could tap dance too and, pausing only to put on her high-heeled shoes, she tap danced naked before him. Tap dancing in high heels is a bit tricksy, but it is a skill that can be learnt. The three main things to master are time, tempo and rhythm, or that is beat, speed and pattern. Sonja demonstrated the straight tap, the forward and backward tap and the shuffle, and her breasts were flapping up and down and Goebbels was laughing as she tapped away. It was such fun! She was sure she could teach Joseph to tap dance! Then she realised what she had just said and the laughter and the dancing came to an end. She remembered how earlier, when the Reichsminister had knelt before her, how difficult it had been for him with that club foot and the leg brace.

Joseph just smiled sourly and gestured that she should rejoin him in bed. Later, she was talking about her hopes to become a great film actress and about how one day she would start on a book about all the films she had been in and her path to stardom. So then Joseph told her that she should keep a diary. He too was going to write his autobiography, the story of his path to power and glory, and he had presold it to a publisher for a huge sum of money. Soon, when the final victory over Judaeo-Bolshevism should have been achieved, he would actually sit down to write it. But to that end, he was keeping a diary. The diary was his gymnasium in which he exercised his mind every day. More than that, it was his friend. He sometimes thought that it was his only friend. Now it was his turn to get up and he went into the next room to fetch what he said was the most recent volume of his diary to have been typed up.

He urged Sonja to leaf through it, so that she might understand what kind of man he was. Sonja hardly needed any urging, for the volume dealt with events of the last eighteen months and she was excited at the prospect of reading about the matrimonial rows with Magda, the slow breakup with La Baarova, Hitler's rage at this liaison with a foreign woman, the weeping, the supplications, Baarova's attempted suicide, the catcalls at the first screening of *The Gambler*, in which Baarova had starred, and finally the Gestapo escorting that woman out of Germany. But sadly there was none of that in the diary. Instead, there was a lot of this kind of thing: 'In the near future Hitler foresees a very grave conflict. Probably with England, which is seriously preparing for it. We must face up to it, to decide the matter of European hegemony. And in view of that, there is no place for any personal hopes or desires. What are we individuals compared to the great destiny of the state and the nation?'

After dutifully leafing through it for a few minutes, Sonja put the diary down and asked Joseph his date of birth. It was October 29th. So that made him a Scorpio, just like Magda and Ewers! And now Sonja felt uneasy with her lover. She supposed that, by and large, people who were Scorpios were just as good as people who had been born under other star signs and she had met lots of Scorpios who seemed quite nice. Even so, Scorpios tended to be jealous, obsessive, suspicious, manipulative and unyielding. She thought that there was always a sting in the tail of a Scorpio.

And Goebbels confirmed her doubt, when he exploded in anger on being told that he was a Scorpio, 'Astrology is trash, my dear! It is a drug that is eagerly consumed by the underclass, for it explains their failures, as well as feeding their foolish dreams of what they might have become, if only the stars had not been against them. It is for housemaids. It is a dream factory, whose production-line prophecies tell the housemaids to be content with their squalid little lives. Whereas I made myself who I am and I owe nothing, nothing at all to the stars. You must do as I do and have faith only in yourself and the Fuehrer. Don't look to the stars. You can become so much more. Look to the Fuehrer, for in submitting to his will, we shall all find our true destiny.

It took Sonja quite a while to calm him down. And later the sad thought came to her that she was most unlikely to feature in Joseph's diary, or his autobiography. She would so much like to feature in someone else's book. That would be almost as good as appearing in films.

But, anyway, Sonja took Joseph's advice and the very next morning she had gone out and bought a little black notebook and started writing in it. If only she had started earlier. Unlike Joseph's diary, hers was not going to be a boring record of political events. She was going to hold nothing back. Also if she wrote in it every day, then perhaps this would give her the mental discipline that she knew she sadly lacked. The trouble was that she had so little practice in writing, or, for that matter, in reading.

That had been a few years back in the good times. It was, she thought, a curious feature of orgasms that, in retrospect at least, they all seemed the same. Thus while the tap dancing and Joseph's tirade against astrology were vivid memories, she could not remember how the sex had been that night. How had she written it up in the first of her many diaries? She had to know. Now she was wide awake and in the grey light before dawn, she reluctantly staggered out of bed and went to the corner cupboard where she kept her diaries and hunted out the first volume in the series. One problem with her diaries was that her handwriting was so bad and, of course, she did not have Joseph's resources, so that she could not pay a team of secretaries to type them out for her. Not that she would have wanted a team of secretaries reading the explosive revelations in her diaries anyway. Ordinary Germans had no idea what Joseph was really like, not to mention what she could tell them about Eva, Ribbentrop, Canaris, Streicher, Riefenstahl, Gründgrens and the rest of them.

She took the first volume back to bed with her. It was a bit difficult in this dim light, but her handwriting did not look as bad as she remembered. But what is this?

'Oh Wieland,' she sighed. 'You are my only Fuehrer.'

She gazed in horror and amazement at what she had written.

'He gave an impression of strength and cruelty... my protests were stifled as he pressed his hungry lips upon mine... I felt myself melting in his arms... I was like a bruised fruit pressed between his strong arms... I reached down for his strong cock... wave upon wave of hot desire swept over me... I had not known it could be like this... now that he had had his savage way with me, I knew that Wieland and I were destined for one another, forever and forever... who can know the secrets of the human heart?... but then it was time for more kissing...'

With difficulty she steadied herself to look more carefully at the handwriting. It was similar, but not hers. And it was in

German, not Dutch. It must be that of Wieland and, as she leafed through the pages, she saw that the notebook which she had thought was hers was full of much worse things. In gleeful detail, Wieland had laid out his fantasy which had Goebbels being summoned to the Chancellery for a midnight meeting with Hitler. 'He is like a dog which runs to his master when the master whistles.' Then Sonja supposedly telephoned Wieland and implored him to come immediately to the villa at Schwanenwerder. She had let him in through the sliding glass doors. To get themselves in the mood for what was to follow, they rummaged around in Joseph's hoard of pornographic films and watched a little of the uncut version of *Extase*, starring Hedy Lamarr. After sex in Joseph's bed and all the kissing, she had gone to the wardrobe and donned Goebbels' party uniform before tap dancing for Wieland's pleasure, as he lounged at his ease against the pillows. Then she rejoined him in bed where she proceeded to describe in contemptuously comic detail the Reichsminister's seduction techniques and went on at some length about his casting couch routines. 'The Goat of Babelsberg has *droit de seigneur* over all the actresses at UFA.'

Sonja had a quick look at other later volumes of her diaries. Some had had additions written in by Wieland, stuff about his philosophy of life and turning the everyday into drama, but others were uncontaminated and just as she had written them. One diary was missing. Wieland must have sweet talked or bribed Giselius in order to get access to her flat while she was at work. It would be easy enough for her to destroy the diary containing Wieland's erotic fantasy and she would find a safe place for those diary entries which were truly hers.

But a cold fear stole over her. Where was the original first volume of her diary, the one which described that night with Joseph when they had watched *Broadway Melody of 1938*? It was nowhere in the cupboard. So Wieland must have it. He had stolen her memories. Much worse, she was in terrible danger. Come to that, so was he, though he was certainly mad enough not to care. As long as he had that diary, he had absolute power over her. It was definitely mostly cold fear that she was feeling, but yet, but yet, there was a small part of her that was thinking what a terrific film this would make: the dangerous madman, the stolen documents, the honour of a beautiful woman in peril and, more than that, vital national interests threatened. Wieland would have to be tracked down and shot in a dark and narrow alley.

Now she realised that when he had turned up at the UFA studios a week ago, claiming that he had something of hers, it had not been her ration card. If only it had been so. It must be the diaries. Would she find time in prison to write *My Life is Like a Nightmare*? She needed help, but whom could she turn to? There was only Tilde. Only Tilde knew what kind of man Wieland was.

Tilde and Sonja met on the Kufurstendam. The grand avenue was not as it had been on the occasion of their first meeting. Bombing had destroyed whole blocks and there were other shops that had been boarded up. It was cold and overcast. So they sat over ersatz coffee indoors in a little cubicle and spoke in low voices. Sonja told Tilde as much as was necessary, though still as little as possible. (The tap dancing and much else was not mentioned.) These days Tilde was somewhat in awe of Sonja, the mistress of the Reichsminister, even though

Tilde now despised the man.

As it turned out, Tilde was not much help. Having listened to all that Sonja felt able to tell her, she said, 'I think that Wieland is a special kind of scientist. He does things in order to see what will happen. You are complaining because he has chosen to experiment on you. I only wish that I received so much attention from him.' She laughed. 'I really wish it was I who was the test tube that was being heated by his Bunsen burner. He is working on a plan to simulate a Jewish ritual murder. He talks of setting up a school for confidence tricksters. Before he was arrested he was also conducting a street survey in which he asked old women about how they felt about being so ugly. He has so much energy and is so brilliant. If he has stolen one of your diaries I am sure that it is for a purpose.'

Sonja hoped that this purpose had nothing to do with Jewish ritual murder.

But what she asked was, 'What star sign is he?' It was absurd that she did not already know this.

'I don't know, but it is certain that he was born under a dark star. I have known him a long time, I share his ideals and I admire his pranks. Whereas you are not for him. To be frank, Sonja dear, you are not intelligent enough and what is more you are a hopeless conformist. People who believe in horoscopes generally are. Sorry. I do still like you. But keep away from Wieland. Remember that I warned you about him.'

'You did. I swear that I have done nothing to encourage him, but still he hounds me. How is it that he is still in Berlin and not in uniform? Why is he not at the Eastern Front?'

'Who knows? He has a way of making himself invisible and disappearing. He has money. Perhaps that helps. I have

187

heard rumours that he has found work with Gründgrens and consequently, as a state registered actor with the Reich Theatre, he is in a reserved occupation. But that may just be a story he is putting about. All I know is that he certainly has recently acquired money.

'Well anyway what can I do now about the missing diaries?'

'You can hardly go to the Gestapo.' Tilde paused. 'It would have to be the opposition.'

'There is an opposition?'

'Well, yes, but no. Not a political opposition, not that I have heard of, at least. No, I mean the criminal underworld. There are people there who can make Wieland fear for his life. What is more, I know that they have a particular dislike of actors. You should take your case to The Court of Miracles,' and, seeing the baffled look on Sonja's face, Tilde continued, 'It is a club in the Moabit quarter. Its proper name is The Tannenberg Club, but everyone calls it The Court of Miracles and that is where the sandwich men and others gather.'

'The sandwich men?'

'For God's sake, Sonja, do stop echoing everything I say. Surely you know about the sandwich men?'

Sonja shook her head.

'You live in a little world of your own,' Tilde continued. 'I thought everyone knew about the sandwich men. You know those little booths on street corners throughout our city where sandwiches are sold. Well, the city's beggars are employed by the sandwich men to report on what they see in the streets and sometimes to shadow targets and just occasionally to pick a pocket to obtain something important, but mostly they just act as the eyes of the sandwich men and they are usually paid in sandwiches. Sandwiches are the small currency of the criminal underworld. Then the sandwich men, in turn, report to the criminal bosses. The biggest and most dangerous of the gangs operating in and around Berlin is known as the Wild Clique and their top men are known as Clique Bulls. They can do the job for you, though, of course, it will cost you.'

'Can I pay them in sandwiches?'

Tilde impatiently waved this away and whispered, 'Only if you want to see your hands lopped off. But you must have money, don't you? There must be certain rewards for... er, consorting with... er... the person you consort with. Hasn't he given you stuff?'

Sonja could see that, though taking her case to The Court of Miracles and enlisting lots of sandwich men and beggars to hunt down and kill the dangerous madman in that dark and narrow alley would make a great scene in the hypothetical film she had running in her mind, in real life it was just not going to work.

'Oh yes!' she replied. 'A copy of *Mein Kampf* bound in red leather and a bronze medallion featuring a profile of himself. He hates waste and extravagance. When he has people to dinner, he makes them bring their ration cards and there is not much food on the table anyway. He is clever, witty and brave, but also very mean.'

Tilde shrugged, 'So then it is up to you. When Wieland next gets in touch, you will have to give him whatever he wants.'

Sonja could see that Tilde was not really interested in her plight. What she really wanted to do was to lecture Sonja on the foolishness of consulting horoscopes in magazines. Horoscopes were a form of social control. They generally offered consoling messages to people, mostly women, who were depressed or unsure of themselves and what their advice was to these unhappy people was that they could easily improve their lives by bucking up and acting more cheerfully. What the horoscopes never allowed for was that people might be depressed because they were impoverished, ill or living under a dictatorship. Horoscopes moralised relentlessly. Horoscopes vulgarised. Horoscopes preached that it was good to be ordinary. Horoscopes were relentlessly petit-bourgeois. But members of the elite were smart enough to pay no attention to horoscopes. Neither Wieland nor Tilde had any faith in astrology.

And having delivered the lecture, Tilde left.

Sonja sat there thinking. It was a painful process. Why has Wieland not already been in touch? Then it came to her that Wieland could not do anything with the diary. If he took it to the Gestapo, they would thank him politely before executing him. Nobody who had read that diary could be allowed to live. If they were both lucky, they would be beheaded. If not so lucky, then, then it would be slow strangulation brought on by hanging with piano wire. But when she thought a little more she realised that Wieland could do something. He could post the diaries anonymously to Goebbels or the Gestapo. But that would be sheer malice. He did not want to see her dead, did he? Besides, when they came to arrest her, she would denounce him. Surely he would be able to see that? So she was safe. All the same, she would feel a lot safer if she had that diary back. And she came back to asking herself why had she not heard from Wieland since that first message?

She slept badly and awoke early. It was Sunday. So there was no need to take the train to Potsdam. She was not going to spend all day worrying about the diary. Instead she was going to devote herself to writing a chapter or two of *My Life is like a Fairy Tale*. What was more, she was going to concentrate on the good bit, the best bit of her life. Hitherto, whenever she had sat down to write, she had started remembering things that could not possibly go into print: misunderstandings, confidences, failures, horrors. This time she would only write about pleasant things. So, for the time being at least, she would skip the Olympic Games and the terrifying outcome of that party on Peacock Island, and she would set herself to write about *Munchausen*.

Chapter Fifteen

'Be happy!' It was Von Baky's watchword. A talented young Hungarian had been chosen to direct *Munchausen*, the spectacular fantasy film which had been designated by Goebbels to commemorate UFA's twenty-fifth anniversary and at the same time demonstrate that anything Hollywood could do, Germany could do better. And they were happy! Even in Babelsberg, things had always been easy and relaxed. In the mornings people used to say, 'Good morning', rather than, 'Heil Hitler!' and things became even more relaxed once the film crew and actors arrived in Venice. As Albers had remarked on their arrival, they were making a film about history's greatest liar... Albers had extraordinarily piercing blue eyes and when Sonja told him that he would have made a much better Fuehrer than Hitler, Albers just laughed.

As so often, Sonja had been given only a small part in the film. She had featured in the harem scene in which she and other naked ladies descended into the bath or rose up out of it, watched by the Sultan who sat painfully cross-legged under the weight of his enormous turban. That had been shot in the studio in Babelsberg. But, though thousands of foreign labourers, effectively slaves, had toiled in Babelsberg to build the Russian and German palaces, the Sultan's harem and the

Moscow fairground scene, exceptionally the Venetian episodes were to be shot on location in Venice.

Really there was no good reason for Sonja to be part of the small group of actors that had been sent to Venice. The massive crowd scenes were to be played by locals wearing the thousands of carnival costumes and masks provided by the German props department and the Italian players got nothing more than free meals for their performances. The only actors who were really needed for the Venetian bits of the story were Hans Albers (Baron von Munchausen), Ilse Werner (Princess Isabella d'Este) and Hermann Speelmanns (who played Christian, Munchausen's faithful servant). But, at the Berghof some months earlier, Eva had put in a good word for Sonja and Joseph had been in an unusually benign frame of mind. Things were going well for Germany. Moscow and Stalingrad were about to fall to the German divisions which had also advanced on down into the Caucasus. The Crimea was already occupied and meanwhile Rommel continued his unstoppable advance on Cairo. *Munchausen* itself was to be part of the Nazi offensive, the crushing response to America's *The Wizard of Oz*.

They were so happy in Venice! It was the summer of 1942. It was a kind of holiday for Sonja and one which she was enjoying in the rococo fantasy that was the eighteenth century, an age of pleasure, sensibility and refinement. The Grand Canal at the heart of Venice had been turned into one vast film set. The whole area was ringed by Blackshirts, *carabiniere* and Gestapo plain-clothes men and, within the enchanted circle created by security, all was ease and contentment. The sky was eggshell blue and the sun danced on the water. The gondola carrying Munchausen and Isabella d'Este was followed by a regatta of other gondolas all festooned with flowers and steered by gondoliers dressed in black and scarlet. The bridges and quaysides were crowded with gaily costumed carnival revellers, all of them in masks. Gobelin tapestries hung from the windows of the *palazzi*. This was to be Germany's third colour film and easily the most extravagant, with a budget of six and a half million marks. It vaguely reminded Sonja of another film that she had seen, also set in Venice, though she could not for the life of her remember which.

As the sun began to set shooting was abandoned. The crowds ceased their revelling and queued to hand back their costumes. Sonja climbed out of the gondola that she had shared with a unit of the camera crew and started to make her way back to the hotel. It had been a wonderful day. But if only... if only she could get a proper starring part in a film. Once again she fantasised about doing a deal with the Devil, one in which perhaps she could sell her shadow to him in exchange for a leading role. It was just at this moment that she glanced back and saw that someone seemed to be following her. She ducked into a narrow alley and then at its end took a sharp turning before looking back once more. There could be no mistake. She was being followed and the person behind her was gaining on her. He wore a tricorne hat, a black cape and a white mask with a grotesquely long snout, the kind of mask that she later learned was known as the plague doctor's mask. In another second the man was upon her and pushed her into the shadows of an archway.

'Who are you? Get away from me! I will scream!'

But then he removed his hat and mask to reveal that 'he' was not a he after all. It took Sonja a little time to recognise the woman who stood before her for who she was, since her face was so pinched and miserable. Then 'Lida!' It was Lida Baarova! She nodded.

'Softly please. Yes, you know me.'

Of course. And now Sonja remembered the name of the film that she had been trying to recall all day. It was *Barcarole*. The word meant a song sung by gondoliers. *Barcarole*, released in 1935, had been set in Venice in 1912. In it Lida Baarova had played the glamorous Jacinta Zurbaran. Gustav Frölich was Count Colloredo, an Italian nobleman, who bets Jacinta's gloomy and jealous husband (played by Willi Fritsch) that he can seduce his wife before the day is out. Jacinta and Colloredo experience one day of idyllic happiness, before on the morrow Colloredo has to fight a duel with the husband, one in which he will die. Then Jacinta, mourning for what might have been, rejoins her husband on the ship that will take them back to Mexico. The plot was silly. Now Sonja thought of it, all the films these days seemed to have silly plots.

Barcarole's budget had been quite small. It had been filmed in black and white and the sets were all built in Babelsberg. Hitler and Goebbels had visited the UFA studios during the filming and it was then that Goebbels had fallen in love with Lida and proceeded to pursue her passionately. He had not only showered Lida with gifts, but he ensured that she got a sequence of starring roles in the films that came after. Sonja, who had been at the premiere of *Barcarole*, had followed Lida's career with bitter envy.

There was little to envy now, after Magda had gone in rage to Hitler and Hitler had ordered Goebbels to give the Czech star up. Lida's final film had been booed by its audience and a little later the Gestapo escorted her out of Germany. Sonja had later learned that Lida had ended up in Prague, but had been unable to find work there. Now the woman who had seemed so beautiful looked much older and hungry.

Lida hastily re-donned the mask and hat and when she spoke again her voice was muffled.

'This place has a thousand eyes and ears. I am allowed no peace. We must be brief. You are here, I think, with Fritz Hippler, Von Baky and some of the other people involved with the big film that they are making here. I am guessing that you have met Doctor Goebbels. Is that right?'

'Oh yes,' said Sonja. 'I have had tea with the Reichsminister and Magda at Schwanenwerder. They have such lovely children, so beautiful and well-behaved and the villa has doors that open and close by electricity, and...'

Lida raised a hand to motion her to be silent, 'We have not much time.' It was like an oracular statue speaking. 'You have a kind face. I think that I can trust you. Here is a letter. When you are back in Germany, can you deliver it to Doctor Goebbels without anyone seeing?'

Seeing Sonja nod, she continued, 'My life depends upon it. God bless you! God bless you!'

Sonja sensed that the mask concealed tears. Lida thrust the envelope into her hand.

'We must not be seen together. So now, farewell.' And with that Lida hurried away.

Sonja walked and walked until she was certain that she was not being followed either by Lida or by the Gestapo. Then she opened the envelope. The letter inside was full of terrible stuff. Sonja smiled and then laughed out loud. Lida's gushing endearments were followed by complaints about being unemployable and these led on to threats of suicide which were in turn followed by declarations of eternal devotion. Sonja reckoned that she could have written a much better love letter. When she had read the letter, she tore it into little bits and let the bits drift down onto the waters of the Grand Canal. In doing so, she was sure that she was doing Joseph and Lida a favour.

The following morning, their last day in Venice, she was due to join Hans Albers, Ilse Werner and a couple of others for a final gondola ride and picnic on the waters. She was hurrying down to breakfast when she was intercepted by two Blackshirts.

'You will come with us please. Herr Hippler wants to see you.'

Even if they knew why they were frogmarching her towards Hippler, their German was not up to saying it. As Reich Dramaturge and Director of Goebbels' film department, Hippler was staying at an even more expensive hotel than the one allocated to the actors and that was where they took her.

Though it was still early in the day, Hippler was at the bar and he was drunk as usual. He perched precariously beside a silver bucket containing a bottle of champagne. He was incapable of rising from his stool, but he gestured that she should take the stool beside him and then pointed to the champagne.

'This is for you. I have had a telegram from Berlin. You are to report to Doctor Goebbels next Tuesday. It has been decided that *Baghdad Capers* is to go into production and you are to be its star. Felicitations!'

She had a couple of glasses with Hippler before hurrying away. She was late to join the picnic party, but they had delayed their departure and were waiting in a gondola moored close by the Bridge of Sighs. She was so happy that she thought she would explode. Yet she felt that she could not talk about the source of her happiness, until she had direct confirmation in Berlin. So, as the boat began to glide over the waters, she and Ilse talked of other things. This was their first proper conversation. Ilse turned out to be Dutch, though she had forgotten most of her first language. She had been born in Jakarta and she thought that she remembered her father talking about Hedas in Jakarta, but that was long ago and maybe she was misremembering. Then they talked about Ilse's other films, especially *Request Concert* and *The Swedish Nightingale*. Ilse, like Sonja, was going to write her autobiography. Ilse was famous for her whistling, and as she whistled something from Offenbach's *Tales of Hoffmann*, Albers tried to join her, though with limited success. Then they argued about whether the eighteenth century really would have been the best time to have been alive. And were the canals on Mars at all like the Venetian ones? Albers amused them by demonstrating how he could remove his shirt without taking his jacket off. And so the day continued. The sun shone, but there was a gentle cooling breeze.

The sun was setting, when Sonja noticed with a start that Ilse was silently weeping.

'Ilse dear, what is it.'

Ilse shook her head and all she would say was, 'When a thing is complete, it begins to fall apart.'

Then Albers, who was trailing a hand in the water, started to recite something:

My Life is like a Fairy Tale

Lord, it is time. The summer was immense.
Now lay your shadows on the sundials' faces
and let the winds roam over field and fence.

Command the final fullness to the vine
and give it two more warm and southern days,
drive it to consummation and then raise
the final sweetness in the heavy wine.

Whoever has no home now will have none.
Whoever is alone now will remain so,
will watch and read, write long letters and then go
to wander through the wide streets one by one,
drift restless like the dead leaves, to and fro.

Later, back in Germany, Sonja got him to write it down for
her as a memento of that last day in Venice. He said it was by
somebody called Rilke. Of course, if she had known then what
she knew now, she would have joined Ilse in weeping. How
could those days in Venice possibly be written up? Her readers
might form a lynch mob and murder her out of sheer envy.

Chapter Sixteen

She was thinking about this writerly problem when she was disturbed by a loud banging on the door below.

'Wieland!' For once she was glad to see him. 'You have my diary.'

'Yes, well, we can talk about that over dinner. I am taking you out to dinner.'

Dinner would be fine, if she got her diary back. So they walked out together. Wieland was looking strangely well. His face, which was normally ash-white, was tanned and he had put on a little weight. He was almost attractive, though not quite.

'I have been skiing in Switzerland', he explained, but, come to think of it, that was no explanation at all. How was it that he had been skiing in Switzerland? And then, to her astonishment, he led her into Horcher's gourmet restaurant on Lutherstrasse. Its walls and curtains were deep crimson, Persian carpets covered the floor and the dining booths were arranged like horse boxes in a stable. It was a perfect place for confidential meetings. It was the last luxury restaurant left in Berlin. The rest had all been closed by Joseph's recent decree, but Goering had intervened to protect Horcher's, as this was the regular haunt of Luftwaffe officers and Goering's friends. And there indeed at the opposite side of the restaurant was Goering himself together with a gang of other people she did not recognise. Possibly the blonde young woman was the famous aviatrix Hanna Reitsch. And at another table there was the actor Gustav Gründgrens.

'Wieland! Are you sure we should be here?'

'Money buys one a table anywhere,' he said expansively. 'Shall we have the lobster?'

Lobster! Sonja was so hungry. Surely she could eat anything, anything at all? Yet at the same time she was terrified at the sight of so much food. She had not had a big meal since… since 1940, it might be, or maybe even longer ago. Was there a word for fear of good food? A waiter arrived and knelt to insert a footstool under her feet. Another waiter came with the wine list and yet another with the menus.

Wieland had to translate the menu which was all in French. In the end they did not have the lobster, but settled on a Horcher speciality, pheasant in a flaming sauce. Wieland was evasive about where the money was coming from, 'I have new friends,' was all he would say.

He was equally unhelpful about the diary.

'Since I know that I am an interesting person, I was really hurt that I featured so little in your diaries. I would have thought that I deserved more from your pen. Even so I wanted one volume as a keepsake. I thought that I must have something that is truly yours. Did you not think that the substitute diary I provided you with was funny? It was intended as a joke. Well, not entirely a joke. I wanted to give you an idea of what it might be like if you came to me after recognising that it was me that you really loved, and –'

'Wieland, what do you think would happen if I left... him for you? How long would it be before the Gestapo came looking for both of us?'

'One night with you and I could die happy.'

This was so selfish. What about her? She certainly was not going to die happy after one night with him.

He placed a hand on hers.

'Also I was quite hurt that you actually preferred Goebbels to me. A romance with someone handsome like Speer... that I could understand. But with that hobbling rat-faced poison dwarf... now, please relax about your diary. Believe me when I swear to you that I have put it in a place where the Gestapo will never find it.'

Though Sonja was not happy about this, they did then talk about other things. They briefly discussed the war which was so boring and they agreed that it had been going on for far too long. Beyond it having gone on too long, Sonja could not have said whether the war was going well or badly, for she tried not to have opinions on things about which she was not well informed. Much of the time Wieland seemed entirely sane, but, talking about the war, he did hint vaguely that it now lay within his power to hasten its end.

But at this point, she thought it better to steer him to another saner topic and she found herself agreeing with him American films were better than German ones. (Joseph thought so too, though Sonja kept that to herself.) How sad it was that American films were now banned – and jazz too! Then Sonja wanted to know what it had been like growing up in a lunatic asylum. As a child, Wieland had actually witnessed the last of the lunatics' balls in 1913, but he was visibly uncomfortable with those memories. The bogus remake of *The Cabinet of Dr Caligari* was another matter. Though it had never been properly edited, Wieland had watched the rushes again and again.

'You actually look more beautiful in black-and-white,' he said. 'And look at you now. I have seen all your films.'

'When we first met, you said that films would not last and that they were like the yo-yo or something.' Sonja's voice was accusatory.

'Yes well, I am an artist, not an astrologer.'

This reminded Sonja that there was something that she had been meaning to ask for a long time, 'Wieland, what star sign are you?'

'Well I used to be an Aquarius, but then I decided to switch to Leo and I have been feeling much better about it since then. I can't remember what I was before I was Aquarius. Maybe nothing, but I really can't remember. Does it matter? What does matter is that I am capable of change, that I keep having new ideas and I get rid of old ones. I was one sort of person when I was Aquarius and now I am someone entirely different. Indeed, when I was Aquarius, I did think that the cinema was a passing fad like the zoetrope or the magic lantern. But I now see that film is the narrative of our age and I see also that it is our joint destiny to have our love story immortalised in a truly marvellous film.'

'But Wieland there is no love story. I am not in love with you and I do not believe that you are in love with me.'

'That will change. You will change. As I have changed. At first I thought that you were a silly, pretty girl on whom it was fun to play tricks. But I now see you for what you are. You are the reincarnation of Leonardo's *Mona Lisa*.'

At this point Wieland ceased talking in a normal fashion, closed his eyes and started to declaim, 'You are older than the rocks among which you sit; like the vampire, you have been dead many times, and learned the secrets of the grave; and been a diver in deep seas, and kept their fallen day about you; and trafficked for strange webs with Eastern merchants. You are my destiny and I am yours.'

Tilde was right! He had remarkably thin eyelids and with his eyes closed he had still been looking at her. Sonja was obstinate, 'I don't have a destiny. I am just ordinary. And I am not in love with you and I want my diary back.'

Wieland was obstinate too, 'You do not yet know that you are in love with me, but you will, and in the meantime your resistance just increases my ardour. The more you say no, the more I will admire you. You are the eternal feminine that draws me ever onwards. The more you spurn me the better the film of our love story will be, since this conflict will be necessary for our story to work. Not every man or woman is privileged to have a story that is worthy to be made into a film. That is reserved for the elite, and you and I, Sonja, belong to that elite. You will learn that you have no choice, since you have been promised to me by fate.'

Sonja was quite certain that she was not the member of any kind of elite and she doubted whether Wieland was either.

'Wieland, this is silly. We are both ordinary. What can I give you in exchange for the return of my diary?'

'Just one night of passionate love,' he replied.

Sonja left most of the pheasant on her plate.

'Goodbye Wieland,' she said and marched out of the restaurant.

When she got home that night, she found that someone had pushed a message under her door. It was from UFA. The studios had sustained some bomb damage on the previous night and it might take a week to clear the rubble and make things safe. So she now had the week off and plenty of time to write about her starring part in *Baghdad Capers*.

Chapter Seventeen

On their return from Venice, Sonja and Hippler had had a brief meeting with Joseph. Though he congratulated Sonja on her forthcoming starring role in *Baghdad Capers*, his mind was elsewhere. The press was full of reports of the triumph of German arms in the East and the capture of Stalingrad was being trumpeted as inevitable and imminent. Joseph was actually worried that the news was too upbeat.

'When Stalingrad does fall, it will just seem like an anti-climax,' he said.

What a thing to worry about! What a strange man he was! But eventually he did manage to brief them on what he expected from the film, 'You are going to make a screwball comedy. You have both been my guests at Schwanenwerder for screenings of *It Happened One Night* and *Bringing Up Baby*. I want something like those films, wacky and fast-talking, full of ludicrous situations and machine-gun dialogue. Only I want your film to be faster and wackier than anything Hollywood has ever managed. And there must be singing and dancing.'

Then addressing Sonja directly, 'You have a great responsibility my dear, for the weight of this comedy will fall on your beautiful shoulders. It is all but certain that in the months and years to come, even though our ultimate victory is inevitable, nevertheless there will be dark moments – times when the German people will find themselves downhearted and they will want to seek solace in comedy and in cheerful tunes. We must not let them down. With this film, Sonja, you will become a soldier in the service of the Reich. I am counting on you to do your bit.'

And with that they were dismissed.

So the film really was under way. From now on, she thought, everything was going to be wonderful. A preliminary planning meeting took place three days later. This was organised by Hippler and was held at the Hotel Bristol. Besides Hippler and Sonja, it was attended by Veit Harlan the designated director, Max Kruse the scriptwriter and librettist, Paul Nikolkoff who was to design the sets and costumes, and Otto Hittmann, an ageing academic who was an expert on oriental manners and customs. Sonja had never met a professor before, unless that clever Mr Speer was one. (He probably was.) Sonja's co-star, Willi Fritsch was not present, as he was away filming in Vienna. She wished that Albers had been chosen, rather than Fritsch, who specialised in comedies and was rather flabby.

As for Veit, Sonja had worked with him a few years earlier when she'd had a tiny part in the ballroom scene in *The Jew Süss*. It was a lovely scene, for it took place in the Ducal Palace in Wurtemburg and everybody was in eighteenth-century costume and there was dancing. Veit's third wife, the Swedish actress Kristina Söderbaum had starred in it. A buxom blonde, Kristina Söderbaum was such a specialist in tragic ends, often as not in brackish waters or dark swamps, that people had christened her the 'Reich's Drowned Rat'. In *The Jew Süss*, after she had been raped by the wicked Jew, she stabbed herself to death. Of course, it would not have been a Söderbaum film if she had not done so. Much later, after the release of *Baghdad Capers*, Sonja learned that Veit had tried to get Sonja fired and secure the leading role in that film for Söderbaum, but Hippler had just laughed and told him that they could not have a comedy film that ended with yet another of Söderbaum's suicides. Veit's first wife had been Jewish and was in a concentration camp. So nobody talked about her. Veit really did not like Sonja and this was probably because he knew that she had got her first break in the film business through sleeping with a Jewish producer.

Otto Hittmann had been called away from delivering a course of lectures on medieval Arabic palaeography at Berlin University and had been told by Veit, who for now was his boss, that his first job was to select plot motifs from *The Thousand and One Nights* that could be recycled in a screwball comedy, and secondly, he had to come up with a good selection of medieval Arab jokes. Otto demanded to know what a screwball comedy was and, once Veit had explained the concept to him, he declared that he did not like the screwball thing and he did not want to do it.

'You do not like it? You do not want to do it?' growled Veit. 'Why then, my dear doctor professor, we are brothers!' And Veit put his arm around Otto's shoulders before continuing, 'I hate the American-style mush. That sort of humour stinks of lewdness, decadence and Jewishness. Do you know who I am? I am the man who made *The Jew Süss,* perhaps the greatest film of this century, and yet now I am under orders to… to…

Veit, momentarily at a loss for words, removed his arm from Otto's shoulders before continuing, 'This is going to be like taking poison and you are going to join me in taking that poison. Unless, that is, you want to join the dirty Jews and gypsies in one of the camps. That can be arranged within the hour.'

Hittmann gloomily muttered that he did not think that the medieval Arabs were good at jokes and anyway he personally did not have much of a sense of humour, so he would be no good at spotting them. Whereupon Max told him that if he could not find old jokes, he would have to make new ones up, as Max was going to need them for his script.

Hippler was absent from subsequent meetings which took place in one of the Babelsberg canteens and it was Veit who presided thereafter. Otto and Max had swiftly agreed on a story from *The Thousand and One Nights* which could serve as a basis for their comedy. This was 'The Story of Delilah the Crafty'. Delilah (to be played by Sonja) is an accomplished thief and confidence trickster who, on learning that the Caliph Haroun al-Rashid has appointed the famous criminal Mercury Ali (to be played by Fritsch) as chief of Baghdad's police, decides to play a series of tricks on him in order to demonstrate that it is really she who should control the police, for women are more cunning than men. But, in the new ending devised by Max, she does not become chief of police and instead she marries Haroun al-Rashid. At the wedding Mercury Ali will be Haroun's best man only after, in the nick of time, he finds the clothes that Delilah has stolen from him. And, though only a few days had passed since the first meeting, Max was already working on the lyrics of a string of songs, including 'Playtime in Baghdad', 'Fritters, give me fritters', 'She has stolen my clothes and with them my heart', 'We are the roaring riff-raff of Baghdad', 'She's no lady', and, above all, Sonja's early aspirational song, 'I know that some day...' The tunes would be plagiarised from Ippolitov-Ivanov.

So far, so good. But then there were problems. Otto was not happy with Max's insistence that Mercury Ali was to be best man at the Caliph's wedding. He said that there would not have been a best man at a medieval Muslim marriage. But Max insisted that Willi Fritsch had to be there in a prominent role in the final scene of reconciliation and rejoicing. The public would expect this. Who cared how things were actually done in old Baghdad? Anyway, what did Otto know? Had he ever been at a medieval Muslim wedding? Veit ruled in favour of Max. But then Veit produced his own bombshell. He had found no opportunities in Max's draft outline script for the throwing of custard pies. There had to be custard pies. Otto looked shocked and said that he had never come across any references to custard pies in the chronicles of the Abbasid Caliphate. He did not think that it had been invented then. Now it was Sonja's turn to join the debate. How would they not have had custard pies in the days of old? They were so easy to make. You just needed milk, eggs, sugar and vanilla extract. She could show the props department how to make them. Everybody looked at her with irritation.

Max said that *Baghdad Capers* was not going to be the sort of film in which custard pies were thrown, as its humour would need to be more verbal. Veit said that the sort of verbal comedy Max was talking about seemed to him to be Jewish. Jewish comedy, the wit of sub-humans, was full of self-deprecation and even self-hatred. Whereas Veit envisaged *Baghdad Capers* as an essentially Germanic film and custard pies were surely very Germanic.

'We are aiming for the belly laugh, not the snigger,' he announced, confident that this settled the matter.

But now Sonja changed tack as she realised that she did not want to be on the receiving end of a custard pie. What would be left of her glamourous image if she received a custard pie in the face? Even throwing them would be no good.

Real stars like Marlene Dietrich and Zarah Leander did not go around throwing custard pies.

So she cut in, 'The Reichsminister has directed us to make a screwball comedy. I have had the privilege of watching a number of such films at his house, including *My Man Godfrey*, *Easy Living*, and *Bringing Up Baby*. I can assure you that custard pies featured in none of those films.'

Veit looked furious, but Sonja's invocation of Goebbels and the reminder that she was on intimate terms with the Reichsminister was enough to make him back down.

And Sonja continued, 'But there was a leopard in *Bringing Up Baby*. Can we have a leopard in the film?'

She had almost said 'my film', but she had stopped herself just in time. She was sure that a leopard beside her would make her look more glamorous, as Katherine Hepburn had looked really good walking around with a leopard.

Otto said that they might well have had leopards at the Abbasid court and Paul Nickoloff said that he would get someone to talk to the zoo.

But the rows continued and Sonja had to fight hard to get tap dancing included in the final shooting script. Since she was good at tap dancing, it would be a waste not having a couple of big dancing scenes, one in the thieves' kitchen and the other in the Caliph's harem. Both sets would need wide staircases for the chorus line to tap up and down on. Otto, Max and Paul groaned in unison and Veit declared that it was out of the question. But Sonja talked to Joseph in bed that night and it was then announced that not only was tap dancing to be included, but Otto was detailed to advise on what an authentically medieval belly dance would have looked like. The film's choreographer grumbled, as he was more used to directing waltzes and polkas. (The Whirling Dervishes, added later, would be an additional problem for him.) After that Otto gave up and he went around saying that he thought the film would be improved by the addition of a troupe of black and white minstrels, a yodelling contest and an aeronautics display. Even so, meetings became yet more acrimonious when Fritsch arrived back from Vienna. He did not want to be Mercury Ali, as he did not want to feature as a man who was constantly being outwitted by a woman and he thought the role of Haroun al-Rashid would be more consistent with his dignity. Veit told everyone who would listen that he had never wanted to make a comedy and that tragedy spoke more about the truth of the German soul. But, he added, the way things were working out, *Baghdad Capers* was definitely turning into a tragedy.

The sets and costumes were another problem. *Munchausen* had overshot its budget and, since little could be allocated for the making of *Baghdad Capers*, Paul was seeing what he could do with material left over from the shooting of *Munchausen*. The lack of authenticity in the costumes enraged Otto who said that it was going to look as though the actors had been costumed from a child's dressing-up box. But what did he know about it, as he admitted he had never actually been out to the Middle East? Whereas Sonja thought that she had a pretty good idea of what the Arab world looked like because she had seen so many films. Manasseh used to claim that stamp collecting was a great way to learn about foreign countries and past times, but Sonja thought that films were better at this and not only had she appeared in *Munchausen*'s harem scene, but when she was younger she had seen Valentino in *The Sheik* and Douglas Fairbanks in *The Thief of Baghdad*.

The Sheik had made a particularly strong impression on her. The Arab was noble and cruel. (Well, actually he was a Scottish aristocrat incognito in the desert, but throughout most of the film everyone thought he was an Arab.) 'When an Arab sees a woman he wants, he takes her.' Lady Diana Mayo swooned in the arms of the 'Arab' and then he raped her. After which she knew he was the only man for her. Sonja could not identify with Lady Diana Mayo (played by Agnes Ayres). For one thing the aristocratic English lady had dazzlingly white skin, something that set her apart from the swarthy Arabs around her. Sonja gathered that the whiter a woman was, the more Arabs would lust after her. More important, when Sonja saw the film on one of her afternoons off as a waitress, she had fantasised about being raped by an Arab and yielding to his cruel desire against her will, but later after the terrible night in the summer of 1936, she entertained no such fantasy.

At first she presumed that Otto found her boring – as Speer had done. But after a while she became aware that Otto was seeking out her company and, as she lost her awe of Otto, she started to tease him, 'Had any luck with your proposal for a yodelling contest?'

Otto only smiled before saying, 'Perhaps you think that I

care too much about the look of this film, for after all it is only a comedy. Well perhaps… but people are going to come out of the cinema asking themselves why the medieval Arabs chose to live in cardboard houses. This film could be so much more! If only we can take our audience out of Berlin with its rubble, its soup kitchens and frightened people and lead them into the dream of the golden city that was Abbasid Baghdad.'

'I think that it would be much better to have lived here in the time of Frederick the Great,' said Sonja, who could not be enthusiastic about going to live in a medieval city full of lustful and cruel Arabs. She had seen lots of films about Frederick the Great. He sat in Sanssouci, his palace in Potsdam, playing the violin and devising plots to outwit his foreign enemies. Everybody going about around him was being elegant and polite. The costumes were beautiful and there was lots of dancing and card games.

Otto was not interested in the Prussia of Frederick the Great and waved his hand, as if he was peremptorily dismissing the Emperor. Instead he told Sonja, 'That is because you cannot imagine what Baghdad was like in its heyday. The city's narrow alleyways, flanked by the stone platforms of the shopkeepers and overshadowed by the wooden balconies with their elaborately framed and shuttered *mashrabiyya* windows, form a labyrinth of possibilities: one of those shuttered windows suddenly flies open to reveal a heartbreakingly beautiful face; the mysterious sound of an oud is heard coming from the top of a minaret and it seems to beckon the listener to ascend; the bazaars double as places of assignation and an old crone offers a fistful of gold to any man if only he would sleep with her daughter; a veiled figure beckons you to follow and a door swings open to reveal a garden in which a carousing party of one-eyed men are passing bottles of wine amongst themselves while they gaze upon a naked snake charmer; a flask is found in the street and, when it is unstoppered, it releases a great dark cloud which begins to reform itself in the shape of a man. In the Caliph's palace you will see vases full of jewels and meet poets who cannot speak because their mouths have been stuffed with gold dinars. And torch-lit paths will take you down to the banks of the slow-flowing Tigris where the glinting reflection of the crescent moon is broken up by the wash of gondolas taking revellers to unknown destinations. You may encounter beggars who had been princes and who might become princes once again, or beautiful young women whose fresh complexions are said to be due to their habit of eating human flesh and you will also find old men in the mosques who can tell you the secret of why you were born. You only have to ask. And there are such smells about you: attar of roses, wine, pomegranates and human sweat and sex. Desire drives men and women down the alleys of this maze of plea-sure in which every possible longing can be met. Half a million stories are there simmering in the heat of a summer night.'

Otto sighed.

'*Eheu fugaces!* The mystery has departed from the world! As I say, old Baghdad was a place of infinite possibilities, whereas the Germany of 1942 in which you and I find ourselves, is a land of rapidly diminishing options.'

Sonja gazed at Otto in wonder. Was this what was taught at Berlin University? If so, it sounded quite fun.

Otto sighed again, 'You are ignorant, but that is not your fault.'

Then Veit came up and, pointing to Sonja, asked Otto, 'Does she look Arab to you?' (At this point Veit must still have been hoping to have Sonja replaced by Söderbaum.)

'She looks beautiful,' was all Otto said and then he walked away.

Her next encounter with Otto was just after they had been shooting the 'or what' scene.

Sonja had been kneeling as a supplicant before the Caliph, when he asked her, 'Are you a virgin or what?'

'I am, oh Caliph, "or what".'

It was one of the very few medieval Arab jokes that Otto had found and he was obviously pleased with it. By now he had quite forgotten his earlier reservations about the film and it was evident that he found all this much more exciting than giving lectures in Berlin.

'I like it here in Babelsberg,' he said. 'Here it is all so pleasant and easy, whereas in the university everyone is watching everyone else, waiting for someone to say the wrong words. Then there are denunciations and disappearances. Sometimes, though not often, those who have disappeared return, but they dare not talk about what they have been through.'

Sonja did not want to hear about how horrible academic life was and, seeing this, Otto changed the subject, 'This film is going to be a great success and shall I tell you why? You. You will carry the film. Your dancing is marvellous. It is magic. When you dance you are like Ariel. You hardly seem to touch the ground.'

(Who is Ariel?)

Otto continued, 'And your singing is entrancing. I know

that you do not want to believe what I am saying and in recent days I have often seen you looking downcast, but you must have faith in yourself and your film. And consider, Veit is at least a capable director, more than capable I should say, and the crew tell me that the lighting man is good.'

The lighting man was good. She knew that. Indeed, she knew him from old, since Ernst had worked with Richard Angst on *Rembrandt*. Even when he had been hardly more than a mere gofer, he had shown promise. Now he was director of photography on *Baghdad Capers*.

'Your job is to be beautiful and my job is to assist you in that,' Ernst had told her. 'It is not often that I work in close-up with such a dark complexion. Mostly we will use a front keylight, but we will also use an eyelight to bring out the wonderful brightness of your eyes. Also lamps and candles and gauze will give an additional sparkle to those eyes. It is not difficult. I will just put gauze filter over the lens. Your skin is still quite good, but the diffusion can enhance its velvety look.'

Ernst's remarks were just a preliminary to hours of testing the lights on Sonja's face. Then Ernst consulted with Fritz, the chief make-up artist. He was less enthusiastic about her skin, but he was confident that a cream foundation and lots of highlights would conceal the lines on her face and make her skin glow.

It was wonderful to be the centre of such concentrated attention and Sonja knew that she was still quite beautiful, but, even so, she felt an undertow of panic rising within her. She found herself thinking back to what Albert Speer had said about how buildings ought to age and the aesthetic grandeur of ruins. Then it had just seemed curious architectural stuff which was of no particular interest to her. But now she was beginning to sense that the body she was living in had just begun the slow and irrevocable process of turning itself into a ruin. Poor diet was playing hell with her complexion and the skin was tightening around her skull. Though she still felt young, she was trapped inside a decaying animal. Was there any way that she could look good as an ageing ruin? Too many years had passed and there had been too many disappointments in those years. For now she was dependent on men who would use camera-magic to make her seem as youthfully beautiful as she truly once had been.

'The Reichsminister does not approve of make-up,' Sonja told Fritz.

'Well, his writ does not run here,' had been the reply.

Oblivious of Sonja's reverie, Otto was still talking, 'You will bring enchantment to the screen and give your audience the hope to dream. This is your big chance. You only have to have faith in yourself. You are a star, whereas somebody like me is destined to moulder away with dull books in unheated libraries.'

Perhaps Otto was right. As the filming went on, things seemed to be pulling together. What did the horoscope say?

'Establishing your supremacy is important. You are tired of working for people who do not appreciate you enough. Surprise those around you with what you can do.'

Yes! The horoscope eerily seemed to echo what Otto had been telling her. Perhaps he should give up his dreary researches into Arabic palaeowhatsit and become an astrologer instead. And the filming was fun. She was taking lots of notes on the production. It was all going to go in *My Life is like a Fairy Tale*.

There were constant retakes of the tap dancing sequences, but that she loved, even though they left her breathless.

So breathless. Partly it was the cigarettes, but mostly it was the excitement. Her wild optimism had fermented with the accompanying tension, so it was like a high fever, but an energising one. Then quite suddenly, during an interval between retakes, she had what she thought of as one of her 'turns'. She was back as a child in Dordrecht. She was remembering the stillness of the place with only the quiet lapping of the water in the canals and distant, muffled shouts to be heard. Soon then it would be dusk and already oil lamps were being lit in the windows. So many years on, the moment still seemed palpable to her when on a late autumn afternoon the sun was beginning its descent towards a thick bank of clouds. Should she have left what now in retrospect seemed a paradise of intense familiarity, limited expectations, small pleasures and little danger? The girl that she was then did not know what she would become. Was it really necessary to her that she be a film star of the Third Reich? She could have been married and had children. Though those days in Dordrecht had passed so very slowly, now it felt as though something malign was pushing hard and hurtling her towards her end. But her turn only lasted a few moments and then she was ready for the next retake.

Almost at the last moment Joseph wanted the script amended, as he decided that it's glorification of crafty thieves might encourage criminality. (Cynical people at Babelsberg whispered that the real fear was that the portrayal of a crafty thief might encourage comparisons with Goering or Streicher.)

Then Joseph wanted Haroun to be presented as the father of his people and a war leader of genius. There was some hasty redrafting of the script to accommodate just a few of the Reichsminister's demands.

Shortly before the film's premiere Hippler had arranged for her to give an interview to a reporter from *The Film Courier*. She had been briefed on what to say:

> 'Playing the part of Delilah the Crafty has been a real challenge, but I enjoy challenges. And it has been wonderful to work with such a team of dedicated and enthusiastic people. Veit Harlan is a superb director and it has been a privilege to have Willi Fritsch as my co-star, but everyone from the director down to the humblest tea-boy has pulled together in order to bring the German people a film which is truly entertaining, but which at the same time is educational, as it sheds light on an exotic culture in bygone days. *Baghdad Capers* will play its part in confirming Germany's pre-eminent role in the international film industry.'

The film's premiere was at the UFA Palace by the zoo on February 1st, 1943. For the first time Sonja's name appeared in big letters above the entrance to the cinema, though of course this was not in lights because of the blackout. She was on the edge of fame. She was moving up to join Zarah Leander and Kristina Söderbaum. What was it going to be like when she became really famous? For the occasion Sonja had donned the scarlet bayadere's dress that she had worn for the big dance number in the thieves' kitchen.

The premiere was horrible. Joseph had promised to be there and to make a speech at the opening of the film. But he was not and merely sent a messenger to say that he was detained on important business. What was more important than her premiere? Then Veit, who was looking grim, muttered something about Stalingrad and Sonja remembered that Joseph had spent a lot of the previous evening on the telephone. Apparently von Paulus and the Sixth Army had surrendered at Stalingrad. Well, it was bad news she supposed, but there had been German defeats before in distant places, like Rommel's defeat somewhere near Egypt in the previous year, but the Germans always recovered. So Sonja told herself, but everybody else seemed to be determined to be depressed. If only von Paulus had waited another day.

The barbiturates that Sonja was taking these days made it difficult to see straight. So what was on the screen was a bit of a blur. The film hardly raised a titter and very few people stayed for the reception afterwards. The times being what they were, those who attended the reception were only allowed one drink each. Except that Hippler had stipulated that he and Sonja were allowed as many glasses as they liked. Sonja was on her third drink and fourth cigarette when Veit came up to tell her what a bad actress she was.

'We did our best with you,' he said. 'But you would ogle the camera. I could not get you to stop doing that. God knows, I tried. And when you had finished one of your big dance numbers, you just had to pause to simper. I was in despair. Only your dancing was all right.'

Then Veit marched off. Otto, who saw that Sonja was looking upset, came over and said, 'Your beauty lit up the screen. It was Veit's direction that was the problem.'

This was sweet of Otto, but only a few days earlier he had been saying what a capable director Veit was. Otto was going on about her dancing, her beauty and how very much he had enjoyed her company. She was desperate for another drink. She glimpsed what looked like a waiter with a bottle in the shadows at the far end of the foyer and gestured him over. As Otto kept talking, she realised that they were dangerously close to re-enacting the roles of Professor Unrat and Lola Lola in *The Blue Angel* and, if she was not careful, she would have Otto in attendance on her dressed in a clown's outfit. The waiter was filling her glass. Thank God. She wished Otto would stop talking.

'The film world is cruel and competitive,' Otto continued. 'It is full of backbiters and slanderers. You are only as good as your last performance. One day you are in and the next you are out. Let me take you away from all that. Marry me. I can offer you security as a professor's wife. It is not nothing to be a professor's wife.'

How to let him down gently?

'That is very sweet of you, Otto and I am touched. But it would never work. I am really quite stupid, you know, and besides I know nothing about the old ography stuff that you do.'

'I have never wanted to go to bed with an expert on eleventh-century Arabic palaeography,' he replied.

(The trouble was that neither had she.)

'Marry me,' Otto said again, 'and let me make you happy.'

Then the waiter spoke, 'You are a complete idiot. You must be the only person in Berlin who does not know that Sonja

Heda is sleeping with the Reichsminister Joseph Goebbels.'

Sonja would never forget the look of horror and disgust on Otto's face. Then he turned on his heel and moved swiftly away. He was almost running by the time he reached the exit.

'Aren't you going to thank me?' said the waiter. Sonja had, of course, already recognised the voice. It was that of Wieland, who had donned a waiter's costume in order to gatecrash the premiere. He now muttered in a low voice, 'I could not get into the film. Is it as bad as people are saying it is? That man was right. You should get out of the film business. Germany is in danger of losing this war and, if it does, you can be sure that people like Harlan and Riefenstahl will be tried as war criminals. So will you, if you are not careful.'

Then suddenly he was shouting, 'Men are dying on the Eastern Front. Nobody should be partying in this time of national peril. The time for frolics is definitely over. Go back to your homes and prepare for tomorrow's battles. Your chatter, chatter, chatter is no better than a machine gun trained on the heart of Germany. You believe that you are swigging away at champagne, but the deeper truth is that it is the blood of our brave young men that you are drinking. In the Russian winter, which still continues, the men's guns jam. Fires have to be lit under engines to de-ice them. If a soldier tries to shit in the open, he cannot, since his bum freezes up. If he takes an axe to a dead horse, hoping for some meat to eat, he finds that his axe bounces off the beast's frozen corpse. The men eat rats and dogs – if they are lucky. They stuff their boots with newspapers in the hope of delaying the onset of frostbite. When frostbite comes, then the fingers, toes, limbs have to be amputated without the use of anaesthetic. The men's bodies are covered with lice, but yet there is no hope of washing in the dreadful cold. Such shelter as there is likely to be booby-trapped. Some of you think of yourselves as artists with imagination. Yet you cannot imagine what it is like in Russia now. What do you think our heroes would make of you all standing round me and smiling at me while you sip your champagne blood?'

She tried to tell herself that Wieland was spoiling her evening of triumph, but of course that was not true. There was no triumph to be spoilt.

As he spoke, shouted rather, Wieland pounded his right fist into the palm of his left hand. His eyes seemed to burn with a passion, though it was not clear whether that passion stemmed from a love of Germany or from a hatred of his audience. The commissionaire was moving towards Wieland and she thought that he was going to usher him out, but then the commissionaire, who was looking uncertain, halted. Apart from Hippler who lurching slightly, came and stood protectively beside Sonja, everybody was edging away and some were already leaving the foyer. She later learnt that people could not decide what was going on. Was the man a member of the Gestapo? Or some kind of officially sponsored agent provocateur? Or a deserter from the Eastern Front? Or a waiter suddenly possessed by madness?

Wieland continued, 'Nobody who is able-bodied has any business being in the film business, now that the hour of destiny has arrived. Are you ready to face the Judeo-Slavic monsters when they come? Are you ready to sacrifice your lives in defence of all that you cherish? It is no time for asking "Make me an omelette, but don't break any eggs". This is a fight for our very existence. You must all swear a solemn oath to the men on the fighting front that the country is behind them with its morale high and that you will give everything necessary to achieve victory. You, Mister,' pointing at Hippler. 'Why are you not in uniform?'

Though Hippler drunkenly stood his ground, a final cluster of the remaining guests broke and hurried out of the cinema.

Wieland swept Sonja and Hippler a bow, 'I can still do it,' he said with satisfaction. 'I was just showing them what real acting is.' And with that he walked out.

A car was waiting to take Sonja back to her flat. It had to swerve to avoid Wieland who was walking away in the dark down the middle of the road, hands in pockets and manically laughing.

Chapter Eighteen

She should have recognised Wieland straightaway. Yes, he had been standing at the far end of the room and the place had been dimly lit, but the sad truth was that her sight was beginning to fail and even when he came and stood close to her, his face had been a bit of a blur. Also she was having to hold papers close up in order to read them. Her whole body was becoming a ruin and she was trapped in it – skin texture, muscle tone, digestion, eyesight, all failing. There was no help for it. She would have to get herself fitted with a pair of spectacles. She hated the thought.

She had been telling herself that there were compensations in being short-sighted and not wearing spectacles. For one thing, short sight helped smooth out the disagreeable features of ugly people's faces and she thought that there were far too many ugly people on the streets. But it was better than that. When half blind, evenings spent at the UFA studios offered paradisal visions, since the brilliant studio lights presented her fuzzy vision with such beautiful effects as aureoles, penumbras, celestial flares, and rainbows. And even when she closed her eyes, bright gobs of colour continued to swim across her lids. Out of the doors there was less joy for the blackout prevailed, but interior visions brought back memories of Berlin and its nightlife as it was when she first arrived in the city. With the flashing neon advertising and bright beckoning windows of restaurants and nightclubs it was a symphony of light. This was the electric age and she had been part of it. This was the future – or so she had thought. Later came the torch-lit processions and the great gatherings in floodlit stadiums. Later yet at the Berghof Speer had boasted to her about how he had created his cathedrals of light. But now it was all just darkness outside and people felt their way cautiously through the streets.

After the premiere, the reviews of *Baghdad Capers* were of course entirely laudatory, if only because some years earlier the Reichsminister had banned unfavourable film reviews. Nevertheless, it was not awarded the status of a 'politically valuable film' and therefore it did not have to be shown in every German cinema and therefore very few cinemas chose to screen it. She will have to write up *Baghdad Capers* somehow. She could quote those reviews and perhaps she could present the film as being retrospectively recognised as a masterpiece. But really *My Life is like a Fairy Tale* was a mess. There were days, weeks and months that she dared not revisit in her story. Why was one not allowed to choose what one forgets? God knows, she has forgotten thousands of names and places. Why not Peacock Island?

She wished that what Wieland had told Otto had been true, but the reality was that it had been some months since she had last been in bed with Joseph. Rökk was welcome to him, welcome to his ugliness, his bitterness, his rages, his meanness. When she had watched him leaving the house in that long trench coat, he reminded her of nothing so much as a rat all dressed up and pretending to be a human. So good luck to the woman who fancied all that. Ah, but he also had a rat-like intelligence. This was something that burned inside of him whose heat she could almost feel and see. He thought so fast and he taught her about things like propaganda. Since his noisy speeches in theatres and sports stadiums and on the streets hypnotised the masses, there was nothing surprising in the fact that his quieter words should hypnotise her. So she told herself. She had been attracted by Rego, Goebbels, Speer and Albers, all intelligent men. Was it not strange to find something invisible such as intelligence sexy? Perhaps not. Some women were drawn by kindness in men and kindness was invisible too. She rather liked the idea that she might be the sort of person who was attracted by something more than good looks or money, though of course she was also attracted by good looks and money. She still needed Joseph to advance her career, but if she was true to herself, she had to recognise that he really was quite repulsive. He was like the frog in that fairy tale, the one in which the princess dropped the golden ball into a well and then had to let the frog sleep on her pillow before he would retrieve the golden ball. Although in the fairy tale he then turned into a handsome prince, that sort of thing was not going to happen in Germany in 1943. Sonja tried to imagine Goebbels leaping into a well in order to retrieve a golden ball for her. She wished that she had a stronger imagination.

Spectacles made women look ugly. By wearing spectacles she thought that she would be transformed into a female version of Heinrich Himmler, though without his rabbit teeth. Yet remaining beautiful while becoming blind hardly seemed to be an option. At least there was no problem in finding an optician, since there was one directly below her flat. After

Manasseh had been taken away the basement and ground floor of the house had remained empty for a while. But one day coming back from the studio Sonja found herself confronted by a pair of giant eyes framed by thick black-framed spectacles. The painted board placed directly over the front door of the place where she lived gave her a shock and even now made her nervous. There was no face behind the spectacles, only the eyes and they seemed to accuse her of having done nothing about her own sight. Vain and foolish woman! She was daily confronted by that silent message. Still, now she was going to do something about it and she was going to get her sight back. This was true, but it was a sad truth for the price had to be the surrender of her youth. Her face might still seem beautiful, but only if she could not clearly see what was in front of it. So now she was reduced to a bargain. Ageing seemed to be a series of deals with the devil. So anyway one afternoon she knocked on the ground-floor door and after a considerable interval the old man opened the door.

'Come in my dear,' and Dr Giselius ceremoniously ushered her into a room off the hallway.

'Please take this seat.'

The room was small and dark and the only lights were on brackets on the far wall set on either side of a small curtained-off area. Below the curtain there were two large open wooden crates. Sonja could not clearly see what was in the crates but they gleamed like silvery fish in the low illumination.

'Ah, the woman from upstairs, Miss Sonja Heda. I take it that this is a professional visit and that you have come to have your eyes tested. You are most welcome.'

Giselius had red hair. In the half dark his eyes under a

thick-lensed pince-nez were invisible. He wore a yellow waistcoat and what might have been a frockcoat of faded bottle green and he looked as though he had spent most of his life in the previous century.

'Are you comfortable? Good. Now, Miss Heda, first I must enquire do you need spectacles for your job? Are you in employment?'

When Sonja told him that she was a film star she had expected a whole slew of questions about what films had she been in and had she met Hans Albers and what was Zara Leander really like and so on, but all he said was, 'Ah yes. I see,' and he clucked his tongue, as if her being a film star was the complaint that had led her to come to him in the hope of a cure.

'Well now, Miss Heda, we must proceed to investigate what may be the problem with those eyes.'

And with that he fitted a heavy metal contraption with two eyepieces over her nose. Then he walked over to the far end of the room and pulled away the curtain to reveal a chart with what at this point looked like lines of black squiggles. After that he started putting lenses into the contraption that rested on her nose and got her to read out the letters on the chart on the far wall.

'Is that clear? Is that clearer? Is that less clear? How about this one? Let us try this one again? Are you sure that it is less clear?'

As the interrogation proceeded, she started getting confused. She was no longer sure what 'clear' and 'less clear' might be and her answers became more random. Finally he sighed and she, looking up at him through a powerful pair of lenses, could see that his eyes under the pince-nez were melancholy. But when he removed the heavy thing from her nose his face was once again indecipherable.

'Now we must see if we can find a pair of spectacles that will fit you. Come over here, if you please Miss Heda.'

She followed him over to the crates and now that she stood over them she could see that what she had fantasised as being silvery fish were actually pairs of spectacles, hundreds of them, perhaps thousands. He started to rummage in one of the crates.

'I thought that I might have a pair specially made for me. I thought that I was being measured for the right sort of lenses for my short sight.'

'Indeed, Miss Heda. In an ideal world that would be so. But things are not so easy now. Zeiss and most of the other firms specialising in the production of lenses have switched over to war production: binoculars, riflescopes, optical guidance instruments, cameras for military use and suchlike. We must make do with what we have here. Doubtless we shall find something that approximates to your need.'

'But Dr Giselius, where do all these spectacles come from? Whose are they?'

'They come from people who have no need of them any more. People bring them on a lorry and sell them to me.'

He rummaged in the crate. Many pairs had to be rejected because the lenses were cracked. She did not care for the pair he finally selected for her, heavy spectacles with a black horn-rimmed frame. No, it was more than that, worse than that, she felt as if she was going to be looking at the world through a dead person's eyes and with her new eyes everything became clear, horribly clear. She could see how threadbare the cuffs of Giselius' coat were. She could see particles of dust floating in the air. She could see what she had never noticed before, liver spots on the backs of her hands. She hastily took the damned things off, paid Giselius and hurried out of the house. She needed some air.

An hour later when she was out of the house and walking along Friedrichstrasse she thought that now she was in the open air she ought to try the spectacles again. When she did so everything seemed so hard-edged and so much more three-dimensional, though she was not sure that she liked things to be that clear. On the other side of the street, she could see every detail of a faded and torn poster for *The Golem and the Dancing Girl*. The dark monster, a clay statue into which the semblance of life had been breathed (Paul Wegener) loomed over the swooning dancer in a long white ball gown (Lydia Salmonova). Goodness. That must be an old film. Then it came back to Sonja. This was one of those old silent films that Hans Becker had listed as having been destroyed or otherwise lost. Yet here it was. Or here its poster was at least. The title was intriguing and she wondered what happened in *The Golem and the Dancing Girl*. But could there be a film to go with the poster any more? Hans had told her that so many films had vanished – an Atlantis of lost stories. Only posters and studio stills remained to bear enigmatic witness to what was gone beyond retrieval. Films, like people, were mortal and one day, soon or late, a masterpiece like *Habanera* would become a forgotten film. One day even *Baghdad Capers* itself should become as if it had never been, crumbled to powder in its canister. The planets roll on and Earth receives messages from stars that died billions of years ago. On a distant planet at the far end of the galaxy a strange creature resembling a giant praying mantis emitted eerie high piping sounds as it tap danced under alien moons in front of the cameras. That was the last film ever and the death of the universe followed. What had Sonja's dancing and singing all been for? She shook her head. She was on Friedrichstrasse. Get rid of these thoughts. She took off her spectacles and, as she did so, the poster vanished.

Chapter Nineteen

Those colourful assemblies: the ball in eighteenth-century dress at Munchausen's Bodenwerder Castle, the court of the Empress Catherine the Great, the Moscow carnival fair, the Sultan's seraglio, the Venetian regatta. And such strange things: the rifle that can kill at 200 kilometres, the clothes that come to life in a cupboard, the baron travelling on a cannonball, the runner who takes an hour to deliver a bottle of wine from Vienna to Constantinople, the Baron's resort to a ring of invisibility, the balloon flight to the moon, the lunar woman with the detachable head, the clock of living beings. Surely this was never the film of a doomed regime? But 'Man is like a cloud of smoke which rises and then disappears'. Though Baron von Munchausen had been given the gift of eternal youth by the sinister occultist Count Cagliostro, at the very end of the film the Baron nobly renounced eternal youth in order to grow old with the woman he loved. Though Sonja found this shocking, she supposed that getting older did not matter so much if one was a man.

She admired herself stepping out of the pool in the Sultan's harem. A little later she wept to see the regatta in Venice on the screen and then she remembered how Ilse had wept on the day after the filming of that scene. Sonja also caught a glimpse of herself on one of the gondolas on the Lido and, though she had seemed impassive under a carnival mask, she knew that she had been smiling then. In those days there were no problems. Although the filming of *Baghdad Capers* only began after *Munchausen* was almost finished, UFA's 'magic kitchen' had experienced considerable difficulties in achieving the numerous special effects that were necessary for *Munchausen* and, since Agfa film was still under development, there were also difficulties in getting the registration of the colours exactly right. In the end Joseph's demand for perfection in this prestige picture led to it being released over a month later than *Baghdad Capers*. *Munchausen's* premiere on March 5th 1943 at the UFA Palace by the zoo was timed to mark the twenty-fifth anniversary of UFA.

The cast and production team had so much fun making it and there had been so much laughter then that Sonja was now startled to realise what a sad comedy this turned out to be. 'Man is like a cloud of smoke which rises and then disappears.' Cagliostro and Munchausen recognised each other as brothers of a kind, for they were both masters of illusion and both of them were acting as frontmen for UFA. As Cagliostro confessed, he was in the business of lending out dreams at ruinous rates of interest. It was not in the film, but in the end Death the Bailiff would inevitably come round to collect what was owing. What strange thoughts she was having! It was better not to think such things, for, after all, thinking is always painful. As the lights came up in the cinema she hastily put away her spectacles.

The gala showing was not like the premiere of *Baghdad Capers*. People at the showing of *Munchausen* were by now ready to put on a brave face and there was laughter. The shock of Paulus' surrender at Stalingrad had been absorbed and the German people had heard Joseph pronounce the glorious epitaph on those who had fallen on the Russian front: 'Life itself surrounded them with a heroic rhythm. Our dead are standing on the other side of life with its light shining upon them. We are the seekers, they have found fulfilment. They have fulfilled their time early, time which still lies before us with a thousand riddles and tasks.'

Anticipating the Ministry of Propaganda's new austerity programme, some of the cast and crew had brought extra bottles with them. Even so, the timing of the premiere meant that it was not exactly a celebration, but more a lament for a Germany that might be about to disappear (and, as it turned out, this was to be the last event at the UFA Palace by the zoo, for a few days later the cinema was wrecked by a bomb). Joseph did turn up for the opening of *Munchausen* and he made a speech. He went on about how the technical miracles to be seen in this film were being matched by similar miracles in the development of new kinds of weaponry and he promised that the German people would be seeing the results soon. Sonja did not bother to listen. Politics and the war were not for her. She thought that if she allowed herself to think about the war then it might occupy all the space in her head and push all her other thoughts out. But she did remember something that Albers had said to her the last time they lunched in the canteen. 'Can Germany lose the war? Unfortunately not. Now we have got it we are stuck with it.'

Instead of listening to Joseph, she hastily put on her spectacles again and anxiously scanned the crowd of guests, afraid that Wieland might be about to reappear in yet another disguise. Only when she was satisfied that this was not so did she start to wonder what might possibly be her next role. Could Albers help her find another part? He was so handsome and debonair – and clever. But it was difficult to have a proper conversation with him that evening, as he kept dodging around in order to avoid being photographed with Joseph or any of the other 'golden peacocks'. She supposed that film stars were beginning to look to their futures after the war. In any case, fewer films were being projected. *The Great Love* and *Paracelsus* were already in production and because of the bombing much of the filming was now being moved to Prague. She had thought she could have died happy if only she could have secured the starring part in *The Great Love*, but it went to Zarah Leander. Dear old boozy Hippler might have found her a part in a new film, but he was not there at the showing of *Munchausen*. Goebbels had dismissed him for alcoholism and growing incompetence. Perhaps the failure of *Baghdad Capers* had contributed to his disgrace.

This was the evening that Sonja first got firm details of the next big film that was being planned. It was rumoured to have an even larger cast and budget than *Munchausen*. It would be the greatest work of art ever produced by the Reich and as such a proclamation of defiance to the barbarous Jews, Slavs and Americans. Yet, though there were so many rumours, Sonja had hitherto been unable to learn anything definite about this, the greatest film project ever. Hippler would have told her. Of course she could ask Joseph, though it was ages since their last assignation. He was so busy now. The Fuehrer was hardly visible these days. But Joseph was everywhere, visiting munitions factories, touring recently bombed out neighbourhoods, presiding at meetings of filmmakers and artists and addressing the nation on the radio. When she found him in this crowd she was going to ask him about his plans for the great film, whatever it was. This might be her last chance. But she would have to finish her cigarette first. He just hated her smoking. If only her friend Eva was here, but Eva never made public appearances and she would probably see *Munchausen* at a private screening at the Berghof. Apart from Albers, had Sonja a friend in the room? She almost wished that Wieland really was lurking somewhere in disguise. The party was so crowded with pushy, anxious people. Where was Joseph? Only when Sonja put on her spectacles once more did she see him at the far end of the foyer whispering to that bitch Rökk and she was laughing. Sonja took off her spectacles and began to push her way towards the whispering couple, but when Joseph glimpsed her approaching he waved her away. The casual gesture made her feel sick.

Suddenly it came to her that most of the people at this premiere party were younger than her. That was the quiet menace of youth. They rose to fill the spaces and edged the older ones out of the way. That morning, as always, she had faced her mirror. These days she did not want to, though she still had to. It spoke to her and told her that Rökk was not only younger than she was but also more beautiful. Then when Sonja put on her spectacles she had seen herself become ugly in the reflection. The mirror, which used to be her friend, had turned against her and these days it gloated at her future – which must be tragic. The mirror was like a man who looked her over before rejecting her. If only she could have left her ugly reflection trapped in the mirror and returned to her younger self. If only. If only…

If only she could have been born a few years after Rökk and Söderbaum, then she would have a good chance at the new big film. But this mental skittering must stop and she must order her thoughts. She was going to have to write this premiere up in *My Life is like a Fairy Tale*. She must take careful note of all the famous actors, actresses and Nazi functionaries assembled here and then, since no one spoke to her, she must invent some conversations to go with the big names. It was a good bet that soon some of them would be in no position to query what she recorded them as saying, since they would be dead. There was no telling in advance whom Death the Bailiff would be coming for.

Just at that moment she felt a tap on the shoulder. It could not be Death, not yet. But when she turned she still felt a flutter of fear. It was Magda Goebbels.

Magda was obviously drunk and a thin column of ash dangled from her cigarette holder. Magda squinted at her.

'We have met before, haven't we? Your face is familiar.'

It was eerie. As soon as Sonja gave her name, exactly the same set of questions that she had been subjected to years ago during their walk from the Berghof recommenced. So Sonja was not German but Dutch. Sonja was a friend of Eva Braun's. Sonja was not married and had no children. Sonja was a film actress. But this time it did not feel like a hostile interrogation. Magda was adrift and trying to remember things and she needed someone to talk to.

'Look at him. He does not trouble to conceal his lust for that tart.'

The tart was Rökk of course, still talking to Joseph and still laughing.

Magda regarded Sonja kindly, 'You are all right. You are not his type.'

That again!

Magda waved her right hand dismissively. Since this was the hand holding the wineglass, some of it was spilt.

'She was born on November 3rd. He only falls for Scorpios.'

Though Sonja had rather wanted to protest that she certainly was Joseph's type, it was obviously best to keep quiet about this. It was ages since her last cigarette and she was desperate for another one.

'I am not deaf and blind,' Magda continued. 'I know that they call him the Babelsberg buck. Others call him the Prince of Lies. That is true. That is the only true thing about him.'

Sonja, who could not think what to say, made what she hoped was a sympathetic sounding noise. Then she begged Magda for a cigarette. This was a mistake, for though Magda was ready to oblige, she found this difficult. She needed to rummage in her handbag which dangled on the arm which held her wineglass. The glass was passed to Sonja who already had a glass in one hand and her handbag on her right arm and then Magda still needed her other hand free in order to rummage. So the cigarette holder was passed to Sonja and, then having found the cigarette packet, and given a cigarette to Sonja, Magda decided that her cigarette holder also needed reloading and with difficulty she eased it from Sonja's left hand, in the course of which only a little of Sonja's wine was spilt and her cigarette slightly dampened and then Magda's hunt in the handbag for a book of matches commenced. Though several of the matches proved duds, finally Magda got the cigarette in her holder lit and was ready to light Sonja's. Since Sonja was still holding both glasses, more wine got spilt in the process. After all this, the cigarettes were a welcome balm. A photographer approached and Magda raised both her glass and her cigarette holder in an attempt to shield her face. Sonja protectively waved the photographer away.

'What is the world coming to?' Magda wanted to know. 'What kind of future will my children face? Perhaps the little ones' best hope is to perish in their innocence so that they may be reincarnated in a better world.'

What was Sonja supposed to say in reply to that? But now Magda must show Sonja their photograph and the photograph was in the handbag. Once again the wineglass and cigarette holder were passed to Sonja. The photograph was found and presented with a proud flourish.

'What do you think?'

But all that Sonja could see was a blur of ghostly shapes. She needed her spectacles which were in her handbag. The only solution was to put the wine glasses on the floor and return the cigarette holder to Magda, before she could get the spectacles out of the handbag and examine the photograph.

The children were pretty, but now that she could clearly see what she was looking at, there was something sinister about it. Helga, Hilda, Helmut, Holde, Hedda and Heide, were posed with their parents. The girls, who were in white party dresses, stared uncertainly into the future. They were indeed lovely, but Sonja had to wonder if they would not grow up to become versions of either Joseph or Magda, or a combination of the two and that would indeed be a frightening prospect. Then again, if the children did die young, what would they be reincarnated as? She needed another drink. Magda, of course, had different apprehensions about the future.

Now that Sonja had her spectacles on she could see what bad shape Magda was in. Part of her face had fallen and when she raised her glass to her lips she swallowed with difficulty. How old was she? Previously Sonja had thought that she could not be much older than her. Magda's voice was slurred.

'You have heard the rumours of our recent development of death rays. They are supposed to be like X-rays only very hot, so that people who are caught in them combust. Well, I can tell you, it is all lies. It is like the gun in the silly film we have been watching that shoots a man dead at two hundred kilometres… all lies. My husband, the father of lies, manufactures these lies. But yet I still love him. These days it is best to live with the lies.'

Though Magda had lowered her voice to confide this to Sonja, this only meant that her voice was deeper, not quieter, and a few people close by edged away.

'There are other rumours, so many rumours. Some people say that we are now reduced to making soap from corpses. It is said that we now have a base on the moon from which we can launch our rockets. According to Joseph, some bad people are spreading the rumour that an actor has taken the part of Hitler after Russian agents assassinated our Fuehrer last year. That is certainly not true. Joseph and I had tea with him three days ago. On the other hand, there is the story that the Fuehrer is a reincarnation of Vishnu. It really is hard to know what to believe. Then there are those strange reports about the sandwich men. I have also heard that a Suicide Club has been established here in Berlin. Have you heard this? People are supposedly paying large sums of money to join it. People, some of them important people keep vanishing without trace. The Gestapo is said to be desperate to track down the leaders and shut the organisation down, so far without success.'

Sonja shrugged. She thought the story of a Suicide Club was ridiculous. The only rumour that she was interested in was the one about the forthcoming big film. But Magda's interest was elsewhere.

'Have you heard anything about a Suicide Club?'

The rocket base on the moon and the reincarnation of Vishnu were neither here nor there, but Magda really wanted to know about this Suicide Club. She stared hard at Sonja, apparently willing her to become more informative. Sonja just smiled placatingly.

'I long for peace. Death is the miracle weapon that will give us peace.' And with that Magda dismissively waved the hand holding the cigarette holder at Sonja and told her, 'I am going to find someone who can tell me about the Suicide Club. You are of no use to me.'

As she left, she kicked over one of the wine glasses on the floor.

Sonja watched her disappear into the crowd. That woman's obsession with death was unnerving. Sonja had in the past fantasised that she was going to live forever, like the High Lama (played by Sam Jaffe) in that film *The Lost Horizon*. She was not like other people and she could envisage herself a hundred years on from now receiving reverent visitors in her luxurious flat in the heart of Germania, the capital of the

Reich. A robot, like that one in *Metropolis*, would usher those visitors into her presence and she would instruct them on how it had been to live in the first half of the twentieth century – a difficult and bloody time which she would be able to look back on with tranquillity. But it was a long time since she had last played with that fantasy.

Suddenly it occurred to her that perhaps the secret weapon that Hitler's scientists had been working on was a kind of cosmic time machine which took the earth back through the years and Hitler had been using it to take Germany back to various earlier points in the war and seeing if, by taking different decisions, he could then get a better outcome. Maybe he kept trying but so far without success. Maybe that was why she was so confused about the sequence of events.

There was so much animation and laughter among the young people at the party. But now she sensed that there was also a whisper of fear amid all the noisiness. The young men might easily be only weeks away from being drafted and sent to the Eastern Front. Conscription and war work regulations were getting much tighter and exemptions were being cancelled. Hitherto film actresses had been exempted from the Reich Labour Service, so that their feminine beauty could be protected in a kind of nature reserve, but the way things were going it was quite possible Sonja's own exemption would soon be rescinded and she would be required to work with some kind of machine tool or even toil on a farm.

At last she spotted a friend in the noisy throng. It was Ilse Werner. She waved and came over. After a few reminiscences about their time together in Venice and some polite chat about nothing very much, Sonja summoned up the courage to ask

Ilse about the next big film. Ilse, who knew all about it, was astonished that Sonja had not already heard. *Kolberg* was to be the next great German film project and its budget would indeed be even larger than that of *Munchausen*. Again it was going to be in colour and it would have a cast of thousands and it was even said that Joseph was planning to requisition troops from the Eastern Front to act as extras in the battle scenes. The embattled citizens of Kolberg in East Prussia were going to defy the might of Napoleon's army. Ilse thought that perhaps it was intended as a magical conjuration. Just as the actors playing the German citizenry of Kolberg would see off the actors playing soldiers in the Napoleonic army, so the divisions of the Reich would see off the barbaric Slavic invaders.

Sonja thought that, since it would be set in Napoleonic times, the men would be in colourful uniforms and the women in those lovely period dresses. So perhaps it would be a bit like *The Congress Dances*, or *Women Are the Better Diplomats* – all ringlets, fans, parasols, long dresses, waistcoats and frock coats and dashing hussars in uniform. It was just the sort of film that Sonja had to be in. But when Ilse told her who would be directing it, her heart sank. It was the director of *Baghdad Capers*, Veit Harlan and, not only did Harlan hold Sonja's acting ability in contempt, but it must be inevitable that his wife, Kristina Söderbaum, would get the lead female part. In any case, Ilse then said that filming had already started in Pomerania.

Sonja told herself that maybe there was still a chance she could get a role as one of the dancers in some big ballroom scene? Or maybe even as a dairymaid or a nurse? She did not really believe what she told herself. It was tragic. Could she present it as the final tragedy in *My Life is like a Fairy Tale*? Not really. There could be no role as a tragic heroine for a small-time failure. Her life, all that mattered in her life, was over. 'Man is like a cloud of smoke which rises and then disappears.'

Since the drink had now run out Sonja decided to leave. On her way out she encountered Hans Becker who was unsuccessfully trying to get in. She told him that he was wasting his time since there was no more drink. He had tried walking in with an empty champagne glass that he had brought along with him in order to give the people at the door the impression that he had only just stepped out of the reception for some air. But it turned out that he was carrying the wrong-shaped glass. This led them on to a chat about gatecrashing techniques. Sonja had got in by attaching herself to a small group who had been entering the cinema and saying something to them as if she was one of their number. But they agreed it was easier for a woman to gatecrash. A trick Hans had used in the past was to give an imaginary name in an inaudible mumble and then point to a name on the list of invitees and say, 'That's me.'

But recently things had got more difficult. Hans said that gatecrashing used to be fun. It was a kind of sport, but now it had become a survival technique.

He sighed. Then he said, 'You will be sorry to hear that Markus has died. You liked him didn't you?'

Sonja made a noncommittal noise that might just possibly be mistaken for an expression of liking or of sorrow. The truth was that she had been terrified of the man.

'He died of a broken heart,' Hans continued. 'The asylum was his whole world and he loved his loonies, every one of them. They were so much more interesting than normal people. He had great hopes of pioneering a new therapy which would involve mesmerism. He aimed to use hypnotism to trick the insane into seeing the world normally. He'd had great success in using hypnotism to cure people of cigarette smoking and he did not see why he should not be able to cure paranoia and schizophrenia in roughly the same way. He was also experimenting with drama therapy and he was beginning to get some results. It was a mad, yet happy place. It was the Nazis who broke his heart when they took over his asylum. As they saw it, since Markus' patients were socially useless and a burden on the state, they could be dispensed with. At first the patients were merely sterilised. Later euthanasia was seen to be the answer and then the wards were stalked by nurses who were also murderesses and, ward by ward, the murdering nurses under Nazi direction administered overdoses of the anaesthetic morphine-scopalomine until the asylum was empty of patients. Though some of the saner patients guessed what was happening, there was no escape. The doctors even made death masks of the lunatics in order to facilitate research into the physiognomy of the insane. The place is now a camp for British prisoners of war.'

Hans paused, 'He was a great man – at least he would have been a great man in normal times. But perhaps that is not the whole story. Markus had great hopes for Wieland. Wieland tried so hard to live up to those hopes and to be interesting – at least as interesting as his father's patients. But do you not find him over-interesting?'

Sonja nodded. ('Over-interesting' was putting it mildly.)

'Perhaps I was a disappointment to Markus also.'

Then Hans wanted to talk about literature. He had heard that Dante's *Divine Comedy* was really good and he had wondered about turning it into a film script, but when he actually started to read it he could not find anything funny in it all.

'Men and women being cut in half, or having their heads chewed by demons, or being turned into trees. Medieval people must have been really sick to laugh at such things.'

Sonja supposed that Hans was right, but since the topic of Dante's sense of humour did not really interest her, she politely said goodbye. It was cold and dark and the sirens were starting up again. She wondered if this would turn out to have been the last party in Berlin. Sonja passed through canyons of dead houses and her shoes crunched on brick dust and broken glass, the litter of destruction. Later that night she tossed and turned in her bed. If only she could get her life in the right order. Time is so horrible. Why does one thing have to follow another? If it must, why cannot time have a built-in plot? Or why cannot everything happen simultaneously? That was her last thought before sleep engulfed her and with sleep came horrible dreams.

Chapter Twenty

A few days later, Sonja received an unexpected invitation:

Dear Sonja Heda,

Would you like to take tea with me next Tuesday? If you
agree, I will send my chauffeur for you at a quarter to four on
that day. I have an interesting proposal to discuss with you.

With best wishes and hoping for a favourable response,

Olga Chekhova

An invitation from Olga Chekhova! She was rather grand. She
was one of Hitler's favourite film actresses, she had been made
a State Actress and she tended to play baronesses and society
beauties. She had starred in *The Haunted Castle*, *Masquerade
in Vienna*, *The Hymn of Leuthen*, *Amorous Adventure*, *Sinister
Desires* and *Bel Ami, the Idol of Beautiful Women*. Chekhova
was supposed to be related to some famous Russian writer. So,
of course, Sonja wrote back immediately accepting. Maybe
they could do a film together.

On the Tuesday the chauffeur arrived in a Talbot

convertible and drove her to Olga's house in the fashionable suburb of Dahlem. Olga met her on the driveway. She embraced Sonja, saying, 'I am sure we are going to be such friends.' Then, gesturing at the Talbot, 'The Reichsminister is trying to stop me using it, as part of another of his austerity drives. But I say that it cheers Berliners up to see me being driven around in it.'

Sonja was led into a room which was crowded with Russian dolls, musical instruments, lacquered Palekh ware and framed photographs. Most of the photos were of Russian aristocrats and officers from pre-revolutionary days, usually clad in spotless white, but there was one picture of Hitler accepting a bouquet of flowers from a little girl and another of Olga looking relaxed as she sat beside him at some official function. In that photo Olga seemed to exude a regal kind of glamour. It was the same when, as now, she was encountered in the flesh. One would have guessed that she was a princess rather than an actress.

'I see little of the Fuehrer these days,' said Olga. 'He always seems to be at that command post of his in East Prussia. But I see the Reichsminister for Propaganda from time to time, as I believe so do you. I am glad you have come and I am sure that this will be the first of many visits.'

A maid entered with the tea things and Olga waited until the tea was poured and the maid had left before continuing,

'So now, how are you and the good Doctor getting on? Have you yet persuaded him to take up tap dancing?' Olga could not conceal her amusement at the look of dismay on Sonja's face. Then she said, 'We like your diary.'

(We? Who was 'we'?)

'It is not great literature, but it is quite charming. Indeed, we would like you to continue your diary keeping, the more detailed the better, and we would like to be the first readers of each volume as it is finished.'

Sonja looked wildly around for something she could use as a weapon. Or would she have to kill Olga with her bare hands? But Olga was taller than her and probably stronger.

Olga continued serenely, 'The diary is not here, if that is what you are thinking. But it is securely held inside a safe in the Soviet Embassy in Berne. We paid your friend, the one with the strange eyes, a good price for it. I wish I could read the whole thing. I have only been told a little about its contents. It seems that you are intimate with Goebbels.'

'We meet occasionally,' said Sonja defensively. 'We have become friends.'

Olga laughed throatily.

'Such good friends!' Then leaning forward and lowering her voice, 'But tell me the truth and I shall keep your secret, do you love that man? Is it possible to love the nasty little runt? What must it be like to welcome to one's bed a man who has returned from a day's work, ordering murders, arrests and tortures? And does he wear a truss?'

Though Olga seemed genuinely curious, Sonja was in no state to reply. Tears were streaming down her cheeks and Olga had to find her a hankie.

'Well, well, to business. I dare say that I will have the answers soon enough. As I say, we wish you to continue your diaries and include in them as much as possible about Goebbels. We are also interested in your friend, Eva Braun and what is going on at the Berghof. You don't have to write so much about the day-to-day business of filmmaking, even though I might enjoy any gossip that does come from the UFA studios. We would also like you to switch from writing in Dutch to German. Once a month or so Arno, the chauffeur, will call for you and you will bring these diaries to me and then it will be my business to see that they reach Switzerland safely. Oh… and on your next visit you will hand over all the volumes of the diary that you have already written.'

Then Olga set to spelling out what would happen if Sonja did not do exactly what she was told to do. Sonja was not really listening any more. Yes, it was obvious that her predicament was dangerous. But what really upset her was the loss of the diaries themselves. In the first place, they had been going to serve as a basis for *My Life is like a Fairy Tale*. That was just going to be the personal story of her rise to stardom. But much later, when Joseph, Eva and Hitler were all dead, she had planned to publish another tell-all account of life among the inner ring of the Nazi elite and that would be her pension. She was keeping a diary, but the diary was going to keep her. And the discipline of making a daily entry in the diary had been so hard for her. Usually when she arrived back at the flat she was cold, tired and hungry, but she had to force herself to write, before she allowed herself to eat or sleep. And often by evening, she had forgotten what had happened in the morning. The days seemed to slide into one another. Maybe Ewers had been right and every day was the same day, though different things kept happening in it. When Olga had asked her whether she loved Joseph, that was such an obvious question. Yet there was no answer to it in her diaries, as she had never dared ask herself that. The heart has its mysteries,

Sonja told herself. Now she thought about it, it was not at all straightforward, discovering what one thought or felt. That kind of investigation would be harder yet, if all the time she had to be conscious of readers over her shoulder. Her diary-keeping would become like a striptease, a striptease moreover that she might now have to perform before Slavic beasts. If only she had a cigarette to hand...

Olga allowed Sonja time to contemplate her predicament before continuing.

'In what you write, you should hold nothing back. By the way, you will be paid. You won't regret this. In fact, since you are a starlet whose career is going nowhere, this is probably the best thing that has ever happened to you.'

The only thing Sonja could think of to say was, 'I am too stupid to be a spy.'

Olga laughed. She was enjoying this.

'But we are not asking you to become a spy. We do not want you to microfilm secret documents. You do not have to try to penetrate Speer's underground factories. You will not decipher codes or have assignations with agents in dark alleyways. All you have to do is keep on doing what you were doing anyway, which was writing a diary. Do cheer up. Now at least you have a chance of being on the winning side.'

The chauffeur, who had brought the Talbot back to the front of the house was standing at the doorway. Sonja had not even tasted her tea. She had no desire for it. Just before Sonja got in the car, Olga said, 'Till next Tuesday then. Welcome to the fight, Miss Heda,' and bent to kiss her on the cheek.

So now Sonja was to be part of the Judaeo-Bolshevik conspiracy.

It was not until she was back at her flat that she realised that the same considerations that applied to Wieland also applied to Chekhova. Chekhova could not denounce her to the Gestapo without Sonja denouncing her. So she was not going to surrender her diaries to the Russians. Instead she would lock those that she still had in a metal trunk and hide the trunk.

The following evening, stuck on a night train held up outside Potsdam during a bombing raid, she thought back to that old poster she had seen advertising *The Golem and the Dancing Girl*. It was an old film and God knows what was in it, but, if she had been around at the time, she could have starred as the film's dancing girl. Now, what might its story be? She told herself that Germany might be in peril from an ancient menace made new again. In the ghetto of an obscure Polish city one of its villainous rabbis has constructed a figure made of clay and, using astrological magic, has succeeded in breathing life into its monstrous mass. This creature, the Golem, is very strong and is even reputed to be invulnerable to bullets. He has been designed to defend the Jews from the German authorities and their police force.

They were going to have to send the Wehrmacht into the ghetto to find the monster and destroy it. A picked force is assembled under the command of a handsome officer who should look just like Conrad Veidt. So the troops advance into the ghetto and, apart from the Conrad Veidt officer, they are all very nervous. (Veidt had gone to America, like Dietrich, Sierck, Lang and so many others. Would Sonja have a chance in Hollywood? Should she try? But getting the right exit papers would be impossible.) Anyway, back to the story. The houses, like the Golem, are all made of roughly shaped clay.

They have windows like eyes and doors like mouths and they seemed to huddle together, propping one another up. Cabalistic signs and stars of David have been etched into the walls. The Jews watching from doors and windows are sullen. Wolfish children follow the platoon from a distance and occasionally throw stones at the troops. Fog is flooding down the narrow stepped alleyways and lapping round the legs of the soldiers. Cut to a scene where rabbis in skull caps have commenced a magical chant. Their chief, a villainous and mad grand rabbi, brandishes a seven-branched candelabra as he speaks. 'The Golem will save us! You will see!' (Perhaps the rabbi might look a bit like David Rego, but with the physique of a gorilla.)

Outside Potsdam the searchlights were weaving across the sky and the anti-aircraft guns had started up, though there was as yet no sound of bombs. It was probably going to be a British raid. Could her train become a possible target? It was better to return to the film that she had running in her head. It was a terrific story, but what happened next and how was she going to feature in it? Well, the troops requisition some houses in the centre of the ghetto and there they will bed down for the night. But they are not ready for sleep. They are too keyed up for that and they have also confiscated a Jewish nightclub. They want entertaining. The officer decides to send for Arabella (for that is the name Sonja has decided to give herself). Arabella is due to perform in the great theatre outside the ghetto and she will have the starring role in *The Merry Widow*. So she tells the officer's aide-de-camp that she is not free to entertain the troops that night. But just as he is about to leave she thinks of her patriotic duty and has a change of heart.

So then she accompanies the aide and his small escort into

the mysterious ghetto. At the nightclub… but what would a Jewish nightclub look like? She has no idea. It might as well look like The Blue Angel in the film of that name and Sonja/ Arabella would be exposing a lot of leg just like Marlene Dietrich in that film. Then the mad rabbi sends the Golem to seek out the soldiers and spy on them. Cut to a scene where one can see the burning red eyes of the Golem who gazes through a window at the soldiers who do not notice him as they are so rapt watching Arabella who sings and dances. She is singing about how the war will soon be over.

The Golem returns to report to his creator and master. He cannot speak for he has no mouth, but he mimes what he has seen. The rabbi cannot understand the strange curving gestures and the shuffling of the monster. Eventually he gives up and tells him that tomorrow he will set him upon the soldiers to kill them all. Now the rabbi is going to sleep. The Golem stands motionless in a corner of the room until he sees that the rabbi is asleep. Then he leaves the room and descends the stair. His every step makes the house shake but still the rabbi does not wake.

He arrives back at the nightclub just as the soldiers were dispersing to their various places. The handsome officer is escorting Sonja to her lodging. The Golem, this thing of shadows, follows them. The officer leaves her at her door. The Golem waits below and while he waits he practices what he thinks of as dancing.

Then, when he judges the coast is clear, the Golem smashes the door of the house and charges up the stairs to abduct Arabella. Though she had been showing a lot of leg in the nightclub, now she was wearing a long evening gown, since its long folds would look good dangling down as she was carried away in the Golem's arms. Now what? Sonja was running out of imagination.

Would the Golem have had a penis? Presumably not. Perhaps he just wanted dancing lessons. Somehow she will be rescued by the officer and his troops. Never mind the detail here. The bullets will be useless against the Golem who has put her on a roof where she may be safe. Perhaps the Luftwaffe will have to be called in. The Golem is blown to bits in the Old Jewish Cemetery and the Jews all lament.

What a great plot! Perhaps she was wasted as an actress. It would be a wonderful film. She ran it over and over in her mind. It seemed so good that it felt as though she had actually lived this story some time in her past. Then, as she continued with the replay, she felt increasingly uneasy. Slowly she was forced to recognise that she had stolen the plot of *King Kong* and she had given herself the part played by Fay Wray in that film. She remembered watching it with Eva at the Berghof. Hitler had enjoyed it enormously and it was one of his favourite films. 'It was beauty killed the beast'. That was one of the final lines in the film. Oh well. Perhaps there was no such thing as a new story. The train was on the move once more on its way back to Berlin. Belatedly it occurred to her that perhaps she should feel sorry for the Golem.

The following Tuesday the chauffeur drew up outside her flat. He scowled at her when he saw that she was carrying nothing except her handbag when she stepped into the car, but he said nothing and they drove off.

Olga too said nothing as they waited for tea to be served. But once the maid had departed, she looked inquiringly at Sonja.

'I am no traitor to Germany,' Sonja said. 'My diaries are my diaries. You can't touch me, for if you have me denounced to the Gestapo, then when I am arrested, I will denounce you to them. It is a stalemate and there is nothing you can do about it. Your bluff has been called.'

(This was terrific. It was just like in a film. In a film one of the two people in the scene would turn out to be the heroine, but which one was it?)

Olga did not look dismayed. Indeed she laughed.

'So Sonja, you have some spirit! But you underestimate me, for you think that I am like you, but I am not like you, for I am the niece of a truly great writer. I have appeared in almost two hundred films. I have starred in *Three from the Filling Station, Masquerade in Vienna, Sinister Desires, Dangerous Spring, Bel Ami, the Idol of Beautiful Women...* but why go on? I am not the whore of Goebbels, nor am I a mere starlet. I am not afraid to die for Russia. I will be proud to do so. It would be the crown of my career. I would glory in the scandal that might bring down the poison dwarf and by that my greatest role as an actress should become known throughout Germany. So now, we will return you to your pokey little flat and you will do as you have been asked. And then I shall give you a little money.'

There was silence for a few minutes. Then Sonja got the giggles. She had been around in the film business long enough to recognise ham acting when she saw it and so what she said was, 'I saw you in *Three from the Filling Station* and in *Sinister Desires* and I did not think you were any good in either of them. Your current performance is no more convincing.'

And with that she rose and left. She had to walk home in

the drizzle, but she was cheerful. It was only when she was back in the flat and had changed her clothes that her pleasure gave way to anger. Then anger gave way to fear. While it was true that Chekhova could not force her to write the diary of a spy, it was nevertheless possible that in order to protect her own identity as a spy she could have Sonja murdered. She could send the chauffeur to do it. Sonja did not sleep much that night.

The following day the Gestapo came for her. Two of them detained her outside the house, where before setting out to the UFA studios, she was just about to light the ritual first cigarette of the day and they marched her off to the SS and Gestapo headquarters on Prinz-Albrecht-Strasse. It was a long walk and Sonja had plenty of time to consider how she was going to face her interrogators. Her first resolution was that she was not going to be tortured. As soon as her torture seemed imminent she would confess everything and agree to anything they said. Secondly, she was resolved that Olga and Wieland were going down with her. She did not think that Olga's grand posturing would last long when the instruments of torture, whatever they were, were produced. Although Sonja generally tried to avoid seeing films in which unpleasant things happened, she had seen *The Lives of a Bengal Lancer* in which Mohammed Khan tortured the brave British officers by wedging sticks under their fingernails and setting light to the sticks. Presumably the Gestapo were more sophisticated and used electricity and other stuff. In films it was always good people who got tortured.

When they arrived at the headquarters she was led into a waiting room and left there. It was large and draughty and there were thirty or forty other people sitting on the benches.

She was given a number and told that when her number was called she would be dealt with. It was ridiculous, yet Sonja felt affronted to be dealt with in such a manner. Surely the seriousness of her offence should have given her priority? Meanwhile would they be turning over her room looking for diaries as she sat here? Was she a good person? Then, having decided that such a question was unanswerable, she switched to wondering how it was that she knew that the Gestapo tortured people. She had never had bad thoughts about the Gestapo before. Why was she thinking bad things about them now? She wished she could smoke.

It was almost two hours before her number was called and she was conducted to a shabby little office. The man at the desk ushered her to sit and stared hard at her. (Was there some food on her lip or a spot on her face?) It was several minutes before the questioning commenced. Her name. Her address. Her marital status. Her profession. Her place of birth. The date of her arrival in Germany. The date of her registration as a resident. Her religion. Her parent's names. Their address. Their religion. Her grandparents' names. Their addresses, if known. Their religion. The man on the other side of the desk, more like a clerk than torturer, wrote everything down. Goodness, the Gestapo were thorough! When was the real interrogation going to commence?

Finally the man put the papers aside.

'You may go. You will be sent for when we have completed our investigation. In the meantime you are not to change your address and you are to report every week to a police station, the address of which I am about to give you.'

She left the building baffled and when she returned to

her flat she was surprised to find no evidence that it had been searched.

The following day there was nothing for her at the studio and she was able to get back to Berlin early. She was tired and hungry. She had spent hours on Saturday looking in vain to buy hair dye. She also wanted an ointment to deal with the weeping eczema on her hands. Quite ordinary things were unavailable in the shops and one had to hunt for what there was. There are so many things that one takes for granted until one notices that they are no longer there: the last piece of bacon, the last tube of lipstick, the last pair of gloves for sale in a shop window. If only Hitler's secret weapon proved to be some kind of vast time machine that could take Germany back to the year before Britain and France had treacherously declared war on it. These days one had to step carefully over the rubble and the horse shit. There were so many horses in the city now. Several times she had even seen refugees driving cattle down the street where she lived. She was looking forward to a smoke and then maybe a little sleep before the nightly bombing raids commenced, but when she got back to the flat she found Wieland sitting on the end of her bed. She hesitated. She did not want to join Wieland on the bed. But then he got down off it and knelt before her. Surely he was not going to propose marriage?

No.

'Olga has sent me. It seems that you have not been cooperative.'

Sonja nodded.

Wieland, on his knees, spread out his hands as if he was about to burst into a Negro spiritual.

'But Sonja, don't you realise the danger that you are in –

the danger that we are in?'

'Oh, I don't think that there is any danger. She cannot denounce me to the Gestapo without me denouncing her as a Bolshevik spy.'

Wieland looked uncomfortable, 'Yes, well, you do not need to worry about that. Olga knows that she cannot denounce you to the Gestapo... the problem is elsewhere.'

He paused.

'So tell me where else is the problem?' Sonja prompted.

'As long as you are alive and not cooperating with Russian intelligence, you are a threat to her continued existence. She is threatening to arrange for you to be bumped off. It will be easy for her to do this. There are communist agents in Berlin and all over Germany and you will be an easy target... it seems that, if she has to go ahead with this, I will also be killed in order to minimise the risk to her security. She knows where you live, she knows your daily routine and consequently your life hangs by a thread.'

Sonja had to think quickly. Thank goodness she had seen lots of crime films!

'I had anticipated something like this,' she lied. 'And as insurance for my life I have given a friend a sealed envelope containing a detailed account of my meetings with Olga. The friend has instructions to post it to the Gestapo in the event of my disappearance.'

Wieland thought for a while, before responding, 'But the trouble with that is that Olga does not know that you have deposited this envelope with a friend. What kind of insurance is that? She is likely to have you bumped off quite soon and will only discover her mistake too late. That way we will all end up dead.'

Then Sonja was astonished to hear herself saying what she said next, 'My life is over. I have no future as a film star. UFA has no future. There are now very few films to star in and soon there will be none. I am ready to die and it will give me some little pleasure to take you and Olga with me.'

Was that her speaking? Now she was sounding like Olga. The words had just come out. She was ready to die. Was this true? She really did not know. Probably it was true and a quick death might be the best way out of her pointless life.

But then she added, 'If it is really your life that you are worried about, then you had better run along now and do as I have done. Write down an account of your despicable dealings with Olga, put it in a sealed envelope and give it to a friend – if you still have any – and then go and tell Olga what we have both done. Do you really want to live? Then you must be quick about it! Hurry! You must do it now!'

Wieland opened his mouth. He was about to say something. Then he thought the better of it and rushed out of the room. Sonja lay down on the bed and started thinking. She hated thinking, but just now she could not stop herself. She rather wished that she had not made up that nonsense about a sealed envelope lodged with a friend. Then she could simply wait for some friendly assassin to surprise her and put an end to her miserable life. It would be nice if it could be a glamorous death, poisoned at a crowded party, shot by a sniper at the climax of a dance number in the film studio… or something, but perhaps it did not matter. Anyway, if Olga's hirelings were not going to come for her, Magda had mentioned a Suicide Club and perhaps she might seek it out, if it really existed.

She took a little comfort from having played a trick on Wieland the trickster. He always took such pride in making things happen, but now she had made something happen to him. He boasted that he did his impersonations and other tricks in order to prevent life from becoming boring. Presumably he was not finding it so boring now.

She had been slow in making a start on *My Life is like a Fairy Tale*. The diaries should have been useful in this enterprise and to a limited extent they were, despite Wieland's marginal scribbles. The trouble was that she had regularly failed to note things that might be of lasting significance: spats on film sets, her rare conversations with Hitler, her friendship with Hans Albers, the impact of the war on her morale and so on. Instead the entries tended to be brief and log such things as the weather, minor health problems, queueing for liver at the butcher and learning a new dance step. Also she found it all but impossible to make the narrative flow from day to day and she had a sense that, in order to make things more interesting than they actually were, she ought to invent stuff, but she had no idea what or how. But at least she was writing about something that really interested her, herself.

Yet when she talked to clever people like Joseph and Magda or Albert Speer, Sonja was conscious that she could tell them little that was of interest to them. And perhaps people would find what she had written so far about her appearances in *The Blue Angel*, *The Gypsy Baron* and *Baghdad Capers* similarly boring. So how could she make *My Life is like a Fairy Tale* more interesting? Now it occurred to her that perhaps she should read some other film actress' memoirs in order to see how it was done. Though she had never set foot in a bookshop before, she had noticed two on Friedrichstrasse. The following day, greatly daring, she went into one and explained what she wanted. It turned out to be like a magic shop, for a few minutes later she was presented with exactly the sort of thing that she was looking for. It was a little book translated from English which gave an account of the life of Mary Pickford that was based on interviews with the great actress herself. The booklet contained blurred photos on grainy paper. The introduction presented Mary as Hollywood's greatest ingénue, but what was an ingénue? Was Sonja one? She must ask Tilde. Could one be both an ingénue and a vamp? Mary became America's sweetheart. Could Sonja become Germany's sweetheart?

Mary used to enchant American audiences with her starring roles in *Rebecca of Sunnybrook Farm*, *Pollyanna* and *Little Lord Fauntleroy*. These were old and forgotten films and Sonja only remembered seeing *Pollyanna*. She must have been fourteen at the time. One of those blurred photos bought it all back. Those big moist eyes all that curly hair. Of course Mary starred as Pollyanna. She was a saintly little girl and, when her father died at the beginning of the film, she was sent to be looked after by a very strict aunt. But she was rarely downhearted for she had been taught by her father to always play what they called 'The Glad Game' and find goodness even in the worst situations. So she made friends with everybody and spread sweetness and light throughout the neighbourhood. But then one day Pollyanna spotted a little girl seated in the middle of the road, playing with her rag doll, and there was a speeding car bearing down on the little girl. She pushed the little girl out of the way, but it was at a terrible cost, as the car ran over Pollyanna's legs.

Sonja had wept when Pollyanna's father died, she wept again when the cruel aunt beat her and again when Pollyanna lost the use of her legs and was confined to a wheelchair and was trying to find something good in being confined to a wheelchair. She wept yet again and more noisily when, at the very end of the film, Pollyanna was discovering that she would be after all able to regain full use of her legs. Is that not strange, that she should weep when everything had ended so happily?

Chapter Twenty-one

The following morning she heard from the Gestapo. This time it was a letter which specified the day and hour on which she was next to present herself at Prinz-Albrecht-Strasse. It was two days hence. Before that there was the premiere of *Kolberg*. There had been nothing for Sonja in this film, not even a role as a dairymaid, but of course she was not Nordic enough to be a dairymaid. Dairymaids had to be blonde. Everyone knew that. What is more the heroine of *Kolberg*, Maria, was both blonde and apple-cheeked. Blonde Kristina Söderbaum who took the role of Maria, was the epitome of German womanhood (though she was Swedish) and not only was she blonde, but she had been blessed with the good fortune of being born about six years later than Sonja.

Kolberg, whose valiant citizens were supposed to have held out against Napoleon's vast army in 1807, was in Pomerania and that was where the external scenes had been. Apparently thousands of troops had been withdrawn from the eastern front and dressed in period uniforms and put to setting off phoney explosions and training horses to roll over and lie as if dead.

But some street scenes and all the interior scenes were being shot in the UFA studios. While Berlin fell to pieces under daily and nightly bombing, the new city of Kolberg was coming into being outside Potsdam, as if conjured up by a wish in a fairy tale. Pyrotechnicians scurried about and vast sets had been built solely in order that they might be knocked down or set on fire. It reminded Sonja of the burning of Atlanta in *Gone with the Wind*.

For Joseph, film was war by other means and the victory commemorated in this film was more important than the reality of imminent defeat. It would be his legacy to future generations of Germans. The message of *Kolberg* was that, in its darkest hour, Germany would be defended not by its professional army (what use were they?), but by a rising up of the Folk. 'From the ashes and rubble, like a phoenix, a new people will arise... a new nation!' That might have been what they did in 1807, but the Folk in 1944 were hungry, sleepless, and resigned to the worst of what was to come. 'The people rise up: the storm breaks!' No, they did not and it did not. At most there was a thin drizzle. Sonja did not care about the Folk. Germany had denied her the stardom that should have been her destiny. Germany did not deserve to survive her. The nation that was soon to be destroyed was like a vast stage set that would echo on a magnified scale her personal defeat. Even if she were to survive the coming debacle, her life, at least all that mattered in her life, would be over.

Kolberg was released on January 31st, 1945. This was also the day of Hitler's last speech on the radio, though nobody knew that at the time. His had been a depressing performance, since, though he had ranted on about the international Jewish conspiracy, he no longer promised ultimate victory. So she was told; she never listened to his speeches. By now the UFA Palace by the zoo was a bombed-out wreck and so the premiere took place at a temporary cinema on Alexanderplatz. There was so little enthusiasm for the film that Sonja had no difficulty in getting a free ticket. Her arrival at the cinema coincided with that of Marika Rökk. When she saw Sonja, Marika smiled and Sonja smiled back. Both smiles were sad, for their rivalry now had to come to an end. Kristina Söderbaum sat with Veit Harlan and Joseph in the front row. The chairs were uncomfortable and the air was thick with cigarette smoke. For years the Reich had campaigned against smoking. Yet by now there seemed to be very few non-smokers left in Berlin. A lot of people were also on amphetamines, also known as 'panzer chocolates', or else, like Sonja, they were taking barbiturates. Those pills she was taking made her sluggish and, despite the spectacles that she now had to wear, the images on the screen still seemed blurred.

Sonja sat beside Marika near the back of the hall. Marika was also out of work, since there was now no call for the sort of musical comedy that she specialised in and she was thinking of going back to Hungary. But for now she sat with Sonja and they sat there hating the film and Söderbaum's part in it. Söderbaum, as Maria, loses the farmhouse she grew up in, as well as her father, both her brothers and the young officer with whom she had fallen in love. So at the end of the film the indomitable Mayor of Kolberg gives her this consolation: 'You have sacrificed everything, Maria. But it wasn't in vain. Death is part of victory. The greatest victory always stems from pain. If one bears the pain, you will be great again. You remained firm and did your duty and did not fear death. You too have conquered, Maria! You too!' And Maria has to listen to all that pap like a good little girl in a Bible class. Sonja and Marika exchanged looks. By now Sonja knew what propaganda was and she found it easy to recognise. As here. *Kolberg*'s message to the men was that, even though there seemed to be no hope, it was necessary to fight on. The message to the women was that a woman does not have to carry a gun in order to serve Germany. She just has to suffer and watch the men die. After the film there was a cold buffet.

On the morning that she was due to present herself at Prinz-Albrecht-Strasse she took a couple of her little yellow barbiturate pills to steady her nerves. Then she hesitated over her costume. How should one dress for an interrogation? She hesitated for so long that eventually she had to hurry for her appointment. Her long black skirt and black bolero jacket gave her a somewhat funereal appearance. A platoon of SS had followed her into the Gestapo building. At the Berghof she used to admire those handsome and efficient young men who had been chosen to attend on Hitler and his guests, but in this new context, they were terrifying. The SS men ignored her and all tramped upstairs and once again she found herself with a number in the crowded and draughty chamber on the ground floor. Though she strained to hear the sounds of torture, she could not. There was just a lot of coughing going on around her. Eventually she was ushered into the same room as before where she was confronted by the same man.

'As you may have guessed, doubts have been raised about your status as an Aryan. You have been reported to us as being probably of mixed race and quite possibly with Jewish forbears.'

'What is an Aryan?' (Though Joseph had explained this

to her, she had forgotten what he had said, except that it had something to do with India.)

'The Germans, the Scandinavians and the Dutch are all Aryans.'

Nothing to do with India then.

'So I am an Aryan?'

'You are understandably impatient. Our investigation was necessarily lengthy, as we not only consulted the records in Dordrecht and Rotterdam, but also made use of the good offices of the Japanese Embassy.'

The Japanese Embassy! What was this? Was she going mad? Or was he?

Then he said, 'You are of mixed race.'

This was horrible. Now Sonja was terrified.

'But I cannot be Jewish!'

The man made a placatory gesture with his hands.

'You are of mixed race. Your grandmother Nurul Dewi whom you called Cornelia Heda was actually a native of Java. But you have no reason to worry about that and neither have we. The Nuremburg Laws do not apply to Asians. Besides you are three-quarters Aryan and, as for your Javan grandmother, Java is now part of the Japanese Co-Prosperity Zone and the Japanese are ranked as honorary Aryans. So a sophist might argue that you are a pure Aryan.

What was a sophist?

The man continued, 'I am sorry that you have been the victim of a malicious denunciation which has been a great waste of our time. I am sorry for that. You may go now.'

She rose to leave, but then he gestured her to resume her seat.

'Just one more thing… I wonder if I might trouble you for your autograph.'

Then Sonja walked out of Gestapo headquarters marvelling at her being an Aryan. Apparently it was something to be proud of. Also having a Javan grandmother made her seem quite exotic. Should she make something of this in *My Life is like a Fairy Tale*? But she soon stopped smiling. She had been the victim of a malicious denunciation. Who had been behind her ordeal? Who was her secret or not so secret enemy? Was it conceivable that Olga would have dared to do this? Or maybe it was Leni? Sonja remembered that Leni had once remarked to Joseph that she looked Jewish. Or could it be Wieland who had once again got his courage up to make mischief? Then there was the awful thought that it might turn out to be Joseph who, tiring of her, may have thought that this would be an easy way of getting rid of her.

When Sonja and Tilde next met, Sonja confessed to crying over *Pollyanna* and confessed also that she sometimes wished she could go back to that time, to those simple times when the ladies in Rotterdam and Amsterdam wore those strange big hats with flowers and feathers on them and the women in the villages wore clogs and traditional dresses; back to an age of lost innocence, before the big financial scandals, before there was marching on the streets and the storm clouds began to gather, when Pickford and Chaplin ruled the cinema screens and before all those films about monsters and murderers. Was not the world a better place then?

Tilde was scornful, 'I remember *Pollyanna*, the first bit of it at least. I walked out of it. That would have been two or three years after the Great War. You may have been innocent then, but the world was not. Those were dark years. In this country the Freikorps were fighting the Bolsheviks. There was a slump and then raging inflation. Bolshevik menace. French occupation of the Ruhr. Ku Klux Klan. Sinn Fein. Freikorps. The attempted coup in Munich.'

As for Mary Pickford, the 'girl with curls', in real life she was not up to the 'Glad Game'. She had two failed marriages, as well as many blazing rows with dictatorial directors. Then the coming of the talkies killed her career stone dead. She hated the addition of speech since it was so unnecessary and she said that it was 'like putting lipstick on the Venus de Milo'. How right she was!

And Tilde added. 'The coming of sound put an end to film as an art form.'

Here Sonja could not agree. She remembered the days of silent film and she was glad that they were over. As a girl she had struggled to keep up with the captions as they came up on the screen. Also she had not liked the piano accompaniment.

Tilde was remorseless. She pointed out that Pickford did not actually write her book but a ghostwriter fabricated the interviews for her. What was a ghostwriter? Perhaps that could be the solution to *My Life is like a Fairy Tale*. Sonja had been finding writing so difficult. In order to describe one incident, one first had to explain something else and that explanation would in turn usually involve further scene setting. And then the incident one had started with would have consequences and those consequences would have to be set out. She found the remorselessness of having to arrange everything in the right order horrifying. But still a 'ghostwriter' was only briefly tempting, since it had a sinister feel to it. Somehow employing such a literary wraith would make her feel that she was already dead, or soon would be. The ghostwriter would be like her double helping to usher her into the Other Realm.

Tilde had recently given up on the National Socialist Women's League. Wieland thought that, thanks to her, he now understood enough about the inner life of the Nazis. Moreover after von Paulus' surrender at Stalingrad Wieland had decided that the Russians were going to win after all and therefore he and Tilde should learn Russian and start to get to grips with the Russian mind. His decision pleased Tilde who had wearied of trying to feel her way into impersonating a typical female Nazi fanatic... no, it was more than an impersonation. For a while Tilde had actually succeeded in becoming a typical female Nazi fanatic. It had not been a pleasant experience. Now she was delighted to resume using lipstick and face powder and she had stopped wearing that ridiculous tie. Sonja thought that it helped to be a Pisces if one had to keep changing whom one was.

Tilde had derisively quoted Sonja's 'friend', Goebbels: 'The mission of women is to be beautiful and to bring children into the world. This is not at all as rude and unmodern as it sounds. The female bird pretties herself for her mate and hatches eggs for him. In exchange, the mate takes care of gathering the food and stands guard and wards off the enemy.'

And Tilde had continued, 'The Nazis say that the idea that a woman should have a career is a Jewish one. No, it is not! It is my idea and I am not Jewish!'

Tilde's abandonment of the ideal Nazi woman act was ill-timed. Just in the last few months Goebbels had ordered the closure of all beauty salons and banned the publication of fashion magazines. Moreover, by now the mahjong craze was long past and it was far from clear what she could do next.

Tilde was faster than Wieland at learning languages and Wieland hoped that she would serve as his interpreter when the Bolsheviks came. Mastering the Russian alphabet had been surprisingly easy for her. But there were so many declensions and, though there was a grammar of sorts, there were so many exceptions to its rules that it might just as well have done without those rules.

'I am trying to translate Stanislavski's *An Actor's Work* and reading extracts about his System to Wieland. Of course, I should be translating *The Collected Speeches of Lenin* or something, but we agreed that *An Actor's Work* would be so much more interesting and it is also a little easier to translate. Now at last with Stanislavski we have practical guidance on inner experiencing, outer characterisation, and the conduct of rehearsals. One should envisage the whole life of a character in the play rather than just what is given in the text. Wieland and I were halfway there already, but Stanislavski has made things more explicit. We now know how to enter our chosen roles more deeply.'

None of this interested Sonja. Nor did Tilde's lecture on Stanislavski's early work as a theatrical director and his productions of plays called *The Seagull*, *Uncle Vanya* and *Three Sisters*. She kept quoting from the playwright whom she was also reading. 'Perhaps feelings that we experience when we are in love represent a normal state. Being in love shows a person who we should be.' And 'If in the first act you have a pistol on the wall, then in the second or third act it should be fired. Otherwise don't put it there.' That was Anton Chekhov.

Sonja made the necessary intellectual leap, 'Is the film actress Olga Chekhova related to this Chekhov?'

'Of course. She is the daughter of Anton Chekhov's nephew. Everybody knows that.'

So then Sonja felt emboldened to tell Tilde first about her encounters with Olga and then about the run–ins with the Gestapo.

'But who could have denounced me to the Gestapo?' asked Sonja. 'Do you think it could have been Olga? I wondered about that. But then she would have run the risk of me denouncing her as a Russian spy.'

'Oh no, it was me who denounced you a couple of months ago. Don't look like that. I thought that you would have guessed.'

'But why? Why?'

'Because I was then a fanatical Nazi. What would you expect a fanatical Nazi to do when confronted with someone she knows whom she thinks might have Jewish blood in her? It was nothing personal. It was my duty. I had to stay in part. But, as you can see, I am no longer that Nazi.'

'I thought you were my friend.'

'I am not sure that you have any real friends. Whenever we meet you just treat me as a sounding board. I would have liked –'

Sonja did not stay to hear any more. As she walked smartly away it occurred to her to wonder whether the business of being faithful to the Nazi role was true, or was it not that Tilde was murderously jealous of Wieland's erotic infatuation for her? Also was it possible for a single event to have more than one cause? And, if Tilde could be whoever she wanted to be, why couldn't she have wanted to be a nicer person?

Later that day Sonja tried to cheer herself up by composing future reviews of her book. *My Life is like a Fairy Tale* introduces the reader to a lost world of show-business glamour... Sonja Heda's stunning autobiography left this reviewer feeling that life is so unfair, for not only can she act and dance, but she can write – and how she can write!... at last the book that takes the lid off the steamy world of German filmmaking... an insightful portrait of the Nazi elite by the beautiful woman who was at its centre... her story is full of tears and laughter. I loved this book and closed it with a smile on my face... an account of a rise from humble origins to stardom that is destined to become a classic... one can only ask, what will she do next.

Two days later there was a post-*Kolberg* conference at the Ministry of Propaganda. The cultural bureaucrats were there of necessity. But a lot of actors, directors and film technicians also attended. These days everyone was having to report regularly to their local employment office. In August 1944 total mobilisation had been declared and all theatre companies had been shut down, throwing thousands of theatre actors out of work. Yet UFA's productions and staff, under the protection of Goebbels, were so far untouched. Still it seemed a good idea to Sonja and the others to turn up at the Ministry and hear the great man speak. Sonja was also hoping that there might be good news, hoping to hear how the Russian offensive was going to be beaten back, hoping even to hear of another major film in the offing. Even if none of these things were going to happen and by now she could see that they were all but impossible, still she hoped to be briefly seduced and calmed by Joseph's brilliantly optimistic rhetoric. The Fuehrer had a plan and the Russians were walking into his trap. There was the example of Frederick the Great and how in his darkest hour he had turned tables against the Austrians. There might be the promise of a secret weapon. That kind of thing. In all of this she was to be disappointed. Joseph, smiling grimly, had brief words of praise for those who had worked on *Kolberg*. The film had fulfilled all his expectations and was destined to be a classic that would be watched and admired long after all the Hollywood trash was forgotten.

But *Kolberg* with all its challenges and excitements was finished and Joseph rapidly moved on to tell the assembled gathering how to prepare themselves for defeat.

'Gentlemen, in a hundred years' time they will be showing another fine colour film describing the terrible days we are living through. Don't you want to play a part in this film, to be brought back to life in a hundred years' time? Everybody now has the chance to choose the part that he will play in the film a hundred years' hence. I can assure you that it will be a fine and elevating picture. And for the sake of this prospect it is worth standing fast. Hold out now, so that in a hundred years' hence the audience does not hoot or whistle when you appear on the screen.'

That was it! It must be so! Sonja was most impressed. Yes, she hated him, but... but... yes, at last he was offering her a part in a major epic and one that was actually real and in colour! What a challenge! Now she must ask herself how she could meet that challenge. How was she going to play what must be her final role. How do the great tragic epics end? *Gone with the Wind* would not do. There was not going to be another tomorrow worth having in April 1945. It might have to be suicide. Then she thought of *Anna Karenina*, that film of the 1930s (a sunnier decade), and how at its end Anna, played by Greta Garbo, threw herself under a train. Garbo knew how to be tragic and in those final moments she was simultaneously sensuous but doomed. (Fredric March played her lover, Vronsky.) Should Sonja throw herself under a train? That could be rather horrible. In the film, the crushing of Anna Karenina's body under the wheels of the train was not shown. Besides Sonja needed to be sure that there would be enough people watching her and paying her proper attention before she performed her tragic act of self-immolation. That might not be possible. It would be difficult to be simultaneously sensuous but doomed in a crowded Berlin station, with the sirens about to go off at any moment and almost everybody around her also looking doomed. Tragedy was everywhere in the spring of 1945. It was the air one breathed.

Then there was that other 30s film, *Cleopatra*. The bite of an asp seemed a more peaceful way to die. At least it did when Claudette Colbert, who had the part of Cleopatra, showed how it should be done. Then there was Kristina Söderbaum. She had had far more practice than Garbo or Colbert at this sort of thing. In her very first film, *Youth* she drowned herself. In *Jew Süss* she drowned herself again. In *The Golden City* she drowned herself yet again. There must have been something about her looks that told directors and scriptwriters what her watery destiny had to be.

How will Sonja's life be viewed by future generations? Hitherto all her roles had been minor ones – apart that is from *Baghdad Capers*. Now she must find a way of making her end a spectacular one. It might be best to die close to the Fuehrer, as he, gun in hand, finally confronted the Russian brutes. Her sacrifice will not have been in vain. As she falls in front of the Fuehrer, she too will have done something that will inspire generations of Germans for centuries to come. And it will all be in colour. They may weep for her but they will also applaud.

Chapter Twenty-two

Having reported to the Labour Exchange, Sonja was told that her protected employment status as an actress on the UFA payroll had been cancelled and that consequently on the following day she should report for work at a soup kitchen for foreign labourers. So that was it. The last wisp of a golden dream was gone. In what was left of the day she resolved to pay one last visit to the UFA studios and say goodbye to her friends. This did not take long. Many of the huts had been destroyed by the bombing a few weeks earlier and there were not many people about. Not that she had ever had that many friends there anyway.

Then, since there was still time before nightfall and it was not far away, she thought that she might also revisit the Brentano Museum of Fairy Stories and Folk Literature. Though the Museum was close, on the other side of a pine forest, it was quite difficult to find, as fog was billowing in and soon it obscured the sun. When she did reach the Museum she saw that it too had suffered heavily from bomb damage. She experienced a thrill of horror at seeing so many mutilated corpses lying around the rubble. It was only when she put her spectacles on that she realised that the 'corpses' were actually some of the Museum's waxworks which had been thrown clear by the bomb blast. Most of the exterior exhibits were undamaged: the wishing well, the log cabin on chicken's legs and the gaily coloured gingerbread house. Set amidst the ageing elm trees and scattered fragments of the waxworks, they all looked rather strange in the gathering fog. Somehow it reminded her of the old silent film of *The Student of Prague* and its scene set in a Jewish cemetery. The ruined museum and its park had a desolate aspect. Surely most fairy tales were rather horrible? Wicked stepmothers, cannibalistic ogres, trolls, ice queens, evil Jews and the Devil. So perhaps she had chosen the wrong title for her autobiography. Then she thought that she would throw a coin into the wishing well, make a wish and then hurry away. She was about to throw the coin when she heard a cough and then a voice, 'So here we are again.'

She turned to find Tilde standing close behind her. She was carrying a knife.

'What are you doing here? I told you that I never wished to speak to you or hear from you ever again.'

'And I have no wish ever to speak to you,' Tilde replied. 'But I must.'

'Go away! Go away, you horrible old hag! You are no friend of mine.'

Tilde responded calmly, 'I am no friend of yours. Indeed I hate you. I am compelled to be here at Wieland's wish and on his behalf. He told me to shadow you and when I found you alone in a secluded place I was to deliver his message. Since you will not let him talk to you, I am his unwilling ambassador. So let me speak. I should say first that Wieland still sees you as you were twenty years ago, not as you are now. Don't look like that. I am showing my age even more than you. As I say, he still sees the beautiful young woman you once were. He has a large blown up old photo of you and he kneels in front of it and he weeps and he looks as if he is praying. He says that he can change, that he is changing and that he will make himself worthy of you. Wieland loves you, yet he also fears you, for I believe that he fears that his love for you may be his death. I fear that too. This awareness of the possibility that he might die is something new for him. From childhood onwards he has liked to think of himself as being at the centre of the world, which revolved around him, an immortal, a god indeed. He had only to wait for his godlike powers to become manifest. But as the years have passed, he has been forced to acknowledge that those powers have been slow to manifest themselves and he now speaks mysteriously of wagering on something else and of leaving a trashy, tedious, beer-sodden Valhalla for something much grander. So the message is be patient and let him come to you entirely transformed.'

'Is the knife part of his message?'

'No, I have faithfully related to you all of his message. I have no choice, I never have any choices, for I am his slave and must always do what he commands.'

Sonja thought that this was like an old film she had seen, *Svengali and Trilby*. Taken as a whole films constituted an encyclopaedia of human behaviour: love, hatred, vainglory, benevolence, stupidity and here servile subjection.

Tilde continued, 'I had thought that when I had delivered his message as I was instructed, I might then kill you and so set him free. But as I shadowed you, I slowly realised that your death would break his heart. It and he would never be whole again. I could not bear to see my man so ruined. Therefore you

283

have nothing to fear. So he says come to him and I say keep away from him, for he belongs to me and I belong to him.'

She made as if to throw the knife in the wishing well, but then changed her mind.

'It is Wieland's and I will give it back to him. He may have a use for it. Perhaps he will use it to cut my heart out.'

Sonja wondered if all this dramatic stuff derived from the Russians and came from Stanislavski or Chekhov, but she said nothing. She threw her coin in the well, made a wish and then followed Tilde at a distance on the road back to Potsdam.

Chapter Twenty-three

Sonja did not go back in time as she had wished. Since she only liked dance music, she never went to classical concerts. But the word had got around at UFA that Furtwangler and the Berlin Philharmonic would give a final concert in a place called Beethoven Hall. It had all been arranged by Speer and, after it was over, he had commandeered transport to get the musicians out to relative safety in the south of Germany, before, that is, they could be drafted into the *Volksturm*. It was also Speer who had dictated the musical programme to Furtwangler. None of this was of any interest to Sonja. Nevertheless, on April 12th she did decide to turn up at the Beethoven Hall and to steel herself to sit through some hours of music that would mean nothing to her. How could one just sit and listen to music that one could not dance to? Come to that, how could one even think about music and take pleasure in it when the Americans were in Hanover and the Russian assault on Bremen had commenced. It was at most a matter of weeks before the Russians would have Berlin surrounded.

Nevertheless she took the decision to walk towards her death. She had to ask directions to the Beethoven Hall which was on Köthener Strasse. It turned out to be not far from Potsdamer Platz and so a long walk, the longer because some streets were closed off by rubble. It was as if British bombers had been doing Hitler's town-planning work for him, night by night clearing away the old buildings and narrow alleys, so that a new Germania might just possibly arise from the devastation. She came across a woman sprawled open-mouthed on a street bench. Some people had gathered round her and Sonja heard the words 'Self-Murder'. She also passed platoons being re-deployed to the edges of Berlin, as well as gangs of the old who been conscripted to dig defensive ditches. Then there were smaller squads who hunted for deserters. She passed a long train of horse-drawn carts bringing in supplies from the countryside. The whole city had begun to smell of horseshit, that and the thick soupy, vaporous stench that came from those corpses that had yet to be dug out of the ruined buildings. Frightened children sat on doorsteps and whispered among themselves. Otherwise there were few people who walked alone among the blackened ruins. It was not safe. Once she came across a gang of men and women dancing in front of a blazing ruin and a toothless old man tried to force her to dance with them. She had to wrench herself from his grasp and run. What had they got to celebrate? She was in a hurry to escape the awfulness around her. What drew her to the Beethoven Hall was the word that Speer and Bormann had arranged for the distribution of poison ampoules at this concert.

The Hall was unheated and unlit, save for the musicians' stands on the stage. Members of the Hitler Youth with torches guided people to their seats. Sonja had not thought to buy a ticket in advance, but Speer had recognised her at the entrance and so it was that she found herself sitting with him, Bormann, Dönitz and the other Golden Pheasants in the front row. Speer was very grand as he was now head of the Armaments Ministry. The programme, horribly long, consisted of Bruckner's Romantic Symphony, Beethoven's Violin Concerto and the finale of *Götterdämmerung*.

What was she supposed to think while listening to this stuff, except about her hunger and the coming of the Russians? Hunger was turning her into an animal. When was the last time she had had an egg? She still had some carefully hoarded butter, though it was beginning to turn rancid. But she supposed that she should make an effort to respond to the music, since otherwise the hours would pass very slowly. Maybe the music could make pictures, landscapes, in her mind and she should try to enter those landscapes. Bruckner's Fourth was first on the programme. The opening horn call over strings suggested a hunting scene and so she imagined herself in a deep, wooded valley. Then there was the sound of trumpets, surely from some castle. So this was a medieval panorama. And trumpets answered trumpets and they summoned up soldiers whose armour gleamed in the moonlight and pennants dimly discerned in the mists of night. The men were going to battle and they were full of hope and the sounds of brass first promised and finally commemorated victory. Sonja had much enjoyed her fantasy and wondered if at last she had mastered the art of listening to classical music. But thereafter she completely failed to visualise anything during the Violin Concerto. The cold and hunger returned. The faint sound of explosions accompanied that of the violin. That was not bombs. It was artillery. The Russians were getting close now. And Sonja allowed herself to be distracted from the music by thinking of Tilde and her new passion for Russian.

Sonja was still thinking about Tilde when the Concerto came to an end. There was an interval and Speer, after exchanging a few brief words with Hitler's doctor, Theodor Morell, turned to Sonja and asked her what she thought of the concert so far. Unfortunately she was honest and she told him that she could make nothing of the Violin Concerto, but that she had quite enjoyed the Bruckner symphony. She felt that it was so medieval and so romantic and she described the images summoned up in her mind by all those trumpets and horns. Had he seen the same things?

Speer visibly stiffened.

'Sonja my dear, you have been so busy creating your own fairy tale that you have not really been listening to the music or understanding it. If you had listened, you would have heard the early duplet-plus-triplet subject that creates a musical tension which is actually heightened in the measured pace of the four movements, only allowing a partial exception for the Andante. For Furtwangler there can be no hurrying towards Bruckner's end with the composer's first-rate mastery of the hierarchies of the finale. There can never be any hurrying towards the end.'

And he went on and on talking the foreign language that was musicology. What the hell was a duplet? What was an andante? What was sonority? How was it possible to actually see radiant orchestral colouring? But Speer soon perceived that he was wasting his musical expertise on her and turned back to speak to Morell.

'It seems that we are getting through our Thousand Year Reich rather quickly.'

The doctor nodded, but before he could reply, the noise of the scraping of strings from the stage indicated that the concert was about to recommence. Sonja clutched at Speer's sleeve and whispered, 'What about the pills? I thought that we were all going to be given poison pills.' She would have liked to have left early. Too late now.

Speer looked angry.

'They will be made available at the end. You must wait for the end, and this time try to listen.'

So Sonja resigned herself to the doom of the old gods. Speer was not as nice as she had thought. But she would try again with *Götterdämmerung*. One could never have danced to Bruckner or Beethoven, but perhaps a slow waltz to Wagner's music might be possible. Act three of the opera commenced. A cyclostyled note told her that Wagner's music represented the perishing of the old gods as Valhalla went up in flames and the Rhine overflowed its banks. She must concentrate and see if she would be able to hear the lapping of the fire and water and the notes of doom.

She had some vague idea of what the Twilight of the Gods involved thanks to many boring conversations with Gunther, as well as that cluster of displays she and Tilde had seen in the Brentano Museum of Fairy Stories and Folk Literature. And she had heard an actor describe Goebbels as 'Wotan's Mickey Mouse'. What did he mean by that? But most of what she thought she knew came from Gunther as he had repeatedly begged her to use her influence to get Goebbels to authorise an animated version of 'The Twilight of the Gods'. Gunther carried his storyboard with him everywhere and so she knew the epic end of the gods from Gunther's hastily sketched images. After Loki engineered the death of Baldur, the gods caught him in a net and so there was an image of Loki bound on a rock beneath a serpent which dripped venom through its fangs and that venom caused Loki to writhe about in agony. Was that what Wagner's music was about? If so, she could not hear it. Perhaps his was a different story about the doom of the old gods.

Then she found herself picturing Goebbels bound upon the rock under the drip of the great serpent's poison. And why not? Perhaps it was Joseph, 'Wotan's Mickey Mouse', who was the reincarnation of shapeshifting, silver-tongued Loki? It was after all Joseph, the eloquent orator, who was one of those who were bringing fire down upon the land. But this fantastical line of thinking was not getting her anywhere. Gunther had regularly but unsuccessfully argued with Joseph. Gunther wanted the German film industry to compete with Disney. Why should Walt Disney and America have a near monopoly over animation films? And they were such childish animations too. Disney's *Silly Symphony* and *Snow White* were so very trivial. The German film industry could and should aim for an animated tragedy in all its full grandeur. Since Joseph would have liked to have competed with Disney, he would listen to Gunther, but there was never any realistic possibility of going ahead with such a project during wartime, since, apart from anything else, Joseph estimated that in order to produce a feature-length cartoon, it would be necessary to train up to 4,000 artists in animation techniques.

Anyway, Sonja had learnt from Gunther how the first world of the gods had ended. First the sun was devoured by the wolf Fenrir. Conventional cinematography would have had great difficulty in portraying the sun being eaten by a wolf and so, according to Gunther, animation was the only way of portraying the doom of the old gods. The gods fought against the frost-and-storm giants and Fenrir, as well as Loki, now freed of his chains. Warriors in Valhalla would be forced to cease their feasting and once again they would don their armour before going to their doom. It would be the last stand of the gods, and Fenrir and Loki would triumph over all, and the fires of Muspellheim would devour everything. But, as the years and centuries passed, the world would be reborn and a racially purer humanity would repopulate the world.

The trouble was that Sonja could not see that the little animated figures in Gunther's storybook had anything about them of tragedy or grandeur. Not godlike, they had no more dignity than *Snow White*'s seven dwarfs. Perhaps that was another reason that Gunther had not succeeded in selling the project to Goebbels.

Suddenly the music had come to the end and yet there was no applause. Most people sat with their heads bowed and some were silently weeping. With a start Sonja realised that she had been thinking so much about Gunther, Loki, Goebbels and Wieland that she had not really been listening to Wagner at all. Only it had been like the background mood music one often got in films, and no wonder then that she had been thinking such gloomy thoughts. She hoped that Speer was not going to quiz her about the orchestration of *Götterdämmerung*.

He was not. The rest of the audience remained respectfully seated while the Golden Pheasants filed out and Sonja with them. At the entrance Speer and Dönitz conferred about what was presumably official business. Dr Morell took up his position to supervise the Hitler Youth who were indeed waiting with baskets of glass ampoules. Sonja picked up one of the ampoules and, wanting to know exactly what it was, took it to Dr Morell.

'That is hydrogen cyanide, my dear. It is best for a quick death.'

'What will happen? Will it be painful?'

'It is different for different people. Perhaps you will first notice the smell of bitter almonds. Then it is really very quick, a matter of a few minutes. Very likely you will experience a headache, then dizziness and your heart will be beating fast. The agony will be brief. Maybe you will vomit, that is quite likely and, if so, it will be the last thing you will know, for as your heart slows you will no longer be conscious.'

Dr Morell's smile was meant to be reassuring, but was nevertheless scary. By now other people were jostling around the baskets and snatching at the ampoules. Sonja tossed her own ampoule back into one of the baskets. This would not have been the glorious ending that she had promised herself. She did not want her last moment on earth to be agonising and she did not want the last thing that she would know on this earth to be that her dress was covered in her vomit. Speer saw her discard the capsule and nodded in approval.

'Life is not a firework to be let off at the end of a party,' he said. Then he bent to kiss her hand. 'But this must be goodbye, for I doubt if we shall meet again.'

Two days later the UFA studios were bombed again. There could be no more films. Any day now Sonja would be called in to one of the employment offices and assigned war work. She would rather die. Then she thought of Magda and what she had been talking about at the premiere of *Kolberg*. She would visit Magda in the bunker.

Chapter Twenty-four

The following morning she set out for the New Reich Chancellery on Wilhelmstrasse. This had been Speer's grand creation, a kind of neo-classical temple to the might of Germany with huge rooms whose walls were of marble and porphyry. The Fuehrer's supplicants had passed below enormous columns which were surmounted by golden eagles with outstretched wings and with claws that gripped swastika shields. It was all now mostly a burnt-out ruin. Just one wing was still more or less intact. Speer was indeed the architect of ruins. Though Sonja knew that the Goebbels family was being accommodated in the vast bunker beneath the New Chancellery, she was prevented by the Reich Security Guard from even getting near those ruins. She was told that the Goebbels family was not expecting nor wanting visitors. So Sonja walked across to the site of the Fuehrer's own bunker which was located fifty feet below the ruins of the Old Chancellery. These ruins were even more heavily guarded than Speer's grandiose creation, but here Sonja was able to get a note sent down to Eva and after a few minutes she was frisked for weapons before being conducted to the stairs in the former butler's pantry of the Chancellery which led down to the bunker. The descent was horribly claustrophobic. There were many levels and so many rooms, all of them very small – guardrooms, dressing stations, kitchens, larders, lavatories, quarters for servants, typists and telephonists. An empire that had stretched from the Caucasus to the Atlantic had shrunk to not much more than this. The walls of the upper levels were covered in graffiti, some conveying messages of despair, others merely obscene. There were also bloodstains. From time to time the metal stairway shook as it registered the impact of a nearby American bomb.

Finally she reached the level reserved for Hitler, Eva and the campaign conference room. Here there was more space and one could breathe easily. Eva, who was waiting for her at the foot of the stairs, gave her a long hug, before showing her round her suite. This was all very different from the guardrooms and sleeping quarters upstairs. Eva had her own bed-sitting-room, bathroom and dressing room. In this last Sonja found herself admiring Eva's racks of dresses. The armchairs in the bed-sitting-room were comfortable and Eva summoned an adjutant and asked him to bring them tea and cakes.

She was humming a tune as she set to clearing a space on the table for the cakes to come. Sonja recognised that tune. Almost everybody in Germany had seen the film. Sonja had sat next to Eva when they had watched it some three years ago at the Berghof. The song was 'I Know Someday a Miracle Will Happen'. Zarah Leander, looking rather bulky dressed in white on a white stage, had sung it towards the end of *The Great Love*. She was playing a professional singer who performed at concerts to keep up the spirits of the soldiers and civilians and she was deeply in love with a dashing Luftwaffe officer who kept being called away on dangerous missions. There were so many hardships and heartbreaks. War kept taking precedence over love and the miracle would be if he returned safely from his latest assignment and they stayed together long enough to arrange to get married. 'A thousand fairy tales will come true.' Meanwhile man must fight and woman must weep and hope. Films taught people how to behave.

Sonja was not surprised when, once the cakes and tea had been brought to the table and the adjutant had withdrawn, Eva said, 'We are not finished yet. Adolf has explained everything to me. The army groups of Schoerner and Kesselring are still intact and in a few days' time General Steiner will lead a breakout and link up with our forces to the south of the city. And General Wenk will soon reach Berlin via the Pichelsdorf Bridge. Our enemies have at last overreached themselves. Right now Adolf is explaining it all to his generals.' She was madly exultant.

Cakes!

Then anxious. 'Sonja dear, you don't think we are finished, do you?'

Sonja, whose mouth was full of cake, just shook her head. She was impressed that Eva had acquired such a grip on the military situation.

Then the light which had been flickering went off completely and when it came on again a couple of minutes later Eva's mood had changed.

'I have been practising shooting with a pistol. If it must be so in the end, I shall be beside our Fuehrer in the last fight... but Sonja, it is so good to see you. How is it with you? What have you been doing these last few weeks?'

Though Sonja was a little reluctant to speak when there was still so much food to be eaten, she mumbled about the destruction of the UFA studios and most of Berlin's cinemas. She thought that, if any films were still being produced, they were being made in Bavaria or Czechoslovakia. In any case her career as an actress and dancer was over.

Eva looked shocked.

'You, Sonja, cannot become one of the defeatists. We will come through and we will make films again. You have been in some wonderful films.'

Sonja sighed.

'Yes, I suppose more films will be made after I am gone and perhaps they will be great. That is not the point.'

'Then what is the point?'

'I am not sure that there is any point. But five months ago in the UFA canteen I met some of the team who were making what will certainly be the last film to be shot in Berlin. I think that it was going to be called *Under the Bridges* and it was going to be about the everyday lives of boatmen on the River Havel. No singing and dancing. Probably quite boring.'

'So?'

'So I got to talking to one of the actresses. She was called Hildegard Knef and she only had a bit part, but she was beautiful, so very beautiful, and she was born in 1925. So she is twenty years younger than me. So the future of film belongs to her and her generation. Whereas, like the zoetrope and the silent films, I belong to the history of cinema, always supposing that I am thought important enough to rate a footnote. I am finished.'

'But you cannot possibly know how things will turn out

for you. You cannot know the future.'

'I know exactly what is going to happen to me because I am shortly going to commit suicide.'

'Suicide! That is silly! There are other things to live for besides your film career. You could dance on the stage. You could become a drama teacher. Live to travel, live to see the sun, live for your friends. Above all there is love. Search your heart and choose to live. I live for love.'

What is love? Love makes things happen in films, like that one starring Zarah Leander. Love is a great plot-mover. But though she had seen it often enough in films, Sonja had never encountered it in real life. She thought that love was something that people picked up from films and novels, a kind of infection. It was just a delusional aura. It was something that people used to dignify the ridiculous sexual act. But what could she say to Eva? Since she could think of nothing, Sonja just shook her head.

Seeing that Sonja was unpersuaded, Eva took another tack, 'Listen to me. You are talking to someone who has had direct experience of what for you is just an idea in your head. I know what suicide is like. I have tried it myself.'

Then seeing the look on Sonja's face, Eva leant forward and seized Sonja's wrists.

'Yes! Yes! I took my father's pistol and, aiming for my heart, I shot myself in the chest. There was blood everywhere, but they got me to hospital and I survived. That was way back in 1932. I did it for love. Adolf had scarcely seemed to notice me, but from then on he did. I thank God for that shot and I thank God that the shot was not fatal, for since then, as you know, I have had a wonderful life. So don't think of dying,

Sonja. Stay with me and keep me company.'

There was a long pause. Sonja was thinking that if Eva knew what suicide was like, it was also the case that she, Sonja, knew what rape was like. The party had been given by Goebbels on Peacock Island to mark the end of the Olympics. Sonja, like other starlets, had been dressed as a pageboy and made to serve as a waitress. Though that had been humiliating, it was nothing compared to what was to come. The champagne and beer seemed to be limitless, far more than some of the SA thugs could handle. She had been cornered on the edge of the island. Her silken breeches and underwear had been ripped to pieces. The face of the first rapist showed green and then red under the light of the fireworks. When she tried to cry out, he dropped a gob of spit into her open mouth. The second man wanted to take her from behind. And so it went on. When they had finished they lined up to urinate over her and then they walked off laughing. Her breasts had been bruised and her lips so swollen that it was days before she could talk normally. Now it would all happen again with the Russians. There were terrible stories about what women had suffered with the arrival of the Russians in Pomerania and Prussia. Many had been gang raped in front of their husbands and children. Often, driven by shame, they had then committed suicide. Sometimes they had even begged their rapists to be so kind as to shoot them. Surely it was better to kill oneself before the rape?

Eva had released Sonja's wrists and sat gazing at her. Then her face clouded over.

'Have you come here just to tell me that you are about to commit suicide? I had thought that you might have come to keep me company in these difficult times.'

But so little time remained to Sonja, so little time, days rather than weeks. Eva would not understand why Sonja wanted her help in getting access to Magda. Eva hated Magda and Magda was indeed horrible. But Sonja's last hope was that Magda had found out something about the whereabouts and membership of the Suicide Club. If she were to confess that she had entered the bunker in the hope of seeing Magda, Eva would be bitterly offended. But the time was so short. So, 'Eva, I have come to you because I need your help. I need to see Magda Goebbels. These are desperate times and there is a chance that she may be able to tell me where I must go.'

Eva sucked in her breath and Sonja steeled herself to face the inevitable tirade. But there was an interruption. A young naval officer was at the door.

'The conference is over and the Fuehrer wishes you to join him, Miss Braun.'

Eva turned to Sonja, 'Don't go. You are quite mad, but we still have so much to talk about. I won't be long.'

But Sonja, having snatched at the last cake on the stand, followed her out of the bed-sitting-room. Grim-faced generals were coming out of the campaign conference room as Eva went in and the door closed behind her. The officer turned to Sonja.

'How may I be of assistance?'

'I need to speak to Magda Goebbels.'

'That should be no problem. Follow me please.'

It was as Sonja had heard. A narrow tunnel connected the two bunker complexes. The tunnel was narrow and poorly lit. Once inside the bunker of the New Chancellery, the officer indicated that his job was done and that she needed to descend one more level to reach the living quarters of the Goebbels family. Down there in its corridor the girls were playing school with their dolls and they were lining them up so that a roll call could be taken. The boy stood apart with his arms folded. Through an open door Sonja could see Magda seated at a table laying out cards. It was probably a game of patience, though she might have been trying to use the cards to tell her fortune. Anyway it was a peaceful and charming scene.

But just then Joseph came out from another door and when he saw Sonja he went white with anger.

'Wretched woman! What are you doing here? What do you want with me? You slut! I will have you shot! But shooting is better than you deserve.'

And he kept shouting. He could not possibly have heard anything that Sonja might have tried to say. The little girls looked up, distressed to see their dear papa so angry. Who was the horrible woman who had spoilt their game? Magda's door was now closed.

At last, noticing his children's distress, he quietened down and now spoke in a low voice.

'Well what is it you have to say to me? It had better be good or I will fetch my pistol and conduct you up to the Chancellery Garden and shoot you like a dog.'

Sonja was so terrified that it was a while before she could get the words out, 'It is not you that I want to speak to. It is your wife.'

'My wife is in no state to receive visitors. Surely you must realise that? And she will not have the slightest interest in whatever you may have to say about us.'

'But it is not about us. All I want to do is to ask what she may know about a club –'

He waved his hand in front of her face to cut her off.

'Above us the Angel of History is beating his wings and yet you are here with your petty emotional concerns! The harpy who has come to gloat over our misfortune. Now I am going for my gun,' he said. 'If you are still here when I return with it then I shall escort you to the Chancellery Garden and I shall do what I have to do.'

As he turned away, she fled upstairs. The naval officer was waiting at their top.

'I heard the shouting,' he said. 'I thought that you might need assistance. I can escort you out through the Hitler Bunker if you wish.'

Sonja nodded miserably.

'We must hurry,' she said. 'He has gone for his gun.'

'I heard the shouting,' he said again. 'What on earth did you want with Dr Goebbels' wife?'

'She might have been able to tell me something. I need to get in touch with some people. It is urgent. There is a club. You won't know anything about it. It is called the Suicide Club.'

The officer shrugged, 'I have never heard of such a thing.'

As they made their way along the narrow tunnel Sonja was trembling and her steps were shaky. It was possible that Joseph might be coming up behind her with his gun. On the other hand, right now she did not want to re-encounter Eva at the other end of the tunnel. There was even the possibility that if Eva told Adolf about their conversation then Sonja might be hung for disaffection and cowardice. But the officer walking a little ahead of her was cheerfully unconcerned and he chatted away. He was sorry that the poison dwarf had been so nasty to her. The officer's name was Jürgen Ostermann. He was a Captain Lieutenant and he was stationed in the Hitler Bunker as Admiral Dönitz's liaison officer. But since Dönitz was in the bunker today and tomorrow, Jürgen did not have much to do.

Then Sonja had to introduce herself. Jürgen was gratifyingly impressed when she told him that she was a film star and then he thought that he remembered seeing her in *The Gypsy Baron*. To Sonja's relief, there was no sign of Eva when they entered the Hitler Bunker. Jürgen insisted on accompanying her upstairs.

'The Fuehrer does not tolerate smoking, he said. 'But I need a cigarette and anyway I want to be in the open air. The place is like a mausoleum. We could all be buried alive down here.'

Once in the Chancellery Garden Sonja gratefully accepted a cigarette. The air in the cratered garden was not so good. Ash and fragments of official documents blew about.

They were talking about their favourite films, when Jürgen abruptly changed tack, 'I have been thinking about this Suicide Club,' he said. 'It just does not make sense. Suicide is such a solitary act. Besides how would they keep the membership up? There would be such a turnover that the club's management would have to advertise on a massive scale. And could anyone join this club? I think that the idea of a Suicide Club is one of those mad fables that are circulating now that we are in the final stages of the war. It is like the story that Germany, in its greatest hour of need, has been deserted by the Fuehrer who, weeks ago, made his way to Argentina in a submarine. Well, that is certainly not true. I saw him with my own eyes a little over an hour ago. The story of a Suicide Club is one of those things which irresponsible citizens spread about either to amuse themselves or in order to demoralise people and encourage treason.'

Sonja silently noted that he had spoken of the war being in its final stages. Then, when he said that he wanted to discuss favourite books, she hastily replied that she had to be going. (She did not have favourite books.) However, not only was he rather handsome, but he obviously found her attractive and he seemed to have a limitless supply of good quality cigarettes. And then there was his sexy, dark blue smartly-creased uniform with golden emblems on the epaulettes and sleeve stripes. He told her that it was his dress uniform and that was why he was also wearing a sword. All that blue and gold together with a sword seemed to promise heroism, decisiveness and reliability. The armed forces were men's beauty parlours. He was almost certainly a Leo.

So she agreed to his proposal that they meet in the zoo in the Charlottenberg district of Berlin the following afternoon, even though she was doubtful that there was anything left of it. But he assured her that it was still being kept open.

Chapter Twenty-five

The UFA Palace by the zoo had been the Berlin cinema for big premieres and Sonja had been there for showings of *Triumph of the Will*, *The Eternal Jew* and *Munchausen* among other films. There was also a large public bunker in the vicinity. So she had often walked past the zoo, though she had never been inside. The UFA Palace by the zoo, like the UFA studios, was by now a complete wreck. Little more of the zoo had survived. A tattered banner hung over the entrance: 'Entire epochs of love will be needed to repay animals for their value and service.' Some of the animals had been sent to other, safer zoos. Many had been destroyed in the bombing raids or put down by the keepers. A solitary elephant survived, also a hippo and some bears. Elderly members of the people's militia were digging a big trench across one of the zoo's green spaces. It was all rather sad. Jürgen had arrived late, having been detained on naval business. This time he was not in his dress uniform and a pistol had replaced his sword.

They paused to smoke and rest on the rubble of the Antelope Pavilion. Jürgen explained that he often visited the zoo to find comfort with the animals. Before he joined the navy he used to hunt stags, elks and boars in the forests of East Prussia. Boar hunts took place in January, but late September to early October was the rutting season and this was the best time for stag shoots. The ancient forests of oak, fir, ash, and, above all, the birches with their silvery leaves and the apple blossom trees of May, all that was his real home, not the sea. Under winter's leaden skies freezing fog curled round the trees and ice-sailing regattas were held on the Masurian Lakes. It was all so beautiful in its bleakness. Jürgen descended from a long line of Junkers. The family mansion was in the heart of a forest and storks built their messy great nests in the trees around the mansion. Often Jürgen would be awoken by the clacking of their bills.

'I should have liked to take you there, so you could see the ancestral home and meet my mother and then we could walk in the forests. But I am pretty sure there is no home to go to. The subhuman Bolsheviks will have pulled it down. They will probably build a cement factory in its place. I do not know whether my mother is alive or dead. In a way, I hope that she is dead.'

Then he abruptly changed the subject, 'I have been thinking more about our conversation on Tuesday. Have you read Pascal?'

Sonja shook her head. Should she confess that she never read novels? If she had to compile a list of her favourite novels, *Ivanhoe* would have to feature on it since it was the only novel that she could remember reading. Was it possible that Pascal wrote *Ivanhoe*? Ah, no, she was forgetting. She had read some of that strange novel of Joseph's, though she could not remember its title. It would come to her in a moment.

Jürgen gave up waiting for an answer and said, 'He wrote this,' and with eyes closed he recited, "Picture a number of men in chains and all condemned to death. Each day some are strangled in the sight of the rest. Those who remain see their own condition in that of their fellows, looking at one another with sorrow and without hope. This is the picture of the condition of man." It seems to me that the Suicide Club, if it existed, would turn Pascal's picture into something real and tangible, with every man and woman in the locked room looking round and wondering who will be next. To see this, to experience it directly... well, there is something desperate about it. But you are so alive and have so much to live for and I cannot believe that you would willingly enter this room full of chained men looking gloomy. So Sonja, forget about the Suicide Club and... if you can, erase Pascal's words from your memory.'

Now he was beginning to frighten her. What an odd assignation this was turning out to be. Jürgen kept on talking about all manner of strange and morbid things. About how comfortable he had been as a void in the void before he had been conceived. And so he would be similarly comfortable when dead. About how strange it was that the death penalty was reserved for the most serious crimes and yet that same penalty was levied on all of humanity, whether guilty or innocent. About how it was shameful to commit suicide for personal reasons, but honourable and heroic to make a fine ending in the service of the Fuehrer and the Folk. About what a disgrace it was that Field Marshal von Paulus did not do away with himself rather than surrender at Stalingrad. He had brought shame on all Germany. How, if Germany was to be defeated, there needed to be something glorious in that defeat. Otherwise the dream of Germany was forever finished. And right now so many of Jürgen's former shipmates were calling to him from the other side. The best men had already given up their lives on the battlefield. Those who were left did not deserve to survive.

Finally he ran out of strange things to say and looked to her and she wanted to know, 'Jürgen, why are you telling me all this?'

'I have been making enquiries. It seems that the Suicide Club may be more than a dark legend. But it is a little dangerous. One has to travel out to the north of Berlin to the district of Wedding. It is a rough and rundown working-class district and it is still thought to harbour Bolshevik sympathisers. In the whole of that district there is just one sandwich man. One has to go to him and ask for one of his cream cakes –'

'Cream cakes! I have not seen a cream cake for at least a year! Even Eva could not produce cream cakes. It is definitely worth making the journey to Wedding. Shall we go together?'

Jürgen smiled sadly.

'There are no cream cakes. The sandwich man has no such thing. It is a code. But if you ask to buy a cream cake, he will direct you to someone who may lead you to the Suicide Club. So I am told.'

'I want to join the Suicide Club,' said Sonja. 'I must seek out this sandwich man, who like other sandwich men, does not sell cream cakes.'

'But Sonja do not joke about it. It is dangerous. In that part of town you might be beaten and robbed even before you found this man. Besides, you may be in danger already. Are you in trouble with the police or the Gestapo?'

'No, I don't think so. Why?'

'We may be being shadowed, or rather you are being shadowed, for I cannot believe that there is any reason that someone would want to shadow me. He was over there by those cages. But I can't see him now.'

Sonja thought for a while.

'Oh, that is probably Wieland,' she said.

'Who is Wieland?'

'He is my shadow, my affliction. I wish I had never met him. Then my life might have been so different.'

'But who is he? What does he do?'

'Really nothing. He is a nobody. He is an out-of-work actor.'

Jürgen looked shocked.

'But today there is no space in Germany for out-of-work actors. We left that sort of Bohemianism behind us when the Weimar days finished. Does he do nothing for the war effort?'

Sonja shook her head.

'Well, if this scoundrel comes near us, I will knock his teeth out.'

Sonja asked herself what she was doing for the war effort these days. It was not even as if she had recently had a part in a film, so she could claim that with her singing and dancing she was making a contribution by cheering people up and improving their morale. She was of no use to the Fuehrer. It was a wonder that Jürgen did not want to knock her teeth out. In any case she could not go on much longer as an out-of-work actress.

But he said, 'I will see you to your place. And if that scoundrel follows, I will see to him.'

She nodded. Was seeing her home a prelude to their going

to bed together? She supposed so. Why not? And there would be more cigarettes.

Soon after they had left the zoo it became apparent that Wieland was following them. Jürgen ran back after him, but Wieland was too quick and vanished round a corner. A little later he reappeared and resumed tailing them at a careful distance.

It was getting dark by the time they arrived at the door to Sonja's flat. A Wehrmacht officer was waiting in the shadow of the door. He was impatient and it was evident that he had been waiting a long time. He thrust a folded piece of paper into Sonja's hand. The note was in Eva's scrawl. Eva was inviting Sonja to a party that very evening, for today was Hitler's birthday. Of course, April 20th!

The officer was impatient.

'The party will have already started. You must come immediately. There is no time to change. We should hurry.'

Sonja had nothing to change into anyway. She took Jürgen by the hand and said, 'He is coming with me.'

The officer nodded impatiently and the three of them set off, the officer using his torch to guide them. Though sirens had started, he would not permit them to seek out one of the shelters. Sonja thought that she saw Wieland still following on behind, but it was hard to be sure in the gathering dark. The officer with them was a major and his name was Reinhardt. Jürgen asked what the great hurry was and Reinhardt replied, 'I need to get drunk.'

The passage across Wilhelmstrasse was perilous. The air was filled with soot and phosphorus fumes and there were puddles of petrol underfoot. A few of the puddles had caught fire. When they reached the grounds of the Old Chancellery, Reinhardt produced a pass, Jürgen was recognised and the three of them were waved through. During all her visits to the Berghof Sonja had never seen Hitler at a party. Would he be at this one?

No, he had gone to bed early. The party was in the canteen on the ground floor of the undamaged wing of the Chancellery. Eva, dressed like a Rhineland carnival queen, presided. Martin Bormann and Dr Morell were there, as well as two of Hitler's secretaries, Traudl and Gerda. But there were many people that Sonja did not recognise. Some were apparently senior officers who had come in from the front to report to Hitler and who had stayed to drink champagne. There were also young men from the People's Militia, no, really mere boys, who earlier in the day, had paraded before Hitler to be decorated by him. Though they wore their medals with hopeless pride, they could not hold their drink. Ironically many of those partying had no idea who Eva was and Sonja was repeatedly asked about her. There was so much champagne and drinking it was a kind of patriotic act since it stopped the Russians getting hold of the stuff. When Sonja wanted to wash the soot off her face, she was told that there was no more running water, but she should use champagne instead and so she did.

Sonja was a veteran of parties. She used to go to everything for which she could wrangle an invitation and she had gatecrashed quite a few others. But there had been very few parties in the last twelve months or so and this one was a strange party. It was a kind of celebration of the passing of the old order. So she thought it was a bit like that early scene in *Gone with the Wind*, the ball at the Wilkes mansion at which the tempestuous Scarlett O'Hara was courted by handsome bucks, many of whom, though they could not know it, were soon to die in the coming war. Then there was that other scene, the ball in Atlanta and the women in ballooning dresses that swirled as they waltzed. And the young men were heroically confident. 'Gentlemen always fight better than rabble'. But a world of grace, honour and elegance would shortly perish in the flames. Fiddle-de-dee. No, the party in the Chancellery was not really a bit like those southern balls, for there was something feverish, even demonic about what she was witnessing in the canteen. For one thing almost everyone was very drunk. In one corner of the canteen three couples were openly copulating. Why not? The dancing was frenzied. Since there were more men than women, some men danced in pairs. Eva danced alone on a large round table. 'Blood-red Roses Tell You of Happiness'. The music came round and round. There was a record player, but just the one record. In the gaps between the playing of the record, the distant sound of artillery could be heard. The foxtrot song 'Blood-red Roses Tell You of Happiness' had been a hit for Max Mensing and the Saxophone Orchestra in 1929. The record had a scratch on it.

Ah, 1929! How was it then? She had been what? Twenty-four. The twenties were still roaring. The talkies were just coming in. Marlene Dietrich had appeared in *The Woman that Men Yearn For*. *The Blue Angel* was a bit later. The talkies were thought to be a fad, something that would not last. Like the dances of the time. David Rego had indulged her passion for dancing, pleased to be seen with such a beautiful woman in his arms. In 1929 Sonja inhabited a body that was never happier than when it was in movement, whereas now her body was her prison. She had once been beautiful and men had found in her beauty the promise of future happiness, or a sign of inner wisdom, or something else that she could not guess at.

Her face was wet with champagne and tears. Jürgen asked her what the matter was. What was not the matter? But she said, 'I am so old.'

'You are not old. What are you?'

'I am forty.'

Jürgen laughed.

'You call that old! Come on, let us dance.'

This was something that Sonja could do. Most of the throng were just jiggling about and usually not even in time to the music. But the foxtrot was in her blood – two steps back, one step sideways, close and repeat. Slow, slow, quick, quick. Slow, slow, quick, quick. Though she was always stepping backward, she was actually leading Jürgen in a flowing counter-clockwise movement round the canteen. As the soldiers became aware that they were seeing a real dancer, they cleared a passage for her and Jürgen. She would have liked it never to end, but after perhaps half an hour it had to, for she was faint with hunger and this was a canteen with limitless champagne and brandy but no food. When they stopped, Eva led the applause from above.

Jürgen and Sonja sat on a trestle table. Cigarettes were the best substitute for food. He fed her cigarettes and told her how beautiful she was. Her sadness was beautiful and the passage of the years had merely emphasised that sad beauty, for her life story was written on her face. He could see that it had been shaped by so much experience, love, laughter, suffering. As life is beautiful, so she was beautiful. She must give up on those morbid thoughts of doing away with herself. And he went on about the beauty of Sonja's soul. He was a great talker, but even so Sonja was pretty sure that she had no soul.

Then he was insisting that they should escape from this infernal gathering and go back to her place and make love as Tristan and Isolde had done. (Though Sonja had heard of Tristan and Isolde, she could not remember who they were.) Jürgen said that their lovemaking would be a kind of consecration of the end of the Thousand Year Reich. Not this ghastly drunken party. Yet Sonja noticed that he was somewhat drunk too, probably too drunk to take her to bed. And now he had moved on to something quite different. He gestured at the heaving throng in front of them.

'This is the end for them. For centuries German bells have been ringing from church towers across the broad fields, over the great silent woods and the mysterious stillness of the Masurian Lakes. But, now that those bells are silenced, we can see that the writings of Goethe and Schiller have been for nothing. From now on it will be as if Bach and Beethoven had never composed. The quest for the blue flower must be abandoned. Civilisation is finished. In the past twelve years all of us here have been part of a great experiment. Our nation's mission was to purge Europe of the twin materialistic poisons of International Jewry and Bolshevism. For centuries Europe has been ruined by wars between neighbouring states. It should have been our destiny to bring about a united Europe devoted to the pursuit of health and beauty. Indeed we fought hard to reach the light. Yet now it is clear that we have failed and all that is good and noble is about to perish. How is it that we have failed?'

He paused rhetorically and then continued, 'I will tell you how. Our cause and our Fuehrer were noble, but we have been badly served by scoundrels, pimps, drug addicts and crypto-Jews. So much idealism has been harnessed merely in order to keep the Golden Pheasants in champagne, drugs and harlots.'

He looked round, daring anyone to disagree with him.

Reinhardt, who was standing close by and who had evidently lost no time in getting very drunk indeed, had no hesitation in disagreeing with him. He burst into raucous laughter and then asked, 'What is it that is so noble about the death camps?'

Jürgen, shocked, replied, 'What death camps? Yes, there are re-education camps and labour camps. In them people work for the Reich and then they come out as better people. But there are no death camps. Stories of such horrible things are slanders put about by subversives. There are actually such people in Germany who would prefer nothing to be done about the Jewish problem. Perhaps you are one of those traitors.'

The party was very noisy and they had to stand close together with their heads almost touching in order to hear what they were shouting at each other.

'What is the Jewish problem?' Reinhardt demanded rhetorically. 'I will tell you. It is that they cannot die fast enough. I have seen a death camp. I have walked about in one and as I did so I noted corpses hanging on barbed wire and the funeral pyres and the gas chambers. I have seen men so emaciated that they were hardly more than skeletons and I have seen dogs set upon those men. I saw a train bringing in another load of people to be killed. I spent hours with the smell of death about me. I saw a baby taken from its mother's arms

314

and its head smashed against a wall.'

'What are you talking about?'

'I am telling you. I am talking about a death camp.'

'There are no such things.'

'Are you an idiot? Can you not understand what I am saying? I have seen what I have seen. It was in August 1943. My regiment was stationed a little way north of Warsaw. There was little for us to do at that time. But then one day there was an emergency and the SS called us in to help. In a death camp called Treblinka, in one of their many death camps I believe, the Jews had rebelled, killed some of the SS and set fire to part of the camp, after that many had escaped into the surrounding forest. So my regiment was called in to help in the hunt for the escapees and prevent them joining up with the partisans. It was a massive manhunt. Only some Jews got away. Most of them were weak and not able to run fast enough. My regiment was successful in recapturing five of the Jews... I wish that my men had been less successful, for we took them back to the death camp where those Jews were made to lie on the ground and then, one by one, their skulls were smashed in with a pickaxe. But you can call Treblinka a re-education camp if you like.'

This was surely some bad dream. Sonja actually pinched herself, before exclaiming, 'Those poor Jews!' She was remembering how police had come for Manasseh.

Jürgen looked at her angrily and said, 'Such vile falsehoods are not fit for the ears of a lady!'

Reinhardt was remorseless and continued, 'What is so very noble about killing defenceless men, women and children? If Beethoven's 'Ode to Joy' and Goethe's *Faust* has led on to this sort of thing, then it would be better for our country if those two had never been born. By now Treblinka must be in Russian hands and, when they see what we have done, they will take a terrible revenge. I look forward to their revenge. I am glad that it will happen.'

Sonja wished she was somewhere else and not listening to all this. She tried telling herself that, even if it was all true, there was nothing she, an actress and now an out-of-work actress, could ever have done about it. Surely she was innocent? In any case it could not possibly be true. It might be that Reinhardt was mad and everything he was saying was some dark lunatic fantasy brought on by the horror and fear of the war. She badly needed another of Jürgen's cigarettes, but this was not possible, for now he slapped Reinhardt's face and hissed, 'You lie, you Jew-loving traitor!'

The slap made Reinhardt's glass slop over. He looked sadly at it and tipped the rest of the champagne away before smashing the glass into Jürgen's cheek. Now others in the canteen were drawn to the fight that had started and they formed a ring round the two men and egged them on. They seemed to think that the fight was about Sonja. She only wished that this might be true. There would have been something chivalric about that, rather than this brawl about the killing of Jews. Perhaps she now needed another drink more than a cigarette. Most of the men were supporting Reinhardt as he was a soldier. But he was terribly drunk and Jürgen was only a little drunk.

Sonja pushed her way out through the ring of men that had formed round the fight and soon she found herself another drink, before abruptly ending up on the floor. Perhaps the signs had always been there for her to see, but she had been too stupid to read the signs. Was stupidity a kind of evil? Had she chosen to be stupid? Perhaps her stupidity had made her life easier. She was now once again in tears. She tried to tell herself that she was weeping for the Jews, but something in her was telling her that she was really weeping for herself and her stupidity.

After only a few minutes the fight was ended by Eva, who was backed up by some of the senior officers. Jürgen and Reinhardt were manhandled out of the canteen. Eva then went over and joined Sonja on the floor and offered her a cigarette.

'I am sorry about the record,' she said. 'I did try to get others, but nobody was prepared to take the risk of leaving the Chancellery and going to look for them.'

Then, 'You will have to choose between them. Jürgen is very good-looking. I like him.'

'It was not about me,' said Sonja. 'It was about the Reich killing Jews.'

'Now you must not talk about such things at my party. In any case those things are not for us to have an opinion on. I trust my Adolf to tell me what is right. Politics, like war, is the concern of men. The job of we women is to be pretty, and to make homes for the men and then to comfort them when things go wrong. God knows that is hard enough.'

And Eva continued her exposition of the role of women in the Reich. There was no point in women duplicating the way men think and feel. Of course, besides being beautiful and providing comfort, the other job of women was to provide men with babies. Eva's eyes were moist. She should have born the Fuehrer a baby. It was far too late now. Sonja had always thought of Eva as being remarkably like her. They both loved films, dancing, make-up, shoes and cigarettes. But now, listening to her, it was as if she was getting alien messages from another planet, for Sonja had never thought of herself as a potential homemaker and comforter of men or a provider of babies. Her job had been to become famous. Why should only men want to become famous? But it was far too late for that now. And her great book, *My Life is like a Fairy Tale*, was barely begun.

As Eva talked various men came up to ask either Sonja or Eva to dance, but they were gestured away. Jürgen and Reinhardt seemed to have vanished. This was just the tail of what had been a twelve-year-long party.

Limitless champagne, music, dancing and cigarettes. This place, which ought to have been paradise, was a special kind of hell and that bloody song about those bloody roses came round and round. It was as if she was in one of those strange films by Josef von Sternberg. Suppose that there is an afterlife and that it is a hell to be faced that will be even worse than the party in the canteen. Or suppose that the party in the canteen *is* the afterlife. Suppose that she has already committed suicide but then forgotten about it. It is easy to forget things when one is dead. But forgetful oblivion would be good. No sooner had Sonja had that thought than she passed out.

The sound of that bloody song about bloody red roses brought her round. By now there were only a few people in the canteen. There was one couple dancing. Reinhardt was squatting beside her.

'Your friend has shot himself,' he said. 'I have his pistol. What was his name?'

He showed her the pistol. This did not make sense. Having

looked at the gun, she closed her eyes again and hoped for the return of oblivion. But this did not happen and she could still hear Reinhardt talking. He said that he needed to explain what had happened. The two of them had been forcibly escorted by a gang of soldiers out into the garden of the Chancellery where they had been urged to make up their quarrel, but this did not happen and instead they continued to argue. The argument turned into a duel, or perhaps a form of Russian roulette, as they swore on their words of honour as officers that the one who lost the argument would shoot himself. The handful of soldiers still standing around and listening agreed to be witnesses to this. Reinhardt won the argument and therefore Jürgen saw that he had no option but to shoot himself. Which he did.

Sonja thought that this was all preposterous. Was Jürgen really dead? If so, she thought it much more likely that Reinhardt had murdered him.

'I had to win,' he said. 'I want so badly to be alive to witness the Judaeo-Bolshevik revenge. I want to see what our punishment will be.' Then, seeing Sonja looking so doubtful, he continued, 'It was not an argument that I could lose, nor was it one that could be decided by words. I had photographs. Look!'

He took them out of his jacket pocket and fanned them out like playing cards in a game. For the most part the pictures were unsensational: an orderly line of huts with barbed wire behind them; women watched by soldiers as they descended from a train carrying children and little bundles; a small hill of discarded shoes; a group photograph of Jews standing in front of a sign saying Treblinka; a gang of Jews pulling a cart up a

319

railway track. There were just two photographs that were not so innocuous, one of naked women standing in a trench and one of a long line of men stretched out on the ground with their skulls smashed in. Sonja closed her eyes again. This was a nightmare from which she would try to escape by going to sleep. But Reinhardt said, 'You must not close your eyes to this. We must all be witnesses to what has happened.'

To which Sonja replied, 'You should not have killed Jürgen. He was going to take me to Wedding.'

'I did not kill Jürgen. What do you want to go there for? That place is one big slum. I am sorry. Were you his girl-friend? He was rather good-looking.'

'No. We only met yesterday.'

Now Sonja looked properly at Reinhardt. He was not as good-looking as Jürgen. He had a foxy face and there were premature streaks of white in his thick black hair. She was good at faces and judged that he was probably a Libra.

'When were you born?'

'What kind of question is that? October 25th, 1916.' He was looking at her as if she was mad.

So a Scorpio then. Not a calmly balanced Libra, but so close. She had been out only by a few days.

When he spoke again, his voice was quiet and gentle as if he was speaking to a mad woman whom he did not want to upset.

'Why is it that you want to go to Wedding?'

'My life is a mess and I want to end it,' she said. But how to explain what kind of mess? She decided to tell him her life story as briskly as possible: her childhood in Holland, her encounter with Wieland –

At which point he interrupted her, 'I should like to meet him. He sounds interesting. He makes things happen.'

She continued with her waitressing in Berlin, her being taken up by David Rego, her appearances in films including *The Gypsy Baron*, *Baghdad Capers* and *Munchausen*. (Was she going on too long?) She had just got to her first meeting with Hans Albers on the set of *Munchausen* when he interrupted her again.

'A splendid chap!'

'You know Albers!'

'Oh yes, I advised Kästner on the script of *Munchausen*. Before the war I was a scriptwriter. I wonder what has happened to him by the way.'

It turned out that Reinhardt was very familiar with the UFA studios. It was a kind of miraculous non-coincidence that they had never encountered each other there. They talked about mutual acquaintances and other film gossip and then it was his turn to tell a little of his life. He had scripted *The Great Sacrifice* and other less well-known films, before being called up in 1940. He had spent most of a year quite happily with the garrison in Paris before being sent to Poland and later the Russian Front. There he kept getting promoted as his superior officers kept getting killed. But while on leave and back in Berlin he had been able to help Kästner with the final tweaks to the script of *Munchausen*. 'Man is like a cloud of smoke which rises and then disappears.'

Then Sonja resumed the story of her life. It was a selective version which did not include the rape on Peacock Island, her going to bed with Goebbels, the encounter with Lida Baarova and her confrontation with Olga Chekhova. Reinhardt was disappointingly unimpressed that she was a friend of Eva Braun. Having met Eva earlier that night, he had decided that she was a commonplace person. But he confessed to a reluctant respect for Goebbels. He'd had rows with him when Goebbels tried to alter or censor scripts. Also that novel Goebbels had published was rubbish. But he was very clever and a supreme master of rhetoric.

'People like me create fictions that merely entertain, whereas he creates fictions which have made him one of the masters of the Reich and one of those who determine what the story of the Reich will be.'

Finally Sonja got to the point where she described how she had heard about the Suicide Club and how she was going to go on a quest for it.

'That is the story of my life,' she said.

Reinhardt was silent for a moment, then, 'But that is not a story. That is just one thing after another. There has been no danger, no hardship. The story of a life should have a plot. Take it from me, for I am a professional plotter. Though perhaps you are right about needing the Suicide Club, for it may be that the only chance that your life will have any meaning will be if you give it an ending. And I do like the idea of a quest. But perhaps your quest is already at its end.'

He fetched a couple of bottle ends of brandy.

'If you really want to die, drink this and, before you have finished drinking, I can shoot you. If you wish, I can blindfold you first and put a cigarette in your mouth.'

Sonja told him that though she definitely wanted to die, she did not want to know exactly when and how she was going to die. That was the attraction of the Suicide Club. Anyway it turned out that he would have had to have gone off somewhere to cadge the cigarette as he was a non-smoker.

After a long silence, he said, 'I will tell you what. I will accompany you to Wedding and together we will try to find the Suicide Club. As I say, I like the idea of a quest. Not that I have any intention of killing myself. But the idea of a Suicide Club suggests something romantic, mysterious and sinister, even though it is perhaps only a legend like the Philosopher's Stone, or the Rosicrucian Brotherhood, or Shangri-La, or Treasure Island. There might be a film script or a novel in it for me – at the very least a short story. Perhaps the story will turn out to be not a murder mystery, but a suicide mystery. And God knows our journey would be dangerous enough… I think that it will soon be daylight.'

They decided to catch some sleep before setting out on the great quest. So Reinhardt went over to the record player and removed the disc which he then smashed against the wall. With peace assured, they stretched out on the floor and cuddled up to one another for warmth and comfort. They were far too drunk for sex.

Chapter Twenty-six

The sun was high in the sky when they emerged from the New Chancellery. Before commencing the long walk, they managed to scrounge a small amount of food in the upper levels of the Old Chancellery. At this point there was some confusion as several people thought that Reinhardt and Sonja were about to lead a breakout to the south in the hope of somehow passing through the Russian lines and reaching the Americans. But Reinhardt insisted that he would be heading north and that he had no hope whatsoever of escaping the Russian siege. Indeed he did not even wish to escape the Russians.

A man was standing in the middle of Wilhelmstrasse and it looked as though he was trying to conduct the sounds of bombs and artillery salvos like a maestro faced with a recalcitrant orchestra. Sonja pointed to him.

'That is Wieland,' she said.

Reinhardt strode over to him. Wieland's arm shot up.

'Heil er... Heil er... oh, confound it! I can never remember what the fellow's name is.' But Wieland was grinning madly.

Reinhardt took this in his stride and he shook Wieland by the hand.

'You are coming with us,' he said. 'We want you with us as we set out to look for the Suicide Club that is supposed to have its headquarters in Wedding.'

Wieland looked reluctant, but then nodded.

Sonja scowled at Wieland and he looked apologetic. As they walked on, Sonja and Reinhardt tried to explain why they were seeking out this strange and perhaps entirely imaginary club.

'You, Wieland, will make things happen,' said Reinhardt. 'So having you with us, whatever does happen will not be a fiasco.'

Before they could set off for Wedding, they had first to go to Sonja's flat, so that Sonja could extract her life savings from inside her bed's mattress. Reinhardt wanted to know what the large padlocked tin trunk in the corner of the bedroom was. Surely that should have been the place for her savings. But she told him that in recent months that was where she had been obliged to keep her diaries. Wieland had the grace to look shamefaced.

Sonja wondered why Wieland was so ready to accompany them on this dangerous journey. Also, what sign of the zodiac did he think he was these days? She asked what had happened to Tilde and he told her that Tilde had finally wearied of what she described as his 'petit bourgeois romantic infatuation' with Sonja and that she had left Berlin heading eastwards where she hoped to find some kind of salvation with the Russians.

'I think that she thinks that all their soldiers read Chekhov.'

It was a bright spring day, though its brightness was sometimes obscured by the dust in the air. Spring and yet there was no summer to come. They linked arms as they walked on. It reminded Sonja of something, but what? Oh yes, it was *The Wizard of Oz*. But Dorothy was trying to find Kansas again, whereas Sonja was marching towards her death. Also, unlike Dorothy, she was horridly hungover. Though there were road checks and patrols who were hunting for draft dodgers and deserters, Reinhardt's rank protected all three of them. His Iron Cross was an amulet that magically allowed them to pass through all obstructions.

No trams were running northwards and it was a long walk to Wedding. Rubble made some streets impassable where bricks had flowed out of houses like frozen waterfalls. The scorched exoskeletons of buildings rose out of the rubble and remaining pinnacles and church towers hinted improbably at a new fairyland. Papers fluttered about and there were occasional dust storms. In life one gets used to the sight of old ruins – castles whose walls were covered with ivy, roofless monasteries and that sort of thing – but these were eerily fresh ruins and no vegetation had yet encroached upon them. Women, dwarfed by what still stood, worked in chains to clear the streets, and passed buckets of bricks down their lines. Twice the three oddly assorted companions passed people who were fighting to get cuts of meat from dead horses on the roads. An imperial city had been reduced to a shambles. Sonja was pretty sure that they had walked by the place where she had once worked as a singing waitress, but nothing remained of it now. The city was saying goodbye to her.

There were bodies everywhere. Wieland paused over the corpse of one of the Hitler Youth and solemnly made the sign of the cross over the dead boy before stealing his knife. One had to watch one's footing all the time and that was tiring. They sat and rested on the sunny steps of some government building. At this point Reinhardt decided to tell them about a script he had been working on while he had been stationed near Warsaw.

'My script was based on a short story called 'The Bottle Imp' by an Englishman called Stevenson – um… no, no, he was Scottish. The story was set in the South Seas and some of it would have been filmed in Vichy Morocco. In the story a Hawaiian called Keawe purchases a bottle from an aged gentleman. Something obscurely moves within the bottle like a shadow and a fire. That will be for special effects to sort out. This magic bottle will grant Keawe everything he wishes, but if he dies with it still in his possession then he will be destined to an eternity in the flames of Hell…'

'Anybody who does a deal with the Devil certainly deserves to go to Hell,' said Wieland.

Reinhardt ignored him and continued, 'The only way he can avoid this is to sell the bottle before he dies for less than he paid for it. Though this seems quite a bargain, Keawe does not wish to risk it, but the old gentleman tricks him into offering fifty dollars for it. Naturally the aged gentleman is glad to be rid of the bottle. Previous wealthy purchasers had included Prester John, James Cook and Napoleon, but by now the bottle was quite cheap. Keawe first tries to jettison the bottle, but, having failed, he wishes for a great landed estate and his wish is granted, but at the cost of inheriting a fortune from a beloved relative who suddenly dies in an accident. Keawe uses this inheritance to set up his estate and then, after he summoned the satanic imp to manifest itself outside the bottle, sensibly sells the bottle at a reduced price to a friend.

Sonja had only been listening with half an ear as she had been brooding resentfully on how Reinhardt had earlier told her that her life had no story and that she had never been in any kind of danger. That only seemed to be the case because she had not told him about the rape on Peacock Island, her sleeping with Goebbels and Wieland's theft of her diaries. Why should she have? It had been none of Reinhardt's business. Anyway, what was the point of this story about selling bottles?

So now she interrupted, 'Reinhardt, why are you telling us this story?'

Reinhardt looked at her sadly and said, 'It is mostly told and, when it is finished, you will see it mirrors the situation towards which you are hurrying.'

'I wish that we were listening to this story in the South Seas,' said Wieland.

'I don't believe in Hell,' said Sonja.

Reinhardt replied, 'Of course not. Neither do I. That is not the point. The story is about something else.'

'I believe in Hell,' said Wieland unexpectedly and he looked as though he wanted to start an argument, but Reinhardt scowled at him and it was so pleasant sitting in the sun. So they relaxed and let him resume the story.

'Anyway, to continue, the camera will linger over the paradisal scenery, palms blowing in the gentle breeze and whatnot. All now seems well and life is now almost perfect for Keawe, when one evening, walking along the beach, he meets a beautiful woman, they fall in love and agree to get married. But then on the eve of the wedding night he discovers that he has leprosy. There will be no alternative for him, but to leave his bride and the great house and go into enforced exile on the island of lepers. That will be a great scene in the film! Or rather there is one alternative. He can buy back the bottle. That was not easy, for his friend having become very wealthy has gone abroad and by the time Keawe has tracked down the bottle it has passed through many hands. The man who has it bought it for two cents. So Keawe must purchase it for one cent, though he assumes that he will never be able to sell it for less than that. But he does purchase it and his leprosy disappears. He is cured but it seems only at the price of eternal damnation. He reluctantly explains his dreadful predicament to his wife. She suggests a sailing trip to Tahiti, since the centime circulates there and the centime is worth only a fifth of a cent. But in Tahiti no one will buy the accursed bottle. So Keawe's wife secretly arranges for a man to buy the bottle from her for four centimes on the strict understanding that she will buy the bottle back for three centimes and this happens. Then Keawe discovers how his wife has tried to rescue him and so he in turn decides to rescue her by taking the bottle from her and he sells it to a drunken sailor for two centimes, with the promise to buy it back for one centime. But when he comes to offer the solitary centime to get the bottle back, the rum-soaked boatswain refuses, for he says that he is going to Hell anyway. I had thought that the sound track and especially the finale should work with tango music, but perhaps some kind of South Sea Islands native music would be better.'

'What has this got to do with my situation?' Sonja wanted to know. 'I have no bottle to sell.'

'Do not pretend to be more stupid than you are,' replied Reinhardt. 'We are of course talking about diminishing options. Every step you take in this direction reduces your options. But, if you will turn back, many options will become open to you again.'

Had Reinhardt made up this story and invented the Stevenson author in order to deliver some message about diminishing options? Even if so, it did not really make sense.

'Your story is ridiculous. I am not like the man in your story, for he was terrified of death and damnation, whereas I am actually looking for death, which will be oblivion, and I have no belief at all in Hell. I want to proceed on to the single final option which beckons ahead of me.'

Reinhardt just shrugged, his shrug signifying 'stupid woman'.

Now it was Wieland who spoke, 'Turn back, I beg you. You must turn back, dearest Sonja. The commandment 'Thou shalt not kill' does not just apply to killing other people. It also includes killing oneself. You are destroying what belongs to God and that is a mortal sin which puts you beyond God's saving grace and you should know that the flames of Hell are real and all suicides are destined to Hell, for by definition it is a sin from which you cannot repent. God has already given you the precious gift of life. You cannot deny… you must not deny God His right to grant you salvation. Sonja, I have only come with you this far in the hope of saving you. Think of the flames and the eternity of pain which is what is really beckoning you ahead.'

Sonja was incredulous. This was a new kind of rant from Wieland. But perhaps it was a great act, like that time when he had turned up in the foyer of the UFA Palace by the zoo and delivered that extraordinary speech about the sufferings of the soldiers on the Eastern Front. That had just been him performing and now this was a new role that he was trying on.

'Oh stop it Wieland, please,' she said. 'You cannot tell me

that you were trailing me and that naval officer round the zoo and all the way to the Chancellery in the hope of saving my soul. That would just be creepy.'

'If it takes a creep to save your soul, then I will be that creep.'

As they were sitting and talking on the steps, a hungry-looking Alsatian had joined them. Wieland absently patted it on the head and continued talking, 'When I was a boy I had a cult of the old Teutonic gods, Odin, Thor, Baldur and so on. I particularly identified with Loki or Loge. Indeed I fancied that I might be a latter-day reincarnation of him and this absurd fancy stayed with me into adult life. Finding the world we live in really rather boring, I have spent much of my life trying to liven it up a bit by inserting some jokes into our everyday existence, and if people were upset or damaged by my pranks, that was too bad. But I was just a joker and only as good as my latest caper or joke and playing the joker is a lonely business. And I now repent this. People being upset by jokes was just bad. I have never been taken seriously, but at this late hour I must be serious. God has touched my heart and I have been attending mass and receiving instruction. If I should live so long, I will formally become a Roman Catholic. But I have the faith and already I believe that I have saved my soul. What is more I believe that I can save yours too.'

Sonja burst out laughing. Here they were sat among the ruins and she was going to her death. Listening to this nonsense was just so funny. Wieland could play any part: Svengali, Charlie Chaplin, the Kaiser, Alfried Krupp, Mephistopheles, Marshal Petain, Hamlet and just about anybody. Surely the sanctimonious Catholic was just the latest of his parts.

331

'Father Wieland, you are just putting on this religious act to tease me.'

But Wieland sounded sad and gestured at the ruins, 'I really do wish that I was joking, but look around you. The time for jokes, all jokes is over. I know that I used to annoy people when I played at being Loki. The odd thing is that now I have become a sincere Christian I seem to annoy people even more. Forgive me for being annoying.'

Then Reinhardt said, 'You certainly are annoying. From what Sonja has told me, you sounded a lot more interesting before you got theology. I suggest you leave us and allow us to go our own way.' Then, turning to Sonja, he said, 'Of course I am not in agreement with your strange actor friend. I merely wanted you to be aware of what kind of story you are in. It is a story of diminishing options and I really want to see how you bring it to an end, for without an ending your life cannot be considered to be fully a story.'

'I am me!' protested Sonja. 'I am not going to be a story.'

Wieland backed her up, 'It is silly to think of people's lives as just stories. It is even sinful to look on people in this way, as if people lived their lives in order to provide other people with entertainment. None of us was born just to have films or plays made out of our lives. We should not be compelled to live a narrative. Indeed it is impossible. Since we only live in the present moment, the life narrative cannot exist. There is in reality no trail behind us and, as for the future, it does not yet exist and it never will. Tomorrow never comes – any more than yesterday does. There is only the present and the present always is. You are Sonja and Sonja is too lovable to be just a sequence of scenes and events.'

Whether this was philosophy or theology, it was making her head hurt. It was her turn to shrug and she said nothing.

When they resumed their walk the Alsatian started to follow them. Sonja had mentally christened it Toto, but no sooner had she done so than Reinhardt turned round and shot it.

'It was just waiting for one of us to fall by the wayside,' he said. 'Then the dog would leapt upon whichever one of us had faltered and he would have devoured that person.'

Yes. Reinhardt could easily have killed Jürgen.

They walked through a lunar landscape. As the sunny day wore on the sickly smell of corpses became stronger. At least it was not raining. That would have made the stink much worse. Some of the corpses hung from street lamps. Deserters presumably. Far off in the west of the city bombs were falling. That would be the Americans. They passed people with heavily laden prams or handcarts heading in the opposite direction. From time to time Wieland and Reinhardt pissed against a wall. Sonja looked for a wall to piss behind. They did not talk. Sonja was fantasising that she was walking between two angels, and the one on the left was evil, while the one on the right was urging her to be good, or perhaps it was the other way round, but then, as she continued to play with the fantasy, it occurred to her that it could easily be that both the angels were evil.

Then she was thinking that she did sort of think of herself as living a story: the story of a brave Dutch girl who, against all the odds, found her destiny in the glittering world of UFA films and her glorious future had seemed assured until various things went badly wrong about a year ago. It was tragic. So now, like Anna Karenina, she was going to have to do away with herself. Surely that was a sort of story? But not the kind one might find in a book. Looking back on her life as she remembered it, it had lots of jump cuts, flashbacks, flash forwards, fades and dissolves. Soon it would be a wrap. Would there be time for a wrap party?

At length they found themselves in Wedding. It was a sullen neighbourhood and the few people who remained scowled at them. Reinhardt's uniform and rank were not in his favour. Sonja had feared that Jürgen might have got the business about the sandwich man wrong, or even made him up, but there was his stand on the far side of the market square. She was about to walk over to the stand when Wieland took her by the arm.

'Please stop. Let us have a conversation. I find that it is always good to chat and this is something too serious for you to rush into. Let us open our hearts to one another.'

This was tosh, but why not pause? It had been a long walk. They sat on a stone bench on the opposite side of the square.

'Give me just fifteen minutes in which to rescue you from yourself,' Wieland said.

Sonja shrugged again and Wieland continued, 'To commit suicide because you are fed up with the world or with yourself is selfish and, worse than selfish, it is a mortal sin. What is more you are quite wrong if you think that you will cease to exist. The Church –'

'Enough, Wieland. Please stop.' Sonja was tired of this stuff and turned to Reinhardt, 'Please tell him that he is wrong.'

There was a lengthy silence. When Reinhardt spoke, he sounded reluctant, 'Well, he is mostly wrong, but not entirely so.' Then he said, 'You will think me mad.'

Yes, the way this day, probably her last day, was turning out, it was pretty certain that whatever was coming next would be mad.

'Though I am no believer in Hell, it seems to me that what is terrifying about it is not its flames but its eternity. Time is infinite and so our world which is finite must recur an infinite number of times in infinite time. According to Nietzsche, "Everything has returned. Sirius and the spider, and thy thoughts at this moment, and this last thought of thine that all things will return." So it is that trillions of trillions of years hence I will once again be a boy in Lubeck, a philosophy student in Göttingen, an apprentice scriptwriter in Berlin and then I shall once more find myself in Treblinka watching the skulls being smashed in, and then eventually that ghastly party in the Chancellery. Since this person will in every possible way be identical with me, it will be me. I will have to make myself tough to face all that again. Trillions of trillions of years on from now you and I will be back in this place having this identical conversation. Though there will be oblivion in between these recurrences, obviously we will not be aware of that. It will be as if we pass instantly from one reincarnation to another. I want to make myself into the man who will be able to endure this. But that is very hard and the prospect scares me somewhat.'

Sonja had heard of Nietzsche. He was a philosopher and philosophy had nothing to do with the real world or anything really. Reinhardt was absolutely right. He was mad.

Now from the far side of the square the sandwich man had spotted them and he was gesturing that they should hurry over to his booth.

'You two can keep arguing. I have heard enough and now I am going to talk to that man over there.' As Sonja said this, she rose from the bench. But Wieland rose too and he ran ahead and turned to block her way. So she said, 'Step aside, Father Wieland.'

He shook his head vigorously, 'Jesus loves you, but not as much as I do. So I am going to save your soul, whether you wish it or not, for, if you go ahead with this and do away with yourself, you will go to Hell, but if now I slit your throat, you will go to Heaven and I will go to Hell! I will do this for you.'

With that he produced the sheath knife that he had taken from the dead boy and he brandished it at Sonja. The next instant his head was blown to bits. A small cloud of red mist was briefly visible in the air. Having shot him, Reinhardt announced in a voice loud enough to be heard across the square, 'That is the fate of all deserters.' Then he lifted the back of his jacket, stuck his pistol under his belt and covered it up with his jacket.

The square was rapidly emptying. Only the sandwich man and a couple of others remained.

Turning to Sonja, Reinhardt said, 'I confess I am surprised. Though I thought that he would make things happen, I did not anticipate this. I have had to be strong. So much for his story, for it is your story and how it ends is what I am really interested in. Let us go and talk to that man, for I see that he has been waiting for us.'

Sonja was bitter, 'Why didn't you let him kill me? I thought that you wanted me dead, so that the somewhat boring story of my life could be wrapped up in a dramatic fashion.'

'No, his proposed *crime passionnel* would have been merely banal. The Suicide Club should be more interesting. I want to see how it works and if it will make a good short story and I want to see how you will manage in such a strange situation.'

'You shot Jürgen didn't you?'

'As an apologist for death camps, he deserved no better.'

And Wieland? Was it that as an apologist for God and Jesus Christ that he deserved no better? She had long thought of Wieland as her ill-luck, but now she could see that it was probably the other way round. Perhaps he really had loved her and his impostures and pranks were the evidence of this. All the same, they were the human equivalent of a cat dropping dead mice at his owner's feet.

Chapter Twenty-seven

They walked over to the sandwich man. With Wieland dead, she now felt as if she was a woman without a shadow. Indeed, she superstitiously looked down to the ground to check that she did still have one.

'What took you so long?' said the sandwich man who seemed to be a rather jolly character. 'I have been watching you over there on the bench.'

Sonja did not reply to this, but said, 'I know you have no cream cakes, but I have to ask you for one.'

'Yes! We have no cream cakes! And today I have no sandwiches either! But I dare say that what you really want is the Suicide Club.'

Sonja nodded. Reinhardt wanted to know what the Suicide Club was and how it worked, but the sandwich man said that there was no time for that and they could see that there were other people waiting. Then he whistled and a boy appeared.

'Two more candidates for the hospital,' he told the boy. The dark was coming on...

Sonja imagined a hospital with white-coated surgeons going about the beds with syringes and administering mercy doses of some poison. She was wide of the mark. Their destination was only two blocks away and the notice over its archway proclaimed that it was The Lippzanner Horse Hospital.

The man who blocked their way was dressed like one of those commissionaires who in better days used to stand outside hotels and cinemas. In fact he looked just like Emil Jannings as he appeared in the early scenes of *The Last Laugh*. Sonja said that she had come to find her death, but Reinhardt said,

'My name is Major Reinhardt Elmdorff and I have no intention of committing suicide. But this is Sonja Heda and she wishes to do away with herself. She is a film star and I am her biographer and I am here to see that she makes a good end and I will write up that end. In the course of my book I can also highlight the achievements of the Suicide Club. Once the Russians get here they will close this place down and those of you who are still alive will either be sent to detention camps or you will be summarily shot.'

The commissionaire, if that was what he was, was un-impressed and would not at first let him pass. 'She can go in, but there are no special allowances for writers. You have to pay and you have to sign a consent form and be aware that you will not come out again.'

Then the commissionaire looked to Sonja. The sum he demanded was a big chunk out of her savings. But so what?

'You might as well have it all,' she said.

He smiled.

Reinhardt had money too, but was more grudging about it.

'I hope this is going to be worth it.'

The commissionaire addressed them both, 'Before you enter the Suicide Club, you must both sign these consent forms which serve as your death warrants. That is the rule. Our club is not for cowards.'

'So be it,' said Reinhardt. 'I must stay with her and I will see this through to her end.'

Though Sonja had been half hoping that Reinhardt would not be admitted, and though the commissionaire was suspicious of him, he cautiously took Reinhardt's money and allowed him to follow Sonja in after signing the lethal document. Then he pointed them indoors to a broad ramp. This led up to a windowless chamber which was dimly lit by kerosene lamps. The chamber's brick walls had been painted black and were partly covered by expensive-looking hangings. Perhaps they had been looted from some grand residence. A board propped up against one of the walls carried a display of swords and knives arranged in the form of a sunburst. Later someone told Sonja that this sort of arrangement was called a panache. Three large stone slabs occupied the middle of the chamber. They must have served as operating tables in the days when horses had been led up here and tiled channels ran in all directions away from those slabs and presumably they had served to carry away the blood of the horses. A range of phials and pill boxes was spread out on one of the slabs. Another was surrounded by crates of champagne. Who would have thought that the Reich had saved so much of the stuff for its obsequies? Most curiously a sedan chair had been placed behind the operating slabs. It was painted in red and gold and the curtains of its windows were drawn.

It was some time before Sonja could take this all in since the place was quite crowded. It was a party scene, though this was not at all like Eva's party. There was no music and dancing and only a few were trying to get drunk. Instead people mingled and talked quietly amongst themselves. The obvious opening conversational gambit was 'What has brought you here?' In some cases it was obvious. There were a few horribly mutilated soldiers, also a couple of SS men who could expect no mercy if they were captured by the Russians. There were a lot of women. Sonja guessed that some were recently widowed, some had been raped and others had been fearfully anticipating it. Oddly there were a handful of aristocratic-looking men and women who gave the impression that they were here because it was the smart place to be.

Reinhardt was derisive, 'What a shower! Ewers would have loved this. But I have no intention of dying in the midst of these bohemians, draft dodgers, cripples and cowards, the flotsam and jetsam of humanity. These people deserve to die. We all deserve to die. But I am tough.'

'You knew Ewers?'

'Of course I knew him. Besides his wretched novels, he did the scripts for *The Student of Prague* and *Of the Seven Seas*. He also did a script for *Hans Westmar*, but Goebbels spiked it.'

Sonja would have liked to have heard more from Reinhardt about Ewers, but just at that moment someone tapped her on the shoulder.

'Sonja, aren't you going to say hello to me?' The man smiled at her.

His face was indeed perfectly familiar and she knew that she knew him, but encountering him so far out of context, she momentarily could not think how she knew him or what his name was.'

'We last met outside the premiere of *Kolberg*,' he said helpfully.

'Of course we did. Hello Hans.'

'What are you doing here?'

But before he could reply, there was an interruption.

An elderly gentleman was being helped by a younger man to clamber onto one of the operating slabs. Another man passed him up a glass and spoon. Once the elderly man had found his balance on the slab he hit the glass with the spoon.

'Ladies and gentlemen, if I could have your attention please. I won't detain you long. It is most gratifying to see so many people here and I find it always a pleasure to welcome a fresh intake. Though I should introduce myself to you, you will excuse me if I do not give you my real name and, after all, many of you are also here under assumed names. I think that I can see some quite famous faces amongst this evening's gathering. But no names, no pack drill. You can know me as the President.'

The President had a fine beard and was in a dinner jacket with a carnation in the button hole. Reinhardt was surreptitiously taking notes on the speech. Sonja was not listening properly as she was wondering if she should tell Hans that his half-brother was dead and that Hans was standing next to the man who had killed Wieland earlier that day.

The President continued, 'It hardly needs me to say a few words in praise of suicide. At a humdrum level it is surely the case that not all suicides are self-murder. A kinder verdict of self-manslaughter is sometimes more appropriate. But that is by the way and of course quite trivial. The more substantial point is that suicide has a long and distinguished history.

Samson was a suicide and so were Socrates and Mark Antony. It would be absurd to denounce those heroes as cowards or criminals, and was Hamlet's famous soliloquy really the meditation of a criminal? I think not. Yet even the fame of these distinguished names pales before that of the world's most distinguished suicide… for The Son of God indeed made himself a suicide and God the Father had created the universe as His gallows and His universe is also our gallows.'

'But enough of such lucubrations. It is estimated that the Russians will get here in about eight days. Unless, that is, the Fuehrer deploys our famous miracle weapon.'

There was dutiful laughter at this.

'None of you can now leave this place except in a shroud. Enough food will be brought in to see you through the next seven days, particularly in view of the diminishing number of you who will be requiring food. Within the seven days, starting tomorrow morning, one by one each of you will be killed. What happens is that the mandarin in the sedan chair will deal each of you a playing card. You will then show that card to the stewards.'

Here he pointed down to the two men who had helped him up and passed him the glass and spoon, and then he continued, 'Those who have drawn the four aces will constitute the first team of killers and they should conceal their card and their role from everyone except the stewards. Having scrutinised all the cards that have been dealt, the stewards will indicate to the bearers of the aces whom their designated victims are. The stewards are also available to advise on how the killings may be carried out. The general plan is that each of you will be killed when you are least expecting it. I think that almost covers the ground. The toilet is over there in the far corner. Mattresses and blankets have been laid out in the storerooms and stables just to the left of the ramp. If you need assistance with anything the stewards will only be too pleased to help and of course they will be removing the corpses as they fall. In closing I would like to thank those anonymous benefactors whose generosity has made the operations of the Suicide Club possible. Well, that is more than enough from me and so without more ado I invite you to form an orderly queue and collect your cards from the sedan chair behind me. Don't forget to show your card to a steward.'

'This is all very elaborate, even rather gothic,' said Reinhardt. 'If the President had any sense, he and his henchmen would make a discreet exit, padlocking the door behind them, and then pump this place full of Zyklon B and scarper with all the money they have collected.'

'What is Zyklon B?' asked Sonja.

'Believe me, you do not want to know.'

The three of them found themselves near the end of the queue. Having introduced Hans to Reinhardt, Sonja asked Hans how it was that he had decided to come to this place. Had he tried to gatecrash this party too?

He shook his head, 'You can see how it is. For people like you and me, our condition is terminal, since the film industry is finished. We have made such great films as *The Cabinet of Dr Caligari*, *The Golem*, *Waxworks*, *Berlin, Symphony of the Great City*, *The Blue Light*, *Rembrandt*, *Amphitryon* and *Munchausen*, but those films will have no descendants. I gambled my life away on the hope of becoming a director and carrying on the tradition of those films. But now, even supposing I survived the war and found work as a filmmaker in occupied Germany, what kind of films would I be making? Silly vulgar comedy films for the American or British market, or the story of two young lovers who only find true fulfilment and happiness when a new combine harvester is delivered to their collective farm – that would be for the Russians. What is more, the great films that Germany has produced over the last few decades will be lost or destroyed by our conquerors – as irretrievably lost as the ruins of Atlantis. The age of the art film is over.'

This did not rate with Sonja. Apart from *Munchausen*, she did not like any of the films he had listed. She preferred films, like *Kora Terry* and *The Woman of My Dreams* that made one so happy that one wanted to sing and dance. The elegy on the death of the art film did not interest Reinhardt either. He said, 'I have been thinking things over. Looking at the situation superficially, we are certain to be killed, but logically it cannot be so. You are going to be killed when you least expect it. What is today? Sunday, I think. So now you cannot be killed next Sunday because by the end of Saturday you will definitely be expecting to be killed on the following day. But the same applies to that immediately preceding Saturday. If on Friday you know that you cannot be killed on Sunday, then it would have to be Saturday, but that then would not be unexpected. Exactly the same objection applies to your being unexpectedly killed on Friday and therefore the same process of reasoning also applies to Thursday, Wednesday, Tuesday and Monday. That means you are safe.'

Hans looked baffled. Sonja thought this was just philosophy again. Though she could not be bothered to think

345

why, it was obviously rubbish and in real life there was no such silly problem. Now they were at the front of the queue. She went first. A yellowish claw-like hand slid out from under the curtain and handed Sonja her card. It was the five of clubs and she showed it to one of the stewards who made a note of it. (Thank God it had not been an ace.) Hans and Reinhardt collected and showed their cards. Reinhardt turned his back on Hans and waited until Hans had wandered off before he spoke to Sonja, 'I am just waiting to see how your life story ends and then I am planning to leave here and go out and see how the Russians are going to finish with Germany. The last part of any script is always the most difficult.'

'You don't really know what my story is. What is more, you are not going to be able to leave here.'

'You wait and see. Or not.'

Sonja was so short of sleep that she slept heavily despite the sound of bombing. The first suicide (or should it be murder?) took place early the following morning before she was properly awake. A young woman had her throat slit. There was so much blood that her mattress had to be taken away to be disposed of. Shortly afterwards an SS officer was poisoned over breakfast. Later that morning a hysterical woman was screaming to be let out. Somehow the stewards dealt with her. There was another poisoning at midday and a few hours later an old lady was found garrotted on one of the mattresses in the storeroom. So then it was time for them to queue up again for their playing cards. Sonja supposed that it was weirdly like some country house party game, not that she had ever been to such a country house. How long had she to live? The champagne had run out. Reinhardt had been hoping that there

346

would be some left over for the Russians. Later that afternoon there was a poisoning that went wrong. The dose must have been too small and there was a lot of screaming before the victim was finally smothered. Sonja wished she had brought with her some spare clothing and some soap. In the course of the next few days the place was going to get very smelly. She had not anticipated that getting herself killed would prove to be such a long drawn-out affair. The President moved among the survivors making vague conversational remarks and trying to keep them cheerful. The sooner the end came the better.

On the second night she lay on her mattress, sleepless for a while and wondering if she would awake on the following day. So it was a strange kind of relief to be woken by someone else screaming towards the morning. It turned out to be a beheading that had been awkwardly executed a few mattresses away. Breakfast was, like the previous day, a hunk of bread and a cold sausage. Reinhardt was insisting that Sonja should serve as his poison taster and he argued that this might double her chance of dying unexpectedly. For two of the remaining company it was their last breakfast. One of them was Hans. There were no more civilised conversations of the kind there had been on the first evening. What will the world look like after she is gone? The idea that it would look like anything was quite strange.

'I don't like it here,' said Sonja.

'You don't like being in the antechamber to death! What is wrong with you?'

Reinhardt seemed to revel in her unease. But he might represent her last chance to become famous. So, 'Reinhardt, you said that you are planning to escape from here.'

'Yes. Admittedly, as death camps go, this is a luxury death camp, but I have always hated sitting around in waiting rooms, so I will soon be off, and now you want me to take you with me.'

'No, it is not that. I am finished. My only wish is that when you get out of here, you will tell my story.'

Reinhardt made a clicking noise with his tongue, 'This place and its set-up will, as I had anticipated, make a terrific short story, but your life is no good for either a book or a film. It is just one thing after another: parties, dance numbers, screenings, more parties. I can't work with that.

Sonja sighed, 'I have not been frank with you and I have kept back all sorts of strange and horrible things that have happened to me. I want the story of my life written. It is all I have ever wanted.'

So now she told him some of what she had left out and, though this was difficult, she exaggerated the horror of the rape on Peacock Island. She also claimed that Goebbels had been passionately in love with her, practically her slave, and that he had been ready to divorce Magda and resign his Ministry in order to marry her. She also told how Olga Chekhova had threatened her life. But she felt that time was short. (How much time had she left?) And her narrative all came out in a gabble.

So Reinhardt said, 'Well, it is too late now. Though I have been listening with interest, your story is all rushed and garbled. If only you had kept a written record that might have given some order to your life – and given me something to work with.'

'But I told you. My diaries, most of them anyway, are in that metal trunk you saw in my flat. Not only did I keep a diary, but I started to turn my diaries into what I hoped would be an autobiography. I know what I have written is not very good. There was never much time and besides I was never taught to write properly. But, even if I am nobody special, I have met a lot of people who were more interesting than me. Please.'

Reinhardt raised his hand in a placatory way.

'Alright, alright, perhaps there is a story. I will see what I can do. Give me the key to your flat and the key to the trunk. I will go and find those diaries and I guess that, when I read them, it will be as if, from the grave, you had written me a long, sad letter.'

She gave him the keys and then said, 'But Reinhardt there is no way out of here.'

'I still have my pistol.'

'I don't think –'

Eighteen months later in Munich

Reinhardt fetched out a sheaf of paper from the drawer of the cabinet and took it to his desk. On the first page he wrote in large elegant letters *Her Life was like a Fairy Tale*.

FINIS